BI

EDNA

GARDEN

A BRITT MONTERO NOVEL

"WONDERFUL . . . A FAST-PACED PAGE-TURNER OF A NOVEL . . . Buchanan knows the life of a crime reporter and the inside of a newspaper room and police department."

Milwaukee Journal Sentinel

"THIS IS A ZINGER . . . The tension never breaks . . . Miami is never dull, Britt does not disappoint, and fans will inhale this book faster than the city's summer humidity frazzles tempers."

Florida Times-Union

"BUCHANAN TELLS GREAT STORIES— HOT, HORRIBLE, HOMICIDAL STORIES."

The New York Times Book Review

"EDNA BUCHANAN IS OUTRAGEOUS AND UNRIVALED."

Patricia Cornwell

"TERRIFYING . . . Buchanan—and Britt—know their stuff when it comes to working the cop shop . . . The plotting is good and the characters capture our interest . . . Read *Garden of Evil* if you can't make a winter visit to the orange juice state, but don't expect it to warm your heart."

Denver Rocky Mountain News

"BUCHANAN IS ALREADY ONE OF CRIME FICTION'S NATIONAL TREASURES."

Newsday

"A TAUT AND SATISFYING NOVEL ON SEVERAL LEVELS . . . Edna Buchanan is so good that the Miami Chamber of Commerce should start banning her books . . . Buchanan portrays Miami with such realism . . . that readers may decide to bypass it when choosing a destination for the family vacation."

Cleveland Plain Dealer

"A PAGE-TURNER . . . crisp . . . fast-paced . . . bizarre and bloody . . . a story well told . . . Her depiction of never-to-be-trusted editors and respected reporters is on the money, and her descriptions of cops, criminals, and crime scenes ring just as true."

Cincinnati Post

"EDNA BUCHANAN COMES THROUGH AGAIN . . . a spiffy suspense tale that has newspaper reporter Britt Montero itching for action."

Houston Chronicle

"A SUPREMELY EXPERT YARNSPINNER."

Los Angeles Times Book Review

"I NEVER MET AN EDNA BUCHANAN MURDER MYSTERY I DIDN'T LIKE."

Austin American-Statesman

"A FIRST-RATE STORYTELLER."
Michael Connelly, bestselling author of *Angels Flight*

"NO ONE KNOWS MIAMI'S VIOLENT UNDERBELLY BETTER . . .
Garden of Evil is a fascinating journey with a female serial killer and the journalist struggling to understand her."
Associated Press Newswires

"SHE UNDERSTANDS THE POLITICS, HISTORY, AND DYNAMICS OF THIS COMPLEX CITY, AND WRITES A BANG-UP STORY TO SHOW THEM OFF.
Her Detective, Britt Montero, is intelligent, attractive, and resourceful, but she has a soft side that is appealing and memorable."
Dallas Morning News

"THE QUEEN OF CRIME."
Los Angeles Daily News

"*GARDEN OF EVIL* TAKES 'UP CLOSE AND PERSONAL' CRIME REPORTING TO A NEW AND NEARLY LETHAL LEVEL . . .
Edna Buchanan, a legendary crime reporter, always brings special insight to her fiction . . .
The Miami scenes crackle with police and deadline action."
USA Today

"AN IRREPRESSIBLY GOOD WRITER . . .
an author who has a unique place in an increasingly crowded genre."
Portland Oregonian

Also by Edna Buchanan

THE CORPSE HAD A FAMILIAR FACE
NOBODY LIVES FOREVER
NEVER LET THEM SEE YOU CRY
CONTENTS UNDER PRESSURE
MIAMI, IT'S MURDER
SUITABLE FOR FRAMING
ACT OF BETRAYAL
MARGIN OF ERROR
PULSE

Coming Soon in Hardcover

YOU ONLY DIE TWICE

EDNA BUCHANAN

GARDEN OF EVIL

A BRITT MONTERO NOVEL

AVON BOOKS
An Imprint of HarperCollins*Publishers*

This is a work of fiction. Names, characters, places, and incidents are products of the author's imagination or are used fictitiously and are not to be construed as real. Any resemblance to actual events, locales, organizations, or persons, living or dead, is entirely coincidental.

AVON BOOKS
An Imprint of HarperCollins*Publishers*
10 East 53rd Street
New York, New York 10022-5299

ISBN: 0-380-79841-7
www.avonbooks.com

First Avon Books paperback printing: October 2000
First Avon Books hardcover printing: November 1999

Printed in the U.S.A.

WCD 10 9 8 7 6 5 4 3 2 1

For Sgt. Christine Echroll,
Viking Princess, Brave Warrior.
She saw the dark side but never faltered.

What is evil lives forever.

—Spanish proverb

The snake stood up for evil in the Garden.

—Robert Frost, *The Ax-Helve* (1923)

One

THE GARBLED POLICE RADIO TRANSMISSIONS HAD been confusing: reports of gunfire, a fleeing car, a traffic accident, and a corpse. Were they related? It was impossible to determine from my dashboard scanner. Cops speak guardedly on the air these days, assisted by sophisticated encoding techniques that scramble their signals and permit outsiders to pick up only intermittent one-sided fragments of transmissions.

Steamy waves of heat rose off pavement that would still be hot to the touch at midnight. It was nearly dusk, the hottest day so far of Miami's hottest June on record. The temperature had shattered weather bureau records every day, all month. The heat index, taking the humidity into account, had settled at a wilting 115 degrees. The backs of my thighs had become one with the vinyl seat and my dress clung damply in unseemly places. Deadline rumbled toward me like an avalanche, and I still had work to do on two other stories.

I parked outside a little family grocery on the corner, left my press card on the dash, and separated myself from the car seat. What had happened here? I scanned the chaos of the street. Spinning emergency flashers and yellow crime-scene tape stretched for blocks into the sunset's red and purple glow, creating a hypnotic, nearly psychedelic effect. To my relief I saw Homicide Detective David Ojeda. Mercurial and savvy, he is a quick study, so sure of himself that he is not afraid to talk to a reporter. He wouldn't stonewall. And he owed me. At least I liked to think so; he probably wouldn't agree. Homicide cops always feel righteous, no matter what. He acted as though the history we shared had never happened, but I wouldn't forget. You don't forget a man who whips out his handcuffs and books you into the county jail.

Ojeda did not look happy to see me. He looked limp, from his loud tie to his usually fierce and bristly mustache. Damp half-moons ringed his armpits. His high forehead glistened. His knowing smile had given way to a scowl. Not happy at all.

A late-model Buick Riviera had slammed into a huge eight-by-ten-foot concrete planter, in what looked like the last stop on a path of destruction.

A woman sat mumbling on the curb behind the wrecked Riviera, head in her hands, so drenched in blood and gore that I thought she must be seriously hurt. Her hair and even the little pink barrette she wore in it was spattered and stained. Uh-oh. Was that a little pink barrette? Up closer it appeared to be a chunk of brain matter. But whose? The medic checking her pulse did not seem unduly concerned.

Other medics surrounded a young man lying in the street. His hair looked as though he had jammed a wet thumb into a light socket. Was it normally that wild or rearranged by whatever mishap left him sprawled on the pavement? What on earth had the not-so-good citizens of Miami been doing to each other out here?

The world is crazy, full of crazy people. Miami has more than its share. My job is to tell the public all about it. My name is Montero, Britt Montero, and I cover the police beat in this superheated sea-level city at the bottom of the map.

The medical examiner and two cops stepped away from the Buick just then and I glimpsed the driver, still behind the wheel. My God! I swallowed hard. Ojeda mopped his face with a handkerchief as I sidled up and murmured softly in his ear.

"Where is his head?"

"Nowhere," he replied, "and everywhere."

"Was this an accident or a shooting?" I demanded. "What happened?"

"Talk to PIO," he said.

"Nobody from public information is here."

"Jesus, will you look at that," he muttered. We stared morosely at adults in the crowd who had hoisted toddlers up high onto their shoulders so the wee ones could better view the carnage.

"Okay." The detective stashed his sodden handkerchief. "Don't tell them I talked to you," he warned. "Here's the four-one-one.

"Our victim, the driver here; his gal-pal Wanda, that's her over there"—he indicated the woman on the curb, whose mumbling was rapidly coalescing into an incoherent rant—"and his brother come bopping into Overtown to buy crack. The brother is riding shotgun, literally. He's in the backseat with a sawed-off across his knees."

"That him over there? The injured guy in the street?"

"Nope. Don't get ahead a me here." Ojeda looked annoyed. "Don't jump the gun. You always do that."

I wanted to argue that he was no one to talk, but didn't.

"He's the street-corner dealer our happy little group in the car is making a buy from when a dispute arises. Our man in the street there is leaning in the car window, negotiating, when our driver apparently tries to take off with both the drugs and the money. Don't know if they planned a rip or if it was some spur-a-the-moment brainstorm. The seller refuses to let go the goods; he's half in and half outa the window, getting dragged. The brother in the backseat starts brandishing the shotgun, the seller grabs it and hangs on for dear life, getting dragged farther into the car as they wrestle over the gun. Then *ba-boom!* It goes off, taking off the driver's head, which explodes onto his girlfriend's lap. The dead guy's foot punches the accelerator and the car peels out, leaving a hundred-and-fifty-foot traila blood back on Second Avenue.''

He stopped to glare at the flies already buzzing the car.

''He slumps, his chest on the horn, foot on the accelerator. They wind up here about a mile later. From what I hear, his passengers were screaming louder than the horn. The dealer's legs are still hanging out the back window, kicking and thrashing. One of our unmarked cars had to swerve up on the sidewalk to get outa their way. They do a U-turn and are following as the car sideswipes a light pole and a buncha parked vehicles, mows down those meters, runs over some news-vending machines, and slams into the planter. The air bag deploys, shoves the driver back into an upright position, and the horn stops.''

Somebody should invent air bags activated by gunfire, I thought, to shield against bullets and shotgun blasts. They could market them in Miami.

''Where's the brother?'' I asked, looking around.

''Our guys following 'em see the backseat passenger crawl outa the wreckage and sprint off into the twilight,'' he said. ''Wanda's still sitting in front, trying to put her boyfriend's skull back together; mosta the pieces were in her lap. His foot's still frozen on the accelerator, engine revving, tires spinning. The dealer, he got flung free, into the street, on impact.''

Ojeda squinted into the fading glow of the dying day. As I scribbled notes, Dr. Vernon Duffy, an assistant Miami Dade County medical examiner, picked up his padded aluminum equipment case and joined us. Slightly stooped and pale, he spends too much time in the morgue.

''Think we'll ever see rain again?'' A New Hampshire native, Duffy looked wilted in the merciless heat. Ocean winds from the east usually keep Miami's summertime highs below the century mark. But no rain or breezes had come this month, normally our wettest. The entire state had withered beneath brittle blue skies and a scorching sun that seared lawns and shrubbery a crispy brown that crunched underfoot.

"Nope, we're doomed. Must be global warming, doc."

He nodded and looked pleased at my gloomy prognosis. "The ERs are full of heatstroke victims. Joggers are dropping like flies."

"What about him?" I indicated the Buick.

"Can't blame this one on the heat," Ojeda said, "unless it made his head explode."

"What kind of shotgun pellets did that?" I asked.

"It's not pellets or bullets," Duffy said patiently, "it's the gas, the high-pressure combustion, tens of thousands of PSIs."

"Well, the pellets sure didn't help," I said. "Why did the car continue to travel for so long after he was shot?"

"Evidently his spinal cord continued to function, responding to his fatal injury with a reflex that slammed his foot down hard on the accelerator."

"Like I said." Ojeda nodded. "Foot froze on the gas."

The sinking sun projected a rosy glow onto palm fronds silhouetted against the sky. No breeze disturbed the blast furnace radiating around us. I felt my sandals melting into the pavement. Yet something was astir, a shift in the crowd. Instead of being lulled, like me, into a sleepy stupor by the heat, there were ominous murmurs and rumblings.

The atmosphere suddenly seemed supercharged, tempers short.

Ojeda and the uniforms on the police line picked up on it too. "Work the crowd," he told two patrolmen. "See who's running their mouth."

"When are you going to move the body?" I asked.

"We're not," the doctor replied. "We're leaving him in the car."

Made sense. The Buick and its grisly contents, along with the little glassine bags of crack strewn across the backseat and the twelve-gauge sawed-off Remington 870, its stock duct-taped, its short barrel crookedly hacksawed by some amateur, would be delivered as is, a not-so-tidy little package, to the most efficiently designed building in South Florida—our medical examiner's office.

Boats that crash, planes that plummet, and corpse-crammed cars are scooped up intact and taken by flatbed truck to Number 1 Bob Hope Road, where forensic scientists examine them in the privacy of a large, well-lit, and air-conditioned hangarlike enclosure far from bad weather, insects and alligators, curious crowds, and reporters.

Ojeda instructed the uniforms to duct-tape two yellow plastic body blankets over the Buick and its contents for the trip.

"Now I gotta go talk a lady outa her clothes," he announced, turning on his heel.

"The lab wants to try out some new blood-spatter techniques," Duffy explained.

The detective's swagger implied a history of success in talking ladies out of their clothes. I trailed along to watch, perspiration oozing from every pore, my sunglasses skidding down my nose. Ojeda asked Wanda, still seated on the curb, if she happened to have a change of clothes handy. He explained that he needed what she was wearing for evidence.

"I tol' Frankie not to wave that gun around," she said. The detective repeated his request. She didn't seem to hear. The keys to the Riviera, she said. She needed them. The Buick was her mother's.

"If she's the registered owner, she can talk to our VIP representative about releasing it," Ojeda said politely.

Uh-oh, I thought. Using the Vehicle Impoundment Program, police seize the cars used in crimes involving drugs, prostitution, or drunk driving. A man caught soliciting a prostitute can lose his car, even if it's registered to his wife. Try explaining *that* to a spouse.

"I got to get that car back home before nine," Wanda insisted and stood up. Her stained T-shirt read REHAB IS FOR QUITTERS. "My mama needs it to git to work." Her mother, she said, worked midnights at the county hospital.

Did she plan to visit Busy Bee Car Wash first? Then there was the crash damage. The Buick was history.

Ojeda answered his cell phone, then covered the mouthpiece to mutter an obscenity. "Word travels fast. It's somebody from the community relations board's crisis-response team."

He then greeted the caller warmly. Miami cops had been instructed by the chief to deal directly with board members to try to keep the peace in this not-so-peaceful place on the planet. It makes me think of our publisher, who insists that we respond personally and with warmth to every call and letter from readers, no matter how threatening or insane.

"That's incorrect, ma'am," Ojeda responded affably to the caller. "No police officer fired a weapon." He rolled his eyes in my direction. "No, this was not a pursuit situation."

He paced as he spoke, his darting eyes seeking out the uniforms dispatched to canvass for troublemakers. I heard only one side, but the conversation was obvious.

"Well," Ojeda said pleasantly, signaling a sergeant with an index finger's slash to his throat, "if somebody witnessed something we don't know about, we'd welcome the opportunity to take their statement. We'd appreciate them coming in. No, it's . . . but . . . but . . . the victim's vehicle passed two of our people at high speed, nearly ran them off the road, they followed. That's why they arrived so quickly at the accident scene. . . . He was already deceas—no. No pursuit." His fingers ran raggedly through his damp dark hair. "The man at the wheel was already . . . I agree. Dead men don't drive as a rule. But in this sit—No, the shooter is not. . . . We have a tentative. . . . During a struggle. Drug deal. . . . We don't know that yet. . . . I don't know, ma'am. We'll certainly check into it. Thank you for the information. I'm sure the chief and internal affairs will be glad to. . . . If someone knows something differ— . . . Bring them in by all means . . . Why wouldn't they want to talk to us? It's the right thing to do. . . . Well, I'm sorry to hear that. . . . Feel free. . . . Ojeda, O-J-E-D-A. Badge number fourteen-ten. Thank you so much.''

He snapped the small phone shut and summoned the patrolmen sent to check the crowd. ''Okay, anybody who tells you or somebody else that they saw something, heard something, or think they know somebody who mighta saw or heard, or *dreamed* they saw or heard something, get 'em down to the station and take their statements. The community relations board is already on our backs. Check with the guys at the initial scene, see what kinda witnesses they have, and if they found the piston from the shotgun shell. The wad is probably still in the car.''

He returned to Wanda and offered a new ensemble for her consideration, curling his wrists as he unfurled it, like a high-fashion designer pitching an original: a plastic-and-paper sunshine-yellow biohazard suit. Every patrol car is equipped with one.

As he awaited her approval, the driver from Double Eagle Towing arrived, waved cheerfully, strolled up to the Buick, and peered inside.

Wanda yelped in indignation. ''What they doing with that tow truck? Git that outa heah! They can't take that car. My mama ain't got nothin' to do with this! I tol' you I needed to git it back to her by nine.'' She squinted impatiently at her watch, then stared at it for a long moment. So did I. Both the timepiece and her arm were encrusted with blood and what appeared to be bone splinters. Her head swiveled, eyes darting wildly at the people conducting the routine tasks sudden death generates. Her shriek, a bloodcurdling, god-awful cry, momentarily froze them in their tracks. Frantically, she tried to wipe her arm clean with the other hand, then saw that it, too, was bloody. She peered down at her clothes, then lunged as if trying to shake off the mess. She whirled, howling and writhing, into a horrible dance, as though trying to escape her own skin.

The detective's cell phone rang again, at the precise moment that a bottle, hurled from the crowd, exploded against the pavement.

The crowd surged forward. Cops held the line as the sounds of screams and breaking glass galvanized the dealer still lying in the street. Despite an IV in one arm and a splint on the other, he suddenly bucked, kicked, and fought. A medic tumbled back, striking his head on the pavement. Others struggled to subdue the patient.

Above the growing din came an eerie wail. Another joined it: two wails, unearthly yet human sounds, working their way ever closer through the crowd. Ojeda's eyes took on the haunted look of a hunted man.

"You know what that is," he said flatly.

I had a pretty good idea.

"Our backseat passenger accidentally blows away his big brother, then runs," the detective said. "Where?"

"Home to Mama," I said. "To tell his version of the bad news."

"And what happens next?"

"Mama and the rest of the family rush to the scene to see if it's true."

Our eyes caught. The detective trotted back to the Buick. "Take it, take it, take it! Go, go, go! Geditouta here!" He kicked at a back tire.

The tow truck operator moved faster than I have ever seen him, glancing over his shoulder as the wails drew closer.

"Don't tape those blankets anywhere we could find

prints,'' Ojeda barked. ''Okay, roll it, roll it, roll it! Before we have a major cha-cha here.''

The truck's motorized flatbed slid back at a 30-degree angle. The ramp dropped, the cable grew taut, the motor groaned, and up, up, and away, just as the crowd parted for a heavyset middle-aged woman and a younger heavyset clone leading a pack of family members loping toward us, their wails a mournful tremolo as they ran.

Time to return to the office. I retreated to my T-Bird and drove into the soft and moist early evening as pink clouds drifted in a sapphire sky and the neon of South Beach glowed rosy across the bay. My neck felt stiff and my right eye twitched uncontrollably. This was the third story I had worked on in a long and troubled day, but the first exclusively my own.

Dead Dominican stowaways, three of them, had been discovered shortly before dawn, their voyage of hope ended in a dark and airless cargo hold deep in the bowels of a freighter off Government Cut. At noon, two customs agents routinely boarded a rickety vessel docked on the Miami River. As they did, more than one hundred and fifty panic-stricken illegal Haitian immigrants burst out and fled in all directions. Some leaped over the side into the water, others pounded through a dockside restaurant, snatching food from the plates of startled diners as they ran, scattering to the four winds. Overwhelmed, caught by surprise, police and customs captured only a few. The city and the river swallowed the rest.

So many people on the run, risking their lives to reach Miami. What would readers think, I wondered, as they perused their papers over their morning coffee? Would they think at all? Or would they be too busy getting the kids off to school, gearing up for torturous commutes or morning sales conferences?

The desk had overreacted as usual and overstaffed both stories, with *News* reporters bumping into each other at the scenes. It's not that I mind sharing bylines, I just like to work alone. Steeling myself against the arctic blast, I stepped into the *News* building's deserted air-conditioned lobby. The effect was as if I had plunged my overheated and sweaty body into a Deepfreeze. This cannot be healthy, I thought, as the elevator rose sluggishly to the fifth floor. My mind raced with all I still had to do. Check the Dominicans' cause of death. More Haitians captured? Did any drown? Any smuggling arrests? And I wanted more information on Wanda, the driver, his brother, and the dealer. The city directory might help me track witnesses who had seen the Buick's wild ride or suffered property damage from it.

"Britt, you weren't out in that heat all afternoon, were you?" Ryan Battle asked softly, his brown eyes registering shock and concern.

Ryan has the face and gentle soul of a poet, too kind and compassionate to be a reporter, which he is. He works general assignment and features at the desk behind mine.

"Yes, I was." I swept aside the mail and messages on my desk.

"How come?" He looked and sounded so innocent.

"What do you mean, how come?" I snapped impatiently. "Covering the news, doing my job. How was your day?"

"Way too hot to be out there, Britt," he said seriously. "I've been working on stories I could cover by phone." His snowy white shirt looked immaculate, his grooming perfect. "They released the new tourism statistics today, and the state candidates filed their financial reports."

"Silly me." I slapped a palm to my forehead. "Now why didn't I think of that? I could have asked everybody to fax me press releases. But, oh, that's right, I forgot, I'm a journalist."

No answer. I resisted the impulse to turn and face the wounded expression in those soft spaniel eyes. In my mind's eye I saw the scar on his forehead left by a brick hurled through the windshield when we covered the riot.

Bobby Tubbs, the assistant city editor in the slot, was impatiently waving me in his direction.

"Where the hell have you been all this time?" His chubby cheeks puckered with annoyance. "Howie's already gone, and we need new leads on the Haitian and Dominican stories for the state."

"I was at that other scene. I called you," I said.

"An accident?" He looked exasperated.

"Yes . . . involving a headless driver who careened a mile through the city with three live passengers, if you count the guy dangling out the back window."

Tubbs frowned. "We're really tight for space. We've got Ryan's tourism piece, and Miriam's out on a breaking story, a nursing home being evacuated because the air-conditioning died."

"People lived in Miami before air-conditioning," I groused. "Didn't anybody ever hear of fans?"

Tubbs scrutinized my sweat-stained visage, wary, as though—maddened by the heat—I might be dangerous. "That was when everybody who could afford it left for the summer, before they paved all the green space and made it hotter."

He pulled up the local page layout, studied his computer screen, and shook his head. God forbid that breaking news should interfere with the layout for his plans.

"Maybe we can fit something in, but keep it tight, tight, tight. There's no space."

I stalked back to my desk, head aching, feeling weary and unappreciated. I finished everything else, then called Ojeda at headquarters.

Between us we put it together. The love story of Wanda and Bucky began when they met in rehab. Their relationship, short though it was, had obviously outlived any rehabilitative effects of the program. When Wanda borrowed her mother's new car to drive to a "doctor's appointment," she had neglected to mention Bucky, his brother—or the shotgun. Wanda's mother, a nice lady, Ojeda reported sadly, was raising Wanda's two toddlers. That was why she worked midnights. And her limited auto insurance covered only immediate family members with valid licenses. Bucky did not qualify on either count; his license had been revoked after his last arrest. The younger heavyset woman who had arrived at the scene with Bucky's mother was not the dead man's sister, as I had presumed. She was his wife, mother of his five children, and Wanda's bitter rival.

"Shoulda seen 'em go at each other," Ojeda said. "It was bad."

Frankie, Bucky's brother, had been spotted downtown, on line at the Greyhound bus station. He ran again but cops tackled him on Northwest Second Avenue, though not before he darted through four lanes of traffic, causing a three-car crash.

I trotted up to the city desk to report the new information. "Okay." Bobby barely glanced up from his editing screen. "I found a hole for it. But make it brief. Two grafs tops. No more than seven lines."

As I stomped off in a snit, he called after me.

"Britt, there's a bulletin, a wire story outa Shelby County, upstate. I'm sending it to your mailbox. You might be interested." I ignored him.

Trimmed to bare bones, my story still came in at three times his specified length. It's harder to write short than long, especially with so much information. As he edited it, I peered over Bobby's shoulder, arguing as he eliminated every human, ironic, or remotely interesting detail.

I called my friend Lottie Dane, who was back in photo after shooting the nursing home evacuation. "Thanks a lot," I said. "You and Miriam managed to push my story off local and into the brieflys."

"Sorry, Britt, but you shoulda seen all the poor old folks, poor thangs. Hell-all-Friday, they are *us* someday. I jist saw what we have to look forward to. It ain't purty."

I always count on Lottie, the best friend I have, to cheer me up. Despite all she has covered, wars and famine, earthquakes and volcanoes—even Jonestown—she is indefatigably positive, always up. Tonight she did not sound like her usual high-spirited self.

''What's wrong, Lottie? What is it?''

She sighed. ''Jist somethin' I married.''

Long divorced, she never discusses her ex. ''Look,'' I said, ''I'm too tired and disgusted to go right home. Let's go for a drink when you get off.'' Something tall and cold with a twist of lime shimmered miragelike in my mind. ''We can talk.''

''Okay,'' she said, ''but I've still gotta soup the film for that Sunday special section.''

''I'll go through my mail and messages till you're ready. Hurry up,'' I said.

I sorted the mail. Why are people with the least legible handwriting the most prone to scribble lengthy letters?

To be perfectly honest with you, a piece of jail mail began, confirming my theory that this phrase almost always precedes a lie, *I was always threatening to kill Charlene—but I never, ever, really seriously meant it.*

I knew the case. Charlene had dialed nine-one-one, screaming that her ex-husband had a gun and was breaking into the house. Shots, screams, and the line went dead. Police arrived and found her rolled up in a rug he was trying to fold into the trunk of his Toyota—more proof that restraining orders are only paper and don't stop bullets.

Despite his guilty plea, he now claimed in a spidery hand that he'd been framed. I tossed it aside. A mauve envelope, good vellum stock, was addressed in an attractive and legible feminine hand.

Please! You have to help me, the letter began. *Somebody is trying to kill me. I have nowhere to turn. The police won't listen. No one will. There have been several attempts. I fear they'll succeed next time.*

I'm frightened and alone. I don't want them to get away with my murder.

She signed it *Althea A. Moran.*

Her name had never appeared in the newspaper, according to our library data base. I reread the note. Another paranoid reader? A lonely senior craving attention? The address was Coral Gables, an upscale bedroom community. I reached for the phone, then hesitated. It was after midnight, when calls are usually bad news or emergencies. One's upcoming murder should qualify, I thought, and punched in the number.

I hoped the bleat of a busy signal meant she was alive and well.

The next letter was also brief and to the point.

I have a friend who is writing, or rewriting, the Bible. You can help him do it. He also needs a wife. You are it. Send me your home address as soon as possible.

Lottie called to say she was on her way out to the newsroom. "Listen to this," I said, and read it.

"Wouldn't hurt to meet the fella," she drawled.

"For Pete's sake, Lottie, he's rewriting the Bible!"

"I know men with hobbies a whole lot worse."

I tidied my desk, snatched up my purse, then noticed a nagging signal flashing in the corner of my computer screen, a message, the wire story Tubbs had sent. I hit the key and scrolled through it.

FLA. LAWMAN KILLED, SUSPECT AT LARGE

Veteran Sheriff T. Rupert "Buddy" Brascom, 54, top lawman in this rural citrus and farming county for more than 21 years, was shot to death Thursday, apparently by a prisoner who escaped from the sheriff's office in the small county jail annex in Live Oak.

Brascom may have been slain with his own service revolver, according to Deputy S. L. Weech, who discovered the body. The sheriff's weapon was missing, along with his wallet, badge and his Chevrolet Blazer.

In his last communication with a dispatcher, the sheriff had indicated he had a woman in custody and was proceeding to the annex.

The prisoner has not been identified. A trucker who knew Brascom later reported seeing the sheriff's white Blazer southbound on I-95, driven by a young woman in her late teens or early twenties. The Florida Bureau of Law Enforcement and deputies set up roadblocks and launched an immediate manhunt.

Sheriff Brascom is survived by his wife, Lugene, four adult children and two grandchildren. Funeral arrangements are incomplete. He is the fifth Florida police officer killed in the line of duty this year.

I read it twice, questions flooding my mind. Was he wearing a vest? Where was he hit, and why was her identity unknown if he had arrested her? Cop killers are rarely female. When they are, they rarely get away. *Who are you?* I wondered. *Where are you? What's your story?*

Two

WE FOUND A SMALL TABLE IN THE DARK AND crowded back room at the 1800 Club and ordered drinks.

"Got a picture?" Lottie's bright red hair was long, wild, and unruly. She wore blue jeans, hand-tooled leather cowboy boots, and an L. L. Bean cotton shirt.

"Picture?" I asked.

"Damn straight, of that Bible-writing bridegroom, the one you're 'sposed to marry. He a stud muffin?"

"No picture, but I seriously doubt he's a stud muffin and don't plan to find out." I complained at length about Tubbs's hacking my story, then asked about Lottie's ex.

Her freckled face drew into a frown. "Guess I jist let it git me down." She jabbed at the ice in her newly arrived drink with a stirrer. "The man never changes. Every coupla years he decides that, doggone, I was the true love of his life! Keeps insistin' we were meant to be together."

"Nice," I said. "Considering how most men feel about ex-wives, that should be an ego boost. Why are you bummed?"

She inhaled the first sip of her frozen margarita, closed her eyes, licked her lips, and sighed. "Cuz sometimes I'm afraid he's right, and if he is, jist shoot me now. With a man like him, you haul ass and don't look back."

"Maybe he's changed. Some people do, you know."

She shook her head vigorously. "He's the back end of bad luck. Can't settle down. Always off on some new crusade, some new adventure. Feels like fun at first, but it gits old fast. Ain't no future in reliving the past. We git together, it always ends the same way, like the battle of the Alamo, with jist as many casualties. He's wild; a-course that's his most excitin' feature. Known each other all our lives but, like Peter Pan, he never grew up. Wasn't easy, gettin' over that man," she said, eyes sad. "I'll be go-to-helled if I'm gonna do it agin. Speaking of men, when will yours be back in town?"

"Next week." I smiled. Miami Homicide Captain Kendall McDonald was attending a ten-week management seminar in Washington, D.C. Our on-and-off romance was on and red hot at the moment.

"We talk every night; he writes every day, swears he misses me *mucho*. We're *muy simpatico*," I said wistfully, "when we're not together. But this time, Lottie, I think it's really serious." Sipping my Dubonnet over ice, I recalled the wire story. "Hear about the sheriff up in Shelby County? Shot dead with his own gun, supposedly by a woman. She got away."

"Lover's quarrel?" Lottie was always quick to link sudden death to sex. Most often she was right.

"Didn't sound like it. Wire story said he'd apparently arrested her. She's young, teens or twenties. He's a grandfather."

"Musta got careless," Lottie said.

"Yeah. Never let anybody take your gun, that's the first thing they teach rookie cops. Wonder what the heck happened?"

"Got a notorious speed trap up there," she said. "Nailing tourists comin' off the interstate is a major source-a local revenue."

"Maybe she got stopped, had drugs in the car, or was

drinking. What on earth could have made her go for his gun, then use it? She must be sorry now,'' I said.

''Maybe not.'' Lottie shrugged. ''Maybe she's evil, somebody born bad.''

''No way,'' I said. ''Nobody is born bad. All babies start out innocent. Other people shape them, outside influences turn them into something dangerous and violent.''

''I've seen it,'' she insisted, shaking her head. ''Some are born that way. They do bad things because it's what they do. They like it. No other reason.''

No point arguing, I thought, realizing I was hungry. ''She headed south, according to the story.'' I squinted at the menu in the dim light. ''Could be on her way here right now. Just what we need, another cop killer.''

''Shelby County's a long way off,'' Lottie said. ''And you know how cops are when one of 'em gits shot. Doubt she makes it this far. More'n likely she's wearing metal bracelets by now.''

It was late when I drove home, fortified by a sandwich and a salad. The temperature was stuck at 90, the humidity smothering when I got out of the car. The surf pounded the sandy shoreline just a few blocks away, but no hint of a sea breeze stirred. I took out my key, walked through the quiet courtyard, and paused to gaze up at the Big Dipper hanging in place, its bowl pointed toward Polaris, the North Star.

Somewhere out there, beneath that star-spangled black velvet stretch of sky, a woman was on the run, hunted—not in handcuffs. Somehow I knew it. *Where are you?* I wondered. *Are you scared and alone? What are you thinking out there?* My skin tingled with an odd sensation; perhaps it was the drinks, the heat, or both, but I felt connected, as though sensing her presence. I could almost hear her breathing.

A sudden movement, a rustling in the dark, startled me. A figure watched from the shadows of the palms bordering the building. "Who is it?" I demanded, instinctively taking a step back.

"Didn't mean to frighten you, Britt."

I breathed again in relief. My landlady, Mrs. Goldstein, age eighty-one.

"What's wrong?" I asked, voice hushed. "What on earth are you doing out here at this hour? Where's Mr. Goldstein?"

"Sleeping. But I couldn't." She lowered her voice. "It's the water restrictions. The banana trees, you know how they need water. They're burning up."

The stream from the hose she had dropped trickled into the scorched grass. The woman had sneaked out like a thief in the night to douse her little banana grove. "I'm conserving water in every other way," she said, "but you said yourself, they're better than supermarket bananas."

They are. My only reservation was that they exploded into perfect ripeness simultaneously, like bomb blasts at foreign embassies, resulting in an overwhelming fallout of banana bread, cake, shakes, splits, and puddings along with bananas frozen, fried, and chocolate-coated.

"Here." I groped for the hose in the wet grass and picked it up. "I'll finish. Listen," I whispered, "if you water at dawn, just before daylight, who will know? And if the water police swoop down, I promise to bail you out."

I hugged her, sent her inside, soaked the trees, then hung the hose on the side of the building. Inside my apartment, the light winked on my answering machine.

"Call me when you get in, babe. No matter how late. Miss you."

McDonald answered on the first ring.

I began to fill him in on the heat and Miami's news stories of the day, but he interrupted with an important question. What was I wearing? Being a basically truthful person, I had to tell him I had cranked up the air conditioner to its coldest setting and stripped down to nothing in front of it. We talked for a long time.

* * *

I forced myself to walk Bitsy early next morning before the fiery sun rose too high and the pavement grew too hot for her little paws.

A tiny white mop of a poodle, she is delighted to go anywhere, at any time, no matter what the weather. Her original owner, my friend Francie, used to smuggle Bitsy onto the midnight shift, to ride shotgun in the passenger seat of a Miami patrol car.

Billy Boots, the cat, normally trailed us at a discreet distance, but today he watched from the shade of the frangipani tree outside my door.

I glared at the pitiless blue sky, willing it to rain. My senses felt numb, my body sluggish, as though the unrelenting heat had shriveled the circuitry in my brain like Mrs. Goldstein's banana trees.

Bitsy, at the end of her lead, lunged fiercely at lizards, as I fantasized about McDonald and what our life might be like if we merged. Would Bitsy get along with Hooker, McDonald's old hound dog? The temperamental Billy Boots might pose more of a problem. I envisioned us all in a house shaded by trees and pink hibiscus, maybe even a pool, and my T-Bird parked next to his Jeep Cherokee. Was I hallucinating, still dazed from phone sex the night before, or had I begun to believe for the first time that it really could happen? The old obstacles remained. I could not give up my job anymore than he could his, but perhaps we were finally ready to resolve the conflicts, or at least hammer out a way to coexist with them.

I studied the morning paper over Cuban coffee and an intoxicatingly perfumy mango sliced into cold, crisp cereal. The Dominican and Haitian stories, with their group bylines and more staff credits at the bottom, got solid front-page play. My story was buried back inside the local section with no byline. Brieflys don't warrant them. Still frustrated, I had to admit the headline was an eye-catcher:

HEADLESS DRIVER CRASHES AFTER WILD MILE RIDE

By far the best work in the paper were the page-one photos accompanying the story of the nursing home evacuation. They focused in tight on the eyes of bewildered and frail seniors, heat-exhausted and frightened, being spirited into an uncertain night by strangers whisking them away from all that was familiar. The credit line read *Lottie Dane/News Staff.* Damn, she is good, I thought.

The story on the slain sheriff ran unchanged on the state page. No late-breaking developments.

I showered, dressed in cool blue cotton, and sipped my second coffee while making telephone rounds of Miami, the Beach, the county, and Hialeah police. The last had a 10 A.M. press conference scheduled.

"What's it about?" I asked Camacho, the public information officer.

"Just get over here." His voice dropped to a confidential pitch. "You're gonna like this one."

"Gimme a hint," I said, "to tell my editors."

"The chief told me not to get into it, just tell everybody to be here."

I hate guessing games. "Okay," I said, "is the chief quitting? Is it about demotions? Oh, it must be about that big internal affairs investigation."

"What big internal affairs investigation?" He sounded alarmed. "You hear something?"

"Never mind. They told me not to get into it."

"Britt! Goddamn!"

"Is it about a homicide? Did it happen during the night?"

"Nope."

"An arrest?"

"You're getting warm."

"In an old case?"

"Nah."

"So it's something new?"

"You're on target."

Bigger than a breadbox? Smaller than a semi truck?

This game was getting old fast. But maybe it was something major, I thought, interest piqued. "The detectives at the press conference. Will they be from homicide?"

"Nope."

"Robbery?"

"Nope."

"Sexual battery?"

"Could be."

He feigned annoyance, pretending to be far too busy a man for this, but I knew he loved it. "They arrested the Silver-Toothed rapist?"

"Nope."

"The Alysian Lakes Rapist? The Pillowcase Rapist? The I-Ninety-five Rapist?"

"Nope, nope, nope," he shot back, rapid-fire.

"Another rapist?" I suddenly felt queasy to the core at how many predators roam free.

"Not exactly. But you'll like this one, Britt."

I didn't. Lottie also attended, crouched near the podium for a good shot. After the usual half-hour delay for TV crews to untangle their wires and set up their lights, the sexual battery commander announced an arrest.

The "subject," he said, in the usual stilted policespeak, was accused of impersonating both a medical doctor and his own patient. Lottie stopped shooting as the details unfolded, wrinkled her nose at me, and slowly crossed her eyes.

The suspect had been calling hospitals and nursing registries, identifying himself as a physician and hiring private-duty nurses for his "patient." The "doctor" told the nurses he had prescribed sexual gratification as an important part of his patient's therapy.

The "patient" asked his nurses to fondle him "for therapeutic purposes," per doctor's orders. A new nurse had reported his repeated requests for rectal exams to her supervisor, who found no record of the doctor. A police investigation confirmed that "doctor" and "patient" were one and the same. They sought publicity to bring other victims forward.

The pale and pudgy suspect smirked through the photo op, peering at the press through thick glasses as he was marched in handcuffs to a police van en route to the county jail.

"Don't he make you glad you're single?" Lottie muttered in the lobby.

He did, and I met yet another reason at Miami police headquarters: recently reelected City Commissioner Sonny Saladrigas. It was a quiet news day. The entire county seemed drugged into inertia by the heat—except for Saladrigas.

He paced back and forth across the lobby, glad-handing cops and passersby and ranting at his political enemies. They included the newspaper, reporters, and anybody else who dared question his dubious campaign tactics, his padding the city payroll with relatives and cronies, and his purchase of luxurious furniture for his city hall office while Miami was going broke.

"I have a story for you!" he announced, eyes probing my breasts. Sonny was slightly overweight, with a receding hairline. He wore too much gold and diamond jewelry and, despite his expensive wardrobe, always managed to look like an unmade bed.

"Write this, write this down," he commanded, standing too close as he launched into a tirade accusing his city hall adversaries of stealing his office furniture and forcing him into the lavish new expenditures for which he was being criticized.

Same old stuff. He had a list of suspects and was insisting on a major investigation, police reports, surveillances, and searches. A waste of taxpayer money, but he would get them, though the cops knew it was all balderdash. The chief serves at the will of the city commission and Sonny was a commissioner. He had even been vice mayor.

"Why do I never see you at city hall?" he breathed in my face.

"Because I cover the police beat." Truth was, it would make sense if I set up shop at city hall. The crime rate there was probably higher than anyplace else in the city. Miami's politicians regularly stole more than desperadoes with guns.

"But you should come to see me," he said softly. "Why is it we have never had lunch?"

"I usually don't eat lunch. Deadlines," I said.

"So," he said slyly, "we don't need food."

"How is Lourdes?" I asked brightly. "She worked so hard in your campaign. She must be exhausted."

"My wife." He shrugged. "She is busy with the children. Call me," he said meaningfully, "anytime you are free. Anytime." He gave me his pathetic attempt at a suave and seductive look as he pressed his damp card between my fingers. It lacked the intended effect. Instead, I wanted to go wash my hands. "Anytime," he whispered again. "Call me." He stepped onto the elevator on his way up to see the chief. I wondered if anybody had called ahead to warn the poor man.

Back at the office I passed along the tip on Sonny's missing office furniture to Barbara, our city hall reporter, who rolled her eyes, and then rang Althea Mason, the woman who wrote that somebody was trying to kill her. Again, no answer. For a woman desperately seeking help, she was annoyingly difficult to reach. I checked the state desk for the latest from Shelby County. A hero's funeral was being planned. In wire photos, grim deputies wore strips of black mourning tape across their badges. Lawmen from three counties and the Florida Department of Law Enforcement were combing north Florida for the killer and the missing Blazer. The mystery woman now had a price on her head. A $25,000 reward had been offered and would probably grow.

Local stories languished in my tickler file, but curiosity sent me flipping through my Rolodex to find a number for Charlie Webster, long-time reporter for the *Shelby County Register*, a small daily.

"Hey, Charlie. This is Britt, from *The Miami News*."

"Britt! Where the hell are ya? Here in town?"

"No, still down in Miami."

"Thought maybe you got them to send you up here to cover the demise of our late great sheriff."

"No way. They're using your stories right off the wire. Enough action here to keep me working twenty-four and seven."

"No doubt. How fare you in the never-ending war against crime, criminals, and cops? Most excitement we usually get round here is posting your stories on our newsroom bulletin board. You do that little gem on the headless driver? Sounded like yours. Had a feeling there was more to it."

"There was. Space problems," I said. "Wait till I tell you about the press conference I went to today." I filled him in. Leaning back in my chair, I focused on the flawless blue sky beyond the newsroom's big windows. "What's the four-one-one on your sheriff?"

"Biggest story here since that rasha UFO sightin's couple years back. Big in every way. Ol' Rupert weighed in at 'bout two hundred and ninety pounds. Wasn't a tall man, only about five foot seven or so, but he made up for it in clout. Hell, we got cops coming from all sixty-seven counties, Georgia, and South Carolina for the funeral."

"He was that well liked?"

"Well connected more like it. A long-time power player in the good-ol'-boy network up here."

"How come they haven't caught the killer? Who is she?"

"Nobody knows. She's one long-gone lady. Musta hit the freeway and racked up a messa miles 'tween her and here 'fore the body was found. Could be anywhere by now. Haven't had a sighting since that trucker put her behind the wheel of Buddy's Blazer. Could be in the Big Apple drinking a beer or down there in Miami sipping a Cuba Libre.''

''Too damn hot to come here,'' I said. ''Maybe she stashed his car and is right there under your nose. Think she's local or some tourist he stopped on the interstate?''

''No way a-tellin' yet. Whichever, I don't wanna be her. They're hot on her tail. A lot of people want that little gal, and most are packing guns.''

''Too bad you don't have her car, that would probably tell you who she is. How come? Wasn't it a violation of procedure to have a prisoner in custody and not run her ID on the air so the dispatcher could check?''

''Hell, Britt, police work ain't as formal up here as in the big city. For one thing, who's gonna tell the sheriff he's violating procedure? Procedure was whatever he decided to do.''

''What was he like?''

''Okay, long as you didn't cross him.''

His voice hinted at a whole lot more.

''What was the scene like? Where was he shot?''

''You writing something 'bout it?''

''Nope. Not unless she shows up here. Just curious.''

''Hell, Britt,'' he drawled, ''she makes it to Miami, she'll get lost in the crowd and nobody'll ever find her. Nobody'd notice another killer in Miami.''

''Don't let the Chamber of Commerce hear you. What was unusual about the murder scene, Charlie?''

''We-e-ll,'' he said reluctantly, ''you know, ol' Rupert, he liked the ladies.''

''They like him?''

''Like probably isn't the right word, but power's a trip for lotsa ladies. You know how women are, specially 'bout cops. Guns and badges are babe magnets.''

''So you think sex is involved?'' Lottie was right. Sex had something to do with everything lately.

"Didn't say that."

Ugly thoughts crossed my mind. "You think maybe some of his female prisoners didn't always stay prisoners, depending on their . . . attitudes about sex?"

"Rumors to that effect made the rounds."

"What was he wearing when he was shot?" I am often accused of having a dirty mind. It's probably true.

"Well, seems ol' Rupert was bare-assed when he bought it. Had his shirt on, but his britches was down around his ankles."

"He'd had sex?"

"Looked that way."

"Where was he shot?"

"You know."

"You mean . . . ?"

"Politely put, shot in the groin."

"Jeez. Sure this isn't a mob killing? Was he shot anyplace else?"

"In the head. Musta dropped after the first one. Who wouldn't? Then the killer put the pistol to his forehead and fired again."

"Ouch. A contact wound? The blow-back must have splattered her with blood. Sounds kind of messy and mean-spirited for a woman. You sure she was alone?" Most women don't like a mess. Those who kill are usually more fastidious.

"That ain't the half of it. Coroner won't say for publication, but they was like mini-shotgun blasts. He got blown away by his own pistol. Always kept it loaded with Black Talon hollow points."

"Whoa." Black Talon ammo is designed to maim. On impact, the slugs peel open, fanning into jagged flower-shaped blades that shred internal organs. Cops favor their stopping power. Targets go down and don't get up, and the bullets are far less likely to ricochet or pass through a body and hit somebody else. Criminals like Black Talons too. Their use of the deadly ammo generated enough public outcry that the manufacturer voluntarily took it off the market back in 1994. Only cops can legally buy it now.

"You sure this wasn't a hit by somebody trying to make it look sex-related?"

"Some things you can't fake, Britt."

"Killed in his own office, right? What's the layout like?" Unconsciously, I had picked up a pencil and was scribbling notes.

"No windows, one door enters off the lobby, another opens into the jail annex where there's four holding cells. No tenants at the time unfortunately, or we mighta had us an eyewitness. Had his desk in there, four file cabinets, a little fridge, a gun cabinet, an evidence safe, a TV—and a big ol' leather couch."

"So your impression is he might have interviewed suspects on that couch?" The infamous casting couch in reverse, I thought. Audition, and maybe you don't have to play the role of defendant.

"There'd been rumors around for years."

"Women he arrested?"

"Females, period. Prisoners, prisoners' wives, secretaries, dispatchers, even female deputies who wanted to keep their jobs or git promoted."

"Eeewwwwwee. You ever write about it?"

"Britt, I keep telling ya, things are different up here."

True. The farther north you go in Florida, the farther south you get.

"What you putting in your story, Charlie?"

"You kidding? Our publisher already handed down the word. Brascom's widow and grown kids live here. Hell, her granddaddy was a pioneer, first preacher in these parts. Buddy's the victim, he got killed, there's no proof, who ya gonna get to speak ill of the dead anyhow?"

"Nobody, probably, unless you ask them. What happens when she gets caught and spills the story at trial?"

"It'd just get blamed on her sleazy defense lawyer; everybody knows how they operate. But that has to happen first. Chances are, you know, cop killers—especially up in this part of the state—usually don't get taken alive."

He was right.

"Specially this one. Not only did she take off with his sidearm, she helped herself to a coupla boxes of his ammo."

"Black Talons?"

"Yeah."

Three

"ALTHEA MORAN, PLEASE."

"Who's calling?" the woman's voice was guarded.

"Britt Montero, from *The Miami News.*"

The silence was so long, I thought she'd hung up, after I'd finally reached her.

"How do I know you're who you say you are?"

I sighed. "Well, if you recall, you wrote to me."

"Yes?" Her voice was irritatingly noncommittal.

"If you're still interested in speaking to me, you can call me back, the number is—"

"Thank you anyway, I'll just call the main number at the paper and ask for you."

She was difficult, probably paranoid. I had half a mind not to answer when she called minutes later. But I did.

"It *is* you. Please forgive me, Ms. Montero, but I have good reason to be cautious."

"I understand. Why do you think somebody—"

"Please! We mustn't discuss it over the telephone."

Here we go, I thought. I knew it. "Why not?"

"The only way to know a conversation is private is to conduct it face-to-face, alone in the same room."

"Yes, but Ms. Moran, this isn't the sort of thing you want to keep private. If what you say is true, the more people who know, the safer you are. Doesn't that make sense?"

Another pause. "Call me Althea." Her voice sounded softer and more vulnerable. "I'm not crazy."

"I never said you were. What's going on, Althea?"

"They've tried to kill me," she whispered. "Twice."

"Who?"

"I don't know."

"Why would someone try to kill you?"

Ryan stopped tapping his keyboard behind me. He was eavesdropping.

"I don't have a clue. That's what keeps me awake at night, driving me . . . wild. I can't think of any reason, any motive."

"Ms.—Althea. In my experience, when somebody wants to kill you, you usually know why." People often deny it, but they know. Like the driver found in a bullet-riddled car, alive because of his bulletproof vest. He insisted to police that he had no idea why anyone would try to kill him. He had no explanation for why he was wearing body armor either.

"I am no fly-by-night," Althea Moran was saying defensively. "I am a solid citizen, a native Miamian." Her voice shook slightly. "I was born here. I am not a person with enemies. You can check your files, my picture appeared in your newspaper—oh, at least a dozen times."

I lifted an eyebrow.

"I was Althea Albury then," she said, as though reading my mind. "I was Orange Bowl queen in 1973."

"Orange Bowl queen?"

"Yes. In 1973 I rode the biggest, most beautiful float in the parade. Earnie Seiler outdid himself that year. Our float was breathtaking, a huge golden sunburst, waterfalls, and swaying palm trees that lit up. I wore glittery silver and white—and the crown, of course; the four princesses, my court, wore pink. You probably weren't born yet."

"Oh, I was there," I said, wondering if she was. "I

was the little girl sitting on the curb in front of the Everglades Hotel."

My grandmother took me to the parade every New Year's Eve. We fought huge crowds, thousands of people. The best always came last: the queen and her court atop the final float, regal and glamorous, wearing long white gloves, smiling, and waving no matter what the weather.

"That was the year we had the cold snap," she said. "It was the first parade nationally telecast in full color. The mayor and the Chamber of Commerce sent somebody to shut down the power to that bank building along the parade route that displayed the time and temperature. They blacked it out so people around the country wouldn't see how cold it was in Miami. They told us to think warm and keep smiling. We almost froze our you-know-whats off—but we never stopped smiling.

"I caught a terrible cold, but it was the most wonderful week. When it was over—the luncheons, the ball, the regatta, and the big game—and we got rid of the chaperone, Richard proposed and we got engaged. It was an incredible year."

Her letter had said she was alone.

"Are you a widow?"

"No. Divorced."

Aha, I thought. When somebody wants you dead, it's most likely a loved one, or an ex-loved one. "Is he local? Still in town?"

"Oh, yes, his practice is here. . . ."

"You think he's behind your problem?"

"Richard?" Taken aback, she gave a little half laugh. "Up till now he's been responsible for nearly all my problems. He might make me wish I was dead, but he wouldn't try to kill me."

"You've reported everything to the police?"

"Oh, yes. I have the police reports."

"Excuse me." I covered the mouthpiece for a few moments. "Uh-oh, my editor is calling me to a meeting. I'll get back to you."

I lied. No meeting. No editor. Cynic that I am, I wanted to confirm what she'd said before investing more time. It defies common sense when people lie to reporters about easily checked facts, but they do, all the time. Probably the same people who lie on résumés, rent applications, and their income tax. They lie about their police records, credit ratings, and marital status. Sometimes they lie for no reason. Trust no one, not even the president. Our competition recently fell for a tale told by a Cuban physician who swore she had treated Fidel Castro for a potentially fatal brain ailment. Not until after publishing the exclusive did they learn she was no doctor, not even a nurse, and hadn't even been in Cuba when she said the "treatment" took place.

Even poor Ryan had been burned. Badly. He interviewed a World War II combat vet, winner of the Congressional Medal of Honor. The aging hero, now elderly and homeless on the mean streets, had been denied treatment at Miami's VA hospital because he had no paperwork. He said he had pawned the medal to eat long ago, but he still recounted with patriotic zeal his colorful tales of heart-stopping wartime experiences. Despite it all, he still loved his country. Editors planned to front-page it on Memorial Day. From hero to homeless, this hell of a story would have wounded the national consciousness, torpedoed heartless VA bureaucrats, and won our forgotten hero the gratitude and support he deserved. He was a reporter's dream—except for one minor flaw. Not a word he said was true. The man had won no medals and had never served his country—though he *had* served time, mostly in jails and drunk tanks.

He was so damn believable that Ryan failed to place the routine call to Washington to confirm the man's Medal of Honor until the day before the piece was to run. Lottie had spent hours shooting our hero, humble and misty-eyed, as he saluted Old Glory at the Bayfront Park war memorial.

The photos were dramatic and touching. Too bad they were seen only on the bulletin board down at security, along with mug shots of other scam artists, crooks, and undesirables banned from the building. Lottie was still barely speaking to Ryan.

I grabbed a quick cup of coffee and trotted down the hall. What used to be the newspaper morgue is called the library now. Stories published before 1982, when it went on-line, were still in the hard copy archives. I browsed the dusty, poorly lit shelves for the name files beginning with A. Sure enough, Althea Albury had a folder of her own. Then I scaled the ladder to O and plucked the fat Orange Bowl file for 1973. I sat at a librarian's desk and flipped them open, the first time anyone had touched them in years.

Orange Bowl Queen Althea Albury smiled up at me, her regal brow serene. A fairy-tale beauty, a University of Miami student, blonde, blue-eyed, and sweet-faced, with a Scarlett O'Hara waistline, she looked demure and pure, wearing the crown and crinolines of a more innocent time, the symbol of old Miami, the Magic City, the tourist mecca, the fun-and-sun capital of the world, before riots, Mariel, and murder made headlines. News photographers long dead or retired had captured the crowds and the floats from dozens of angles as the parade progressed. Scanning the faces, I searched for myself, the little girl seated on the sidelines along Biscayne Boulevard, wishing my dad was there to lift me up higher for a better look at the queen floating by in all her magnificence.

Her engagement announcement appeared at a time when no one had to pay for its publication. My waves of nostalgia crashed on the rocks of reality. Newspapers not so long ago truly chronicled the three times in life when most people got their names in the paper. Birth announcements, wedding notices, and obituaries are all paid ads today.

Only celebrities count, along with those who can afford to pay. Landmarks in the lives of those who cannot afford to pay do not exist for the newspaper.

Althea Albury definitely existed.

Richard Moran was a cardiologist, a fact not lost on the society-page writer, who reported that the handsome young doctor who mended hearts had lost his own to the Orange Bowl queen. Where, I wondered, did this story-book romance go wrong? Did anybody ever live happily ever after?

"Hey, whatcha digging for back here?"

Lottie had a stack of photos in her hand. She peered over my shoulder.

"Purty woman. What year was that?"

" 'Seventy-three," I said.

"Probably a grandma by now, or wanting to be. Didya know that Dean Martin's first wife was an Orange Bowl queen way back when? Saw her on the float, it was love at first sight, and off to Hollywood. What'd this one do?"

"Claims somebody's trying to kill her. Don't know if it's true yet. Hear anymore from your ex?"

Lottie sighed. "Quit taking his calls. No point in picking up. He'd only sweet-talk me into something I'd regret. They catch the woman who shot the sheriff yet?"

"Nope. But wait till you hear the latest. She might surface with an abuse excuse. The sheriff may have a history of coercing sex from women, including prisoners."

"Think she got scared, managed to git his gun, and shot 'im?"

"It's a theory. If it's true, she's probably terrified. She's in a whole lot of trouble no matter how it happened. Even if it was self-defense, chances are no jury up there would believe her. Somebody might even shoot her before she can tell it. Smartest thing she could do now is surrender on neutral turf where she can tell her story and try to get public sentiment and some feminist groups behind her.

She needs the best damn lawyer she can find and a definite change of venue.''

''Wouldn't mind covering the story; sounds like you wouldn't either. Maybe she'll come down here.''

''We can only hope.'' I closed Althea Albury's folder. ''I've had a real dry spell between big stories lately. I don't know how the justice team deals with it,'' I told her. Four reporters are assigned to the team that works only on sensitive investigative projects. I secretly suspected them of being lazy, taking advantage of the unlimited time they are given, without deadline pressures, to produce a story. ''They've been working on something for weeks now,'' I said. ''I like to see my work in the newspaper every day. It's been so long since I've had a solo front-page byline that I expect my mother to call any minute now to ask if I still work here. I'd love to know what really happened up in Shelby County. Let's look up the sheriff.''

The wires had moved a head shot after the shooting and we found older photos, taken at Florida Association of Chiefs of Police conventions and at dedication ceremonies at the Florida Sheriffs' Boys Ranch.

We spread them out on the desk, images of the murdered lawman at various stages of his lengthy career. Heavyset and stern-looking, T. Rupert Brascom was square-jawed, jowly, and thick across the middle. His wedding ring was clearly visible in several.

''Some people in power get away with abuse for so long they think they're entitled, that they're above the law.''

''Looks like the type,'' Lottie said.

''What do you mean?''

''Well.'' She sniffed and pointed a number-three pencil at one of the photos. ''See here, that thin upper lip? My daddy always called that a sure sign of meanness.''

''Oh, that's certainly scientific.''

''Never fails. And looky here, see the whites of his eyes

beneath his pupils in this one? An indication of criminal behavior. Ya see it in mug shots all the time. Ever notice?''

''It's only the camera angle, the tilt of his head,'' I argued, trying to remember the eyes in the hundreds of mug shots I'd seen. ''You'd sure be a fair and impartial juror.''

''I'd acquit in a minute,'' she said. ''Probably give her a medal for marksmanship.''

''She didn't need to be much of a marksman, they were contact wounds,'' I said. ''You just have a mad on for men at the moment. Wonder what really happened? Hope she doesn't get killed or commit suicide before she tells.''

I grew restless back at my computer terminal. The newsroom was too cold and too dangerous. Frigid air cascaded across my desk from an air-conditioning duct overhead, and Gretchen, the assistant city editor from hell, might glance up at any moment, decide I did not look busy, and shoot some cockamamie assignment at me like a bullet with my name on it. I watched her, one hand on her hip, leaning on the city desk, head tilted, as she spoke on the telephone, showing off her perfectly coiffed hair and crisp designer suit. How did she manage to arrive here untouched by heat and humidity? Did she tunnel her way into the building? Did she sleep sitting up? As the editors filed into their afternoon news meeting, I called Althea, left word with the city desk clerk that I would be out following up a story lead, and made my getaway.

Her address was on Alhambra. The city of Coral Gables has several: a drive, a circle, a way—and no street signs. Names like Alcantarra, Algaringo, Almeria, and Alhambra are carved into low dusky-colored coral rock curbstones, difficult to read in daylight, invisible at night, the attitude being that if you are lost you don't belong in the city beautiful.

The house, an architectural gem from the twenties, was

a two-story DeGarmo, painted white with green shutters and a coral-rock facade. The look was charming old South, with a slight air of neglect. Dead fronds dangled from the stately royal palms lining the driveway. Oak trees shading the east and west sides of the house needed trimming, as did bamboo clumps along the property line. An aging Cadillac sat in the shady driveway. Rust bubbled its cream-color finish and had begun to erode its way around the windows.

I rang the doorbell but heard only distant strains of classical music. Rang again. Listened. Nothing. Paint was peeling and some of the screens needed to be repaired. I knocked, rapping my keys on metal.

Was she lurking inside, watching? Wondering if it was really me?

"Ms. Moran?" I wondered if she might be in the backyard.

"Who is it?" the voice, startlingly close, came from just inside the foyer.

She opened the door after I identified myself and slid my business card inside. "Hope you weren't out here too long. The doorbell stopped working. I have no idea what's wrong with it."

She was the woman in the photos, fighting time and Mother Nature: the clear blue eyes a bit faded now, hair still blonde but poorly cut, figure still good, though heavier. In her casual slacks and matching blouse, Althea Moran could have passed for the mother of the young beauty with the crown and scepter.

Smiling graciously, she offered iced tea, and bustled off to the kitchen.

The house smelled slightly musty, hinting at roof leaks temporarily stayed by the drought. A twelve-foot brick fireplace dominated the great room. Hanging over it was a large framed portrait of Orange Bowl Queen Althea Albury, expression expectant, as though anticipating a regal future.

I was studying it when she returned. "Richard took the best artwork with him," she said good-naturedly. We both gazed up at her youthful image. "That's when I reigned over the parade. Now somebody's raining on my parade."

We talked in an enclosed porch at the rear of the house. She called it the reading room. A ceiling fan, a floor fan, and shady landscaping made it tolerable. The classical music came from a radio on a small corner table. I settled on a wicker love seat, notebook in my lap, and she sat in an armchair across from me, a smoke-colored cat with a red leather collar rubbing against her ankles.

"Okay, what's happening?" I asked cheerfully. "What makes you think you're a target, that somebody wants to kill you?"

She looked self-conscious for a moment, then spoke softly. "In the light of day, in this sunny place, listening to Vivaldi, the birds singing outside, my cat purring in my lap, sometimes I can almost make myself believe it's not happening."

I nearly spit up my iced tea. Was she saying she imagined it? That it was all a bad dream? That I came out here for nothing? Maybe she should meet Ryan's war hero. They could stroll into the sunset trying to top each other's stories.

"But that's denial, wishful thinking," she went on. "The sort of attitude that could prove fatal." She looked directly at me, hands folded properly in her lap. "The first incident was nearly two months ago. Here, in this house. But it's odd, I think it actually began sooner. I had a peculiar feeling for several days, as if something was about to happen or that I was being watched. Sort of an instinct that something was wrong. I'm no psychic, but I've been right about such things over the years. Call it woman's intuition. I knew at once when Richard was unfaithful—and they say the wife is always the last to know. . . .

"There is only one night a week that I arrive home after dark. I volunteer at the county hospital several days a week, helping to feed and nurture the AIDS babies. They're short-staffed and those babies need attention, cuddling, and holding. Many are abandoned at birth, just left by their mothers. The nurses are too busy, and the work is fulfilling. I enjoyed being a mother. It's been a long time. On Wednesdays, we go out to dinner afterward, several of us volunteers, nothing elaborate. We go to a diner nearby or grab a pizza."

She leaned forward, her expression serious. "I would have come into the house alone as always, but that night, as I pulled up, the Adlers, my neighbors down the street, were out walking their dog: Emma, her husband, Arthur, and their son, Kenneth. He was visiting from New York. I hadn't seen the boy for years. He and my daughter Jamie grew up together. I wanted him to see pictures of her baby, so I invited them in for a glass of wine.

"The house was quiet. We were talking and laughing. When I arrive home, I always come directly to this enclosed porch to feed the cat. Instead, I went to the kitchen, got out the wine and the good glasses, then dashed out here for a decanter on that shelf." She indicated a shelf that held several decorative platters and a pot of flowing ivy. "I wanted to decant the wine," she said, lowering her voice, "because what I had in the house was not exactly a prizewinning vintage. I haven't entertained in some time.

"I walked out here without turning on the lights, took the decanter off the shelf, and then I saw him, standing right there." She indicated the corner next to where I sat. "He was wearing one of the those black Boston Strangler–style knit masks, with eyeholes."

A chill rippled down my spinal cord, raising gooseflesh on my arms as she went on.

"I screamed and dropped the decanter. It shattered on the tile floor; it was crystal, Waterford. We'd had it forever, a wedding gift, I think. My guests called out, then came running. I simply stood there, frozen, as he fumbled at the door, trying to unlock it. I'd been having a problem with it. It sticks. I think the wood is warped. For a moment I thought he was going to smash his fist through the glass panel, but then he did manage to open it—and ran."

"What did he say?"

"Nothing, not a word."

"The others in the house, they all saw him?"

She nodded. "Kenneth wanted to chase him, but his mother screamed and hung on to him. She's the nervous type. She kept saying, 'What if he has a gun? What if he has a gun?' "

"Did you see a gun?"

She shook her head.

"What happened next?"

"We called the police." She shrugged. "Two officers came. They said we had surprised a burglar and frightened him off. There have been burglaries in this area, they said, though not on this block. A detective called a few days later. He asked me more about the man's description. There wasn't much I could tell him."

The black mask sounded ominous. I had written several stories about a rapist striking just east of the Gables, in Coconut Grove. He wore a black ski mask. His MO was to break into houses and wait for his victims to come home alone. Was that what the detective was thinking about when he called?

"Did they say they had any suspects?"

"No. But later, particularly after the second incident, I began to think about it. . . . The intruder took nothing. The police assumed we had surprised him moments after he broke in. But that isn't true. He expected me to be alone. He had been inside, waiting for some time. Waiting for me."

"What makes you think that?"

"He had come in another way; he didn't know the porch door would stick. I saw his panic when it didn't open. Worst of all, I discovered later that a knife from the cutlery block in the kitchen was missing, the sharpest one. It was there that morning. He must have had it and was waiting for me with it in the dark. He took it with him."

"You're sure it wasn't missing before?"

"Absolutely. I always felt safe here. I must say I haven't felt the same about this house since. But I believed it was an isolated incident, until it happened again, a week later. I've always grocery-shopped at the supermarket here in the Gables, but prices are higher, and I had some cents-off coupons only redeemable at Dixie-Mart, so I went to the store on Coral Way, in Miami. I finished shopping and was walking to my car. It was twilight, just before the floodlights go on in the parking lot. I thought I heard footsteps, someone running, but when I turned I saw no one. As I put the bags in the car, a man's voice suddenly said, "Excuse me." When I looked up, he was right on top of me. He grabbed me. He wore the same ski mask—"

"It was the same man?"

"I believe so. He was the same height. The mask looked the same. I dropped the groceries, struggled, and tried to call for help from a driver who had pulled his car up right behind mine. I thought he had seen what was happening and was coming to my rescue. But the driver hunched over, and when he came up he was also wearing a mask. The first one had me in an armlock, dragging me toward the car. The masked driver opened the door. I struggled, trying to hold on to my own car, screaming, 'What are you doing? Let go of me!' Something like that. That's when the other one jumped out of the car and came running. He wrenched my hand free from the door and twisted my arm. They were dragging me into their car.

"I saw the look in their eyes, Ms. Montero. They were going to kill me. They didn't want my purse. They wanted *me.*"

She blinked back tears. Sensing her distress, her cat sprang into her lap, where it curled up, fixing a baleful amber-eyed stare on me.

"One put his hand over my mouth, and I bit him. We scuffled, bouncing off both cars, with me yelling as loud as I could. That's when a stranger, a woman in a car, started blowing her horn and screaming at them to stop and an old man with a grocery cart shouted, 'What are you doing? What are you doing?' And then a bag boy came running, yelling, 'Hey! Hey! Hey!'

"Somebody set off a car alarm, and a little old lady blew her police whistle.

"With all the commotion, they let go of me and I fell, broke the heel on my shoe, and landed among the groceries scattered everywhere. I was crying, scratched up, nails all broken, bruised for two weeks. The bag boy got their license tag number as they pulled out of the parking lot. The Miami police came."

"What did they say?"

"The car was stolen. They said it's not unusual for stolen cars to be used in—what did they call it?—an attempted strong-arm robbery. They insisted that the men were thieves trying to rip the purse off my shoulder. They said that women often get dragged that way when the strap is sturdy and doesn't break. I could not get them to believe that those men were not after my purse, they wanted me." Anger tightened her voice.

I understood her frustration. Police used to ask which way the bad guys went and tried to catch them. Now, even if witnesses point and say, "They just ran around that corner!" cops will first ask for the victim's name, address, and social security number. The only cops I've seen actually run after anybody lately were performing for *COPS* or *America's Most Wanted.*

"I was furious," Althea was saying. "I showed them my purse, gave a weak little tug, and the strap tore. It was an inexpensive little vinyl knockoff, not some well-made leather bag like a Coach or a Gucci."

"What was their reaction?"

"I believe they took me for a hysterical woman."

The cops didn't buy the story, and I wasn't sure I did either. Why her? It all boiled down to motive. There was none. Richard was apparently happy as a clam with the younger woman he had dumped Althea to marry. They had a new baby, almost the same age as Althea and Richard's recent grandchild by their daughter, Jamie, who had also married a doctor.

"It's wonderful to have a grandchild," Althea told me wistfully, "but we don't get to spend much time together. Jamie and her husband are much closer to her father and his new family now. Richard," she said, "has the money and the power. My son-in-law is on staff at the same hospital. Richard's new wife, Moira, and our daughter have so much in common. Nearly the same age, with new babies. They socialize, even go skiing together."

Richard was apparently too busy reliving his youth to be trying to kill his ex-wife. If anything, *she* should be gunning for *him*.

"A lousy deal," I said.

She shrugged bleakly.

"What else has been going on in your life?"

"The only thing out of the ordinary is that I served on a jury in a big drug case in criminal court a few years ago, a fascinating experience. In fact, I saw the jury foreman again just recently, bumped into him at the post office."

"You think the defendant might be out of prison and stalking members of the jury that put him away?"

"No, we acquitted."

Money was no motive. She had none. The divorce settlement awarded her the house and her car, but her monthly alimony was not nearly enough to maintain them. Her pride wounded, angry at being dumped, she had not demanded more, naively believing she could make it on her own. She'd been wrong.

"It's not so easy to land a job when your only work experience in the last thirty years is riding a float." She laughed ruefully. Richard's checks often came late; his new wife kept forgetting to write them. Althea used to donate her old clothes to the Junior League Thrift Shop; now she shopped there. She was taking a computer course, hoping it would lead to a job. She was barely getting by.

I thought about my own mother, widowed when I was three.

Althea Moran did not seem the type to inspire murderous passions. She agreed.

"I do not go to bars at night to pick up strangers," she said quietly. "I don't quarrel in traffic, drive fast, or argue over parking spaces. I don't take foolish risks. But I saw it in their eyes—they wanted to kill me. You're my only hope," she pleaded. "No one else will take me seriously."

I wasn't sure what to believe.

On the way back to the office I thought about how both Althea and the crown of Orange Bowl queen had been phased out. The tradition died when women invited to join the Orange Bowl Committee found the queen and her court demeaning. I never understood their objections. What's demeaning about being queen? The world has always had goddesses. Hell, I wouldn't mind riding a magnificent float down Biscayne Boulevard, waving Happy New Year to thousands of cheering celebrants. I could suggest half a dozen more important issues for feminists to fix, but nobody asked me. Althea had been phased out by feminists, her unfaithful husband, the cops, and the world in general. I wished life were kinder and that fairy tales always had happy endings.

I decided not to mention Althea Albury Moran to the city desk yet, in case there was no story.

A message waited. I called Charlie Webster back.

"Thought you might be interested," he drawled. "They found the sheriff's Blazer down in Alachua County, in a ditch out near Turkey Creek."

"Did they find her? Have they got her?"

"Nope. The lady's long gone again. But she did leave her calling card."

"What?"

"Dead man. Britches around his ankles. His wazoo shot off, then shot in the head, just like ol' Buddy Brascom. Took his car too. Thought you'd be interested, cuz it appears she headed south again, coming your way."

four

THE UNIDENTIFIED VICTIM HAD PULLED INTO AN I-75 rest stop at midmorning. The coffee-shop waitress saw him soon after, chatting with a vivacious young woman. The busy waitress did not see them leave. Five hours later, the pilot of a crop duster spotted the roof of a sports utility vehicle in a dry drainage ditch off a back road bordered by woodlands.

The Alachua County Sheriff's Department and the Highway Patrol dispatched cars, hoping to find the Blazer sought in the Shelby County murder. They did. What they did not expect to find was a dead stranger in his late twenties or early thirties sprawled beside it. His pockets were empty, his car gone, apparently taken by the killer, but no one knew what he had been driving.

The manhunt intensified. I swiveled my chair to study the Sunshine State's gun-shaped outline on the three-by-five-foot map mounted on the wall next to my desk. I found a box of red pushpins in the wire room and inserted one into the map in central Shelby County, the site of the sheriff's office, and another to the south, at the rest stop just off the interstate, where the second victim was last seen alive.

I regretted that the story was unfolding outside our circulation area. Not my turf. I opened a file anyway. Was it wishful thinking or because I know that those on the run are inevitably drawn here? I heard someone say once that it is the carrion smell of the corpse flower that attracts the dregs and bottom feeders who drift inexorably toward south Florida. The amorphophallus, now in bloom, resembles a phallus and smells like something dead. Its sickening spoiled-meat odor attracts flies, in the jungle and in Florida gardens.

I drove home at twilight. Looming clouds blackened a tumultuous western sky but failed to keep their promise of rain. The heat evoked dreams streaked by lightning and rocked by distant thunder—or was it gunfire?

I woke up dazed, at daylight, Bitsy barking a warning. Moments later an urgent pounding rattled my front door.

"Britt! Britt! Help me!"

Mrs. Goldstein. In trouble. The gun. My mind blanked in a moment of confusion. Where was my gun? Nestled in the glove compartment of the T-Bird, parked outside. Normally I bring it inside, but the night before I had been lugging a grocery bag, notebooks, and my purse.

I threw open the door. "What's wrong?"

"Look! Look what they've done to the amaryllis!"

The yard was alive with huge black grasshoppers with garish yellow and chartreuse racing stripes, red-tipped wings, and orange warning dots. The stuff of biblical plagues, they swooped and swarmed, stripping away succulent leaves.

"Look at their size!" I said. "It must be this crazy weather."

"They've already eaten all the new growth off the day lilies!" she said. "I haven't seen them like this for years. Nothing kills them!"

Some societies prize grasshoppers as a delicacy. Too bad ours is not one of them.

"The only way to kill these babies is with a small-caliber pistol, but don't try it," I warned.

Assurances that they would soon swarm off to greener pastures didn't stop Mrs. Goldstein from swinging a broom at them. She was still at it when I left early to go to a scene.

"Stay in the shade," I urged. "Are you wearing sunscreen?"

She shook her head and sighed. "I'm leaving soon anyway. The Jam and Jelly class at the Fruit and Spice Park starts at ten. You're off to work?"

"Yes. McDonald sends a hug. I talked to him last night."

"Your handsome captain. He'll be back soon?"

"Few more days." That got her attention. Romance always does. She's been trying to marry me off for years.

"I knew it." She looked thrilled. "I always knew he was the one for you."

She's right, I thought. I knew it too.

Lost and looking for a street in South Miami, I stopped to give the right of way to a land crab invasion. They skittered across the road, claws clicking like castanets. I see them less and less frequently now. They're fast disappearing, their habitats paved over, poisoned by pesticides, or crunched by cars.

I finally found the right small, neat house. The owner, a seventy-seven-year-old widow, reclined outside in a lawn chair. A neighbor had seen her lounging there, then noticed the widow still seated in the same position nearly thirty-six hours later.

The remorseless heat had dried her lips, drawing up her mouth as moisture evaporated from her body, shrinking the skin on her face, thinning her nose. Her fingertips had shriveled, darkened, and hardened, the first stages of mummification.

"Doesn't anybody ever die inside an air-conditioned

building anymore?'' Dr. Duffy grumbled, as he mopped his brow.

It didn't seem that way. Mother Nature continued to crank up the heat. A woman walking outside the criminal justice building on her lunch hour glanced into a parked car—and screamed. Other passersby joined her, trying to smash the windows. The first cop who arrived shattered them with his club. Too late. The temperature inside had soared to more than 140 degrees. The baby girl, still strapped in her car seat, was dead.

The mother was in an air-conditioned courtroom with her older children, ages three and six. Investigators from the Division of Children and Family Services had recently returned all three, finding no basis for neglect charges against her. Her caseworker had assured the mother that her court appearance, ''a mere formality,'' would result in a quick dismissal, so she left the little one in the car. The court calendar, as usual, was log-jammed and lengthy.

DCFS supervisors refused comment. When I returned to the T-Bird, the steering wheel was too hot to touch. I could have fried eggs on the dashboard. Pets and people didn't stand a chance.

I had no time to call the Adlers, Althea Moran's neighbors, until after the early edition deadline. Son Kenneth had returned to his New York job; his father wasn't home yet.

''That man could have had a gun,'' Emma Adler said.

''What did he look like?''

''Well, when I say I saw him, it's just a figure of speech. It was a glimpse, a shadow disappearing into the dark. That's all any of us had, a glimpse. None of us really *saw* him.''

''What was he wearing?''

''Dark clothes, I suppose. You're not actually going to put any of this into the newspaper, are you?''

''I'm not sure.''

''Well, don't you use my name. I mean, we don't have

crime here. This is a good neighborhood. We all take excellent care of our homes. Nobody wants anything in the newspaper that could bring down our property values or tarnish the image of our neighborhood."

"You saw his mask?" I persisted.

"I couldn't swear he had one. All I know is what Althea said. Who knows if that's right?"

"Why wouldn't it be? You think she lies?"

"Well, you know"—her voice dropped to a confidential tone—"she hasn't been herself since her husband ran off with a younger woman."

"I'm aware she's divorced."

"I told her then not to keep that house." She spoke louder, disapproval permeating her words. "It's far too big, too much for a woman alone. But would she listen? No. Told her to hire herself one of those tough divorce lawyers and go after big money. Could have had herself a nice waterfront apartment and enough to be comfortable the rest of her life. Did she listen?

"Look, what happened at Althea's happens every day, but not in our neighborhood. We scared off a burglar. That's it. No big news. If it was a burglar."

"If he wasn't, who would he be?"

"Maybe some man she knew."

"Is she seeing someone? Dating?"

"Not that I know, but it wouldn't be the first time something like that happened."

"Why would she scream and call the police?"

"Who knows? Maybe she was embarrassed or had herself a drink or two."

"She's a drinker?"

"Well." She paused. "I wouldn't know, but she was pretty quick to invite us in for a drink that night."

"Did it appear as though she'd already been drinking?"

"To tell you the truth, I didn't notice, but she was coming home alone, after dark."

"I thought she'd been volunteering at the hospital," I

percent on class-one crimes last year. That's something you can write about. We credit our success to the community awareness programs we—''

''Lieutenant, do you think somebody tried to kill Althea Moran?''

''Hell, no.''

''But two incidents? So close together?''

''You've been around long enough, Britt, to know things happen. She could be either overreacting or craving attention. Sometimes, when women reach a certain age and are alone, that happens. I'm not saying that's definitely the case here,'' he added quickly, ''but we had a divorcée once, lived over on Sopera, used to dial nine-one-one every damn night. Heard prowlers, noises, thieves, whatever. Just lonesome. She wanted some young good-looking police officers to come by so she could flirt with them.''

''How'd you handle that?''

He guffawed. ''Had a no-nonsense policewoman respond to every call from that location. Didn't take long for the calls to quit.''

''Do you know Althea Moran's ex-husband?''

''Dr. Moran? Sure. Excellent surgeon. Operated on my father-in-law, triple bypass. Nice fella. City manager plays golf with him from time to time.''

Lieutenant Randy Springer, in the city robbery division, recalled Althea Moran clearly once his memory was jogged.

''Oh, yeah, I remember her,'' he said. ''Started out real ladylike, but went a little dramatic on us—ripping up her own purse, trying to demonstrate that it couldn't have held up if a purse snatcher had yanked on it.''

''What happened?''

''Oh, the strap snapped right in two, whole thing came apart.''

''How do you explain that?''

''They dragged her around by that strap and they weakened it; it was already starting to come apart. Look, Britt, she's a nice lady from a nice neighborhood. I understand her fears. This city, as we both know, gets a little scary sometimes."

"So you patted her on the head like a good little girl, sent her home, and told her not to worry?"

"That's not fair, Britt. We did all we could. Even talked to the Gables, just to be sure. Look, we had two thousand strong-arms in the past year. There's been half a dozen in and around that parking lot since Easter. We've been meaning to send in CST, the crime suppression team."

"The other muggings there—were they by the same guys?"

"Hard to say."

According to Springer, the getaway car belonged to a college student and was stolen off a South Beach street while he partied there with friends the night before. Other witnesses in the parking lot did confirm that at least one of the muggers was masked.

"Isn't that odd?" I asked him.

"A little out of the ordinary, but I wouldn't go as far as to call it odd."

"Any other recent muggings done by masked men?"

"Not that I'm aware of."

"I'm just trying to determine her credibility, Randy. I don't want to run with it and get burned. What do you think?"

"Honest opinion? Two unrelated, isolated incidents. It happens. Remember that tourist, got robbed three times in one day? Hey, the mayor's car has been stolen twice. Remember the married couple, had both their cars stolen the same day? Shit happens. It was her turn."

"You don't believe anybody's trying to kill her?"

"Hell, no. She's not the type, doesn't live the life, far as we know. I mean, we talked to her. Her divorce was no war. No reason for anybody to kill her or have her killed. And if those jokers were hired hit men, you'd have to admit they were pretty sloppy."

"She seems convinced."

"Like I said, nice lady. Something did happen. Twice. Maybe she's just taking herself a little too seriously, a little paranoid. Or she's looking for sympathy from her ex. Gotta go, staff meeting's about to start."

I read through all my notes, wavering on Althea's story. My cynical mean-spirited self thought: spoiled society wife gets dumped, is lonely, has a couple of bad experiences, thinks life as she knew it is coming to an end, and wants the world to join her pity party. But then I remembered the look in her eyes. Her desperation was real. What if—? My telephone rang.

"He's here!" Lottie hissed.

"Who?"

"O'Rourke!"

"Who?"

"Tex O'Rourke, my ex-husband."

"In Miami?"

"Hell-all-Friday, Britt. In the building!"

I scanned the newsroom for a sinister face. "Where?"

"The lobby, five minutes ago. Chip from security called. O'Rourke was at the front desk asking to see me. I told 'im not to let him come up, to say I was out."

"So he's probably gone."

"Britt, the man called from Fort Worth last night. I said don't come. Told 'im I was engaged, booked up, knocked up, screwed up, had gained seventy-five pounds, and had chicken pox. He's here anyway. You think *our* security kin stop him?"

She had a point. News security guards routinely demand that I present my ID card to enter the building, but their record of challenging suspicious strangers who could be heavily armed mad bombers was not a distinguished one. I recently saw a violent repeat offender, free on bond and awaiting trial, busily using our newsroom copy machine.

A stack of legal documents he needed to copy for his lawyer, he said. When I asked how he slipped by security, he looked puzzled. Security?

"Where are you?" I asked Lottie.

"Under a desk in the sports department," she whispered. "Photo is the first place he'll go."

"Let's meet for coffee in the cafeteria."

"Wish I had a disguise."

Lottie's wild and frizzy mane of flaming red hair was hard to hide. "We'll go to a table back in the corner where the pressmen sit," I suggested. "Take the freight elevator. Meet you there in two."

I arrived first, poured myself coffee, and got her hot tea in a Styrofoam cup. She appeared as I stocked up on napkins and plastic spoons. I signaled her, then stared. Her hair, brushed and shining, was sleekly pinned back on one side with a silver and turquoise clip. Her lashes were coated with inky black mascara, her lips were creamy coral, and she had discarded her khaki vest, the pockets always crammed with film canisters and camera lenses. She even walked different. Her usual easy long-legged stride had been replaced by smaller, more dainty, almost mincing steps.

I whistled under my breath, then muttered, "You sure have a peculiar way of scaring this guy out of town. Wouldn't it be more effective to paint on whiskers?"

"Jist want 'im to see what he's missing," she murmured self-righteously, as we sat down. "Got any blusher on you, Britt?"

"No, but I think there's some in my locker upstairs. I don't believe you," I said, still staring.

She watched the doors behind me as we talked.

"How 'bout this?" She opened the top two buttons of her L. L. Bean blouse, exposing a hint of cleavage. "Look okay?"

"Enough," I said, as her fingers moved to the third button. "You don't want to be too obvious."

She settled down enough to launch into a diatribe against the mother of the dead baby in the car.

"Ought to string that woman up," she muttered. "I'll do it. Why spend money on a trial? Better yet, they oughta stick her in an oven and turn it up to broil. Animals take better care of their young'uns."

She sipped her tea carefully, so as not to smear her lipstick.

"Hear they identified the second guy shot by the woman who killed the sheriff?"

"No, where'd you hear that?"

"Hid out in the wire room awhile, read everything that came across. He wuz driving down to Orlando from Live Oak for a job interview. Never showed up. Got a description on his missing car. Shouldn't be long now. They'll git 'er."

"Be interesting as hell to find out who she is, what she's all about. I thought maybe she panicked and shot the first one defending herself, but jeez, another one makes her look like a stone-cold killer."

"Maybe some man done her wrong." Lottie shrugged.

" 'Member that Orange Bowl queen?" I said, and told her all about Althea. "What's weird," I mused, "are the masks. Muggers and burglars don't wear them. Shit, you see convenience store robberies on TV all the time. They walk in, pull guns, knowing there are security cameras, but even they don't bother to wear masks."

"Maybe he wuz trying to look like the Grove rapist," she said. "So if anybody saw him, the rapist'd git the blame."

"But why target her at all? She's got no money, no insurance, no enemies, no friends—except for that neighbor; with a friend like that she doesn't need enemies. Why would anybody want to kill her?"

"Something to do with her being Orange Bowl queen?"

"Twenty-six years later?"

"Her picture was in the paper, on TV. She was every

man and boy's fantasy back then. You telling me she didn't have a stalker?''

I sighed, shaking my head. ''That was way before stalking became the national pastime.''

''Then it's gotta be her ex-husband or something she's not telling you,'' Lottie said.

''The husband got a good deal, must feel lucky he's not paying through the nose. And why would she hold anything back when she's the one looking for help?''

''What does the desk think?''

''I'm not mentioning it to them until I'm sure she's not nuts and that there really is a story. For all I know, she's as phony as Ryan's Medal of Honor winner.''

''Do not mention that man to me.'' Lottie's eyes flashed fire. ''Saw him panhandling downtown the other day and nearly stopped—and not to pin a medal on 'im.''

''The guy's one hell of a storyteller. I sat right there while Ryan interviewed him. Believed it myself. So did the staff at the homeless shelter; they're the ones who tipped Ryan off about 'im.'' I checked the clock. ''Looks like your ex isn't in the building after all. He's probably on a plane by now.''

''Think so?'' She looked disappointed. ''He's outside, I betcha, watching the exits. Wish I'd lost that ten pounds I've been meaning to drop. You kin drive me to my car. I'll hide in your trunk.''

''No way, the trunk is not comfy. Why are you so determined to duck him?''

''Cuz if I see him, I'm a goner,'' she said, focusing on the door behind me.

''The guy's probably fat and bald by now. What does he look like anyway?''

''Like that,'' she whispered, and licked her lips. ''Jist like that.''

I followed her gaze. A man stood at my elbow, facing her.

"Carlotta Samantha," he drawled, in a gravelly baritone. "Make a wish." Their eyes locked.

"Why, if it isn't Austin Jeffrey O'Rourke," she replied, with an air of total surprise.

He was tall and lean, his black hair curly and his piercing eyes intense. He wore blue jeans and hand-tooled leather boots and exuded a magnetic energy. So did she.

How perfect they looked together, I thought. I was clearly in the way.

"Sit down," I offered, pushing back my chair. "I was just leaving."

He thanked me without taking his eyes off her. She returned his smoldery stare. Neither noticed when I left.

Two messages from Althea waited in the newsroom. I pushed them aside and read the wire copy on the rest-stop murder. Roland Miller, age thirty-six, had been driving a beige Ford Taurus. When he failed to keep his appointment for the Orlando job interview, the company contacted his home. His worried wife called the highway patrol to ask if he had been in an accident. They matched his description to the dead body in Alachua County.

Charlie was not at his desk but returned my call minutes later. "We've got us a helluva breaking story here." I heard the excitement in his voice.

"Did the Shelby County detectives go down there yet?"

"They were all over it the minute the Blazer turned up. It's the break they were waiting for. I just caught up with 'em twenty minutes ago."

"What'd they say? How many times was the victim shot?"

"Twice."

"Where?"

"You probably already guessed."

"The same?"

"He died a happy man—at least till she pulled the gun on 'im."

"Why—"

"Maybe she's a man-hater."

"I just saw a short wire story. Why aren't they releasing more?"

"They're about to. Britt?"

"Yeah, Charlie?"

"She shows up on your turf, you sharing information?"

"Sure. We're not competitors. The street runs both ways."

"Okay," he said. "The sex angle's about to hit the fan. We're running with it too. But there's something else. Medical examiner down in Alachua saw something that didn't look right in the cavity at the front of a hollow-point Black Talon he dug outa that poor bastard."

"What?"

"A pigment that didn't look right. Not blood or human tissue. He had the detective take it right over to the crime lab and they identified it."

"What was it, Charlie?"

"Lipstick."

"Lipstick?"

"They're thinking she kissed the bullet, left traces of lipstick on it, 'fore she loaded the gun."

"But why?"

"Send a message, I guess, such as in kiss-your-ass-goodbye. I don't know. But it was too good to stay a secret. Somebody leaked it, it's been all over local TV down there. With that and the sex, they're calling her the Kiss-Me Killer. Ain't that something?"

The Kiss-Me Killer. I stared at the map above my desk and at the red pin nestled at the rest stop just off Interstate 75. The highway rolls on south through Ocala and divides near Wildwood. The main branch, I-75, runs west to Tampa, down the Gulf coast, and across Alligator Alley. The other jogs southwest of Winter Garden, cuts through Sebring, and snakes around the great Lake Okeechobee south near Belle Glade. The two roads reunite en route to Miami.

Five

SHELL HUNTERS FOUND ROLAND MILLER'S MISSing Ford Taurus the following day, at the end of a no-name road that runs off Canoe Creek, outside of St. Cloud in Osceola County, about a hundred and fifty miles south of Alachua. The powdery-sand road, where local kids like to mud-slide when it's wet, according to the wire stories, skirts the outer edge of a giant stand of bald cypress. As it winds deep into the swamp, the road is lined with an assortment of discarded appliances, furniture, and the rusting hulks of abandoned cars and trucks. Locals use the area for target practice, taking potshots at squirrels, snakes, and swamp rats. Three teens collecting used cartridge shells to repack and use themselves had seen the vehicle. Thinking it was occupied by lovers, they gave it a wide berth. Hours later, when the car was still there, they grew curious.

The doors were unlocked. They might have considered a joy ride but were distracted by swarms of flies buzzing in a nearby clearing. Miller had kept a yellow blanket in his trunk for weekend beach outings. Spread out beneath the live oaks as though for a picnic or romantic woodland rendezvous, the blanket was now saturated with the blood of a stranger, who sprawled atop it staring cross-eyed at the sky.

Two hollow-point Black Talon nine-millimeter slugs had shattered his lower forehead and the bone structure around his eyes. With no anchor for the muscles that hold them in place, both eyes turned inward.

The dead man, about forty-five years old, had been well dressed before removing his trousers and undershorts, folded neatly nearby. His genitalia had been mutilated by a close-range gunshot blast.

According to Charlie Webster, crime scene technicians from the Florida Department of Law Enforcement found the Taurus wiped clean of prints. How could she spend more than a day and a night in a car without leaving telltale evidence? Hair, fiber, the scent of her perfume? I had a hundred questions.

Attempts were under way to construct a composite of the Kiss-Me Killer, based on the uncertain recollections of the coffee-stop waitress, who had been working a full counter at the time, and merchants with whom the killer had used her victims' credit cards.

The dead man's pockets were empty, his vehicle, if any, missing. Technicians attempted to photograph a second set of tire impressions at the scene, but results were not promising due to the dry weather.

Teams of lawmen from north and central Florida had coalesced into a task force. The FBI was working up a psychological profile, and the reward had grown to $100,000.

The story, with its reports of Black Talon bullets kissed by the killer and the victims' "sexual mutilation," caught fire. The *St. Pete Times* and the Tampa and Lakeland papers assigned teams of reporters. Fred Francis did a report for *NBC Nightly News*, and CNN sent in a crew. TV in Miami was already following the case, and the *News* was allotting it more space on the state page.

The speedy and all-out response from law enforcement

and the media was interesting, I thought. Murdered women are frequently found along remote roadsides or in canals. Roving serial killers often achieve double-digit body counts before law enforcement begins to link cases and seriously question whether a monster is at large. Was the early and extraordinarily speedy mobilization in this case because the victims were men? Was there major media coverage because most publishers, executive editors, and news directors are men?

Lottie had taken comp time to spend with Tex. The state of their rekindled relationship was so far so good, I learned, when I called her. They had gone parasailing and water-skiing and were planning to scuba dive under a full moon. I reported the latest on the killer and her most recent victim.

"Hell-all-Friday, somebody sure has pissed her off. Maybe," Lottie suggested, "a man infected her with AIDS and she's getting even. 'Member that story a couple weeks ago? Four out of ten people infected with HIV don't tell their sex partners—and two-thirds admit to not using condoms. Could be she's positive and pissed."

"Could be anything," I said. "The victims seem to be strangers unlucky enough to cross her path. Doesn't sound like they look alike. Maybe they say or do something that triggers her. Or maybe she just wants to rob them and doesn't like leaving witnesses."

"What about the sex?"

"It can't be at gunpoint," I said. "Not many guys could perform under those circumstances."

"Unless they find it excitin'," Lottie said cheerfully. "I once knew a guy who liked—"

"Spare me," I said. "Gotta go."

My destination was an Opa-Locka nursing home. The eastern horizon blurred beneath a reddish-brown haze that looked like smog as I drove the interstate north. The annual migration of red African dust had begun. A monster cloud five hundred miles wide had ridden trade winds and air currents more than three thousand miles from the coast of West Africa. The sky would be milky by tomorrow, with a whitish haze. People with respiratory problems would have breathing difficulty, and Miamians would find their cars coated with a thin rougelike red powder.

Detectives were still interviewing employees at the Golden Sunset Nursing Home. Two elderly patients, one suffering from advanced Alzheimer's, the other a helpless stroke victim, had been wheeled as usual to a remote spot on the landscaped grounds at 9 A.M., for a few minutes of fresh air and sunshine while an aide changed their beds. The temperature had already climbed to 96 degrees but the spot was shaded and the ritual brief. Today, unfortunately, their aide was interrupted by a telephone call. Her child's grade school principal insisted that she pick up her sick youngster from school at once.

The aide left in a hurry, harried and upset, assuming fellow staffers would look after her charges. Not until 4 P.M. did someone note that they were not in their room. A search was launched. By then, the shifting sun had done its brutal work. Still strapped in their chairs, their deaths were apparently due to heat exhaustion.

I remembered Lottie's words about what we have to look forward to and imagined how it felt to be helpless and forgotten in the merciless heat. If only it would rain, I thought. Life would return to normal. Instead, tempers frayed, motorists fought in traffic, and as I listened in my car, City Commissioner Sonny Saladrigas mouthed off on Spanish-language radio, branding the mayor, his former ally, a crook and a Castro spy.

Three days and counting until Kendall McDonald returned. I stopped to shop on the way home. At a liquor store I spent too much on a bottle of good champagne. In Burdines' lingerie department, I bought a frivolous new nightgown, short silky lavender trimmed with fine pale lace. The champagne in the fridge and the gown wrapped in tissue paper in a bedroom drawer, I awaited his call.

The phone rang late. I was dozing.

"Hi, love," I breathed into the mouthpiece.

"Didn't know you cared." The braying laugh came from Bobby Tubbs in the night slot.

"What is this, an obscene call?" I grumbled, and checked the time: nearly 2 A.M.

"Not unless you want it to be." He sniggered. "Seriously, Britt, I'm just closing up shop and I know you've been keeping tabs on those killings upstate. There's a development. Sorry, thought you'd still be up."

"They identify that last victim?" I felt suddenly alert and awake.

"No, but they've got a new one."

"Where?"

"They found this guy near Clewiston, up in Hendry County."

I visualized my map. Clewiston was near the south shore of Lake Okeechobee, closer to Miami than the last one. "Are they sure it was her?"

"Cops seem to think so, same MO. Want to make sure you'll be available if she shows up here. Heard you talk about taking comp time next week."

McDonald and I had discussed driving across state to Sanibel Island in the Gulf of Mexico. The first place we had ever been truly alone together, it was away from Miami, far from our jobs. If the man planned to propose, that's where it would happen.

"Think she's headed here?"

"Who knows? They could nail that crazy bitch tonight, but I need to make sure we're covered, just in case. This is turning into a major national story, and I need to get somebody working on a-matter in case it breaks here and you're not available."

"I'm available." I spoke quickly, staring into the dark.

"I think she'll be here, Bobby. I have a feeling about this one."

"Me too."

What were the chances of the Kiss-Me Killer and McDonald showing up in Miami at the same time? I wondered, Remote, I told myself. I wanted McDonald; I wanted this story. Is this why you should always be careful what you wish for? How could I juggle both? But how nice it would be to break this professional drought and have a front page byline again. I switched on a light. "What play did my story on the nursing home fatalities get?"

"Well," he began slowly, "you're aware that we've got space problems again."

"It's an incredible outrage story," I said accusingly, sitting upright.

"Yeah, I know, could be anybody's grandmother, but we just don't have the space. And we won't know for sure that the heat killed them until after the autopsies tomorrow."

"Oh, sure! They just happen to die simultaneously of natural causes after being left out in the sun all day. It *did* make the paper, didn't it?"

"Sure. Six-B, the obit page."

Not even the local front.

"So," Bobby said, "we can count on you? Your plans won't interfere if the Kiss-Me Killer story breaks in Miami?"

"For sure," I said bleakly. "Count on me." Hell, McDonald hadn't even called.

I tossed and turned, waiting for the phone, then dreamed of endless ribbons of bloody highway streaming south beneath a hazy sky tarnished by African dust.

McDonald called at 8 A.M. "Sorry, babe. Dozed off; by the time I woke up it was way too late. Didn't want to call in the middle of the night and scare you."

"It's never too late for you to call me," I said softly. "Scares me more when you don't."

"You sound so good," he murmured. "Man, do I miss you. Two days to go. I'll drive straight through. Then you'll really have something to be scared of."

Coffee brewing, I ignored my story, buried with the obits, and focused instead on the story stripped across the top of the state page:

BLOODY SIX-DAY THRILL SPREE LEAVES FOUR DEAD.

Few details on victim number four. The story broke late, but Bobby had managed to fly in a new lead as presses rolled.

The upstate sexploits of the Kiss-Me Killer led the radio morning news, followed by stories on the record-breaking heat and a shoving match between Commissioner Saladrigas and a valet car parker at the Inter-Continental Hotel.

The valet asked Saladrigas not to leave his Mercedes on the hotel ramp. Sonny went into a tirade and, witnesses said, shoved the valet. When the valet shoved back, Sonny made threats and displayed a gun tucked in his waistband.

Gone by the time police arrived, Sonny, reached at home, denied everything and blamed his political enemies, "the tools of Fidel Castro," for trying to discredit him.

I pitied the valet, who was expendable. Hotel management probably would not risk offending a powerful politician known for his long memory and his bad temper. Sonny, I thought, could get away with murder.

A wave of heat washed over me as I stepped from my apartment. My damp skin felt coated with an invisible film of African dust before I slid into my ovenlike car. The police beat seemed relatively quiet so I beelined for the office, eager to find out more about the Lake Okeechobee murder. I read the wires and made some calls.

Victim number four was young, a first-year college student on a football scholarship at the University of Florida. He was working for the summer in his father's all-night service station, which answered motorist-in-distress calls from the nearby highway. An attendant who worked with him took the tow truck out on an emergency call at about 10:30 P.M. When he returned shortly before midnight, the door was locked and the office dark, though the exterior lights still burned. A late-model Cadillac he had not seen before was parked behind the station. The college football player's red Trans Am was gone.

As he wondered whether to call the owner, a local trooper drove in to buy a soft drink and write an accident report. He shined a flashlight through a barred side window and saw blood.

She must have assumed he would not be found until morning. She was on the run in a red Trans Am, with little head start. The chase was heating up.

The lime-green Cadillac was registered in Osceola County to the Reverend Jeremiah Truesdale, the wires said. Victim three, the man on the yellow beach blanket, had now been tentatively identified. An evangelical preacher, Truesdale had not been reported missing by his wife because he often disappeared for a day or two, she said, on missions to save the wicked, preach the gospel, or perform impromptu baptisms. It was unclear to me which of those he had been attempting on the yellow beach blanket when the killer sent him to meet his maker. Family and friends had not linked the preacher to descriptions of the unidentified corpse found dead at the sordid woodland scene. This was a man of God.

I jabbed the fourth red pin into the map, studying the trail of the killer's odyssey. She'd stuck mostly to main highways, with brief, deadly excursions into rural areas and small towns. It seemed doubtful she was from out of state; she knew the terrain too well. Settling at my terminal I checked anyway. No similar cases reported anywhere in the United States. Sheriff T. Rupert (Buddy) Brascom had apparently been the first. I focused on the map again, trying to think like her. She could have gone north or turned west to the Gulf. She might be halfway to Biloxi. In my heart I knew she was not. She was coming our way.

Unconsciously toying with a red pushpin, I pricked my finger. It drew blood.

Eager to clear the decks while I could, I asked the slot to beep me with anything new and drove to Miami Beach. I am no detective or social worker. Why, I wondered, was I wasting so much time on Althea Moran? If what she believed was true, it was an intriguing story. But was there a way to prove it? Was I that hard up for a story? Or curious? There was something about her. Did she remind me of my mother? Or was it just that I always want answers?

Dr. Richard Moran and his second wife lived on swank La Gorce Island, where Cher had recently renovated a home. Moran's landscaping, bright and lavish, appeared well watered, despite the restrictions. Some rules don't apply to all of us. The water view was breathtaking, even with the milky haze that transformed large sailboats into mysterious sulfurous ghost craft, disappearing and vaguely retaking their shapes on the horizon. A racy cloud-colored Jaguar in the driveway looked as if it were doing sixty miles an hour standing still. No pink plastic flamingos here.

A uniformed maid answered. The lady of the house was not far behind, an adorable infant in her arms. My jaw must have dropped. A sweet-faced blonde, the young mother was a dead ringer for 1973's Orange Bowl queen. No wonder Richard didn't miss Althea. He had found himself a younger version of the same woman.

She wore a raw silk turquoise blouse, white linen slacks, and a wide leather belt that flattered her figure and her tan, both flawless. She stared, uncomprehending, as I introduced myself.

"We already subscribe," she said, narrowing her eyes at the Spanish-speaking maid who let me in.

"No." I smiled. "I *write* for the newspaper, I don't deliver it."

"A reporter?" Curiosity crept catlike across her face and then blossomed into a welcoming smile. "You're here about the Heart fashion show and winter gala!"

Before I could deny it, she handed off the baby to the maid, who disappeared with her. "It's a bit early for publicity," Moira Moran said, leading me into a spacious great room. "We're still nominating committee members, but I am chairman this year."

"How wonderful," I said. "But I'm actually here about what's been happening to the first Mrs. Moran."

"Althea?" She spoke the name as though it were something she had stepped in. "Oh my God! She went to the press!" she blurted out, then spun around, venting her frustration in a small frenzy. "That woman! She goes to the press because her goddamn check is late?"

"That's not it at all. It's the other things."

"She even had the nerve to annoy our attorney just because of a few days, maybe a week. . . . What other things?"

"I'm sure you're aware of the intruder at her house, the attack on her."

"Attack?" Moira sneered. "The woman was mugged. My God, it happens. Happened to me once. A lowlife took the Rolex right off my wrist outside of Neiman's in broad daylight. You get over it."

"I wondered if you or your husband might know of any reason someone might want to harm her."

She rolled her eyes impatiently and checked the time on what had to be a gold replacement Rolex. "You'll have to talk to my husband about that."

"I tried his office. They said he was in surgery all day."

Moira Moran's response was to steer me toward the door. "The woman is a pain in the butt," she said, "but I seriously doubt that anybody would waste the time and effort. She's trying to make us look bad. She has the house. She has the car. I'll see that she has her check. What she really needs is to get a life."

She had one before you came along, I thought.

"It's not easy being a second wife," she said pitifully, as I left.

Richard, I thought, not his trophy wife, was the culprit. How often, I wondered, did he call his new wife Althea? They deserved each other.

I could have walked, but I drove half a shaded block and pulled into the old Chicago-brick driveway of a smaller but still impressive house, on the dry side of the street. Flowerbeds flourished; the status symbol in this driveway was a BMW.

Jamie Moran Wagner answered the door herself. Petite, her wavy brown hair frosted with golden streaks, she looked less like her mother than Moira did. Her smile faded fast; I was obviously not the person she expected. A baby cried, comforted by someone in another room.

Jamie sighed in distress at mention of her mother. She took me into the kitchen, where she was fixing a bottle for the baby.

"It must be nice to live so close to your dad," I said.

She smiled again. "It's grand," she said. "It's why I told Lawrence that, no matter what, we had to have this house. I didn't see much of Dad when I was little, he always worked so hard. Now we have kids the same age, his wife is my best friend, and my husband his colleague. It's a blast. We double-date and go to medical conventions and conferences together. Moira and I keep each other company when the guys are working."

She flipped the top off a can of premixed formula and paused. "I know it's hard on Mom, especially holidays and stuff, but you can see how awkward it would be to have them all in the same room."

"Isn't it uncanny how much Moira resembles your mom?" I perched on a kitchen stool and watched her pour the contents of the can into a disposable plastic baby bottle and screw on the nipple top.

"You noticed." She laughed. "I keep telling Mom it's a compliment that he was attracted to someone just like her."

"I'm sure she'd have felt more complimented if he had kept the original."

She rolled her eyes. "You know how it is with some men. They get to a certain age . . ." She shrugged. "Dad's really a nice guy. You'd like him."

We sat across from each other at the little breakfast bar.

"I admit," she said softly, the plastic bottle in her hands, "I've been so busy with the baby and everything that maybe I've neglected her some. But that's not a news story; there's no mystery stalker. If you wrote something, it would just embarrass everybody. When things slow down a little, I'll spend more time with her, take the baby to see her more often. I mean, she can't come here. Moira could pop in the door at any minute."

My face must have betrayed my thoughts.

"Look," she said earnestly. "I'm happy now. My own family has to come first, and when I'm happy, they're happy. When Moira—when this whole divorce thing came up, Mom was bummed. She used to cry a lot. It was such a downer, I couldn't handle it."

She excused herself to take the bottle in to the baby, then rejoined me.

"It's no crime to want to be happy. Mom had her time. She will again. She has to build a new life for herself. She's overdramatizing, wanting our attention, especially Dad's. She won't—can't—let go. Don't you see? Psychology One-oh-one. She has to snap out of it. Nobody can do it for her. Not me, not you. She's a good woman, a nice woman, I love her, and I'm sure Dad still does in his own way—nobody wants to hurt her." She consulted her Rolex. Had there been a fire sale? I felt suddenly aware of my own wristwatch, a Heinz novelty model, the second hand a tiny dill pickle.

"You'll have to excuse me," Jamie said. "Moira and I are going to Bal Harbour. Saks is having a sale."

The cloud-colored Jag rolled up the driveway as I left.

Althea needed time, attention, and moral support. That's what family, friends, and shrinks are for. That's not what I am paid to do.

Lottie had reappeared in the newsroom, svelte and radiant. Love always made her lose weight. She claimed she hadn't slept.

"It was nothing but sex, sex, sex," she drawled, drawing instant attention from Ryan, at his desk behind me, and Howie Janowitz, who was passing by. "Coral sex."

"Coral," I informed them, speaking succinctly. Both looked disappointed.

Coral sex occurs only a few nights a year, when the moon is full and the tides, temperatures, and other conditions just right. They had gone diving to watch elkhorn and star coral spawn.

"You shoulda come with us, Britt. Underwater blizzards, millions and millions of teeny tiny pinkish balls—sperm and eggs connecting in the moonlight. Eventually they settle down and build a reef."

"Sounds like you and Tex are a hot item," I said.

"Nothing but sugar and honey so far," she said. "Way I figure, it's probably jist about time for the bottom to drop out. Happens every time." She sighed. "When he's good, he's so-o-o good. Then he gets involved in some wild adventure or decides to save the world and it's time to run for the high timber."

"Maybe he'll surprise you."

She shook her head. "When he was twelve he got his picture in the paper for being the youngest student body president ever elected at our school. Same week he got expelled for flying a glider he built off the roof. That's how it's always been, like he can't stand success.''

Clucking sympathetically, I thought of McDonald, who would never disappoint me.

I bought thick steaks at Epicure on the way home and scrubbed my apartment to a shine. I gave Bitsy a bath, brushed Billy Boots, trimmed his claws, and then did my own nails. Everything had to be perfect.

He called late. I whispered sleepily that champagne on ice awaited his arrival. ''One more day,'' I said.

''We need to talk about that.''

''Yes-s-s,'' I purred.

''Something really great has happened. I've been invited to take part in an FBI/State Department symposium on terrorism. I talked to the chief today and he was really enthusiastic, heartened by the offer. The more cooperation we can foster with these guys, the better off we are.''

''When is it?'' Was rain about to fall on my parade?

''Starts tomorrow,'' he said briskly.

''How long?'' I held my breath.

''I'll be up here another week.''

''A whole week?''

''It's an excellent opportunity to work with these guys, good for the city and good for me personally. Because of the department's past troubles, the FBI hasn't trusted us or wanted to work with us. You know how it's been. And you know how important mutual cooperation is on some of those extraditions we've been trying to make from south of the border.''

His spiel had begun to sound like an official presentation.

''But we were—''

''A chance like this doesn't come often.''

''And me you can see anytime, is that it?''

''Believe me, I'm as disappointed as you are.''

When did all this come about? His invitation to participate didn't arrive at midnight. Why didn't he tell me before I scrubbed the apartment, washed the dog, bought the champagne, manicured my nails, requested comp time, and practically picked out a silver pattern? He prefers terrorism to me, I thought furiously. I'll show him terrorism.

"The best things are worth waiting for, babe," he said. "We've got the rest of our lives."

He got me with that one.

I stared at the ceiling later, disappointed and surprised at my own sweet understanding. That is how good police wives are, I told myself. Wait and wonder, swallow disappointment and worry, smile bravely, bear up and behave like a trouper. Did they actually find fulfillment in that?

In the morning I called to ask my mother to dinner. She'd been on my mind since I visited Althea. Also, I didn't want to dine alone on the night McDonald and I should have been together. And, most importantly, someone had to see and appreciate my spotlessly clean apartment.

"Sweetheart! I've been thinking about you," she said cheerfully. "Kendall McDonald isn't back in town yet, is he? What will you be wearing when he arrives? Make it memorable, something he'll always remember you in."

I did not mention my new nightgown. "I thought, maybe my navy blue—"

"No, no, no! Something glamorous, unforgettable, in some lighter shade of blue. A bias cut, with a draped neckline, a romantic little soft jersey dress that skims the body. Something like that would be absolutely darling on you, with your figure."

"He's delayed," I said glumly. "Won't be back for another week. Want to have dinner here tonight? I'll cook."

"You darling, but I have to settle for a rain check. Roger is coming in from New York, and we have plans. I wish you'd called sooner."

"You didn't return my last call," I complained. When

did our relationship take this 180-degree turn? I wondered. Her chronic complaint was always that I didn't call or see her enough. These days, with her high-fashion job and burgeoning social calendar, I had to make an appointment.

"Who the heck is Roger?" I grumped.

"You remember, I told you about him, recently retired, relocating to Aventura."

"I thought you were seeing that fellow from the cosmetics firm."

"Warren," she chirped. "We're doing brunch on Sunday."

"Well," I said. "Sounds like you're all booked up."

"What's wrong?" She said it so spontaneously it startled me. "I'll cancel on Roger if you need me, Britt."

"No. Don't be silly. I'm really glad one of us has a life. Have fun."

"I saw that dreadful story about the baby in the parked car. Everyone was talking about it." She clucked. "If you could just write something pleasant for a change, I'm sure you'd feel much better about yourself."

That was the mother I remembered. Somehow I felt better. For a moment there, I thought she'd gone sensitive and caring on me.

My mom had a date. Everybody I knew had happily paired off. That I was not totally alone in my misery and frustration was small comfort.

I called a kindred spirit from the office. Althea sounded relieved. "I was so worried when you didn't return my calls."

Her words irritated me, probably because I woke up irritated. The state map with the red pushpins hung over my shoulder, a dark presence behind me, casting an imaginary shadow over my desk.

"Look, Althea. I really think I've gone as far as I can go with this. I don't think you're in any danger, anymore than any of us on any given day."

"But Britt, surely you're not—"

"Hear me out, please. You got a raw deal in a lotta ways, but look at the big picture. You are still a helluva lot better off than ninety percent of the people on the planet, and certainly better off than most people I write about every day."

"You don't believe me either."

The raw pain in her voice made me feel like shit.

"Althea, murder is a big deal." I glanced up at the map as if for confirmation. "People go to prison forever for murder, or to the electric chair. A lot of times we hear the reason for a homicide and shake our heads because it sounds so stupid and trivial, but trivial or not, most killers have some sort of motive. Nobody has a motive to kill you—unless there's something you're not telling me."

"No, there's nothing, that's what makes this—" Her voice broke.

"You see? Sometimes terrible things happen to us, a death, divorce, illness, and when more bad things follow we tend to take it personally and maybe get a little paranoid. What you need to remember is that life is cyclical, tides turn, good times come back again, sometimes bigger and better than ever, if you just hang in for the long haul."

"If you survive," she whispered hopelessly.

"You're smart, healthy, attractive. You'll be fine," I enthused, with all the gusto I could muster.

My cheerleading did not produce the desired effect. She said nothing.

"I met your daughter, Jamie. A lovely young woman, all wrapped up in being a wife and a new mother right now, but she loves you and cares about you."

"You saw the baby?" she asked eagerly.

"No, I didn't, but if she looks like the rest of the women in the family, she must be gorgeous."

"She is. Thank you for trying to help. I'm sorry I troubled you."

"No trouble. Just take care, don't allow yourself to feel or look vulnerable. Go on out there, chin up, determined to break this bad cycle. Maybe you should see somebody, a counselor or a therapist, just to talk things out."

"I wish it were that easy. Goodbye."

The mention of a therapist motivated me. I made a call, then drove downtown, stopping to pick up half a dozen jelly donuts on the way.

Dr. Rose Schlatter met me at her office door. She wore her usual dangly earrings and low-cut blouse over a tailored skirt. With her bright blue eyeshadow and thick smeary lipstick, she looks more like a faded stripper or aging cocktail waitress than a well-known forensic psychiatrist who specializes in sex offenders. Her eager eyes settled immediately on my offering.

Shc took the Dunkin Donuts box, lifted the lid as though expecting pearls, and reacted as though they were diamonds. "Jelly!" she exclaimed, in her breathy Marilyn Monroe voice. She smiled. "You remembered."

We poured coffee from a pot in a tiny cubicle near the unmanned reception desk and carried the cups into her office.

"Where's your secretary?" I asked.

"I sent him out on an errand that will take some time." She winked, displaying her eyeshadow, took the first bite, and crooned softly with pleasure.

I must have looked puzzled.

"He watches me like a hawk," Dr. Schlatter explained, patting powdered sugar from her lips with one of the pink-and-white paper napkins. "Saves me from myself. He's tough as nails. Wouldn't let me near these things. Wouldn't allow them in the office."

"Why not get a new secretary?" I said.

The mascaraed eyes above the rapidly diminishing jelly donut widened. "But that's part of his job description," she said, chewing. "I assigned him to stop me. It's a question of health. I have to lose weight because of my high blood pressure."

"Oh, okay." Now I felt guilty.

She held on to the donut box while pushing aside a thick folder.

"Just refreshing my memory on an old case coming up again soon. You may remember, Siegfried Olson."

"The shoemaker. If his plumber hadn't been nosy, they might never have discovered the body parts in his septic tank."

"Yes, he had such a fascination with victims' shoes that he sometimes left the feet in them. You have a good memory." Nodding in approval, she sank her teeth into another donut.

"I'd like to forget him. He still writes to me."

"Jail mail." She sighed. "I guess you would get it too. It makes sense."

"All the time."

"Ever answer?" she asked.

"Never," I said. "Despite our publisher's policy. You?"

Coyly she sucked the powdered sugar off her lower lip. "Depends a lot on the case."

"Why is Siegfried coming up?"

"Doctors at the state hospital say he's competent now and quite harmless, as long as he remains on his medication. Since he was found not guilty by reason of insanity, he's coming up for release."

"Oh, swell. And who will insist that he take his medication if he's released?"

"Not if." She swallowed, patted her lips again, and smiled. "When. But I'm sure you're not here to discuss him. What's on your mind today, Britt?"

Her eyes lit up when I mentioned the Kiss-Me Killer. "I've been following the case in the news media. Absolutely fascinating. Now *she* is someone I'd certainly like to meet."

"What do you think makes her tick? She may be coming this way. She could already be here, for all we know."

"Yes," Dr. Schlatter said, nodding slowly. "A glittery big city like Miami, widely known for sex, drugs, alcohol, and violence, would attract her. Hunters like to go where the game is—the wild life, so to speak. As for what makes her tick, that's more difficult to answer. Historical records on female serial killers go back for centuries, but their murders were most often poisoning or baby killing.

"Most modern serial killers of the female persuasion have been health care workers or companions to the elderly, not women out trolling the highways and city streets for victims like the men do. Remember the woman in South Miami who took in elderly boarders, buried them in her backyard, and continued collecting their Social Security checks?"

I nodded.

"And the teenage baby-sitter who smothered half a dozen or so infants—all attributed to SIDS—before somebody finally took note that she was present every time? Others have been the more passive partners in couples that kill for cash or thrills. And then there are the Black Widows—like Florida's own Rita Lee Hutton."

"I remember reading old stories about her."

"Oh, she was a piece of work, that one." She absently bit into a fresh donut, the red jelly oozing out onto her fingers and crimson fingernails. "Charming and quite likable, actually; the girl next door. I got to spend some time with her. Poisoned her father, a husband, a fiancé, a son, and, I believe, a couple of neighbors, one of them a nosy retired cop. Total lack of conscience, no guilt, no remorse. Managed to justify everything until the day she died. She might have been capable of something like this, except in those days it just wasn't done. A woman's choice of weapons was most often poison."

"What about this one?" I asked impatiently, as she licked her fingers.

She paused, eyes resting fondly on the cardboard donut box.

"There's so much we don't know. So little research has been done. Most serial killers are white men in their twenties and thirties. We know their numbers are proliferating and that most of their victims are white women. But this is something new. Do the backgrounds and psychological afflictions common to male serial killers apply equally to females with similar violent patterns?" She shrugged. "She's fascinating."

"But the MO, what we know so far, what does that tell you? Apparently she's attractive."

"Of course, so many are." She smiled. "Rarely do they resemble monsters, which is what they are, of course. That's how they manage to get away with it long enough to become serial killers."

She whisked crumbs from her sleeve and leaned back in her chair.

"Probably intelligent in a street-smart way, even though she didn't do particularly well in school. Suffers from an inability to relate sexually to others in a normal way. Likes the publicity. Most likely follows her own exploits in the press. May even save news clippings, keep a diary; perhaps she even risks revisiting murder scenes, though this one certainly seems to stay on the move.

"One common ritual in serial murder is the taking of keepsakes—either as trophies, to commemorate a successful hunt, or souvenirs, used later to fuel masturbatory fantasies. Would this apply equally to a female? I don't know.

"Mutilation, damage to the face and genitals, is often inflicted to depersonalize the victims. The way these bodies are left exposed apparently is to make a statement—either to society at large or to the authorities. It's interesting," she mused. "Male victims of homosexual killers are often found with their pants down.

"It's dangerous to theorize. Generalizations are always risky, you know. This country makes up five percent of the world population, yet we account for nearly seventy-five percent of the world's known serial killers. Twenty years ago, an estimated thirty or so roamed the United States. Today the FBI estimates there are about five hundred. What's going on out there, in the suburbs, the malls, and on the highways? What are we breeding here? She is totally new turf. I've been wondering if she is an aberration or a harbinger of things to come.'' She smiled dreamily and reached for the last donut as chills rippled down my spine.

''If you should meet her first, Britt, would you give her my card?''

She was joking, of course. Or was she? She plucked a few business cards off her desk and dropped them in my jacket pocket on the way out.

''One other thing, Britt.'' She frowned as she followed me to the door. ''Are we certain our killer is a woman? Has the possibility been ruled out that she could be a female impersonator?''

''I don't know. No hint of that from the police.''

She shrugged. ''I doubt it too, but it would be comforting if she were. Just a thought. Spell my name right. Thanks for coming by. And Britt—'' she smiled—''bring a dozen next time.''

She was busily disposing of the evidence as I closed the door, sweeping crumbs off her desk and crumpling the distinctive box and paper napkins.

Six

I STUDIED THE MAP AGAIN BEFORE LEAVING THE newsroom that night. *Come out, come out, wherever you are.* I projected the message as my eyes drifted idly up the narrow peninsula. When would she be caught—or would she? What if she repents, I wondered, finds Jesus and becomes a model citizen, leaving her crimes unsolved mysteries like D. B. Cooper or the disappearance of Jimmy Hoffa?

Or what if she is here now, strolling the Miami Beach boardwalk, flirting with tourists, wriggling painted toenails in the sand or shopping the big sale at Saks in Bal Harbour? She might be rubbing elbows with the Moran women at this very moment.

I called Miami homicide. Detective Ojeda picked up. "The Kiss-Me Killer," I said. "Have you heard any bulletins on where she last used her stolen credit cards?"

"Why? You hear something?"

"Thought you had. I heard that's how they're tracking her, working with credit card security, keep coming up just a step behind her."

"They're putting a BOLO out now," he said. "You must be psychic—or psycho. I can never figure out which one."

"Very funny. Where'd she use them last?"

"The Seaquarium, right over here on Key Biscayne; stocked up on souvenirs like a regular tourist. Bought a plastic alligator, a giant orange beach ball, a dolphin mug, and pink flamingos."

"Are you ser—? Damn it, Ojeda!" I nearly believed him for a moment.

He chortled. "Had you going, didn't I?"

"Where? Where'd she use it?"

He dropped his voice. "Fort Lauderdale. Yesterday."

"Lauderdale!" My heart skipped a beat. Twenty minutes away.

"Yep, pumped 'er own gas at a Chevron."

"Is she still driving the Trans Am, the last victim's car?"

"Correctamundo. Then whipped out his card at a Big Daddy's. Bought four bottles of tequila—José Quervo Gold—and a six-pack of Coors."

"What's your plan if she shows up here?"

"The plan is, her ass goes to jail. We don't mess around, like those rubes and rednecks upstate. She shows up here, she's ours, and the minimum that's gonna happen to her is jail."

"She's got chutzpah. How'd she get this far driving a cherry-red Trans Am the whole world is looking for?" I said.

"She's lucky, and she hasn't run into me," Ojeda said. "I hope she makes a big mistake and shows up here."

I alerted the slot and our police desk, where an intern named Jerry monitors more than forty law-enforcement radio frequencies in a small soundproof alcove outside the newsroom, and then called our Fort Lauderdale bureau. They said the adjacent county had had three homicides in the last thirty-six hours: a domestic fight to the death, a dice-game stabbing, and a terminal fit of road rage. Nothing remotely connected to the Kiss-Me Killer. I pushed a blue pin into the map at Fort Lauderdale to designate the sighting. I'd replace it with red if a body surfaced. Then I called the Miami/Dade County Medical Examiner's office to inquire if any male victims had arrived with bullet wounds to the genitals and/or face.

"You talking about that woman leaving bare-assed bodies all up and down the state?" the night-shift attendant asked. "She coming here? Tell me she ain't."

"Just checking," I said. "You never know."

I searched traffic for a red Trans Am on the way home. Restless and tense, I changed into jeans and a T-shirt and walked Bitsy, wearing my portable police scanner clipped to my belt so I didn't miss anything. The sky was overcast, the heated air thick and suffocating. I stood the scanner on my kitchen counter while I fixed dinner.

Police radio traffic was relatively routine, yet there was a tension, an electricity in the air. I heard cops check out several Trans Ams, none the right car. I wanted to make a sandwich, but the bread was stale and the mayo expired. Could it really be that old? A jar of what appeared to be long-frozen soup had sprouted an icy beard. I held the jar up to the light to better scrutinize its contents. What were those green things? Maybe it wasn't soup. Could it have been a sauce? Something brought by my Aunt Odalys? A butcher-wrapped package beckoned. I could eat McDonald's steak. Serve him right if I did.

I stared bleakly into the frozen wasteland and then closed my eyes and simply inhaled the frigid air. A *media noche* was what I craved. Warm and fragrant cheese, ham, and pork on crisp bread. A cup of chicken soup on the side, Cuban style, with carrots and lots of noodles. Then silken flan, sweet, smooth, and syrupy.

Cono, I thought, why didn't I stop at that little Cuban restaurant near the Boulevard? The more I thought about the enticing aromas from its kitchen and the flaky *pastelitos* on a covered tray atop the counter, the more ravenous I became. Was it worth venturing back out into the heat and driving across the causeway? Yes. My mouth watered.

No stars in sight, the moon in hiding, a thick wet blanket of muggy air pressed down on South Florida as though Mother Nature, like a homicidal baby-sitter, was trying to smother us all. Heat lightning leaped madly across the horizon, pirouetting like a ballerina on speed, as distant thunder rocked and rumbled ominously. If it did rain, the weather story would lead the morning paper.

La Estrella glowed, a beacon for hungry, lonely, and displaced people seeking a taste of home. Cubans dine late, and the tables were busy. Two Miami patrolmen sat at the counter, their uniforms a comforting sight. Robbers rarely hit places with police on the premises.

"Uh-oh," they chorused on seeing me, "we know nothing"—my second most frequent greeting from cops. They sipped their Cuban coffee and rehashed the Marlins' fall from the top while I studied the menu and other people's plates. Everything smelled so good. One of the cops raised his walkie and amid the crackle and hiss of static, I heard him instructed to change frequencies, to "car-to-car" transmission, which cannot be monitored by outsiders.

"Need you here right away." The tinny voice sounded oddly familiar; the address, the Jolly Roger Motel on the Boulevard, not five blocks away. "We got us a dead big shot, a VIP homicide. Get over here on the double."

The cops exchanged glances, avoiding my eyes, hoping I hadn't heard.

"Hey, wait a minute!" I said, but they ignored me and left in a hurry, without finishing their coffee.

The motherly waitress stood before me, order pad in hand. "Never mind," I said, already on my feet. "I'll be back."

I made a U-turn, followed their flashers, and pulled into the motel parking lot right behind them. Another patrol car and an unmarked were already there, along with some other cars, one of them a red Trans Am. Breathless, I followed the cops up an outside open staircase to the second floor.

Halfway up, a deafening crack of thunder rattled the building, the wind gusted wildly, and a fat wet drop spattered my cheek. Rain, or condensation from a room air conditioner?

Ojeda answered the door, tie flapping in the sudden burst of wind. "How the hell did you get here?" he demanded. "You bring her with you?" He scowled at the two cops.

"I was driving by and saw their car pull in," I said quickly. "What happened?"

His face looked odd. I saw a rumpled bed in the dim light behind him.

"'Member what we talked about a few hours ago, *chica*?" He studied me for a moment, then took a small step back. "This is big," he said. "Really big. The world is about to descend on this room. You were never here, Britt. We'll all swear to that."

"It's her, right? Did she kill another one?"

"See for yourself."

I stepped gingerly across the threshold, knees shaking.

"That's it." He stopped me with a cautionary gesture. "No farther."

A single step into a space that small was enough. The room reeked of sickening cigar smoke—and something else that churned my stomach.

"Guess who? Your friend and mine." Ojeda gestured, as though politely introducing me to the remains on the floor beside the bed.

"*¡Dios mío!*" I breathed. No introduction necessary. The corpse had a familiar face. Sonny Saladrigas looked astonished, mouth open in surprise. Naked from the waist down, his penis resembled a bloody flower, its stem broken. The gaping wound dead center in his forehead added to the bewilderment of his expression.

His wife smiled warmly, as did their three small daughters. Their wallet-size color photos had been spread out over his skin. The picture of his smallest child, wearing pink and clutching a teddy bear, was stained, propped against what was left of his penis.

"Did she get away?" I whispered.

"That she did," the detective said. "Sick bitch."

"What is that smell?" My eyes watered and I swallowed hard.

"Looks like somebody shoved Sonny's cigar up his ass," Ojeda said. "A lotta people been wanting to do that for years."

"How do you know a copycat didn't kill him?" I asked, certain it was really her.

"We don't. But it's her," he said, slowly turning to the grisly tableau behind him. "Ballistics will say for sure."

"And what is that?" I squinted in the poor light. Sonny's dress shirt, unbuttoned and open, exposed his thick, dark, curly chest hair in which something small and blue nestled.

"Not that I have any personal knowledge or intimate acquaintance with such things, but I think that's gonna turn out to be a Viagra tab. We're gonna be holding back on that for now, so don't mention it till we give the okay. And that"—he gestured toward the dresser top—"appears to be crack cocaine. Not unusual for Sonny, from what I hear, except that this little party got rough at the end. This is a major cha-cha." He nodded grimly. "The chief, the brass, the mayor, the city manager, and all their advisers are on the way. No way we can keep the lid on long. Once the press runs with it, it's showtime, a three-ring circus. Now you're outa here, Britt."

A hulking shadow loomed in the doorway: Ojeda's partner, Charlie Simmons. "What the hell are you doing here?" he demanded, my number-one most frequent greeting from cops.

"Who?" Ojeda said. "She ain't here, never was."

Simmons grinned at the others. "Guess this shit-cans

the chief's memo on no more overtime. *Ka-ching! Ka-ching!*'' he crowed. ''Unlimited OT! Who'da thought Saladrigas would turn into a cash cow?''

''What'd you get?'' Ojeda asked impatiently.

''Good news,'' Simmons said. ''They had tape in the security camera. The bad news is the quality. You can hardy see 'er. But maybe the lab can enhance it. That's not for publication.'' He turned to me. I was still staring at the corpse.

''You still here? Out! Now!'' Ojeda's walkie squawked persistently. ''Be cool,'' he muttered. ''And don't say I never did you any favors.''

Grateful to breathe fresh air again, I didn't even notice the pounding rain as I ran down the stairs to my car. The oppressive high-pressure system that had hovered motionless over the state for weeks, its westerly winds inhibiting the sea breezes that deliver thunderstorms, had shifted and begun to drift away. The heavens had opened.

The dry spell that had kept me off the front page for weeks was over; the weather would not be the biggest story in the morning paper. Summer rains had finally arrived, but so had something else.

Seven

I CALLED THE CITY DESK FROM A LAND LINE, A nearby pay phone. Minutes later, by the time I parked in the shadows beneath the building, the paper's lawyer and a half dozen editors were en route. The state's most wanted killer and Miami's highest profile politico had collided head on, right on our deadline for the final. The newsroom, usually winding down at this hour, became a frenzied beehive of activity.

"Britt said the killer would come here," Bobby Tubbs babbled. "She knew. But who'da thought she'd cross paths with Sonny Saladrigas?"

The story was breaking too late for TV at eleven. With any luck, the competition still knew nothing. South Florida and the world would wake up to the shocking news on our front page. First I had to convince my bosses. Despite my assurances that I had seen the body, they wanted official confirmation.

Fred Douglas, my city editor, called the mayor at home. He was out, gone to "the terrible tragedy," his wife said, warily declining to elaborate. At the same time, the police chief made the mistake of answering his cell phone. My heart pounded.

"Is it true that Commissioner Saladrigas has been murdered," I asked, "apparently by the Kiss-Me Killer?"

"Where did you get that information?" he blustered. "How'd you find out so fast?"

That was enough. They ripped up the front page to display news-photo high points of the dead commissioner's political career and used head shots, off the wires, of the other victims.

Editors hovered around my terminal, peering over my shoulder as the words appeared on the screen, exclaiming and muttering, reacting to what they read as my fingers flew across the keyboard. We had only minutes to wrap it for the final.

In a running debate as I worked, they decided that we would appear insensitive and mean-spirited if we focused on Sonny's dubious political practices in the initial report of his brutal murder, since the two did not appear to be directly related.

His frequent official trips to our sister city south of the border were mentionable, but not the allegations that his dedication to the program was linked to the city's abundant supply of teenage prostitutes. Sonny's seedy side surely played a role in his own demise, but there would be time and space in which to explore that later. For now, the more sordid details were judiciously edited. My references to the "controversial commissioner," his "partially clothed" corpse, and his "gunshot to the genitals" stayed in; details about the cigar did not. Family photos arranged on the body were acceptable; precisely where, was not.

"Remember," the publisher said piously, "this is the story his children will read someday." He had arrived in the newsroom clad in black tie, straight from some charity fund raiser at the Fontainebleau hotel.

I turned in the copy and fished a cotton blazer out of my ladies' room locker to dress up my jeans and T-shirt as best I could. Not tired, not hungry, I was flying—on the adrenaline high achieved when you are first with the biggest story in the state. I hoped Lottie would be assigned, but she didn't answer phone or pager, which was totally unlike her. Another photographer, Villanueva, was assigned instead.

I returned to the crime scene as the blessed downpour soaked parched ground, drenched moisture-starved foliage, and flooded the streets. Miami was back to normal: hot, wet, and weird. I called Charlie Webster on the way. "She's he-e-e-re," I crooned.

"Who is this?" he grumped sleepily. "Britt? Tha'chu? What the heck time is it? She catch another one?"

"The biggest so far," I said. "A Miami city commissioner, the former vice mayor. She's still out there. No time to talk, but check our story. I already filed it. Later, Charlie."

The entire parking lot and the Boulevard in front were roped off now, traffic diverted. City and county cars and crime-scene vans were clustered everywhere, their flashers bouncing off buildings and rain-slick streets.

The mayor and the city manager scuffled with cops guarding the scene, trying to push their way into the room to see Sonny's corpse, then turned on each other with flailing fists. Another Miami moment. Villanueva captured their antics. Ojeda, Simmons, and two prosecutors from the State Attorney's office flatly refused them entry.

Along with Sonny's executive assistant, they demanded access from the chief. To the man's credit, he backed his detectives, explaining that the murder case could be lost if the defense impugned the crime scene's integrity due to alleged contamination by unauthorized civilians.

A Spanish-speaking TV crew rolled up, clearly tipped by the mayor or the manager. Word was out. By dawn, reporters outnumbered cops.

The rain faded as a rosy blush softened the horizon and swarms of invading news choppers hammered the air overhead.

I never hinted that our story was already landing on wet

lawns. Instead, I mingled with my peers who were clamoring for information and official confirmation of the victim's identity.

The county mayor, other politicos, and their hangers-on began arriving to express their shock and to take advantage of the photo ops. Swarmed by reporters, they lamented the loss and extolled Sonny's virtues. The man had sprouted a halo and wings. He would have loved it.

It is the norm for Miami politicians, exposed, indicted, even convicted, to be overwhelmingly reelected by voters who are apparently brain dead or, in some cases, literally dead, as recent voter fraud investigations revealed. Sometimes, a felony record seems a prerequisite for holding office.

Sonny was the classic comeback kid. Stung by scandal, sued by the state, blasted by the press, indicted by the feds, and down for the count, he always bounced back to the top.

He would not be back from this one.

Shortly after their return from notifying the widow, the chief and the two detectives agreed to talk to the press. Politicians rushed to join them, pushing and shoving, jockeying for position in front of the cameras.

The chief grimly confirmed that the victim was indeed Sonny and introduced the detectives, who acknowledged that the Kiss-Me Killer might indeed be the suspect. They disclosed only the barest of details. The cigar and the Viagra went unmentioned, along with other specifics. They acknowledged the cocaine, which had field-tested positive, only after direct questions from reporters who knew Sonny's reputation.

They asked for the public's assistance in locating the commissioner's missing midnight-blue Mercedes-Benz C43, a sleek high-performance model, top speed one hundred and fifty-five miles an hour and zero to sixty in six seconds.

The midnight shift remained on overtime, the day shift

had arrived, off-duty personnel had been mustered, and a grid search of the entire city was taking place, street by street, alley by alley. Private security guards in golf carts scoured the parking facilities at condos and apartment complexes.

She had never stayed long in one place, and I wondered why they focused on the city. I envisioned the Mercedes, its powerful engine whining, flying low across the Seven Mile Bridge in the Keys. Continuing south would be a mistake, I thought. There is only one road in and out of Key West and no place left to run at the end.

Miami's more muscular mayor wrestled the microphone away from the county mayor and upstaged him, announcing that the city was posting an additional $25,000 reward for arrest and conviction of the killer. He made an emotional plea for calm in the face of this latest crisis.

"We are sending a message," he said, "that we will not tolerate violence against our duly elected officials or any citizen of this great city. This heinous crime will not go unpunished. We will not be cowed by those who . . ." and so on and so on and so on. Blah-blah, blah-blah, blah-blah-blah. The press corps stopped taking notes, eyes glazing, until somebody showed up with a copy of the *News*. They crowded around.

The headline, in six-column 72-point Bodoni:

MIAMI COMMISSIONER SLAIN AT MOTEL

with three lines of 30-point subhead:

SALADRIGAS POSSIBLE FIFTH VICTIM
OF NOTORIOUS KISS-ME KILLER;
FEMALE SUSPECT FLEES IN HIS MERCEDES

Howls of protest rose. Complaints from news directors and station managers would surely follow, charging Miami police with favoritism and demanding to know why we had the story first. Who would believe that I happened to be in the right place at the right moment—that I was meant to own this story?

The medical examiner's van rolled up, exciting the TV

crews, whetting their appetites for the footage they crave. Sonny Saladrigas, covered by the same purple blanket, would be maneuvered down the stairs on the same stretcher, plopped onto the same gurney, and slid into the same morgue wagon by the same crew that removes countless anonymous victims whose deaths go virtually unnoticed. Nobody holds press conferences or authorizes overtime to solve their murders.

No reason for me to stay. I drove to the Saladrigas home in Coconut Grove. Lottie had finally surfaced and met me there. She looked tired but radiant.

"So where were you during Sonny's last date?"

"Tex chartered us a boat," she murmured, rolling her eyes. "The captain, a Cuban guy he met somewhere, took us out to one of them little spoil islands, built us a campfire. Brought everything: music, blankets, gourmet food and wine. Had our own private beach. Then the captain says *Adios, muchachos,* he'd be back when Tex beeped 'im."

"What about the rain?"

"For a while I wasn't sure they didn't arrange that too, like movie crews do. The rain was like a mirage, a fantasy, like being trapped by a typhoon on a deserted tropical island with a handsome, sexy stud. We ran for cover, a lil' tin-roofed shelter. Shoulda heard the rain pounding on that tin roof, the wind whistling, palms bending in the storm. It got a little chilly, so we had to keep each other warm—"

"I get the picture," I said.

"Left my beeper behind," she admitted. "For the first time. So, naturally, the biggest damn story of the year broke. Dad blast it, just my luck."

"You never choose romance over a great picture. This must be serious. Did he propose?"

"Only about two hundred times. But I'm still waiting for the other boot to drop. If I hadn't lived through all this before, I'd be trousseau-shopping right now. Can't believe the Kiss-Me Killer nailed ol' Sonny. Musta been like the last ten minutes of a bad horror flick. Lordy, if it didn't have her name on it, the lista suspects'd be so long they'd never figure it out. Who *didn't* want to kill Sonny?''

Cars packed the circular driveway. The house was crowded, with people speaking both English and Spanish. I didn't expect the widow to be receiving the press, given the circumstances. I was wrong.

Pale and wan, clutching a damp handkerchief, her bewildered and photogenic children clustered around her, Lourdes Saladrigas continued to do what she had done for years. She campaigned for Sonny.

''He was a wonderful husband and father and he loved this city and its people,'' she said tearfully, seated on a sofa, wearing a simple black dress and holding her children close, the youngest on her lap. I shuddered slightly, remembering the last time I had seen their innocent faces, in the photos at the crime scene.

The little one squirmed. So did I, along with other reporters, at the widow's version of events.

''Sonny never met a stranger.'' She smiled sadly. ''He was always so generous, so quick to help anybody in trouble. He could never turn away from anyone in need.''

Waymon Andrews from WTOP-TV caught my eye and lifted a brow. The Sonny we knew was always so quick to pick a pocket, pocket a bribe, or pick up a hooker.

''He was set up,'' the widow said, ''by people who knew what an easy mark he would be.''

''How do you think he was set up?'' Andrews feigned interest and perplexed concern.

''Sonny could never pass by an accident scene . . .''

True, the Bar Association had censured him twice for pressing his business cards on the survivors of crash victims while bodies were still trapped in the wreckage.

'' . . . or a stranded motorist without stopping to help.''

Only, I thought, if she was young and pretty.

"If it is this . . . person they suspect," the widow said, repositioning little Yvette, determinedly trying to wriggle off her lap, "they say her MO may be to fake car trouble. Then she murders any good Samaritan who offers help. Sonny must have stopped to assist a woman driver stranded in the dark, helped her find a motel room, and was seeing her safely to her door when . . ." Her dark eyes brimmed and she paused, lips trembling, to stroke her toddler's hair.

"So you're saying this might have been a conspiracy? That Sonny was specifically targeted and not a random victim?" I asked.

"Definitely. His political enemies would do anything to stop Sonny. Anything." She nodded, voice barely audible. "Some are even in the press. They know who they are." Her moist eyes roved the room. "I gave the detectives their names. The police promised to do everything they can."

I wanted to ask how Sonny's enemies managed to find the most hunted and homicidal woman in the state and convince her to target him, but the widow had no more to say. Handing the children over to a relative, she opened her arms to new arrivals at the door. Sobs resounded as an older woman fell weeping into her embrace.

"She talking about the same Sonny Saladrigas we all knew?" Waymon Andrews asked, as we walked down the gravel driveway to our cars.

"I guess she loved him," I said. "Is it loyalty or did she really believe all that? How could she live with the man and not see what he was?"

"Love is blind," Lottie said, suddenly glum. "Could be she just wants her kids to grow up loving their daddy and believin' that's what really happened."

"I bet it's her platform," Andrews said cynically. "You know, good Samaritan's widow appointed to serve out his term. If she doesn't get the appointment and they decide to hold an election to fill his slot, I betcha she runs for it."

"No way," I said. "She's got those little kids to raise without a dad . . ."

I drove home. Mrs. Goldstein, bless her, had fed the animals, walked Bitsy, and left a department store catalog with a note suggesting I register for china and silver patterns.

McDonald had left two messages on my machine. I'd call him from the office. I showered, put on fresh clothes, brewed myself some strong Cuban coffee, and went back to work. I stopped at La Estrella on the way. The same waitress studied me suspiciously.

"I said I'd be back," I chirped brightly.

She said nothing, solemnly taking my order of more Cuban coffee to go; an Elena Ruiz, a turkey sandwich with cream cheese and raspberry jam; guava and meat *pastelitos*; and a double order of *maquiritas*. I needed energy. Hell might break loose at any moment. Time was running out for the killer. Nobody can run forever. Soon she would be cornered, caught or killed. I hoped it would be before lack of sleep overtook me. Chewing would keep me awake. I added a side of ham *croquetas* to my take-out order, paid the check, and stepped out onto the steamy sidewalk. The downpour had failed to cool the city. The temperature was an enervating 97 degrees and still climbing.

"Hell of a story this morning, Britt." Ryan watched me place the food containers atop the two-drawer file cabinet beside my desk and sniffed appreciatively. "You brought lunch for everybody?"

"Touch any of this and I'll chew off your fingers," I warned, brushing aside messages from Althea. Not now, I thought. Doesn't the woman know I'm busy? Doesn't she read the newspaper?

Fred Douglas, the news editor, paused at my desk. "Nice work, Britt. How the hell did ya manage to get the jump on everybody? One of your police sources call you?"

"I was hungry," I said. "Long story . . ."

"Well, we beat 'em bad." He rubbed his hands together briskly. "But that was yesterday. Keep it up. We want to stay ahead of the pack."

I nibbled my sandwich with scant appetite. The story was what I hungered for. For the early edition, delivered to racks and convenience stores by 7 P.M., I focused on the widow's comments, the massive manhunt, and the growing reward. Funeral arrangements went into a sidebar with eulogies for Sonny and expressions of shock from politicians all over the state.

The task-force detectives had hit town to work with the locals, but I couldn't find them. I did find the Jolly Roger desk clerk, whisked away by the police that morning. Henry Mead was back on the job.

Thin, stoop-shouldered, in his forties, he wore stubble on his weak chin and looked as if he hadn't slept or changed clothes. He knew who Sonny was when he had checked in using a name not his own. He had been there before. He signed the name of a former prosecutor who had tried to nail him in a corruption case. Sonny must have thought it funny to use the prosecutor's name at a hot-pillow joint. This time the joke was on him.

Sonny only wanted the room for an hour or two. So when Henry Mead, the desk clerk, saw that the commissioner's Mercedes had left the parking lot, he climbed the stairs to change the sheets and found the body.

"Changed my life," he said, shaking his head. "I'm giving notice, getting myself into some other line of work." He assumed Sonny had picked his companion from the herd of hookers who strut the Boulevard. He had sneaked a look out his office window as they went up to the room but didn't recognize her. She wore very high heels, a short tight skirt, and had skipped energetically up the stairs. Nice legs, he said, but he never actually saw her face. On the security tape, which he had viewed with detectives, she was little more than a grainy silhouette, face turned away, to the dark. But he heard her laughter. It sounded free and easy, like she was having fun, a good time, he remembered thinking.

"I'm getting out." He shoved back his stringy too-long hair. "Going on home to Iowa. This town is no place for a God-fearing family man."

"You have a family?" I asked.

"No, but I'm thinking 'bout getting me one."

"But you are God-fearing."

"I am now."

Ojeda and Simmons were out in the field. I kept missing the task-force detectives, at city homicide, their hotel, the morgue. Where the hell were they?

Back at the office, Barbara, the city hall reporter, said the commissioners had met and were leaning toward appointing someone to serve out Sonny's term. Several names had been mentioned.

"Tell me one of them is not Lourdes Saladrigas," I said, massaging the back of my neck which had begun to cramp.

"How did you know?" she asked.

I snacked, drank more coffee, and checked my messages before settling down to write for the final. They were from Althea, my mother, Charlie Webster, and the usual faithful readers, weirdos, and anonymous callers reacting to Sonny's death. One of the latter had left a terse message: *Dead lawyers don't suck.* And another from McDonald. Damn, I had forgotten to call him. I swallowed the last of the guava pastry and reached for the phone. It rang first.

"Dead lawyers don't suck."

"I got the message." I hunched my shoulders, rolled my head around, and listened to the bones in my neck crunch. "Who is this?"

I needed sleep or more food. I reached over to rattle the bags from La Estrella and see what was left.

"A reader, pissed off as hell." The husky, whiskey-throated voice had an accent so southern that *hell* had two syllables.

"What about?" The last ham *croqueta* felt cold and greasy, so I dropped it in the wastepaper can. What could I lead with for the final?

"You. You're Britt Montero. You wrote those stories about the murder, right?"

"Yes, I did."

"Well, you can't believe anythin' you read in the paper. Don't you people ever check anythin' out?"

"I'm on deadline right now," I said frostily. "Why don't you write a letter to the editor?"

"Well, la-di-da. Too damn busy to discuss how you write all this inaccurate bullshit, huh? That man went right straight to hell where he belongs, and you're probably fixin' to write another story makin' 'im sound like a god-damn saint. You can't shine shit! Good husband? Wonderful father? Dedicated public servant? Bullshit."

"Those were not my words," I told her. "I never said that; those were accurate quotes from people who did. I'm only the messenger. Commissioner Saladrigas was a controversial figure," I conceded, "and he certainly had his share of problems. But it's only natural for people to speak well of the dead." I silently cursed the editors who insisted we tread lightly when it came to his character in the initial story. "I'm sure you'll see that future coverage is more balanced."

For the final, I vowed to get in his indictments, his trials and tribulations, maybe even his recent skirmish with the hotel car jockey. Maybe I'd call the valet for a quote.

"A lot of people disliked him," I added.

"Damn right. That Sonny was a pig—smellin' up the whole room with that damn rotten stinkin' cigar. Why the hell didn't he stay home with his precious wife and kids?"

I swallowed a mouthful of coffee. It tasted muddy, not even lukewarm. "His wife is left with three small girls to raise," I said wearily. "What would you . . ."

I paused.

"How did you know about the cigar?" Was that in the paper? No. Or was it? I reached for a copy of my original story and knocked over my Styrofoam coffee cup. The murky dregs splashed across my desk and notes as I rolled my chair back to avoid the spill.

"How d'ya think?" Her seductive voice hinted of dark secrets. "I was there."

My stomach churned as I snatched some paper napkins to mop up. "When? When were you there?"

"You figure it out."

I scanned the newsroom. Was another reporter playing games?

"Oh shit," I whispered.

"What's wrong?" she demanded.

"I spilled my coffee."

She laughed. "Gotcha going, huh?" She laughed again, free and easy, like somebody having fun. "You've got a nice voice," she said. "Kinda sexy, younger than I expected."

"Look," I snapped. "I don't have time to play games. I'm on deadline here, and I'm tired."

"Been busy, huh? Me too."

"Who is this?"

"Who do you think, genius?"

"Are you saying you know something about the case?"

"Sure do," she teased.

"What?"

"Everythin'."

"Listen." I exhaled, eyes focused on the big clock overhead. "We get a lot of crank calls; what makes you think I'd believe—"

"He'd already popped one-a them little blue pills 'fore we got there," she said, interrupting. "Then he comes on real pushy cuz he took it and is horny as a toad. Smellin' up the room with that stinkin' cigar.''

''You've got my attention,'' I said quietly.

''They tell you what I did with it?'' The question sounded like a smirk.

''I heard.'' My eyes darted wildly around the newsroom for somebody to signal. That made no sense. What could anybody do? Quietly, I slid my desk drawer open to look for my tape recorder. Not there. Where did I have it last?

''Shoved it where the sun don't shine,'' she murmured. ''You know so much, why didn't you put that in your story? How come you didn't write that?''

''The police like to withhold some details,'' I said, voice thin. ''Specifics that only the killer knows.''

She laughed. ''And you work right with 'em, like a good little girl, doin' what they tell you.'' Her voice was mocking. ''What kinda reporter is that?''

''I don't work with them. In fact they're pissed off at me most of the time.''

''They're assholes,'' she said, sniffing disdainfully. ''Bullies who like pushin' people around. Most of 'em aren't smart enough to find their own ass in the dark.''

''I wouldn't underestimate them,'' I said. ''If you were with Sonny, what happened? What were you thinking?''

''Maybe I wasn't ready, maybe I changed my mind and didn't want it, maybe he just got a bit too damn pushy. The guy was a crack monster. You know, he wanted to rub coke on hisself to keep him hard longer—Viagra, booze, and all that too—what was *he* thinking? That's the question. That sumbitch never even tried to hide his weddin' ring.''

''But you had sex with him, right?'' I said, scribbling notes.

''Sure.''

''And the others?''

''They were all asking for it, pushy as hell. That man,

Sonny, he was using cocaine. Hell, I might pop a few pills, drink a little booze, but that stuff'll mess up your mind."

"Yeah," I said. "You wouldn't want to do that."

"Don'chu talk down to me, lady. I'm not stupid."

"Sorry. If you are who you say, you're *not* stupid. Every cop in Florida is looking for you; you've got them all as frustrated as hell. And if you're lying, you've got me snowed and I'm a trained cynic."

She laughed again, free and easy. "Don't believe me, huh?"

"You plan to turn yourself in?"

"You lost your mind, woman?"

"That would be the safe thing to do, for everybody, yourself included."

"In your dreams. Read it right there in your story, everybody's talkin' capital punishment, 'count of this asshole in Miami and that piece-a shit up in Shelby County. Oh, sure, turn myself in. That makes a lotta sense if you're suicidal."

"Why did you call me then?"

"For a goddamn retraction! Admit it. You got it all wrong. Write the real story and tell 'em what a slob Sonny was."

"People know all about Sonny. They're interested in you." My heart thudded. "Your story is the one they want to read. It couldn't hurt you, public relations-wise, to have people see you as human, not a monster."

She paused. "Have to think on it."

Bobby Tubbs approached my desk. I saw him coming out of the corner of my eye. I frowned and tried to wave him away. It didn't work.

"Britt?" He loomed over me. "I need your story. How much you gonna have? How many inches?"

"Who's that?" My caller sounded wary and distant.

"My editor. He wants the story I'm working on."

"Tell him I'll show him how many inches."

This seemed surreal.

"Hang on," I said.

"No, I can't. But guess whose phone I'm using?"

"What?"

"Check it out. You know how to do that, don'chu?" She hung up.

I quickly punched star sixty-nine. The number came back, and I matched it to a card in my Rolodex. It was the number of Sonny Saladrigas's missing cell phone, last seen in his missing Mercedes.

"Britt?" Bobby gestured impatiently. "Where's that copy? How can I lay out a page without a length? What do you want me to do?"

"Call the police," I said.

"Come on. Don't be a wiseass," he complained. "You're not the only one who's had a long day."

"Call the police," I repeated, raising my eyes to his.

Eight

"THINK SHE'LL CALL AGAIN?" OJEDA LOOKED RED-eyed from lack of sleep.

"I hope so. She likes to talk."

"Sure, she's lonesome. Stranger in town, all her acquaintances are dead," Simmons said.

"We got nothing," Ojeda said glumly. "Been waiting for the magic phone call. Didn't think she'd be the one who made it. Work with us on this, Britt. Don't try anything cute."

"Have you ever seen me cute?" I snapped irritably.

"Came damn close a few times." He winked.

I agreed to forward my office calls to my car, then home. They wanted her on tape and said they would apply for a court order. It's illegal in Florida to record conversations without the other party's consent or a court order. Hell, the way our justice system works, the killer would go free and I'd do jail time. But I agreed to hook a recorder up to my office phone and sign out another from supplies to take home.

"She calls again," Ojeda said, "try to establish a rapport, draw her out. You know, act interested in her welfare, her feelings, relate to her. Hell, you know how, Britt, you do it with us all the time, trying to get information."

They would get the court order and apply for traces on my numbers, he promised, as they left to go wake up a judge.

The call went unmentioned in my story. Tubbs phone-conferenced with Fred Douglas; Murphy, our managing editor; and Mark Seybold, the paper's in-house attorney. They wanted to be sure, rather than rush into print and risk copycat callers tying up our lines. What's more, if she was the real deal, she might call back.

Cops in the newsroom seemed to trouble my bosses more than a killer on the phone. They had eliminated name plates on reporters' desks years earlier, as a precaution, in case cops or prosecutors ever tried to seize a reporter's notes or tapes. Editors scheduled a meeting to discuss this development in the morning.

I drove home, giddy with anticipation. The superheated night was sultry and starless, saturated with the overpowering scent of night-blooming jasmine as intoxicating as exotic perfume. How close was she? Did she smell it too? My skin dampened with perspiration in the few steps between my car and front door. My phone rang as I approached. I fumbled with the keys, pulse pounding, as it continued to ring. Inside at last, I lunged through the dark, groping for the phone, stumbled over Bitsy's exuberant greeting, dropped the tiny tape recorder, and snatched up the handset.

"So, you're alive and well," McDonald said.

For the first time since I met him, I was disappointed to hear his voice. "You won't believe what happened!"

"I heard."

"How? I just left the office."

"You're talking about Sonny, right? The homicide commander called to brief me. It's been all over the TV news up here. More bad press for Miami—"

"McDonald, listen. I might have . . . I'm sure I just talked to the killer!"

He did not respond with the enthusiasm I expected as I filled him in.

"How many reporters ever get to talk to a serial killer still at large?" I demanded. "I'd love to interview her!"

"Wait till after she's behind bars," he said. "You can do it then."

"Oh, sure, when her defense lawyer is warning her not to talk to the press, or some TV tabloid is offering her big bucks for an exclusive interview. I've been down that road."

"Let homicide handle it, Britt. They're good detectives, and she's dangerous. Stay out of their way. Let them do the job they're trained to do. Our main concern is that some traffic cop will pull over a pretty girl in a flashy car, without realizing who he's stopping, and wind up dead."

"I'm not in their way. They need me."

"So do I, babe."

"What are you wearing?" I murmured, in a blatant shift of topic. No way did I want to argue with this man, especially about something unlikely to happen. Sinking into my comfortable chair, I made smoochy sounds into the mouthpiece.

"Not much," he said. "Just stepped out of the shower."

I couldn't sleep later, plagued by conflicting thoughts, obsessing about the killer. Who was she? A throwaway kid, come back to haunt society? An abused child striking back against all men as abusers? Probably one of those disposable people no one cares about, like a puppy dog abandoned at the side of the road. Or was she a pioneer in her field, something new and monstrous, spawned by a mad, disordered, barbaric age? I agonized at all the questions I could have, should have, but never asked during that brief golden moment of opportunity, and prayed for another chance.

* * *

Awake before dawn, my thoughts haunted by odd and nameless anxieties, I listened for the reassuring plop of the morning paper against my front door. I called homicide. Nothing new.

Coffee brewing, I reread my story, trying to see it through her eyes. What would she think? How would she react?

The phone rang. Recorder in place, I pushed the button, hands shaking.

"Good morning, Britt. Hope I'm not calling too early. I really didn't think you'd be in yet. I merely intended to leave a message."

"Althea?" Thanks to simple telephone technology, every call, every crank, every complaint, would follow me home, intruding into my private space. Now Althea, with all her fantasies and fears, real and imagined, was in my sunny yellow kitchen.

"Yes, a call to you was on my list of things to do today," she chirped. "Good news. I guess." She added the last two words wistfully. "I've made up my mind. I'm putting the house on the market. It's something I never wanted to do," she said slowly. "I came to this house as a young bride, raised my daughter here. The happiest times of my life took place here. But it's scary to come home to alone now, I can't really afford it, and it will be *such* a relief not to be poor anymore."

She was trying to convince herself, so I helped.

"A new start is a good thing," I assured her. "A new life in a new place, with new neighbors." She could certainly use the last, I thought.

"Yes," she said. "Perhaps a nice little apartment in a gated complex, with security . . ."

"Excellent choice for a woman alone."

"I guess I just harbored some foolish fantasy about keeping the old homestead in the family. You know, in the event my daughter or her children ever needed a place to come home to. But she's well fixed now, and nobody . . ." Her voice quavered.

"I hear Gables real estate values have soared through the roof in the past few years," I broke in cheerily. "And interest rates are at rock bottom. You sure picked the right time."

"That's what they tell me," she whispered miserably. "I'm meeting with a realtor today."

Her future would be secure and happy, shared with new friends, I thought, after we said goodbye, so why did I feel her pain? Change, even for the better, is always hard. That had to explain my own nagging sense of impending chaos, I thought, stepping into the shower. McDonald is coming home—to me. My life might soon change. Why did I feel so uneasy? Happiness is possible. Other people find it. Happily ever after does happen. Look at Lottie, how radiant she was lately. Althea could be happy. So could I.

At the Villa Deli I spied on others who were eating breakfast. Those with newspapers went straight to my story. The best-read story in town, the one on everybody's lips, and it was mine. I stepped out onto the steamy sidewalk, ready for whatever the day might bring.

The meeting was already under way, around the big conference table in Murphy's office: Fred Douglas, half a dozen other editors, including Gretchen Platt, and our lawyer, Mark Seybold. All looked somber as I was summoned into the glass-enclosed office.

Did I believe my caller was the killer?

"I'm pretty convinced," I said primly, a fresh notebook open on the polished tabletop before me. "Not only did she appear to have details that only the killer could know, she seemed genuinely indignant at what she felt was our too-flattering portrayal of Sonny. She seemed to feel she'd done the world a favor."

"There are those who would agree with her," quipped Stan Potter, the state editor.

They were concerned about police tapping our telephone lines. ''What are the chances she'll call again?'' Murphy demanded.

''I'm not sure. I think she might. As a reporter, I'm hoping she will. I don't believe she'll turn herself in,'' I offered. ''And if they can't stop her, there will be more victims; at least that's true of most serial killers.''

''What concerns me,'' Douglas told the others, ''is that we have confidential sources calling in on some lines. For example, that tipster from inside the Department of Agriculture and the justice team's source in that jury bribery investigation.''

''We're not cops,'' Gretchen said. ''We shouldn't be doing their job. This could be risky to our sources, our credibility, and a waste of time. This caller could simply be another of Britt's cranks.''

Mark nodded, his intelligent brown eyes magnified by the thick lenses of his gold-rimmed glasses. A train buff, he was wearing his favorite tie, the one with little locomotives. ''I would need to see heavy-duty guarantees,'' he said, ''that they will absolutely isolate these calls from everything else that comes in here.''

Uh-oh, I thought. I understood their concerns, but I had my own. The detectives didn't care who else called this newspaper, all they cared about was their case. If the paper threw enough roadblocks in their way, they'd feel jerked around, and they were the people I sought information from every day.

''These police officers have been very helpful,'' I pointed out. ''We wouldn't have broken the story first without them.''

''Any possibility of a quick arrest?'' Fred asked. ''It would make all this a moot point.''

''Only with some off-the-wall lucky break,'' I told them. ''They seem to have no major leads. They went to obtain a court order for the phones last night.''

''We could successfully block it,'' Mark said confidently. "Crimes are committed every day, but the constitution guarantees a legitimate expectation of privacy. They'd be violating the privacy of law-abiding citizens."

"But it would only be my line," I protested.

"Even if they could isolate a single line off the main trunk coming into the building, what about your sources, all your other calls, personal and professional?" he said.

For a sobering moment I imagined cops who knew us both eavesdropping on me and McDonald.

"There has to be some mechanism," Murphy said, "for weeding out what they're not supposed to get."

"A system that enables Britt to simply press a button that triggers the tape and a trace only when the right call comes in," Fred said. "Is that technology possible?" They all looked at me.

"I'll find out," I said. "I'm sure they can make it happen."

A short time later they presented their conditions to Ojeda, detectives from SIS, the Special Investigations Section, and two telephone company employees, a security expert and a technician. All looked pained.

"It's doable," the security expert said slowly, "but extremely complex to install that type of call tracing system on a public business exchange, a PBX. You've got two thousand lines coming into this building. This will take us at least twenty-four hours to set up. Ms. Montero will have to tell us the precise time the call came in, after the fact. Then it will take us about a day to trace it back."

"A day?" Ojeda objected. "Our suspect is constantly on the move."

"What about all those TV shows?" Douglas frowned. "They trace the call, identify the point of origin, and surround the suspect while he's still on the line."

"That's television," the phone man said. "And on individual lines, not a setup like you've got in this building. Sometimes there's a technical glitch," he added, "and the trace won't work at all. Another thing: older cell phones can be traced to an area a few blocks square. But those new digital phones? They're untraceable."

"So even with all this, we're screwed anyway if she keeps using Sonny's phone." Ojeda rolled his eyes.

The phone man was equally pessimistic about call forwarding.

"Every time we step down a generation it becomes more complex," he warned, "from the PBX, to the office extension, to the car phone, to the house phone." He shook his head and looked grim.

Nonetheless, all agreed and shook hands.

"Sorry about the suits," I told Ojeda later. "I had no idea it would be this difficult."

"Don't worry about it," he said. "These technical experts always like to tell you how impossible a job is, so when they do it they're heroes."

I walked him to the elevator, hoping to learn what the crime lab had found. "Not for release," he said, "but they've got lipstick traces on both bullets, just like all the others since Shelby County. The class characteristics could even give us the brand name. And if they both smoked the crack pipe, they should be able to get her DNA."

"Remember, she said she doesn't use crack, only pills and booze. Doesn't want her mind messed."

"Well, we'll be getting her DNA anyway."

"How?"

"A real long shot." The doors to the empty elevator yawned open and we stepped aboard. "We got lucky. Sonny's genitals were pretty messed up, with all the blood, but they took smears and when the ME looks for sperm on one of the slides, he sees what look like female epithelial cells, from her vagina. He calls the crime lab; they check their slides and see the same thing. They do something like a Pap smear, and lemme tell you, Britt, what they can come up with is awesome."

"Like what?"

"They can run DNA. They can determine if the cells are pre- or post-ovulatory, even tell us when she's menstruating."

"So what are you going to do, put a wanted poster in every feminine hygiene department? Put her picture on Kotex boxes like missing kids on milk cartons?"

"Very funny." He scowled. "You never know when some of this physical evidence is gonna be important. The scientific stuff goes over great in court. They're gonna try to match up her DNA with the other cases."

"So she's having unprotected sex with them."

"Right. The college kid apparently had condoms, even opened one, but never put it on. Maybe he was in a hurry."

"Why weren't they worried about HIV and all those other sexually transmitted diseases?"

He shrugged as we stepped out into the lobby.

"But," I said, remembering what the clerk had said about Saladrigas being a frequent guest. "Sonny could have infected his wife and kids. What's wrong with you guys?"

"What's wrong with women?" he retorted. "A guy goes out, meets a pretty face, has a few laughs, hopes for a little horizontal mambo, and winds up inside a chalk outline. Romance ain't what it used to be."

Miami's police chief appealed to the state's Violent Crime Council for at least $100,000 to help defray expenses. Cops had already logged hundreds of hours of overtime and costs were mounting in a city nearly broke. The reward had climbed to $200,000.

I caught my breath every time the phone rang, but she didn't call. Charlie Webster did.

"Looks like the rumors 'bout 'ol Buddy were true. They ran a test in his office to detect the presence of semen stains."

"Right, a UV light," I said. "Ultraviolet fluoresces old semen stains just as luminal reveals traces of blood even though it's been cleaned up."

"That's it. Appears ol' Rupert was pretty reckless with his seed, so to speak. They went in there in the dark, shone that light, and the place lit up like high noon."

"Where?"

"You name it. Found stains on the carpet, the couch, his chair, the walls, even his goddamn desk blotter. Had he been a younger man and the ceiling hadn't been as high, they probably woulda found it there, too."

Sonny's viewing was set for noon to 9 P.M. at the Caballero funeral home. Lottie picked me up down in front of the News building.

"Quick," she said, as I slid into the car and slammed the door, "you still got a number for the Hemlock Society?" She looked pale and haggard and sounded hoarse.

We both had taken CPR, First Aid, even a class on the Heimlich maneuver. Now there are courses on how to end your life. We had done a story on suicide sessions. "If it's the last thing you do, do it right," instructors urged. Their recipe called for pills, booze, a plastic bag, and an elastic band.

"What's wrong? Don't think I have the number on me, but I can probably find you a plastic bag."

"Good, don't fergit the booze and the pills." Lurching over the speed bump into traffic, she cut off a circulation truck whose driver hit his brakes.

"Wish you had mentioned you were suicidal," I said, fastening my seat belt. "I could have driven my own car."

"Didn't I know it all along?" she croaked. "Didn't I tell ya from the start?"

"Is your throat sore?"

She nodded. "From all the screaming."

"Oh, jeez. Tex?" I inquired.

"Who else?"

"Tried to call you last night, late. Figured you two were out."

"We was supposed to go to dinner at Sambuca, then hit some-a the South Beach hot spots, Amnesia, Liquid, and Bash. I'm all dressed up and he shows up late—"

"But he did show up?"

"Wait," she said. "That ain't nothin'. He tells me we have to make a stop first. Some dinky li'l dive in Li'l Havana. Wait in the car, he says, and traipses off. So I'm setting there in the car by myself, checking it out, and there's thangs rattling around in the console. Thangs 'bout the length of a pencil and big around as a quarter. Guess what they were?"

"Oh, I don't know, Lottie, don't make me guess. I have a lot to tell you."

"Okay! Fine. If you don't wanna hear it . . ." Her pouty face crumpled. She who, this morning, had been my exemplar for happiness.

"Shut up, slow down, tell me everything."

"I seen 'em before when I was shooting stuff for AP in Colombia and El Salvador."

Whatever they were, they weren't good. I blinked and waited for the punch line.

"Fifty-caliber slugs, the ones for sniper rifles. Kin take out a target a mile away."

"Aw, shit."

"Exactly what I said."

"What on earth is Tex doing with that kind of ammo?"

"Helping plan an assassination," she said matter-of-factly.

So much for happiness, I thought. "Who do they plan to assassinate?"

"Fidel."

"Oh, for God's sake."

"I know! I told 'im. Only reason Fidel is still alive with all the plots hatched outa this town for the last thirty years is cuz every damn one of them exile groups is fulla spies. Some are all spies, spying on each other."

"What's his role?"

"Flying them to Margarita, an island off Venezuela, just before Fidel's visit next month."

I winced. "You know the feds will never let them get off the ground with that kind of firepower. They'll swoop down, arrest them all, and seize his plane. He may end up the only one prosecuted because everybody else involved is working undercover for various government agencies."

"Ten of the guns and lotsa ammo were in the trunk."

"Yikes, Lottie, I'm sorry. What did you do?"

"He had an extra ignition key on the floorboard. Always did that. So I stole the damn car, drove out to the old Dodge Island bridge by the port, high heels and all, and heaved each and every one a them guns and all that ammo off into deep salt water."

"Jeez, Lottie, why didn't you call me?"

"No point getting you involved. That's jist it, he calls me the love of his life and takes me out riding around with all that shit in the car. A cop had pulled 'im over we both woulda got busted. My career'd be down the toilet. I'd sure never get Secret Service clearance agin."

"That SOB."

"Damn right. Against my better judgment I go back to Li'l Havana, where he's running up and down the street like a wild man. He's thrilled to see me and the car, till I tell 'im I found guns and ammo that somebody musta left in it before he rented it, so naturally I got rid of 'em, to make sure he didn't git in trouble."

"How'd he take it?"

"Not good. Tells me the whole story and wants to know what I done with 'em. Wouldn't tell 'im, a-course, I could jist see 'im and his new *compadres* under the bridge with a dive boat. That's what he'd do. We sorta made up, but driving over to South Beach for dinner he starts making calf eyes, trying to sweet-talk me into telling 'im. Instead, I tell 'im 'bout federal prison, his next stop. Damn it to hell, Britt. He ain't got no flag to wave here. The man jist can't help getting involved in stuff he's got no business being involved in. So we git in a big wrangle."

"Bummer."

"That ain't all. I was so mad I coulda swallowed the devil, horns and all. His hardheaded, obstinate streak jist made me want to scream. So I did. Screamed at the toppa my lungs to drown him out. Then I screamed again. You know, the long-drawn-out one with the little yodel in it? He could never deal with that one. We're trapped in bumper-to-bumper traffic on the MacArthur, I'm screaming and yodeling, and he throws open the driver's side door to jump out and take a walk."

"Oh, no."

"Ain't the half of it. As he does, a Beach motorcycle cop come roaring up through traffic, 'tween cars, on his big Kawasaki eleven hundred and slams right into it."

"Oh, no!"

"Blows the door clear off that new rental, the Kawasaki goes down, the cop goes ass-over-teakettle skiddin' down the pavement on his backside, flying glass everywhere."

"Oh my God. How bad is the cop hurt? Who was it?"

"Young guy, name-a Larkberry. Real stud. Seen him around before in them high boots and tight pants. Won't be wearin' them for a while. Had him some road rash. Wearing a neck brace and stretched out on a backboard when they slid him in the ambulance, but I think he'll be okay."

"Was Tex arrested?"

"Got a buncha tickets. I called a cab from the Coast Guard station and left his sorry ass there, his hair fulla broken glass. Coupla hours later, he called. Was at Bash, you could tell he'd been drinking. Wanted me to join him."

"What'd you say?"

"What didn't I say? Stay outa my life, you freak! Haul ass back to Lone Star and don't bother looking back. I screamed and yodeled till he hung up. Even the dog was howlin'. Far as I know, Tex is still out there, drinking and dancing with the beautiful people. Once he's on a tear, he don't slow down for days." She whistled. "Would ya look at this. Sonny's sure pulling 'em in."

The parking lot was full, the streets around the funeral home clogged with cars.

Local movers and shakers, all the politicos, and their entourages were working the spacious velvet-draped room, greeting each other, shaking hands, and ignoring the corpse, which was just as well. Sonny looked lousy. They did a good enough job covering the hole in his head with putty or something, but his complexion was gray and unnatural. Enough to turn you off open caskets for good. Me, I'd just as soon be dipped in bronze and stood in Bayfront Park at the edge of the water, with seagulls and pigeons for company.

The widow refused to speak to me, and other relatives made rude remarks because of my last story. I blamed my evil editors for mentioning Sonny's peccadilloes. At least we weren't barred from the premises, as were a few of Sonny's political enemies, stopped at the door and banished after minor scuffles. The press was in full attendance, with TV news crews interviewing local dignitaries in the meditation room. Lottie disappeared into the garden of standing floral arrangements to shoot the politically powerful discreetly as they approached the bier to pay their respects.

The police chief, in full dress uniform, was reluctant to discuss Sonny's case. "We're doing everything possible," was all he would say, the same sound bite he'd given the TV crews. During our chat, however, he mentioned a new development in another case I had written about.

A Chicagoan, one Jeremy Sullivan, had driven his ex-girlfriend to Miami months earlier. She was in the trunk.

He was trying to borrow a shovel when police intervened. He told Miami police he had killed her before leaving Chicago. So local cops charged him with failure to report a death, a mere formality to hold him for Chicago homicide detectives. When they arrived, he confessed again, saying he'd murdered her in Miami. No one could prove if it was either city, or somewhere in between. Prosecutors in both places backed off, fearing that if he confessed at trial to committing the crime in the other jurisdiction, the case would be thrown out, double jeopardy would apply, and he would walk. Instead, since nobody could prove where the crime did occur, he did walk. He had just been released.

A great outrage story.

As political adversaries scuffled at the door, Lottie nudged me. "Let's go," she whispered urgently. We went.

"You won't believe the great quotes I've got for your story," she said, as we emerged into the blinding sunlight and chaotic traffic sounds outside. "Listen to this. I'm behind the flowers and the potted palms when the mayor comes up to the casket alone, kneels, genuflects, then gives Sonny the bird and says, 'You son of a bitch, you deserved it. Where the hell is the money?' "

"Wow! Did you burst out of the bushes to ask 'What money, Mr. Mayor?' "

"Hell, no. He never knew I was there."

"Could be cash from that payoff at the port. Remember all the rumors?"

"Or kickbacks from the big developers on that Brickell Avenue project. Everybody knows something fishy was going on there."

"Or the missing money from the Overtown restoration project. Sonny mighta been holding it, until it was safe to divvy up."

"Yeah, coulda had it in a safety deposit box under an assumed name."

* * *

The mayor emphatically denied everything, of course. Not only would he never say such a thing or make such a gesture, he thundered, it was a flagrant violation of privacy to shamelessly spy on the bereaved *compadre* of a slain public servant during this tragic and emotional time. This was another example, he said, of a vicious conspiracy to undermine his administration, and he threatened to sue. He and his lawyer protested to the executive editor and the managing editor and even stormed through the newsroom to protest in person to the publisher.

At the afternoon news meeting they kicked around the ethical question of Lottie failing to make her presence known. As if she was expected to push her face through the palm fronds and identify herself before he spoke. She may have misheard, they said. The room was noisy, the organ playing, and the man muttering under his breath. They decided not to go with it.

Instead, the political reporter would be assigned to nose around to see what else, if anything, could be unearthed.

Lottie and I were furious. She heard him, at a public gathering, an event where the press was welcome and in obvious attendance. The paper had no *cojones*, no faith in us. Had one of those editors overheard it, would they have had the same reservations?

Ojeda instructed me to contact him through dispatch if the killer called, no matter what the hour, but nothing. I stayed busy tracking down the slain Chicago woman's irate relatives by phone, along with the prosecutors and detectives in both cities.

"He killed her in Chicago and drove her down here," the Miami detective said.

"They drove to Miami, where he killed her," the Chicago detective insisted.

Everybody agreed something should be done—by somebody else.

I wrapped the story for the early edition.

The phone man and the cops were still at work on the

system when I forwarded my calls and went home. The phone rang as I got ready for bed.

Heart pounding, I answered. "Turn on Channel Seven, right now!" Lottie said. She stayed on the line.

Waymon Andrews, in a live shot in front of the funeral parlor, was introducing this "amazing piece of tape recorded earlier, a Channel Seven exclusive!

"This was actually recorded earlier today at the casket of slain Miami Commissioner Sonny Saladrigas," Andrews said, over footage of the mayor solemnly entering the funeral parlor. Despite the soft sweet strains of organ music and the background buzz of conversation, the mayor could clearly be heard saying, "You son of a bitch, you deserved it. Where the hell is the money?"

Lottie and I shrieked in unison. The television crew, Andrews explained, had planted a tiny mike amid the floral displays "to pick up the tears and endearments from friends and supporters bidding a final farewell to the veteran politician. As you just heard, we picked up more than we bargained for."

They played the tape over and over, then played it again. They played it over footage of the mayor and Sonny together, over Sonny in full rant at a commission meeting, over shots of the morgue crew bouncing his covered corpse down the stairs at the Jolly Roger, and over a sentimental scene of the mayor consoling the widow and her darling fatherless babies. The mayor, according to Andrews, was refusing comment. The widow had issued a statement. The mayor must have been misunderstood, she said, the tape doctored. He and Sonny were lifelong friends, since childhood in Cuba. The tape was an obvious fraud and the work of—what else?—political enemies.

"Ain't that enough to bring a tear to a glass eye?" Lottie demanded.

I unloaded my frustration on the hapless McDonald, who called to say good night. His input was being well received at the terrorism sessions; he was learning a great deal, forging excellent contacts, and sounded elated. He agreed that the killer had probably left town, based on her prior MO, listened to my complaints about my editors, and ordered me to bed. I needed rest, because when he arrived, he promised, we would make up for lost time. He would take me dancing and dining and walking on the beach. Even that brought little comfort.

Tape recorder in place, I willed her to call. She had moved on, I thought. It was over. The story I led the pack on had slipped through my fingers. I blew my chance.

I tried to drown my negative thoughts with a stiff drink from the Jack Daniels Black Label stashed under the sink, then went to bed.

She called at 3:48 A.M.

Nine

"HI THERE." SHE SOUNDED GENTLY AMUSED. "Asleep at your desk, or having your calls forwarded?"

"Who is this?" I mumbled, suddenly aware of the answer, wide awake and groping blindly for the record button.

"Were you thinking 'bout me when you went to bed?" she whispered suggestively. "I was thinkin 'bout you. Read your story. That son of a bitch. Hope to hell I meet up with him." Her smoky voice took on a hard edge. "I'd give him a few things to think about."

"Who?"

"That prick from Chicago who got cut loose cuz nobody knows which town he was in when he killed her. In the early edition, tomorrow's news tonight. Ever notice there ain't no justice when it's a woman who gets killed?"

Switching on my bedside lamp, I found and gently pressed the tape recorder button.

"What was that?"

"I turned on the light." Is the trace working yet? I wondered frantically.

"A woman after my own heart. I don't like doin' it in the dark either." The seductive timbre of her voice sent a peculiar thrill through my body. Billy Boots suddenly hurtled off my bed and darted into the hall, as though sensing my fear.

"Where are you?" I asked, wishing to God that the cops were listening, knowing they were not.

She laughed softly. "The Beach. I love South Beach," she said. "The partying never stops. My kinda town."

"I live on the Beach," I blurted stupidly, eager to keep her talking. If only I had some coffee.

"Maybe I could come by for coffee or a drink," she said, as though she'd read my mind. "Just you and me."

"We could talk," I said, wondering wildly what to do if she agreed.

She chortled slowly. "See the TV tonight? Even the mayor spoke the truth about Sonny—'cept he didn't know anybody would eavesdrop. What a hoot." Her voice faded as though she had turned away from the phone, attention diverted. By what? I wondered. I thought I caught a snatch of distant music in the background.

"We had that information," I said. "Our photographer heard him say it at the funeral home, but my editors wouldn't let me use it in the story."

"Them assholes again. Ever notice how men do not listen to you unless you got something they really want or you're jammin' the barrel of a gun up the side of their head?"

The image chilled my blood.

"Oh, they listen then. You get their absolute attention then." She sighed, expelling a short impatient breath. "I guess you'll probably hear 'bout it soon enough."

"What?" I scribbled in my bedside notebook in case the recorder failed.

"Somethin' that'll win you points with all your police friends."

"They are not my friends."

"Oh, sissy, don't gimme that. Think I'm stupid? When you're sleeping with the captain, the one that's out of town? Hell, I know all about it. Chapter and verse."

"About what?" My mind reeled. What was she saying? Was *she* tapping *my* phone?

"Never mind, sweet sister. I'm watching you. Just remember, I know a whole lot more than you think."

"What do you mean?" I demanded. "How did you . . . ?"

"Like that sporty little T-Bird you drive?" she said. "And don't git me started on Lance Westfell, the big movie star you dated when he was makin' a flick down here. Now tell me, what is that man like in bed? We got to have a heart-to-heart, a blow-by-blow, pardon the expression, 'bout that sometime."

"How . . . ?" I gasped, speechless.

"Tol' ya, sugar. Where you think I'm calling from? Know that pay phone down the street? I can almost see your front door from here."

Pulse pounding, I swallowed hard. I knew the phone. If she was there, I could see her from outside. My eyes darted toward the door. Perhaps police were listening, they don't always follow the rules. Maybe . . . if only . . .

She sighed, the long-drawn-out sound of a much maligned woman, overworked and misunderstood. "I met another asshole tonight." She sounded exasperated. "Yep, this town is full of 'em. They're everywhere."

"What happened?" I asked. Ojeda had said to relate on a personal level. Hell, this was entirely too personal already. "Are you all right?"

"Why, thank you, Britt, for askin'. Nobody ever does. The son of a bitch tried to slip drugs in my drink, Blue Nitro. You know, the one that's like Ecstasy, but you come down faster. That stuff's dangerous. Makes you warm and tingly all over at first; then it heightens your sexual response, then you could die: I caught him, a-course. Shoulda known better. I mean, he's 'sposed to be a big hotshot sophisticate, one of South Beach's suave and urban beautiful people."

"You get around," I said. "Didn't take you long to learn the lay of the land."

"Sure. Oh, yeah. Don't take me long to settle in, feel at home, get to meet and greet, find out people's stories."

"So how did this date go?" I stared at the door, knowing what was out there.

"The son of a bitch was like a dog after a piece a meat. Once he got the scent he was all over me. You know how they get. Pawing at your nipples, sucking on your neck."

"How is he?" My voice was thin and uncertain.

She made a derisive little sound. "Well, his pulse is a damn sight slower." She paused. "His pulse rate is like"—she stopped to think, then, and erupted with a gurgling laugh at her own joke—"maybe, zero."

"But why . . . ?" I whispered, stomach churning.

"He deserved it."

"Did the others deserve it too?"

"They had their problems."

"Do you?"

"Don't we all?"

"God didn't intend this for you," I said quietly. "You're somebody's child; you must be breaking your mother's heart."

"Don't you bring up God to me—or my mother—ever!" Her voice rose. "You got no business. . . . Why, I worshiped that woman. When she walked out of a room, the light went with her. She's dead. My life woulda been a whole lot different if she hadn't been taken from me when I was just a little kid."

"I'm sorry," I said. "It must have been rough on you."

"Happened a long time ago. I was just a little kid. Anyhow"—she sniffed impatiently—"you want the scoop on this asshole tonight or not?"

"Tell me," I said.

"Well," she began casually, "if you wanna eyeball this dude 'fore the circus starts, he's right where I left 'im at, far as I know. If the tide ain't washed him out while we been chit-chattin' here. Hell.'' She laughed, slow and relaxed. ''He could be halfway to Cuba by now. And he ain't swimming, either.''

''Who is he?'' I whispered, eyes closed.

''Nobody now. See, met him at this South Beach club. I'm already talking to somebody, but he muscles in, gets pushy. Tries doping my drink, then wants me to walk down the beach with him in the moonlight. Only he ain't much on walking and there ain't no moon, 'cept for his own fat ass. Wants to stop and get it on at one-a the cabanas at the Sea Sprite.

''We got what we wanted. Him first. Then it's my turn. He seen the gun—you ever see a fat man run? Really comical. Arms swinging back and forth like he's running fast but his legs and ass ain't keeping up?''

''Nobody heard you?''

''If they did, they didn't check it out. Everybody's inside, air conditioners blastin' this time-a year, I guess. He was huffing and puffing too much to do a lotta yelling, and we wuz down by the water where the breakers boom. God, I love the ocean,'' she said dreamily. ''Shot 'im through a cushion from one-a the lounges. Muffled the noise some. I have to say, despite the conditions, I'm a helluva shot. So that's it. There's your story. Gotta go now. Places to go, people to see.''

''Wait! When can I interview you?''

She paused. ''I may be a fool for askin', but ain't that what we just done?''

''No, I want your story. You, your background, what you're thinking, how this all began and why. Your side.''

''Maybe later. Gotta go. Why don'chu head on down to the beach by the Sea Sprite and check 'im out?''

She hung up. I scrambled from my bed and dashed barefoot to the door. Stepping gingerly into the jasmine-scented night I stared out into the darkness, then trotted toward the street, straining to see. Nobody at the pay phone on the corner, no car leaving, no footsteps retreating.

An electric current of fear surged through me as some small nocturnal creature skittered through the cherry hedge. I backed toward my door. I hadn't noticed before that the streetlight at the curb was out, plunging the block even deeper into darkness on this moonless night.

I retreated inside and bolted the door. Call return said only that the killer had called me from a "private number."

I punched in the number for Miami dispatch.

"Patch me through to Detective Ojeda!" I told the operator, breathless. "This is an emergency!"

"Your IBM number?"

"I'm not a police officer. This is Britt Montero from the *Miami News*."

She paused. "He's not on duty. You have to talk to PIO."

"No, no, PIO is closed at this hour. Don't—" She had transferred the call. It rang in an empty office.

The Sea Sprite was only a few minutes away, at Collins and the ocean. I pulled on shorts, a T-shirt, and sneakers, snatched up my notebook, and ran for the car. Bitsy, still a police dog at heart, squeezed out the door with me, scrambling into the front seat, eager for action, her exhilaration in stark contrast to the dread in my belly.

Fumbling with the phone, I dialed 911.

"Miami Beach Police. What is your emergency?"

"There's been a homicide!"

"What is your location?"

"I'm in my car, on the way to the Sea Sprite Hotel."

"Your name?"

"Britt Montero, from the *Miami News*."

"The media?" She sounded dubious.

"Somebody's been shot! Send a car."

"What is the location?"

"Somewhere on the beach near the Sea Sprite."

"What makes you think there's been a shooting?"

"I got a call. Just send a car!"

"Did you see a victim?"

"No," I said. "Send a car! Send homicide!"

"You heard gunshots?"

"No."

"What is that location?"

"He could still be alive, for God's sake!" I hung up, frustrated. Yet as I raced toward the recently refurbished Sea Sprite Hotel, I also felt a guilty sense of relief. This was still my story. I still led the pack.

I checked the glove compartment at the next stoplight. My gun was still there. I left it unlocked, floored the gas pedal, and ran the red light.

I parked at the foot of the street, as close as possible to the sandy beach. No police. Few people in sight, only a city street-sweeping machine grinding its way slowly up Collins Avenue. A strolling couple, arms intertwined, meandered at a distance. Overhead, a giant jet rumbled out of sight. It was impossible to see where black sea ended and fathomless sky began. A single light blinked in the distance, a freighter far out at sea.

If no dead man was here, this was a trick to lure me out alone. I took the gun with me, its dead weight uncomfortable in my waistband. "Come on, Bits," I said, comforted by the sound of my own voice and her company.

We trotted up the stairs to the boardwalk, paused to scan the beach, then jogged down the other side. I moved quickly toward the water, eyes straining, relying on Bitsy to bark if someone was waiting.

In the dunes, I nearly stumbled over lovers on a blanket, in lusty flagrante delicto, naked bodies glistening in the dim light from the hotels and condos behind them. The one on top cursed. The other man gave a small startled yelp.

"Sorry," I said, and kept moving.

I spotted the lounge cushion first, discarded in a patch of sea oats, burn marks radiating from a jagged hole in the center. Then, at the edge of the surf, where breaking waves foamed across hard packed sand, I saw a smooth curve of pale skin, like the carcass of a beached sea creature tossed earthward by the sea. The man's trousers, attached to only one ankle, were already afloat, swept back and forth by the action of the waves. The incoming tide had cleansed the blood from his head wound, which now resembled a grotesque third eye in the center of his forehead. Bitsy stopped two feet from the corpse. Daintily avoiding getting her paws wet, she watched me over her shoulder, waiting expectantly.

I used the cell phone, scooped up my dog, and ran back the way we came.

"You should get dressed," I told the lovers. "The police are coming."

Ojeda, Simmons, and two burly task-force detectives were furious. Not only was I already at the scene, but so was Lottie and the Miami Beach police, who had also called in the FBI, even though the feds had not assumed jurisdiction. The victim, and possible clues important to the case, were saved from the tide, but not from the first two cops to arrive. Tracking through existing footprints, they caught the dead man's ankles and dragged him halfway up the beach. One picked up the lounge cushion I had been careful not to touch, handed it to another, who lobbed it to a third, who tossed it to the newly arrived sergeant, who stashed it in the trunk of his cruiser.

Lottie had appeared, hair wild, sans makeup, minutes after I called her. I shivered in the T-Bird, despite the 94-degree predawn temperature, replaying in my mind what the killer said about McDonald, Lance Westfell, and me. Only the detectives would hear the tapes tonight, but transcripts would be made and circulated through that rumor mill of a department. Copies would go to other law enforcement agencies, including the Beach. They would become part of police, prosecution, and state court records, accessible to other reporters. The transcript could be published nationwide. I thought about McDonald, returning from D.C., hoping to be appointed major. I thought about his career and mine, and our reputations.

Lottie was shooting pictures before the tide could obliterate the footprints and drag marks. I joined her and pressed my house key into her hand.

"You've got to do this for me," I whispered. "The killer knows all about me. It's on the telephone tape, next to my bed. Go there now. Erase it. Make sure the whole thing is blank."

"You sure?" Her honest brown eyes were troubled.

"Absolutely. I took notes. Erase it all. I'll tell 'em it was a mistake. Take Bitsy along. I'll say you took her home for me."

"You got it." She stuffed my keys into the pocket of her jeans and took Bitsy's leash.

"And, Lottie," I added, as she turned to go, "you can listen to it first."

"I was gonna anyhow."

She trotted up the sand, Bitsy running to keep pace with her long legs.

There was a brief flurry of excitement when the lovers on the beach informed the cops about a strange woman they had seen, but it was me.

"What the hell's the matter with you? You trying to sabotage the entire case? Trying to win a Pulitzer at our expense?" Ojeda was steamed. "You shoulda called us first. You never, ever shoulda come out here alone. Now the Beach has screwed up the scene and we got the FBI horning in. What do you want to bet, when we track her down, they'll try to steal our arrest. What the hell were you thinking?"

"I did try to call you," I said for the second time.

"I know. Dispatch dropped the ball at shift change. But that's no excuse. . . ."

"I had to know," I said. "I wasn't even sure there was a body. If so, he might still be alive. It seemed right at the time."

"Well, it sure as hell wasn't. If we're going to cooperate on this," he said, "you're not supposed to think. You call us and we tell you what to do. You got the tape?"

"Back at my apartment. She really got me rattled. Claimed to know where I live. I don't know if she was blowing smoke or not, but she even told me what kind of car I drive."

He shot me a sharp look, his brow beaded with sweat. "How could she know that?"

"I don't know."

"Something here you're not telling us?"

I shook my head.

He looked around. "Where'd your pooch go? I suppose he peed on the body too; everybody else did." He stopped to glower at a Beach cop sipping a soft drink from a vending machine outside the cabanas. "Nice to know that if our victim and killer shared refreshments from that machine before things turned nasty, their prints are now obliterated."

"She," I said numbly. "Her name is Bitsy. She didn't pee on the body. She was Francie's."

He gave a little nod of recognition. "I remember."

"Lottie took her home for me."

"To your place?"

"Yes."

"So the killer may know your address and you send your friend there alone. Very nice. The redhead with the camera don't need any enemies as long as she's got you for a buddy. See?" He turned to his partner. "This is why amateurs should stay outa this business. Let's go get that tape."

I promised the Beach cops I would come to the station shortly to make a statement.

* * *

Lottie answered my door all smiles. She had combed her hair and brewed coffee. Bitsy greeted the cops like long-lost friends and the atmosphere was cozy, until they played the tape and heard nothing but the hiss of the machine.

"You sure nobody was in here after you left?" Ojeda thundered.

"The dead bolt was locked when I got here," Lottie said primly.

"I'd been sound asleep," I explained, hoping to sound sincere. "I'd given up; I didn't think she'd call. I don't know, I must have pushed the wrong button. I could have sworn the tape was rolling. But don't worry, she said she'd call back, and my notes are still here." Luckily, only I could decipher them. I read them a censored version and promised a transcript.

The pay phone down the street proved to be out of order, so she had not called from there. She doesn't know where I live, I thought, relieved.

"Probably trying to psych you out," Ojeda said. "Every place on the beach has a pay phone down the block. She's being cute, but to be on the safe side we probably oughta move you outa here."

I opted to stay, refusing to be run out of my own space.

"We can ask the Beach cops for a watch order," Simmons said.

"Of course you know what that means," Ojeda added. "You live or die on your own." He ran his hand through his hair. "We need to know how she picked up that other stuff about you."

Seated across from him at my dining room table, Lottie raised her hand like a schoolgirl.

"I think I know," she said. "I'm sorry, Britt."

We all stared.

"Who do we know," she asked, her stricken eyes on mine, "that's been partying hard in South Beach for the past thirty-six hours and probably still is? Who do we know who would spill his guts to some sexy stranger in a bar? Who do we know with diarrhea of the mouth and poor judgment to boot?''

''Who?'' Ojeda and Simmons chorused.

''Tex,'' Lottie and I said. ''Tex O'Rourke.''

They found Tex facedown on the floor of his Sunny Isles motel room. He was alive but wished he wasn't. Still reeking of booze, he was suffering from the mother of all hangovers.

A leggy blonde passed out half naked on his bed woke up to drawn guns. A model from Amsterdam, she had a purse full of pot and a passport showing she'd arrived in the USA just two days earlier.

''Yellow Rose,'' Tex moaned fondly, on seeing Lottie. He blinked and winced painfully. The two cops helped him to his feet as he studied the carpet beneath them, his handsome face bewildered. ''I thought my back was to the wall,'' he mumbled, ''but that was the floor . . .''

He eased over to sit on the bed, wincing again when he saw it already occupied by the blonde model, who looked equally dazed.

''Who's that?'' he croaked to Lottie. ''Never saw her before in my life.''

''Sure,'' she replied quietly. ''You've gotta talk to these detectives, darlin'.'' He focused on them, slowly, with great effort.

''You turned me in to the cops?'' he asked in hurt disbelief.

''Tex, honey.'' Her voice dripped syrup. ''Now, why would I turn you in to the police? Bustin' up ain't no crime. No crime at all,'' she said succinctly. ''They just need to ask you about a woman.'' She swallowed hard, struggling to keep it together.

''You're the only woman, darling. Whoops.'' He lurched, unsteady, to his feet. ''Got to go talk on the big white telephone,'' he mumbled, bouncing off the wall as he made his way into the bathroom.

Ojeda jerked his head at Simmons. ''Take care of him. Hold his head, then throw 'im in the shower.''

''Why me?'' Simmons grumbled, as he opened the bathroom door to the sounds of retching.

After establishing that Tex had met the Dutch model only a few hours earlier, at Bash, they flushed her pot and put her, protesting, into a taxicab driven by a Jamaican in dreadlocks.

Tex's cuts and bruises were unrelated to his encounter with the serial killer. ''I ate the asphalt,'' he recalled, thoughtfully fingering a scrape on his chin. Clad in a terrycloth bathrobe, his curly hair was still wet from the shower.

'' 'Member the other day,'' Lottie prompted, ''we wuz catching up and I told you all about my friend Britt here?'' He squinted up at me. ''Well, then you went and talked to somebody in a bar 'bout her, didn't you?''

''You shot me down, Yellow Rose, you shot me down,'' he protested plaintively, eyes swimming. ''I was hurting and all alone.''

The detectives finally asked Lottie to step outside, to prevent personal feelings from inhibiting his answers. ''The only woman I ever loved. There she goes,'' he crooned as she left, her eyes reddening. ''She's walking away.''

His memory improved after the door closed. ''Oh, yeah,'' he said. ''I think I 'member her. Real sweet little thang, a honey babe. A blonde?'' He looked up at the detectives questioningly.

''You tell us,'' Ojeda said.

''Maybe dark-haired, or one-a them funky shades they use now. Hard to tell under them colored lights. But she was a doll baby, can tell ya that. What happened? That guy didn't hurt her, or nothing?''

''What guy?'' the detective asked with interest.

"Some chubby fella. I'da cleaned his clock, 'cept I was so bummed. My woman had just dumped me." He sighed. "I was hurting, hurting bad, and this gal was real sweet. Good listener. I was telling her all about Yellow Rose, how she shoots pictures for the newspaper and all, and somehow Britt's name came up. I said she just happened to be a friend of a friend. This gal was a good talker, real curious, a big fan of the newspaper.

"We was hitting it off. So it surprised me when this other dude come outa the VIP room and starts coming on to her. I'da kicked him from here to Kansas, 'cept she starts flirting back. Finally she says, 'So long, sugar,' pecks my cheek, and takes off with 'im. Shoulda seen 'im, proud as a puppy with two tails. Didn't boost my morale any, I tell ya. Guy was kinda pudgy, red-faced. Big spender, bragging 'bout his brand-new Jag, could be what attracted her. I was so bummed, so down and out of it . . . I jus' let her go."

Forehead in his hands, he looked green around the gills.

"Mighta been the first smart move you made lately," Ojeda said. "All I know is you're the first witness we've got who had a good look at this suspect and can put her and one of her victims together right before a homicide. I know you don't feel so good right now, but you're alive. He ain't. She's the Kiss-Me Killer—and he's lying dead on the sand. If he did have a new Jaguar, she's probably driving it. What'd she look like? What name was she using? What was she wearing?"

"Said 'er name was Keri, or Kelly. Somethin' like that. Nice body."

"What did she look like?"

"Really nice body. Wearing one of them little . . ." —his hands moved clumsily in a circular gesture—"you know, one of them little sexy things." He squinted up at them, red-eyed. "Nicely built. Friendly. Liked drinking tequila, liked to talk. Real sweet little thang. You say he's dead?"

* * *

The dead man was Tommy Karp, age forty-five, the self-proclaimed "King of the Night," a club and events promoter on South Beach. His 1999 black Jaguar, credit cards, and digital cell phone were missing.

By midmorning, Sonny's Mercedes surfaced on the third level of a South Beach parking garage near the club where Karp and the killer met.

"A motherless child," Dr. Schlatter said thoughtfully, when I called to pick her brain. "How interesting. Serial killers—usually male, of course—are more likely to grow up with absentee fathers and domineering mothers. Hmmm. . . .

"Maternal separation can profoundly affect brain chemistry in the young," she said, "with lifelong consequences. Studies on Romanian orphans in state institutions showed dramatic results, with extremely high levels of stress hormones. Other studies revealed that the brain cells of baby animals deprived of a mother's nurturing touch and loving care may actually commit suicide. Did she say at what age she lost her mother?"

"All she said was 'little kid.' " I wondered if any of this really applied to homicide. I hadn't heard about any Romanian orphans on killing sprees.

"Did you ask about her father?"

"No. I'll try if she calls again."

"She will, I think, unless other circumstances intervene. Sounds like you've done an excellent job in establishing rapport. Good work. Try to make her feel you share things in common. Did you mention my name, give her my number?"

"There was no time."

"She has so much anger in her," the doctor mused.

I didn't need a shrink to tell me that.

"Her selection process is quite remarkable," she went on. "The way she spared the first more sympathetic, more attractive, and less threatening man and took the other.

Clearly her victims are not selected at random but must meet certain specifications to fit her fantasies."

"Think I have anything to worry about?" I felt embarrassed to ask, but my fears the night before had been real.

"Probably not. You've stroked her ego and she would consider you a confidante, the vehicle by which to tell her story. She wants to use you. But I would advise extreme caution. She's volatile, totally unpredictable, and homicidal."

Schlatter agreed that the killer probably did not know where I lived, since Tex did not.

"It's just her way of keeping you off balance," the doctor said.

"She talked about a face-to-face meeting."

I heard a passionate little intake of breath. Either the idea took her breath away, or a donut had crossed her field of vision. "Feel free to suggest my office," she said quickly.

Tex, still hung over, worked on a composite with a police artist. But too many beautiful women had crossed his path as he partied his way through South Beach thinking of only one. Every sketch looked like Lottie. Ojeda was furious.

The massive manhunt came up with nothing. South Beach is full of beautiful girls in bustiers and leather skirts. Promiscuous, hard partying, and hard drinking, the Kiss-Me Killer had fit right in, disappearing into the atmosphere of sexual abandon, foam parties, and drugs.

I was on the phone, trying to reach Tommy Karp's ex-wife in New York for more background on him, when Gloria, the city desk clerk, said I had a call transferred from the sports department.

"It's me," the killer said abruptly, taking me totally by surprise.

I pushed the button. The phone man had said the system

might be in place by this afternoon, but could it trace a call transferred through the sports department?

"Do you ever sleep?" I asked.

"I took a nap," she said, "but I'm wired. Fired up. Hear all the bullshit they're sayin' on TV? See the news at noon? That skinny prick from Channel Seven had the balls to call me every man's worst nightmare. What the hell does he know? Some ugly-ass piece of shit from the Chamber of Commerce or someplace said I was scum. That black guy on Channel Ten called me 'a homicidal hooker.' Where do they get that shit? Hooker?" Her voice rose as she worked herself into a fury. "They don't even know who I am! I'm gonna tell you what it's really like! I want everybody to know."

"Nobody's heard your side," I agreed. "Let's tell it."

"Damn right. Face-to-face, you and me, one on one. No tricks, no games, no cops."

"That can be arranged," I said, voice calm, but so giddy I nearly fell off my chair. "I'll have to talk to my editors."

"Those assholes again."

"Right. My bosses."

"There's protection, laws for reporters, right? It's like talking to your lawyer or priest. Nobody, not even the cops, can make you tell anything confidential. Right?"

"Good reporters go to jail before giving up a news source," I said. "You name the time and place."

I closed my eyes to block out Gloria, who was waving that I had another call.

"Now, I'm only gonna talk to you. Private, one on one—me to Britt. You can bring one of them little computers with you, a laptop."

"Sure, I can do that."

She spoke rapidly, words tumbling over one another. She sounded manic, probably using drugs. I heard a TV in the background.

"All this pressure, this whole thing, is driving me nuts.

You'll get the exclusive. I'm sick of this shit on TV. They don't know squat."

"I believe you."

"Got that right," she muttered. "Talk to your editors, do what you have to do. I'll put it all together. I have to think. Be around, call you later. I might have something else to tell you."

I recoiled. "Wait," I said. "What do you . . ." But she was gone.

Ojeda and Simmons played the tape in a conference room.

The call had come from Tommy Karp's digital phone, according to call return. The system, now in place, could not pinpoint its location. The detectives arranged to have his phone disconnected, hoping she would switch to a land line.

"I'll go meet her," I told them. "I want to do it."

"I don't like it," Ojeda said. "But it could be the only way to get the break we need. We could set a trap."

The chief agreed. Ground rules would not include me interviewing her first. They would swoop down to make the collar the moment she appeared.

"We'll do everything we can to protect you," Ojeda said, "but you've gotta listen to us, do exactly what we say, and forget any crazy stunts. You can talk to her all you want after she's in jail."

"Oh, sure, as if she'll speak to me after I lead her into a trap."

I had nearly forgotten the other call Gloria had signaled me about. McDonald was late for a session by the time I called him back. No time to explain. I could fill him in later.

"Two more days," he said cheerfully, "and I'll be ringing your doorbell." I heard the smile in his voice.

Suddenly I wanted to blurt, Come back! Now, before it's too late, before I'm sucked into something way over my head. I swallowed the words, and the moment passed. Was it because there was no time to explain, or because I knew he would object?

"Hey," I murmured, instead, "be cool on the road, sweetheart. No picking up hitchhikers or pretty women in distress."

The two detectives and their lieutenant met with my editors and Mark Seybold. I had already briefed Fred. Nobody smiled. Eyes troubled, they spoke as though I wasn't there.

"My concern is obviously the safety of the reporter," Fred began.

"Normally we wouldn't ask a civilian to take this kind of risk," the lieutenant said, "but we've got nothing else. Saying that our only hope is that next time the killer will make a mistake is acknowledging that there will *be* a next time, another victim. Nobody wants that."

Harvey Holland, the publisher, shook his head. "It's one thing to send reporters and photographers into war zones, but it's another to dangle a reporter as bait."

This, I kept thinking, is the story of a lifetime.

"It would help us immensely," the lieutenant said earnestly. "This investigation has already cost taxpayers more than a million dollars, including rental cars for detectives, overtime, and sophisticated lab tests. More than seven hundred people have been interviewed statewide, thousands of leads followed. And this is the best we've got."

"Speaking of money," Gretchen said, frowning, "what if this should lead to an arrest? What about the reward? Could a reporter claim it?"

"If a staff member became eligible, it would have to go to charity," Holland said dismissively.

"Of course." I shrugged. I never gave the reward a thought.

"I don't feel right, encouraging a reporter to do this so we can have the story," Murphy, the managing editor, said.

"Nor do I feel right saying she can't do it. It's more an individual moral choice, a weighing of the pros and cons."

"We can't allow reporters to become swept up in their own stories, to lose their detachment," Fred argued.

"The goal we should all have," Ojeda said, "is to take this murderer off the street before she kills again."

"We're not the police, that's not our job," Murphy said.

"But you always say," I told him, "that journalism is personal—that a single reporter, a single edition, a single story can make a crucial difference."

"If you're going to quote me, Britt, quote me accurately. I believe I said the toughest, wisest, and best journalism," he said gruffly, then turned to the lawyer. "You've been quiet up to now, Mark. Give us your opinion."

All eyes on him, Mark Seybold took a deep breath, as I held mine. He removed his gold-rimmed spectacles and began slowly to polish the lenses with his handkerchief.

"I would say the newsroom has almost no standing here to take a position one way or the other. It's not a question of journalistic ethics. This should be between the police and the reporter, to consider the pros and cons and make an informed judgment. You've got a great story with or without this, Britt. If you want to help the police bring in a dangerous killer, do it as a person, not as a reporter. That said"—he paused, eyes troubled—"I tend to envision worst-case scenarios. This scares me. The police always say nothing will go wrong—but as we know, it almost always does. Not as general consul for this newspaper, but as your friend, I would point out that you're not trained to do this. As your friend I would try my damnedest to talk you out of it."

The cops fidgeted in their seats, eager to interrupt, argue and rebut.

"Hear me out," he said, stopping them. "You, Britt, have got to ask these detectives all the tough questions."

In the end it was my choice.

Ten

NOW WE WAITED FOR THE KILLER'S CALL. SWAT, the police chopper, and the undercover detectives were poised and ready to roll. I was to deal for as much time as possible and refuse any location impossible to surround or surveil. The police did not want me out of their sight for a moment.

The hours crept by.

Ojeda and Simmons stared in dismay at the contents of my refrigerator, or lack thereof, then tried to sleep on folding cots in my living room. The phone rang once, and I thought my heart or bladder would burst as we scrambled. Despite the hurt in her voice, I asked my mother not to call again until I finished my current project, adding that I loved her and would explain later. I took a call from McDonald in my bedroom, door closed. I told him I was tired when he asked what was wrong. No lie there, though I did neglect to mention the detectives in the next room. Primed for the trip home, he talked about new grant possibilities, new colleagues in Washington, and urged me to get some rest.

Caffeine, adrenaline, and the delivered pizza took their toll. Padding barefoot into my dark kitchen for a glass of warm milk at 4 A.M., I found a shadowy presence at my kitchen table. Ojeda couldn't sleep either.

"What do you think motivates her?" I murmured, as we shared the last of the milk. "Why kill total strangers? What turned her into a monster?"

"I don't know, and I don't care," he said. "I don't need to know what makes her kill or if it can be cured. All I want to know about her is information that helps me identify her and apprehend her. I want to arrest her, and convict her. That's my job. It's not up to me to figure out what makes her tick. I really don't give a shit."

I wanted, needed, to know it all, as though the answer would place everything into perspective and I would be able at last to figure out why people do the things they do to each other. I went back to bed and left him alone in the dark, both of us awaiting the call that did not come.

Had she changed her mind? Was this all a game to her? Had she left town?

The detectives trailed me to the office next morning and Simmons fetched our breakfast from the cafeteria. It was Ryan's day off so they ate at his desk. Then they waited, feet up, perusing out-of-town newspapers.

I worked on other stories but found it hard to focus. I kept checking the time. Where was she?

At 10:30 A.M., Gretchen, cool and crisp in black and white linen, sauntered over to my desk. "I guess you're not as plugged in as you thought." She shrugged smugly and handed me a slip of paper. "The police desk just called. The Beach had another one."

"Another homicide?" The detectives were on their feet.

"You think it's her?" I asked.

"That's what they say," she said breezily. "That's the address."

The detectives cursed and Ojeda snatched the address from my hand. South Beach, a dozen blocks south of the last murder scene, not far from where Gianni Versace took his final morning stroll.

"We asked them to notify us of any development at once," Ojeda muttered, slamming a fist into his palm.

"Guess they forgot." Gretchen shook her shiny blonde mane and strutted smartly back to the city desk.

He was Carlos Triana, a model.

He had failed to appear for a catalog shoot when the early morning light was just right on the Boardwalk. The furious photographer notified Triana's agency. Someone was sent to the model's subleased condo. No answer at the door. Triana's Mazda was missing from his parking space. Then the young agency assistant recognized Karp's Jaguar in visitor parking. The sedan had been on TV; everybody was looking for it. He called his boss, who called police.

Neighbors had complained in the past about loud parties in the second-floor condo apartment. This time the sounds of doors slammed in the wee hours had actually been gunshots.

His live-in fiancée, a psychology major at the University of Miami, was away, visiting her family in New York.

Tall, athletic, and handsome, Triana worked hard, played hard, and had it all. He was twenty-seven.

I joined the rest of the press amid the crowd gathered outside the yellow crime scene tape. Ojeda ducked beneath the tape to talk to Beach detectives while Simmons hung out close to me, in case the call came.

The South Beach crowd differed from the gawkers at most murder scenes. Kids on summer vacation mingled with curious senior citizens wearing little umbrella hats and plastic nose protectors against the brutal sun. Promoters and entrepreneurs complained bitterly to reporters and each other about what a blow this was to business. Triana's agent, Melinda Mowrey, worked the press, helpfully distributing her cards and copies of her late client's modeling composite. Impressive. Clad in tennis whites and brandishing a tennis racket, he flashed a blinding Pepsodent smile. The man had been a hunk.

He was a regular on the Beach nightlife scene that had blossomed after the modeling agencies moved in, attracting beautiful women and the players who orbit around them.

Fiercely competitive clubs, bars, and discos all crowded into a small district battled soaring rents, parking nightmares, and each other for survival. Independent promoters hired to make places happen dreamed up innovative specialty-night party themes, papered the city with posters, and packed as many as two thousand hot bodies a night into certain clubs. Like head hunters, the promoters were paid a percentage of the night's take for delivering high body counts.

The Kiss-Me Killer had just single-handedly changed the meaning of the term.

Karp's death had sent shudders through the beautiful creatures of the night. Now this. Murder is a turnoff, sudden death a bummer.

Triana was definitely a hot body. He had entertained his killer in his hot tub. That's where he was found. As a parting gesture, she had turned up the temperature. Way up. His groin wound had severed an artery and he bled out, the contents of the tub cooking into a very nasty soup.

''Be glad we ain't working that scene,'' Ojeda told Simmons back at the paper. ''Be very glad.''

Why hadn't she called me as with Karp? The detectives feared she was gone. I feared she was talking to someone else, another reporter about to break the story.

''She's killing the clubs,'' promoter Ziggy Solomon complained on the TV news at six.

This body count meant no business, no crowds, no big bucks. The promoters, business owners, and managers were demanding that the city, the Chamber of Commerce, the Tourist Development Commission, and the cops take immediate action to make the city safe once more for rampant decadence.

Most commissioners had fled the steamy city for the summer, but the mayor called an emergency session of his advisory committee for the following morning.

Beach clubs were subdued that night, the streets deserted. The desk assigned Howie Janowitz to do a piece on it. Normally I would have wanted that too, would have wanted to do it all, but I was exhausted. So were the detectives. On the way home, I cruised Ocean Drive, the detectives trailing in their unmarked. The neon-filled night was hot, but there was no breeze off the sea and no action. Business was dead, the outdoor cafés empty, chairs stacked.

A small Beach weekly hit newsstands next morning with the headline: HARD-PARTYING ANGEL OF DEATH, KILLS SOBE CLUBS.

Tex bombarded the photo department with yellow roses, accompanied by cards threatening to leave Miami forever if Lottie continued to ignore him, which she did. Kendall McDonald was already on the road home—and nothing.

I had been right not to tell him, I thought. We replayed her last call over and over, trying to figure out why she changed her mind. She had sounded so certain. Dr. Schlatter advised not to give up hope.

I did a brief phone interview with Triana's hysterical fiancée, Stephanie, about to fly home to a terrible truth and a very messy apartment.

"Oh my God. Oh my God," she repeated. "It can't be true, he can't be dead." He had lived a swinger's lifestyle before her, but that had all changed, she said. They were settling down. He would not invite another woman into their home. They had talked at seven the night he died. He had been elated because of a second call-back audition for a national margarine commercial. He was sure he would land it. He had wished she were there so they could celebrate.

He must have decided to celebrate without her.

Ojeda was in the men's room and Simmons dozing in a desk chair when my phone rang again.

"¿Como está?" she said, in a bad accent. "Sorry I haven't touched base lately."

"Where've you been?"

I pressed the button, gesturing frantically at Simmons, whose eyes were nearly closed. He snapped awake, donning the earphones to the extension they had set up.

"I thought you forgot about me," I said. The hair prickled on the back of my neck.

"Would I do that, girlfriend? You been on my mind all the time." She sounded serene, relaxed. "Just took a day off to wind down, get a little rest. Nothin' like a good soak in a hot tub. Feelin' much better now, I tell ya."

Ojeda was back, scrambling for his earphones.

"I was surprised to hear about you and that model, Carlos. You didn't call. I was the last to know."

"Awww, did I make ya jealous, girlfriend? Thought you were sharp. Guess I shoulda called. Hate to see you git scooped by other reporters. Us working girls need all the help we can git."

"Weren't you scared? That guy was in great shape, had a black belt in karate."

"Scared?" She repeated it as if it were a new word. "Fear," she said, "is like water. You need it. And it's good for you, as long as you have the right amount."

"What about our interview?"

"I'm callin' you, ain't I? Somethin' you're gonna have to understand 'bout me, Britt, if we're gonna get along. When I give my word, I live up to it, unlike some people." She chuckled. "Unless I change my mind, a-course . . .

"My main concern," she said, her tone becoming more businesslike, "is that a nonbiased individual, like yourself, hears my story and tells it right, as purely as I can refine it from opinion to a true and solid perspective. A-course, over a period of time, I expect we can talk about the significance of everythin' I tell you. Perhaps somethin' can come of it, somethin' significant.''

Her little speech sounded oddly rehearsed.

I stole a look at Ojeda, who was nodding in mock agreement, lifting his thick eyebrows.

''That's exactly what I'm hoping for,'' I said, thinking of McDonald on the road, pushing for home. ''When do we start?''

''You sound like a lady in a hurry,'' she said lightly. ''How 'bout this afternoon?''

My body quaked, as though doused by icewater. This was what I wanted, what I was living for. Wasn't it?

''Sure,'' I said. ''Sounds great.''

Ojeda gestured, a slow-down-let's-take-our-time signal.

''Let's see.'' She pondered, as though consulting a timepiece. ''It's eleven thirty now. Hm. Know where Michelangelo's Garden is?''

Ojeda's hand wobbled in an I'm-not-sure signal.

''I think so,'' I answered slowly. ''Where they make the good pizza?'' Michelangelo's Garden was a combination service station and pizzeria on South Dixie Highway.

''Yeah, yeah, that's the one.''

''I've never been there, but I think I've passed it. Hear it's pretty good.''

''Not bad,'' she said.

''You get around, don't you? Thought you spent most of your time on the Beach.''

''I cover the waterfront,'' she said. ''I get bored easy. Never stay too long in one place, that's my motto.''

The tense cops in their earphones had caught the attention of the city desk. People had stopped work to watch. Somebody must have called Lottie. She appeared in the hall between the newsroom and photo, near the wire room, watching, poised like a deer, ready to bolt for her gear and her car. She would hang with the cops and shoot the arrest as it went down.

"So," I said. "We meet for pizza?"

"I tell ya"—she sighed—"I'm not much for Eyetalian. Right now I could go for eggs over easy, with bacon and grits on the side. But tell you what." She sounded almost eager. "I got to get my act together here. Let's make it Michelangelo's this afternoon, four o'clock sharp."

Ojeda nodded, big smile, thumbs up.

"Okay, you've got it."

"Look casual," she said. "Wear jeans. Don't look like a reporter. Don't wanna 'tract no attention."

"I'll just carry a notebook in my purse and leave the laptop in the car?"

"You got it. You'll be driving your T-Bird, right?"

"Yep. How will I know you?"

"Well, I sure as hell ain't gonna carry a sign. You just pull up in that T-Bird, I'll find you. It's white, right?"

"Luminescent Pearl is the official color," I said.

"Okay, park as close to the front door as you kin get, but park legal for God's sake, then come on in. I'll be waitin' at a table near the front. You git there first, you grab one. Shouldn't be too crowded then. And Britt. I smell cop, and somebody's gonna wind up hurtin'—bad."

"If you see a police car anywhere, just chill," I said solemnly. "Because if you do, he's not with me, he's on routine patrol."

"Don't tell anybody, I mean *anybody*, where you're goin'."

"Okay. My editors know we plan to meet, but I'll tell them when it's over, when I get back."

"Good. See ya in a bit. Remember, I'm trustin' you."

"You can count on me, like a rock."

As she hung up, Ojeda bowed his head, hands in a prayerful position, then hurtled jubilantly out of his chair and high-fived Simmons. "Okay! Okay! Right on, Britt!"

Fred watched from the door of his glass office. Mark Seybold was with him. I gave them the thumbs-up.

Ojeda was already on his radio reporting the location, confirming that all systems were go. Luckily, I had a pair of jeans in my locker. I changed into them, then called Mrs. Goldstein to ask her to feed and walk Bitsy and Billy Boots because I had to work late. I told Fred I'd be back by six o'clock, seven at the latest, to write for the final. There would be more reporting to do: checking out the killer's identity and background, reactions from next of kin and other police agencies. I hoped McDonald got off to a late start. This would be a long night. I'd have to start reporting for the second-day story early in the morning. Then I would be free. We could be together. It could all work out.

As we tore out of the newsroom, my phone rang. The detectives and I stared at each other, then I dashed back to catch it. Breathless, I answered.

"Britt, thank God you're there!"

I winced. Why hadn't I been faster out the door? "Althea, I'm running out right now on a really important story."

"They tried again! They tried to kill me!" Genuine terror shook her voice.

I sank hopelessly into my chair, shaking my head at the detectives, who had started for the earphones.

"What is it?" I said impatiently. "What happened now?"

She hesitated, probably startled by my lack of sympathy. "I—I was walking into the beauty parlor. I had just stepped off the bus. My car isn't running, something with the transmission. I haven't found a buyer for the house yet, so I have to wait to get the car fixed. So I took the bus over to the beauty school downtown, the one where you get cut-rate haircuts from students in training. I hadn't ridden a bus in years, if ever. Well, it was quite an experience. Some of the—"

"Oh, God, Althea," I said, my head dropping to my chest. "Could you please just get to the bottom line?"

"As I walked into the beauty parlor, I dropped my magazine. As I bent to pick it up, I heard a sound. . . ."

Why me, I mourned, forehead in my hand. Would this woman ever get to the point? Ojeda and Simmons glared, gesturing at their watches, as jittery as thoroughbreds at the starting gate. Lottie was with them, carrying her equipment bag.

". . . I thought it was a car backfiring. I heard glass tinkling but thought nothing of it. Well, I walked in and thought I was all alone. It looked like the place was empty. Everybody was on the floor. The window was broken. The police said it was a drive-by. Britt, it never occurred to me that what I heard was gunfire. I never even saw the car, but I heard it speed up and turn the corner. They said the only reason I wasn't killed was that the magazine slipped out of my hands—"

"Anybody hurt?"

"No."

"What did the police say?"

"They don't believe I was the target. Lieutenant Springer was out; I was unable to reach him. They took my name and the other case numbers and said they would check it out, but, Britt, I don't think they will. They said it was teenage gangs shooting at each other. That there have been a number of drive-by shootings in that neighborhood. But I had just gotten off the bus—"

"Oh, Althea, maybe you should believe them. Things happen."

"But Britt, they were shooting at *me*, I know it. They were!"

"Did you talk to your family?"

"My daughter?" she said uncertainly.

"Yes. What does she say?"

"That it's my fault, that I shouldn't have been in that area in the first place."

"She's probably right."

"No!" Althea said abruptly. "Why won't someone listen?" She paused, as though collecting her thoughts. "They say the first half of our lives is ruined by our parents and the second by our children; what about husbands? It's Richard's fault—I know he isn't doing this, but I also know that none of it would be happening if he hadn't left, if I wasn't alone, if he hadn't just walked . . ."

She was on the verge of hysteria. I gazed beyond the newsroom out the picture windows at blue sky, swooping gulls, and shafts of light glinting off the mirror-bright face of the bay.

"Althea, maybe being lucky three times is a sign. Maybe it's over. In any case, I don't have time to go into it with you again right now. I'm working on a really major story. I'll talk to the cops about what happened if I get the chance, but really—" Ojeda frowned and called my name. "I've got to go." I hung up before she could protest. I could listen to her later, after this was over.

My phone rang again as we left. I didn't look back.

"That former Orange Bowl queen, the one whose husband dumped her, says somebody tried to kill her again today," I explained on the elevator. "She was nearly caught in a drive-by downtown."

"She's sure living the perils of Pauline," Lottie drawled.

"Ain't we all," Ojeda said.

Lottie and I took our own cars, met the detectives in the lobby at headquarters, and were whisked to a war room I didn't know existed, adjacent to the fifth-floor detective bureau.

"We have an alternative," the homicide lieutenant said in greeting. "A policewoman who resembles you from a distance can drive your car."

"No way!" I blurted. "I set it up, made the contact. If I can get one good quote from her before you guys drag her away in handcuffs, I want that chance.'' Secretly, I hungered for more, but that was probably the best I could hope for.

''We're not in the business of catering to the newspaper's desires,'' the detective commander said coldly. ''We don't need your cooperation at this point. We can use any white T-Bird and do this without you.''

''Sure. What if she knows what I look like? What if she knows my tag number? What if this is a test and she calls me at the Garden? Why take a chance on spoiling it now? Let's just do it as planned. I'm the one she's talked to; she knows my voice. We made a deal. I've had detectives in my living room—''

''It's your safety and the safety of the entire operation that we're concerned about,'' the commander said.

''There'd *be* no operation if it wasn't for me, and I'm following the plan to the letter,'' I said.

''Right. Under no circumstances do you get creative and start improvising,'' the lieutenant warned. ''You absolutely do not go anywhere or get into a vehicle with her. You're covered from the moment you leave here, and we're with you, even if you don't see us. Should she approach you prematurely, before you enter, you push your hair back with your right hand, like this.'' He demonstrated. ''We move in the moment she identifies herself. Otherwise, you walk in, sit at a table close to the door, and order a Coke. When she approaches and identifies herself, you make the same hand signal. The cashier, the waitress, and most of the customers will be cops.''

''But she's been there and knows the place.''

''She won't have time to notice any big difference. Now, if civilians who might be endangered are present, our people might wait until it's safe or until you exit together. That'll be our judgment call. But if that happens, we take her down before you approach your car, her car, whatever. Be assured, you will never be out of our sight.''

I nodded. ''Okay, but remember, the detectives talk to

me exclusively, referring the rest of the media to PIO until morning.'' That was their sole concession, that others in the press would receive only a brief release while we had all the color and details.

They went over and over every last item, to the point of tedium. Using a laser pointer and a map of the neighborhood, the lieutenant indicated the positions of the SWAT van, the mobile command post, and a vacant lot where the bird could land if necessary. Lottie would ride with the SWAT commander to shoot the capture. I would wear a body bug to record any possible admissions the killer might make to me. A global positioning device would be installed so my car could be tracked by computer. Nothing was left to chance. Another uniform entered the room almost unnoticed and listened from the back. I did a double take: McDonald.

Tall, long-legged . . . *guapismo!* I caught my breath and wanted to go to him, touch his face, hold him. This was our time. The place was all wrong. Our glances caught. He did not smile.

''I'm aware I'm in the minority,'' he said, when the captain called for comments. ''But as you already know, I don't like it.''

''Your objections are noted,'' the commander said.

I greeted him as the meeting broke, trying not to be conspicuous. ''Didn't know you were in town,'' I said.

''Just rolled in a short time ago,'' he said. ''See you in my office?''

I sat on a hard wooden chair in front of his desk. The familiar smell of his soap and shaving lotion left me lightheaded. He leaned forward, speaking softly. ''Don't do this, Britt. It's too risky. It's not worth it.''

''I didn't know you were back.''

''I came in early, to surprise you.''

''I didn't mention this to you, because it was uncertain and I didn't want you to worry. I didn't think it would really happen.''

"It *is* happening. No story is worth dying over."

I leaned back in my chair, crossed my legs, and wished I was wearing something more glam than old blue jeans. "You have no idea what Miami has been like with her here. The Beach is in an uproar. The whole mess with Sonny has turned the city upside down. The prosecutor's office is subpoenaing the mayor's funeral-parlor tape—"

"I tried to call you." His eyes said more than his words.

"It was hectic. I left the office in a hurry. I'm sorry. Look, it's going down in broad daylight with every piece of hardware and backup the department can muster. The chief guaranteed my bosses that every precaution is being taken—and believe it or not, the killer likes me. She's never harmed a woman."

"We don't know that," he said, his hands on the desk in front of him.

"Evidently, she hates men. Probably for good reason," I said, hoping to lighten up the conversation. "You know I can handle myself," I said persuasively. "Your chief and my editors agreed."

"They're fools. She's homicidal, a totally unknown quantity. Your editors and the chief don't feel the way I do."

I knew the longing in his silvery blue eyes was mirrored in my own.

"I can't tell you how many operations we've had, where every possible precaution was taken," he said, "and things went terribly wrong. These operations, no matter how well planned, can turn to shit in a heartbeat. You know that. Hell, you've written about some of them. There's always that unpredictable human factor. And she has nothing to lose."

I shifted impatiently in my chair. "She targets men, not women. She relates to me. Wants me to write her story." Why couldn't we talk about what was really important? I wondered. Us.

"Even if that's all true, and we don't know for a fact

that it is, she's more unpredictable than most serial killers. The men have been studied up, down, and inside out, giving us lots of resource material. But this female is rare, we don't know enough—''

''Which is why we need to find out. Shrinks are lining up to pick her brain. I'm as eager as they are. How many reporters ever get this sort of chance? And it's the right thing. Even the chief said there's nothing more they can do until she makes a mistake. How many more victims will die?''

''Leave it to us, Britt. We'll send in a professional. I don't want you involved.''

Why was he being so difficult? Was it my safety he was concerned about, or his ego, because I didn't tell him?

''If you had the opportunity to bring in this killer, or any other notorious fugitive,'' I said, ''and you were the only one who could do it, would you pass on it because I said it was too risky, that something might go wrong? No way.''

His head snapped back, as though he'd been slapped. ''That makes no sense, Britt. That's my job, what I'm trained to do. You're comparing apples and oranges. This is dead serious.''

''Oh.'' My voice sounded stone cold. ''And my chance at a once-in-a-lifetime story is not?''

He paused, studying my face intently. ''For weeks,'' he said slowly, ''I've wanted to be close to you.''

I thought of the champagne and how long I had waited for those words. ''Tonight,'' I said, yearning to reach out to him. ''Later. After deadline.'' Why did fate and timing always conspire against us?

''I can't dictate what you do,'' he said. ''I can only ask.'' He watched me.

''We would have been together already,'' I said, ''but you stayed longer in Washington because it was important to your career. Well, what about mine? Is this how it will be, yours always more important than mine?''

I knew at once I had gone too far. I had seen this look in his eyes before, when he found me in the chaos after the hurricane—with someone else. The rival this time was a stranger.

"I can't stop you." He rolled his chair back abruptly, as if to distance himself from me.

"I'm glad you're back. See you later?" My words sounded as shaky and as uncertain as I felt. I thought of the lacy lavender nightgown.

He blinked, then shrugged.

Sudden panic seized me as I stood up to leave. Can I live without him? I wondered. Will I have to?

"For God's sake, Britt, be careful," he said, as I reached for the door.

"Sure," I said, almost flippantly. "You too."

For a moment outside his office, I hesitated, bewildered. Where was the intimacy we had shared long-distance for weeks? What was I doing? I turned to go back, but Ojeda and Simmons hailed me from across the detective bureau, their faces expectant.

"Britt, it's getting late! We gotta get it together!" They were eager to test the body bug and needed my car keys in order to plant the tracking device. There was no time to dwell on personal matters. I had an important assignment, the most important of my career.

Detective Marcia Anders and Sally, a chubby-faced technician from the Special Investigations Section, wired me for sound, securing a beeper-sized unit to the small of my back with medical tape.

"This is a lot easier," Sally said cheerfully, "than taping guys with hairy backs. You should hear 'em scream when it comes off."

The wire, held in place by tiny strips of tape, ran up the back of my neck, hidden by my hair, around, and down into my bra, where a clip like those worn by TV anchors held the mike between my breasts.

The receiver, built into a slim aluminum briefcase,

would be with the detectives in the primary car, an off-white Isuzu Rodeo, trailing me as I drove to Michelangelo's Garden. They also placed a voice-activated tape recorder under my car seat. The global positioning unit concealed in the trunk would transmit my car's location in approximate street addresses to a portable computer screen.

Instead of the conspicuous SWAT trailer, a smaller cargo van disguised as a delivery truck would be parked in a lot behind Michelangelo's. Ojeda and Simmons would be with the brass, supervising from a staff car concealed on a nearby side street. A jet ranger helicopter, borrowed from the sheriff's department, would be airborne. Miami police lost their air support to budget cuts when the city went bust. All the technological apparatus seemed like overkill to me, but, as Lottie said, big boys love toys.

The Rodeo and two other unmarked cars, each with two detectives, one driving, the other concealed in back with a shotgun, would escort me through traffic. Two would leapfrog behind me, frequently passing each other, pulling up and falling back. The lead car would range blocks ahead.

My face looked pale in the mirror during my third visit to the rest room. Too much coffee, too much waiting. I was eager to see her, to look into her eyes just once while she was still free, before her features became the expressionless mask worn by humans in captivity. The drive would normally take fifteen minutes. Allowing for rush hour, they gave it thirty-five.

McDonald and I exchanged glances but had no chance to speak again. He would be with the others at the command post. Ojeda jabbed a fist gently at my shoulder before leaving with the brass.

"Break a leg, kid. Just stay cool and remember the rules. No screwups. See ya later."

The sky was broad and blue, the sun relentless, and the pavement scorching as I drove south on Interstate 95. I could see the Isuzu Rodeo in the rearview mirror—its stubby little black antenna tuned in to me—riding high in traffic four or five cars behind me. A middle-aged detective named Boggs was driving; a younger one, named Rodriguez, rode shotgun. I felt as secure as the president, surrounded by Secret Service.

"Look at the traffic," I said aloud, aware they could hear me. "We're lucky it's not raining." The heavy stream moved smoothly. I stayed at the speed limit and watched passing motorists. What would they think if they knew where I was going and why? I thought of Althea for some reason. In all the excitement I had forgotten to ask the cops about the drive-by. What would my mother think of this? Would she be proud, or would she redouble her efforts to talk me into some other line of work? What was McDonald thinking right now?

I squinted into the sun on the approach to the SW 16th Avenue exit, where traffic swooped down off the interstate onto South Dixie Highway. Even with sunglasses the glare was brutal. Would the killer try to scratch my eyes out when she saw the cops? I was to step away quickly when they made their move. Humph, I thought, if they had their way, I'd have no chance to speak to her at all.

I hoped for the scenario the lieutenant had mentioned, a delay due to innocent bystanders. That would give us time to talk before the inevitable. I had so many questions. How did life lead her here? Was she remorseful? Was it men she hated? Or sex?

Merging into the far right lane, I slowed and signaled for the exit. Once off the interstate, past Vizcaya, Michelangelo's would be seven traffic lights ahead. The place was well-known for its policy of buy one slice, get one free. Tomorrow it would be famous for something else.

My lane of traffic inched toward the exit ramp. I braked as a shiny red Mitsubishi Mirage with a blaring stereo suddenly cut in front of me. "You jerk!" I muttered at the driver. Then he braked as another motorist, a cute teenager in a blue Camaro, cut in front of him. What is this? I thought impatiently. I'm on a mission here!

Butterflies swarmed through my intestinal tract and I wished I'd visited the rest room one more time. The problem was not the task ahead, it was the damn waiting, the blinding sun, the slow-moving traffic.

"How do you guys deal with this?" I asked the microphone in my bra. "You get all psyched up for action, then sit in traffic. This part is so boring. I hate rush hour."

I checked the rearview. The surveillance car, the Isuzu Rodeo, was seven or eight vehicles behind mine in the bumper-to-bumper crawl. The other, a Ford Explorer, was so far back I didn't see it. The ramp, a single-lane bottleneck at the exit, would broaden into two lanes on the descent.

The red Mirage in front of me literally vibrated with the sounds of rap music. The driver looked like a gangbanger: young, with big shades, a baseball cap worn backward, and the mother of all stereo systems. Did he open his car windows in this weather to bombard us all with his taste in music? Or were the windows closed? Was the volume so high we could hear it anyway? Were his eardrums still intact? What happened to the city ordinance against noise pollution?

He played drums, his hands slapped the steering wheel, his head jerked to the beat, as I inched down the ramp behind him. The girl in front of him suddenly slammed on her brakes, and the vibrating Mirage rear-ended her Camaro with a loud *bam!* "Damn," I said aloud, hitting my own brakes in time. A bumper thumper.

Those of us behind them sat at a standstill in the heat, rush hour building all around us. The girl, out of her car now, wore a fast food uniform. Must be on her way to work, I thought. She checked for damage. I couldn't see from my vantage point, but at that slow speed it couldn't be bad. He got out and joined her, leaving the music blasting. Christ, I thought, what if I'm late? I gave the surveillance car in the rearview an exaggerated shrug, as if they could see me from there.

Neither of those two drivers should have a license. I fumed. This was Miami, they probably didn't. Their heads were together now. He took a quick step back, apparently irked at something she said, and began to gesture. He stalked back to his car and opened the door, releasing more throbbing bass into the superheated atmosphere. She said something else. He stalked back and appeared to be intimidating her. The son of a bitch was twice her size. I didn't like the looks of this. A cacophony of car horns sounded behind me as the drivers exchanged angry words. She walked past his car, ponytail bouncing, as though in search of something. He followed, red in the face, shouting words I couldn't hear. His car still vibrated. The least he could do, I thought, is turn down the volume.

She approached my T-Bird, a flowered straw purse swinging from her shoulder, and motioned for me to roll down my window.

"Do you have a cell phone? I have to call for help." She rolled pitifully worried eyes back at the angry gang-banger, who was bellowing something just two steps behind her.

"Sure," I said. "Want me to call the cops?"

"Think you should?" she said timidly, near tears. "I was just gonna call my boyfriend. It's his car. He's gonna kill me."

"Okay, but make it fast, you've gotta move the cars." She smiled gratefully as I handed her my phone. Somebody behind me leaned nonstop on their horn, adding to the earsplitting din. I sighed impatiently as she placed the phone on my car roof and reached into her straw bag to find the number. Instead, in a split second that seemed like slow motion, she drew out a gun, swung it over her shoulder, and shot the hulking gang-banger square in the face. Blood flew as he was hurled back. I heard the screams of other motorists as he crumpled to the pavement, a messy hole just above the bridge of his nose. The gunshot and the music resounded up and down the concrete barriers of the ramp.

Her eyes so wide I saw the whites, she wrenched open my car door. "Move over!" She swung the gun at my head. The still smoking barrel looked huge. "Move over, damn it!" She shoved her way into the car without waiting for me to obey. At the last moment, she turned, aimed, and fired another shot at the young man, whose body still jerked on the scorching pavement. A middle-aged motorist, half out of his car, ducked back inside and slammed the door. As I scrambled for the passenger-side door, the gun was back on me.

"Don't you move, Britt!" she shrieked. "I'll cap you! I'll cap you right now!"

How does she know my name? I wondered stupidly. Then I knew who she was. The detectives, I thought; they must have heard the shot.

She turned the wheel hard and hit the gas as I looked back. Boggs, a gun in one hand, his radio in the other, and Rodriguez, with the shotgun, were charging down the ramp on foot.

Terrified motorists trapped in traffic were screaming, ducking, hitting other cars in escape attempts. They had to think they'd been caught in a gang war.

She threw it in reverse and slammed into the front bumper of the car a few feet behind me. My cell phone flew off the roof as she wheeled around the red Mirage and ran over something: the man she shot. My T-Bird dragged him until she cut the wheel again and swerved past the Camaro. The driver's-side door scraped noisily along the concrete barrier as she floored it.

"My car!" I gasped. "I don't let anybody else drive it."

"Well, excuse *me*."

Behind us, Boggs stood shouting into his radio. In front of us, the squeegee men working the ramp scattered, fleeing for their lives. Rodriguez was still running, despite the growing distance between us.

"He won't shoot," she panted, grinning. "Too many people around, includin' you. Wouldn't worry if he did, most cops can't shoot worth shit . . .

"Hah! Look at that!" she yelped gleefully. "See that? The stupid son of a bitch with the shotgun tried to take over somebody's car and they peeled out to git away from 'im. Aw right!"

Hunched forward, peering over her shoulder like a race-car driver, she gunned my T-Bird into the emergency lane, rocketing by other traffic.

"Wasn't that good shootin'? Damn, I'm good! You best remember that, girl!"

"Wish you hadn't shot him," I mourned. "You ran over him, too. Think he's dead?"

"Most likely. That's life. You can be fine, fine, fine, then—*boom!* You're dead!" She shrugged her slim shoulders philosophically. "Didja hear that music?" Her pert nose wrinkled in disgust.

I saw now that she was no teenager. But she was young and sweet-faced, with a dimpled chin and engaging grin. Somebody you would smile back at in a mall. Her cuteness wore off fast. I took a deep breath and tried not to be sick as the car lurched and swerved. I didn't see the Rodeo or the Blazer behind us, but they would overtake us any second now. She would have to surrender when surrounded, I told myself.

She slowed into the flow of traffic and swung off Dixie into a residential neighborhood.

"Why are you taking Seventeenth Avenue?" I asked, for the cops who were listening.

She reacted violently and hit the brake, tearing crazily at my blouse with her right hand, the gun still in her left. I shrank back but not before she yanked out the body bug, ripping my blouse in the process.

"You bitch! You think I'm stupid?"

I wanted to say yes, shooting strangers is stupid, but she wasn't. She had just outsmarted me, the SWAT team, and the entire Miami Police Department.

''Fuck you, assholes!'' She kissed the tiny mike with a noisy smack, chortling as she lobbed it out the window.

Another right turn, then a left into the nearly deserted parking lot at Shenandoah Junior High School, where she braked and turned off the engine. We stared at each other for a moment. Without makeup, she had a shiny fresh-scrubbed look with high broad cheekbones sharp enough to cut glass, lashes long and curly, eyes a watercolor blue.

''Hi,'' I said, to break the silence.

Her smile was cynical. ''I drove by the Garden and saw the van. Never expected you not to bring the cops, but I hoped maybe you might surprise me.'' She sighed. ''But you didn't.''

''Sorry,'' I said. ''Can I take my notebook out of my purse? I have some questions.'' They would be here any second.

''No, give it here,'' she snapped, and took it. She checked the mirror. ''Git out! Now remember, I kin shoot the eye out of a squirrel at thirty yards. You and me, we're takin' a walk. Git out real slow, then you lean on the car. Forgit your purse, leave it right there. I'll come round to your side. You ain't gonna be the first human to outrun a bullet, so don't even try it. You do, and you're gone. Go real slow now.''

I did as she said. I closed the door and heard the locks snap down. She wiped off the steering wheel and the rear-view mirror with something she stuffed back in her purse, then slipped out gracefully. She watched me over the car roof, one hand in the straw purse concealing the weapon. I saw no one in the adjacent neighborhood. Residents were inside, air conditioners humming.

''Stay right there.'' She eased around the car.

''Can I see the damage to the driver's side?''

She shook her head.

"Is it bad?"

She didn't answer.

"Where are we going?"

"Shut up!" She slapped me so hard it rattled my teeth and sent my sunglasses flying. "Don't move, don't talk! Shut up and listen! Do what I say!"

I didn't dare try to pick up my glasses. The impact of her surprisingly strong blow and her sudden rage struck mortal fear into my heart.

"Let's just take a walk," she muttered. My knees shook as she steered me away from the car, then stopped near a parked Monte Carlo, white with a blue vinyl top. Slightly taller than I am, she stood about five six, with a strong, tight-looking body that did not appear muscular but had no visible body fat.

"Okay," she said, in a hoarse whisper. "No tellin' how wired your car is for sound. We're changin' vee-hicles. We can do this easy, or do it hard. Behave, and you kin ride up front with me. Or you kin ride in the trunk. Your choice."

I felt a rush of fear at being locked in the trunk. "I want to ride with you, up front."

"Well, you just remember that, sweetie. Let's move." She shoved me into the driver's side ahead of her.

"Get in, get in! Stop wastin' time. Move over!" she snapped. "No talkin' till I tell you to. I need a little peace and quiet."

As she turned the key in the ignition, I thought I heard a chopper in the distance but couldn't be certain.

She pulled out of the parking lot onto a residential street. I noted the time on the dashboard clock. Unbelievable. Less than five minutes had elapsed since the bumper thumper in traffic.

I had been told not to get into a car with her, but nobody had mentioned what to do if I found myself in that position. I decided not to stay. When a traffic light bloomed red up ahead, I tensed, ready to jump out and run when she stopped. Would she chase me? Shoot me in front of witnesses? Based on all I knew, all I had seen, yes. I decided to wait for the professionals.

They were on our tail. They would be here momentarily. We continued south, but at the Palmetto Expressway she entered a north-bound lane. She unpinned her ponytail and shook out her hair. Longer than I had realized, it was chestnut brown and lustrous. I watched for the chopper, squinted ahead for the roadblock, expecting sirens. Without my shades, the blazing afternoon sun made my eyes tear.

She picked up the Dolphin Expressway, proceeded east through heavy traffic, then north on Interstate 95. A Miami-Dade police cruiser passed us in the fast lane. A K-9 officer, with his four-footed partner in back, he never gave us a glance.

At the Golden Glades interchange she continued north on 95, into Broward County. She switched on the radio, a country-and-western station. I wanted to change it but thought better of it as she hummed along with the music.

What was McDonald thinking now? He was right. How could I be so stupid as to open the window and hand over my cell phone? Would a policewoman make the same mistake? Was it my fault the kid was dead? They had to stop us soon, or I would not make it back to the paper by seven. How would I write for the final? Mark Seybold was right. Plans do go wrong. Another man was dead, and here I sat like a jerk, waiting to be rescued.

Eyes tearing, I fingered the bruise on my cheekbone where my glasses had been knocked off.

"What's the matter, Britt? Nothin' to boo-hoo about, just a little bitch slap, that's all."

"It's the glare," I said. "I lost my sunglasses back there."

"Well, honey"—she shook her head in exasperation—"whose fault is that now?"

I wanted a SWAT sniper to shoot her right where she

sat, then prayed that, if we were in their sights, they knew which one to aim at.

Not until we crossed into Palm Beach County, sixty miles out of Miami, still headed north, did I admit to myself that nobody was coming. No police chopper was tracking us. SWAT did not have us in their gunsights. They had no clue.

Eleven

HER DEADLY AND UNPREDICTABLE VIOLENCE TERrified me, but she was eager to tell her story, I reasoned; that was why we were here. Dead reporters don't write. If she did harm me, what other journalist would listen to her? Seated beside me, humming along with a soulful country ballad on the radio, was the story of the year—perhaps of my life.

I felt a thrill of fear, along with something more powerful. She might have me, but I had her—all to myself. I had met murderers and interviewed killers, behind bars. They manipulate, color, and tamper with the truth for their own scheming self-serving reasons. There is a difference between observing a wild beast confined to a cage and one still roaming free in its natural habitat. This could be my access to the candid confession of an unrepentant serial killer willing to expose the dark side of her own sick soul—a journalist's dream.

Urban landscape gave way to rural Hobe Sound. At Palm City, south of Stuart, she took the Sunshine Turnpike, two high-speed lanes through farm and cattle land.

As the sun set, blood red over the Everglades, she reached beneath the seat and came up with a brown paper bag. She twisted off the top, took a swallow from the bottle inside, and exhaled deeply, a satisfied sound. "Tequila," she said, voice husky. "Needed that, for my nerves." She offered the bottle.

"No, thanks," I said.

She looked offended.

Show no fear, I told myself. Never behave like a victim. "One of us has to stay sober," I said. "I'll be the designated driver."

She laughed, a warm, infectious sound. She took another swig, air conditioner blasting, country music still playing, the spirited fiddles beginning to grate on my nerves. "Okay, wha'chu want to know?"

"Your name first. What do I call you?"

The bottle wedged between her thighs, she fumbled on the floorboard, retrieved my notebook, and tossed it to me with my pen. We were driving through citrus groves and farmlands in St. Lucie County.

"Keppie," she said, and spelled it out.

Tex had nearly remembered it.

"What else?"

"Everything," I said. "From the beginning, your earliest recollections. It all contributes to who you are today."

Taking another drink from the bottle, she inhaled deeply. "Unlike most people you meet here, I was born in Florida. Upstate. Lived here all my life."

"Me too," I said.

"I think being deprived caused a crisis 'tween my physical and my mental self. That contributes to who I am today. Yeah." She grinned wickedly and cut her eyes at me. "I'm deprived of somethin'. Maybe it's sex with my father. He didn't live long enough for that. I kin hardly remember him."

"Me too," I said again. Dr. Schlatter was right. "My father was killed when I was three."

"Git outa here! Who killed him? Was he a son of a bitch?"

"No. But Fidel Castro thought so. He had him executed by a firing squad."

"Man! See, I knew we had lots in common." She punched the accelerator, looking pleased as she swung around a dawdling motorist. "Not that Feedel had anythin' to do with it in my case. Okay, now you answer me one." Her voice dropped to a salacious whisper. "How was Lance Westfell in the sack? As good horizontal as he looks standing up?"

This interview would be too long if she got to ask a question every time I did.

"He's good," I said.

She took her eyes off the road, expression expectant.

"Well," I said slowly, "not as good as you might expect from seeing his movies, where he's thirty feet tall on the screen and everything is all—well, bigger. He's just a man," I said. "A nice one. Now, how many men have you killed, and why?"

"Jesus Christ, lemme see." Smiling to herself, she cocked her head and appeared to be thinking, like a prom queen asked to list her dance partners.

"You mean there are others, more than the seven—eight, counting today?" That possibility stunned me. Would I need another box of red pushpins? I wondered if anybody back at the office had plugged one in at the exit ramp off I-95 at SW Sixteenth Street.

"Oh, sure. I've never been real good at numbers," she said casually. "We can git into that later. *Why* is somethin' else again." She frowned, voice cold. "None of 'em were man enough to turn me on. Buncha pigs and cheaters, just scum. They deserved what they got."

"But that kid today, you didn't even know—"

"Him? Well, he just got in the way. It was his turn, that's all. When it's your turn, God taps you on the shoulder."

"God didn't tap him on the shoulder," I said quietly. "You put a bullet in his head."

"You here to argue with me, girl, or to write down what I tell you? I mean, you heard that music! I shot 'em in the brain—that thing they think with. Write that down!" Her glance was meaningful, eyebrow arched, lip curled. "And I ain't talkin' 'bout them head shots either. I been shootin' since I'm nine. Started out with a little bitty rifle my daddy bought me."

"I thought you didn't remember your father."

"The daddy that raised me," she snapped impatiently. "There you go again. Damn!"

We passed a sign: NEXT REST STOP, GAS, FOOD, 7 MILES.

"Can we stop?" I asked, unable to ignore nature any longer. "I need to use the rest room. Too much coffee."

She pulled to the side, the car up close to the guard rail.

"Here? I meant the rest stop."

"We don't need gas yet," she said. Headlights pierced the soft twilight in both directions.

"But where—?"

"Come on." She got out, trotted around to my side, and unlocked it with the key. "The car door will give you some privacy. Come on!" she urged impatiently. "Drop your jeans and do it. Nobody's watchin'."

Nobody but her and a few dozen passing motorists.

She laughed and waved back when a high-riding trucker hit his air horn.

"I think it's somethin' I was born with, or developed when I was real little," she said, when we were back on the road. "I always had the feelin'."

"What feeling?"

"Like, you know, when it's gonna happen."

Her voice almost dreamy, she slowed down and dropped back behind a battered old landscaping truck.

"You wanna know what it's really like? Unless it was something that had to happen, like today, I kin always tell when it's coming on." It was dark now, and I couldn't see her eyes in the dim light from the dash. "I can tell, it's—it's like colors are brighter''—she shifted sensuously in her seat—''and my skin feels more sensitive. Things start happenin' in slow motion, like being underwater. It's a real high when I do it—but when I come down, I feel bad: you know, depressed.''

''Remorseful? Sorry that you did it?''

''Hell, no!'' she said emphatically. Waves of light from somebody's high beams washed over her profile. ''Just empty, sorry the high didn't last longer.''

She glanced at me.

''Ahhh, for Christ's sake,'' she said, ''what I do ain't all that bad. It ain't like there's a shortage of men or nothin'. I mean, shootin' people is just—it's kind of a thrill, I guess. I like bein' in control.'' She sipped from the bottle again. ''I guess maybe I was born that way, just a little different.''

''They say the average brain contains a hundred billion cells with a quadrillion connections,'' I said, wondering if she was already contemplating an insanity defense. ''It's hard to say exactly where something goes wrong.''

''So it's probably something I was born with.'' She nodded, her tone sober.

''But they might be able to tell,'' I said. ''They do a lot now with MRIs—those imaging machines that scan the brain. Rosemary, our medical writer, did a story recently where doctors used it to actually see schizophrenia and obsessive-compulsive disorder—you know, the people who are always washing their hands.''

''I don't do that,'' she said quickly.

''No, you have other quirks.''

She laughed easily, shrugging her hair back over her shoulder. ''I ain't crazy, that's for damn sure. I may have some problems, maybe from drinkin', been doing that since I'm eleven. But I ain't crazy.'' She brought the bottle to her lips again, then replaced the cap, licking her lips. ''You know who was crazy? That goddamn cop today, runnin' down the ramp wavin' that shotgun. That's a good way to get that shotgun crammed up his butt and the handle kicked off. I coulda taken him out just like that.'' She snapped her fingers for emphasis. ''Even with his bulletproof vest. I'm s'prised they didn't give you one.''

I shrugged. Thank God, I thought, that no cop was shot. ''So you weren't scared to see them?''

''Cops? I tol' you before, they can't shoot worth a damn. I don't worry about a police bullet with my name on it, it's the one outa nowhere, the one that says *To whom it may concern,* that's the one that worries me. . . .

''Hungry?'' She squinted in the rearview. ''I'm thinkin' to stop, git us some chicken from the colonel, and find us a place to stay the night.''

''I thought you were going to drop me off somewhere,'' I said, edgy. The drive back to Miami would take hours. It was already late. Maybe the cops or the paper could arrange a flight. ''I've got to get back.''

She did a double take. ''Thought you wanted the story. We ain't hardly begun. 'Sides, it ain't bad havin' company on the road. Believe it not, it gits lonely out here sometimes. You kin go home tomorrow.''

My heart sank.

She left the turnpike at Yeehaw Junction. I remembered one of the FBI tips compiled for executives who travel in countries where ransom is a main source of revenue. If offered a choice of menus, ask your abductors for fried chicken and French fries. Your greasy fingerprints may help investigators build a case later.

''Don't you try pullin' anythin' or givin' anybody any high signs,'' she warned at the drive-through. ''I am damn irritable when I'm hungry. Hate like hell to shoot people before I eat. But I'll do it, no bout adoubt it.'' She grinned.

Her voice dripped honey as she ordered a barrel of extra crispy, cole slaw, fries with extra catsup, and Cokes to go, paying cash from what appeared to be my wallet. ''Now,'' she said, as we rolled out onto the main drag. ''I recollect a darlin' little place right up here somewheres. Nothin' fancy. Just a place to sleep.''

The Sunshine Motel, a semicircle of tiny green-painted cottages, was surrounded by orange groves. The sign boasted COLOR TV IN EVERY ROOM.

I had wanted a vacation from the word factory, but this was not what I had in mind.

''Now be a good ol' girl.'' She stopped in front of the office. ''We're gonna register. 'Member, I got the gun and ain't too shy to use it. Don't do nothin' stupid.''

The sweltering night was alive with sounds, frogs and crickets. She had to sleep sometime, I thought. Nothing stopped me from walking out after she drank enough tequila. No point endangering anybody now.

''We're plumb tuckered out,'' she told the elderly night manager, adding that we were vacationers from Naples. ''Need to git us some shut-eye. Ya got somethin' away from the others? We don't wanna git a lotta noise.''

He barely glanced at us, took the money, and handed her a key. Our cabin smelled musty. But the chicken smelled good. I hadn't realized I was hungry.

The small room had twin beds, a nightstand, a dresser, two chairs, a small closet, and a tiny bath. Keppie tinkered with the aging room air conditioner, coaxing it to full blast, while I unpacked the food on the dresser top, laid out the napkins, and opened the Cokes.

''Now Britt, I hate to have to do this to you . . .''

Her words struck fear into my heart.

''. . . but till I can trust you''—she took a set of handcuffs out of the duffel bag she had brought in from the trunk of the car—''you're gonna have to wear these.''

''You can trust me,'' I protested. Where was the gun? I wondered. I wasn't sure. She stood between me and the locked door. ''You don't—''

''I'm sure I can,'' she said sweetly, the metal bracelets

clinking as she approached, "but it's just the way things are till you prove yourself."

"How will I eat?"

"You'll manage," she said comfortingly.

"Where'd you get these?" I asked, as she snapped one around my left wrist. They looked like police issue.

She brightened. "A date I had didn't need 'em anymore." Chortling, she clicked the other side around the armrest of a bulky vinyl chair. "Now sit down and eat," she said, as though I were a child. "It's almost time for the news."

"The sheriff," I said, stomach tightening. "Buddy Brascom. Were these his?"

"Maybe so." She turned on the TV and perched on the edge of the only other chair, which she had dragged up close to the screen.

The local news seemed a thousand light-years from Miami, but they keyed to the story—The Kiss-Me Killer Strikes Again in Miami—at the top of the hour and reported it a few minutes into the newscast.

The dead driver was twenty-two, a reformed gangbanger who had become the much-loved counselor of a summer program for underprivileged kids. Why is that always the case, I wondered? Somebody finally gets their act together, then *bam!*

"See that, see that? They always do that!" Keppie protested, waving a chicken wing at the screen. "They make 'em out to be heroes! He was an asshole!" she informed the TV news reader.

Footage from a sister affiliate in Miami included aerials of a door-to-door police search in the neighborhood surrounding Shenandoah Junior High. "I knew it, I knew it!" She kicked her bare feet furiously in delight and hammered her fists jubilantly at the air.

"They're beatin' the bushes back in Miami!" she cried. "Hee-hee-hee-hee."

I watched with a mouth full of chicken as the anchor mentioned me.

"Prospects appear grim for a Miami reporter who had apparently attempted to interview the killer and has not been seen since the fatal traffic argument on the expressway off-ramp. The reporter's identity has not been released pending notification of next of kin, but our sources tell us it was a police reporter from the *Miami News*."

Oh, swell, I thought. Next of kin: my mother. "I should call my mom."

"Shush!" Keppie warned. "It ain't over."

We watched aerials of the monumental rush-hour traffic jam at the shooting site, the prerequisite footage of the covered body being removed, and shots of my car surrounded by police and dogs in the school parking lot. I thought I glimpsed McDonald, huddled with the homicide commander and the chief and what looked like the back of Simmons's head, but it was all too brief. I couldn't be sure.

"I have to call my mother." I put the chicken down, appetite gone.

Keppie glanced up from flicking channels. "Well now, missy, maybe you shoulda thought about that 'fore you started playin' policewoman." She stood, one hand on her hip, the other operating the remote. "Man, it's hot in here. You feel that AC at all?" She glared grimly at the lone air-conditioning vent in the ceiling. "It's like a hundret damn degrees in here."

She peeled off her tank top. A pendant, a large and ornate silver cross, hung from a long black silk cord around her neck. Something another date no longer needed, I assumed. Probably the preacher.

Keppie padded barefoot to the duffel bag to unpack. The initials on it, A.J., were those of the college boy slain at his father's service station. She unplugged the telephone, wrapped the cord neatly around it, stashed it under her bed, and began meticulously arranging small items around the tequila bottle on the tiny nightstand.

"I thought you were going to let me call my mother."

"Did I say that?" she snapped.

"I just want to let her know I'm all right. She's a widow. I'm all she's got."

"You're lucky, you still have your mama." She slipped gracefully out of her shorts, exposing lacy thong panties and a tiny butterfly in flight tattooed just below and to the right of her navel.

She caught my glance. "Like it?" She assumed an exaggerated model's pose. "Had it done in Daytona, at the big biker rally last spring." She wet her lips. "Wanna see it up close?"

"No, thanks," I said evenly, still seated in my chair, my left wrist chained to the armrest.

She shrugged, returned to the duffel bag, and bent over its contents. She had one of those rare firm-fleshed bodies that look great in a thong. "Bad news, Britt." She straightened up.

"What do you mean?" My mouth went dry.

"Only one toothbrush." She waggled it at me. "We'll have to share." She smiled.

"That's okay," I said. "I can wait till I go home tomorrow."

She shrugged, padded into the bathroom, flushed, brushed, and gargled, then emerged, brushing her long hair. Seated on the bed, tequila bottle beside her, she opened a fiery red bottle of Max Factor nail polish and began to paint her toenails, occasionally pausing to glance up at the late-night TV show.

Thoughts of my mother, combined with the odors of chicken, mildew, and nail polish, made me queasy. I picked up the notebook.

"You didn't seem afraid out there today, on the ramp," I said. "What does scare you, Keppie?"

"Truthful?" She regarded her glistening toenails for a

moment. "I don't want you to put it in the story, but truthful? Death Row. I ain't a big believer in capital punishment."

Well, duh, I thought, wonder why.

"It ain't fair, keepin' people for years, torturin' 'em. Bein' a prisoner is my biggest fear. Yeah. But I do believe it ain't gonna happen." She retouched a smudged nail. "Cuz I won't let it. Kinda weird. I don't think about it a whole lot, but like today, you just do what you have to do so you don't go to jail. In jail you're somebody else's property. You can't even think or write your own thoughts. You lose touch with real life and become antisocial."

God forbid you should become antisocial, I thought, scribbling notes.

"Nobody knows how hard I try to be a good person," she lamented, her young face earnest, the tiny brush poised in her hand. "But that don't matter now. They're sayin' terrible things 'bout me on TV and in the newspapers. And they don't even know me. But they make me look bad to everybody who hears 'em, and it makes bad people glad to greet me on their level."

Not quite sure what she meant, or if she knew herself, I dutifully wrote it down.

"I like eatin' good," she was explaining. "In jail, they feed you pure crap. Boiled potatoes, powdered eggs, mystery meat in watery gravy." She wrinkled her nose and began work on the other foot. "I'd go crazy. Now, what scares you?"

I would not admit it was her. "People don't read anymore," I said finally. "They get the news online or from TV. Good papers keep folding all over the country. We've got big cutbacks at ours. Sometimes I'm afraid my profession is in its twilight years. If newspapers die before I do, how will I make a living?"

"That's it?" She looked skeptical. "That's what keeps you awake nights? Hell, you kin go on TV. You're better lookin' than some on there. How 'bout your love life? That cop who was out of town."

"I'm afraid I'll lose him. Maybe I already have. He didn't want me to do this."

"Now there's a damn cop might have some sense. Maybe there's hope for one yet," she said.

"He's back in town. This was supposed to be our first night together in a long time."

She capped the polish, poured a healthy shot of tequila into a glass from the bathroom, sipped, and made a sympathetic sound.

"Some plans just don't turn out." Her voice husky, she rolled onto one side to watch me, her body a long sensuous curve. "One door closes, another opens. It kin still be a good night. You don't have to sleep alone."

I stared at her.

"Hell, we can push these beds together."

"I don't think so," I said. "I'm straight. I never—"

"Okay, have it your way—for now," she said lightly. "But don't knock it till you've tried it." She opened a pack of Benson and Hedges and lit a cigarette. "You like that outfit?" Exhaling smoke, she focused back on the TV screen and a skin-tight ensemble worn by an actress being interviewed. "And lookit her eyebrows. I could do mine like that."

She painted her fingernails.

"Want me to do yours?" she offered. She shrugged, when I declined, then sat and smoked. Finally she switched off the TV and turned to me, still chained to the chair next to the food.

"Guess it's time to get you undressed for bed. Now, Britt, I'm gonna be real nice and let you be comfortable. I'm only gonna cuff one wrist to the headboard. But you have to understand, I don't sleep much, and when I do, it's real light and fitful. You make any kinda move or start screaming, the best thing that will happen to you is you'll sleep out in the hot car trunk, both hands cuffed real tight, with your ankles tied and duct tape across your mouth." She reached into the duffel bag and dangled a roll of duct tape. "And that's the *best* that can happen to you. Got it?"

"I understand, but you can take the cuffs off altogether. I'm exhausted; all I want to do is sleep. You can trust me."

She feigned surprise. " 'You can count on me, like a rock.' Ain't that exactly what you tol' me when we agreed to meet? You're damn lucky to be still livin' and sleepin' in here, in this air-conditionin', such as it is."

She released me from the chair and watched me undress.

"Where'd you get that?" She scrutinized my bra.

"Department store," I said, self-consciously rubbing my wrist.

She stripped me of my clothes and cuffed my right hand to the leg of my bed below the mattress. I wanted to sleep in my T-shirt, but she took it. She slept naked too, kicking off the thong panties before she put out the light. I watched her cigarette glow in the dark long after she said good night.

"Hey," she murmured, her voice drowsy, as I thrashed around trying to get comfortable. "With all the shit going on, women's lib, men's lib, gay power, and all that crap, what do you think is the basic difference between men and us?"

"I don't know," I said fitfully, my shackled arm extended awkwardly over the side of the bed. "I guess we have dreams and men have desires."

"Yeah." The glow of her cigarette punctuated the dark. "You got it," she said. "We want Prince Charmin' to ride up on a white horse to rescue us. And all they want is sex."

"I really wish you wouldn't smoke in bed," I muttered. "If your mattress catches fire, how the hell do I get out of here cuffed to this bed? This place would go up like a tinderbox."

"Bitch," she said. "That's the least of your worries if you don't shut up and go to sleep."

My mind raced back to Miami. What had gone wrong? No one knows better than I that the world is a land mine ready to explode beneath your feet. What had happened to the little watchdog in my brain that triggers fear, protecting me from threats and danger? It had never failed me before. How could I have been so stupid? So stubborn? I prayed that the cop who took the news to my mother was McDonald. She never liked me being involved with a cop, until they met. He had totally won her over. Now they fit together like springtime and rain. He would be the only one who could comfort her. She was never close to my father's warm and close-knit Cuban family. I was all they had in common. The only way for me to get through this was to make the best of a bad situation and do a helluva job on the story later. If there was a later. It was nearly dawn when I finally dozed.

Something startled me awake, totally disoriented, my right arm and hand both numb.

"Time to rise and shine!" Keppie stood at the foot of my bed, wearing shorts and a midriff top, the room key in her hand. She grinned. I groaned.

This was real. No nightmare, I tried to cover myself with the sheet as my feet found the floor and I tried to sit up.

She laughed. "You look like crap, Britt. I've seen people ready for body bags who looked better."

"I need to use the bathroom."

"Just sit there a minute. I'm gonna run out to the office, git us a newspaper and some coffee. Be right back."

I sat there, a terrible taste in my mouth and a dull pain in my stomach, as brilliant daylight spilled between the outdated blinds. Keppie bounced back minutes later, oddly buoyant and energized for somebody who had consumed so much tequila the night before.

"Got the paper," she announced, all perky, "but the coffee machine is busted." The story was at the bottom of the front page of the local *Press Journal*. She leaned against the doorjamb, reading it aloud while I used the bathroom. Not much that was new. The police had released very little, protecting me and themselves, not yet admitting their role or mine in the ill-fated events. The dogs must have followed our scent to an empty parking space, I thought. They had to know we drove away. The search had to be expanding; the BOLO must be statewide.

"Wanna shower?" Keppie invited. "We kin take one together."

"No, thanks. I'll wait until I get home."

"Suit yourself." She shrugged and took a long slow sudsy shower while I sat on the toilet seat, handcuffed to a pipe.

Expertly wielding little pencils and brushes, she applied makeup, eye shadow, and blusher, curled her lashes, and stroked on mascara. With her hair long and loose, wearing shorts, platform sandals, and a midriff top, she was a stunner, far from her fresh-scrubbed look the day before.

I desperately needed a hit of one of the world's most potent and lethal forms of fuel, Cuban coffee. I was not likely to find it here.

Keppie bagged the leftover food for the garbage, emptied the ashtrays, tidied the room, and made her bed. A neatness freak, a trait you'd never guess from the crime scenes she left behind.

I had thought about tucking a note between my sheets, tipping the cops that we'd been there and describing the car we were in. I was glad I didn't when I saw how thoroughly she checked everything.

She insisted I apply lipstick and comb my hair before we went into a Denny's for breakfast. "I'm trustin' you," she said. "If you wanna go home in one piece, don't get any smart ideas.'' She insisted again that I slide across the car seat and exit her side.

We sat at a table by the back window, overlooking the parking lot. She devoured eggs over easy, sausage, toast, and grits, eyes alert and watching every time someone passed our table. I drank black coffee and ate an English muffin with marmalade.

I sipped a second coffee as she downed a glass of milk, like the all-American girl she resembled, and pored over the newspaper's entertainment section.

''Lookit here,'' she said enthusiastically. ''They got the annual Bushwhacker and Music Festival up in Pensacola this weekend. I wouldn't mind going to that. And the Possum Festival and Fun Day over at Wausau. We could make 'em both. Butcha know where I really wanna go again? Over to that Tragedy Museum in St. Augustine. Wanna see if they got any new displays. I been there twice. You ever go?''

I shook my head. The morning sun glinted off the cars in the parking lot, hurting my eyes. I missed my sunglasses. I wanted to go home. What was she talking about?

''Man, you oughta see it,'' she said. ''It's amazin', they got this big ol' Buick Electra that Jayne Mansfield was ridin' in the night she got decapitated by a tractor trailer over in New Orleans. Took 'er head right off. Got it right there, on display, with a copy of the police report.''

''Her head?''

''Good God, no!'' Her infectious laughter rose and bubbled over, turning the heads of other diners, who smiled, especially the men. ''The car! The Buick! Wake up, Britt.''

I laughed myself. I was so dopey I hardly knew my name. We laughed like a couple of girlfriends.

''And they got the actual Chevy that Lee Harvey Oswald rode in on the way to the Book Depository the day he shot JFK, and Bonnie and Clyde's last Ford—it's got one hundret and sixty-seven bullet holes. That's accurate, I counted 'em myself."

"Death on wheels," I said. "No wonder you like it."

She shrugged.

"I hate to be a party pooper," I said, "but this is not a vacation. We're working on an interview."

She looked disappointed. "Who said we can't have fun while we're at it?"

"Thought you wanted to see your story in the newspaper."

"Okay, okay," she said. "Ask me questions."

"Did you grow up an only child?" I asked. "Or do you have brothers and sisters?"

She looked solemn. "Had a baby brother once, but he died."

"So your father died when you were four and you lost your mother a few years later," I said, scribbling notes.

"I thought that woman hung the moon and made the stars shine," she said reverently.

"So when did your baby brother die? Before or after your dad's death? What was the cause?" Was it suspicious that only she had survived her immediate family? Or had a tragedy-filled life led to greater tragedy?

She toyed with an iced-tea spoon. "It was after my father," she said. "Hell, you know how it is with babies." She shrugged matter-of-factly. "Sometimes they just die."

"Do you have any family left?"

"The aunt and uncle who raised me. And another uncle, Bobby. Was a repo man. Used to help him out when I was a kid. We'd steal cars right outa people's driveways at night." She grinned. "Kinda weird, how folks react. Never know if they're gonna come runnin' out with a shotgun or sneak up to get the drop on ya. Had one guy, he worked nights. Figured he was asleep and we wuz about to take his pickup in broad daylight, but he come runnin' out. Bobby told 'im we had to take it. No two ways about it. So he agrees, then all of a sudden jumps in that truck and takes off like a bat outa hell with us chasin' 'im. Bobby don't git paid a dime till we bring it in. So we're chasin' 'im all the hell over Sopchoppy, in and out, up and down all those backwoods trails in the tow truck, till he finally gits hisself stuck in the swamp, way back up there in the dark woods all alone. Bobby and me are pissed as hell."

"What happened?"

"Anythin' can happen back up there in those woods." She raised an eyebrow coyly.

"Is Bobby still in the repo business?"

"No, he hurt hisself, got disabled, but he's doin' real good last I heard, real good. Got hisself a little cottage industry. Works at home, makin' temporary license tags, sells 'em to people who can't get tags otherwise, you know, cuz they don't have the paperwork. Beauty of it is, there's a big repeat business. The tags're only good for thirty days."

"Counterfeit?"

"A-course."

A trio of noisy truckers came in, loud and laughing, and took the table next to ours. Keppie had a way of flicking her hair back with her fingertips, lowering her lashes, and stealing glances. They all noticed.

" 'Bye, boys," she teased, with a twitch of her hips as we walked out.

The sun, an eye-piercing orange blaze, could blister your eyeballs. I felt a blinding headache minutes away.

"See that?" she asked indignantly, as she let me into the car. "Ya see them damn pricks drooling all over the place?"

"You're like a fisherman who throws out bait and then complains about all the damn fish that keep coming around," I said. "You have to admit you put the idea in their heads."

"You don't put that kinda idea in a man's head. It's already there." She slammed the car into reverse.

I sighed, pulled down the visor to cut the glare, and picked up the notebook. "Okay, tell me about your first sexual experience," I said, pencil poised.

She eased up on the gas. "Just curious?" Her pink tongue flicked across her perfect white teeth. "Or is this part of the interview?"

"A relevant part."

"Lemme see now. Well, when I was little, a neighbor, an old guy everybody called Duke, offered me twenty-five cent to go in the chicken coop with him. I was 'bout six, I think."

"How awful," I said, thinking of the small orphaned girl. "Were you very traumatized?"

"Hell." She cocked her head and grinned. "That was the easiest twenty-five cent I ever made."

She stopped at a liquor store to stock up on tequila and limes and then gassed up the car. On the way back to the turnpike, she slowed to turn left into a small shopping center. "We need a couple more things," she said.

"Why don't we just keep on?" I said. "I'd like to finish this up." I was eager to discuss the individual homicides and tote up the numbers. Did it all begin with the man she and her Uncle Bobby had cornered in the woods?

She looked hurt. "I just thought you might want a new pair of shades."

"Sure," I said eagerly. "And some aspirin would be great."

It was a combination general store and souvenir-selling tourist trap, next door to a Christian book and gun shop. Across the street, a marquee on the House of Prayer warned, DUSTY BIBLES LEAD TO DIRTY LIVES.

"Mind your manners," she said as I slid out her side.

The man at the cash register only glanced up from his book as we browsed. I tried on sunglasses from a revolving rack next to rubber alligators and Sunshine State T-shirts. Keppie roamed nearby.

"Britt, what size underpants you wear?"

"Five," I said, selecting a pair of wraparound Ray-Bans with lightweight lenses.

She sauntered up to the counter with a stack in various colors, along with several T-shirts, a halter top, and three pairs of shorts.

"Like these?" she trilled, holding up a pair of see-through bikini panties with the word TUESDAY lettered on one hip. " 'Member, you need a toothbrush," she said. "And some toothpaste, too. We're nearly out . . .

"Want a bathing suit?" she asked, as my heart went into a free fall. "That little flowered two-piece would sure look good on you. Oh, and we need a few more note-books," she told the clerk, "those thick black-and-white ones."

I stared. I wasn't going home today. That was never her intention. Stricken, I turned to the cashier, eyes plead-ing until he blushed. Keppie warned me with a look, then reached abruptly into her bag. The gun was inside. My stomach roiled, and I regretted breakfast.

Instead, watching me, she withdrew a credit card and paid. As I climbed into her side of the car, she grabbed my wrist in an iron grip.

"Don't you ever pull that shit again!"

"What?"

"I saw what you were doing with that guy," she hissed. "I'm not stupid."

"You don't understand," I said. "I'm upset. I have to go home today. My mother must be hysterical. My bosses have no idea where I am. The man I care about is in limbo—"

"Thought you wanted to do this story right," she said, driving toward the turnpike.

"I do, but we could finish today. I could be home tonight."

"In such a big hurry to spill your guts to your cop friends," she said sarcastically.

It had been a mistake to mention McDonald. "It's not

that," I said. "I need to get back home. I'll lose my job. I have a little dog and cat. Nobody's feeding them." Mrs. Goldstein was caring for them, I knew. But the good woman must be bewildered and worried sick. Tears sprang to my eyes.

"Now don't let's have a pity party here," she said. "Haven't I been nice to you? Feedin' you, buyin' you stuff, givin' you a decent place to sleep? All of that, after what you tried to do to me!" Her voice rose dangerously, as she worked herself up into a rage.

"You *have* been decent," I said calmly. "And I agree, we both want the story to be good, whatever it takes."

I desperately scanned the unfamiliar streets as the landscape slipped by. This was Dixie, the Bible belt, light-years away from the Gold Coast condos and the bodegas of Little Havana, a place where raising sugar cane, citrus, cattle, and vegetables was a way of life, where Yankees and city slickers from Miami were mistrusted, if not unwelcome.

In Miami, I knew every back street and alley, every squalid night spot with blood on the floor. I am part of the city and share its heartbeat, but I was out of my element here, disoriented, lost, and flat-out scared.

Where was the best place to jump from the car? Which way to run? I had no idea, but I had to do it before we hit the high-speed turnpike with its long desolate stretches. I had no identification. Notebook in my lap, pretending to check my notes, I scrawled the city desk number on my palm, in case I was injured, unconscious, or worse.

FLORIDA TURNPIKE TWO MILES. It had to be now. An intersection ahead, Chevron station on one side, mini warehouse on the other, a pickup with two men and a gun rack behind us. I would run for the truck. If they didn't stop, I'd try for the gas station. The red light might change. I had to do it now, as she slowed down. I wrenched the door handle, to hurl myself out and roll. My body jammed up against the door. It did not open. Fumbling frantically, I tried to unlock it.

"Hee-hee-hee-hee." Keppie laughed and hit the gas as the light turned green. "Wondered when you'd finally figure out it didn't work."

She had dismantled the door handle. It would not open from the inside. She slowed to let the pickup pass. She grinned, looking relaxed until it did, then turned on me screaming, yanked out the gun, and slammed me in the face. My own blood flew as I shrieked and tried to struggle.

"You bitch! I'll kill you right now! I'll kill you! You'll never go home!"

She pointed the gun at my head.

Twelve

"Now see what you made me do!" she screamed. "You're bleedin' all over the damn car!"

I had deflected the blow's full force by throwing my hands up protectively, but the gun butt had struck the side of my face and my nose, which was bleeding profusely. She'd also yanked out a handful of my hair and slammed me in the right eye with her fist.

She reached into the backseat for a box of tissues and flung it at me. The hand holding the gun shook in fury. I fought hysteria, wanting to lunge at the weapon, try to wrestle it away, but I knew if we fought for it in such close quarters one of us would die, more likely me. *Don't let me die in this strange and unfamiliar place,* I prayed. *I want to go home*. I wanted never to have had this story.

"Look at you now!" she screamed, as I tried to stop the bleeding. "Look what you've done!"

"I don't think it's broken," I snuffled.

"Shi-i-i-t!" She tossed her hair back. "More goddamn proof that no good deed goes unpunished. Here I'm tryin' to give you the scoop, tryin' to make you comfortable and help you get to go home, and you . . . put your fuckin' head back or you'll bleed all over the goddamn notebook!"

I did as she said, applying pressure with a wad of tissues.

"Please don't point the gun at me anymore," I managed to say, my voice muffled.

"Give me one good reason not to."

"I know what kind of ammo it's loaded with. I've seen what it can do."

"Well, you just remember that, missy, and how goddamn lucky you are to still be alive. You wanna stay that way, you do what I tell you. What's wrong with you?"

"I won't give you anymore trouble," I said.

She perked up, with another 180-degree mood swing, after we hit the turnpike. Her tequila bottle by her side, she sang country-and-western at the top of her lungs along with the radio, songs about trucks and trains, honkytonks, cheating hearts, prisons, and dead mothers. Thoughts of my own mother made me want to weep. When not singing, smoking, or swigging from the bottle, she ranted angrily against men one minute and spouted jokes the next, as we careened north.

Finally out of range of the radio station, we resumed the interview.

"What was it like," I asked, "the first time you killed somebody?"

"Hell, I had no clue what I was doing," she murmured, smiling as though in fond reminiscence. "Me and this guy, we'd been oofing in the back seat. Man, I was drunk, wasted, trashed, out of control, ripped, sauced, hammered. It felt real sweet, I tell you, cuz I knew what was gonna happen. I'd been thinkin' 'bout it for a long time, hypin' myself up, gettin' ready, boostin' my adrenaline, blockin' everythin' else out. But I tell you, I panicked that first time. I was runnin' around, kep' hearin' gunshots follerin' me, till I realized it was me shootin'. Had to calm down and lift my finger off the trigger, cuz every time I moved, it kept goin' off!" She broke into a peal of laughter and lifted the bottle, as grazing cattle, farmhouses, and orange groves flashed by.

I shuddered at how many times the gun had been pointed at me.

Wavy shimmering-wet mirages rose off the pavement ahead.

"Was that the sheriff?" I asked.

"Hell, no, I was a lot younger then," she said. "He wasn't all that bad a guy. We used to fish for striped mullet. He was tall and lanky, had hands twice as big as most guys, huge bone structure, but he was clumsy, walked like somebody put him together on strings, like a puppet. Really dumb, too, but he wasn't that bad. Most of 'em have wanderin' minds and rovin' hands. There was this other guy, a lawyer—one real sick puppy—wanted me to dance for him. Wanted to be handcuffed and masturbate." She talked nonstop, jumping from one topic, one man, to another.

"Ever see a dead body 'at's been out in the woods a long time? Some of it rots, but other parts get like cork, like a big hunka flesh in a pant leg, just like cork. I could show you one," she offered. "A couple ain't too far from here. It's kinda weird. The nose—the nose just collapses when he decomposes, and he looks like he's got no nose at all."

"There are others who haven't been found yet?"

"I know a few still out there," she responded cheerfully. "Cuz I been back to see 'em. You know, when I'm in those areas, I go by to visit. It's kinda weird." She grinned and waved at the driver of an eighteen-wheeler, who flashed his lights as we passed.

"How many are there?"

"Hee-hee-hee," she chortled. "That's for me to know and you to find out."

"Your MO, shooting them in the genitals, leaving lipstick on the bullets: is that a ritual or some sort of message?"

She looked startled. "It's for the press," she said. "That son-of-a-bitch sheriff got shot sorta spur of the moment. Sorta coincidental where he got hit. You know, I was mad as hell and all. But the press made such a big deal out of it that I kep' it up. It sounded good. The lipstick on the bullets was kinda weird. See, after I done my makeup I was reloadin', happened to hold one-a the slugs between my teeth for a sec. Didn't even notice the lipstick on it. Then that Kiss-Me Killer shit got started; it was in all the stories. I hadda play along—you know, give 'em somethin' to write about. You can't disappoint 'em."

That sobering possibility had never occurred to me.

"Keppie, did you ever wish your life was different?"

Her brow furrowed. "Sometimes," she said slowly, "when I was younger, I almost wished I was a neuter and could erase my sexuality, cuz my feelings, my passion, was so strong. I used to study men with an unreal cravin' that sucked in every bit of information without me knowin' it—but what I could never see is how I would fit best with one. I had so many conflicts, tryin' to decide what is meaningful to a man and how one could be meaningful to me, without endin' up bein' a tragedy."

"What made you think a relationship with a man would end up in tragedy?"

She shrugged. "Just saw so many, hearda so many mental and other kinds of tragedies between mates. I felt paranoid about the sexual aspect."

Her psyche was a mystery to me, but I dutifully jotted down her ramblings word for word. The side of my face throbbed, my nose was swollen and congested. What would happen, I wondered, if I saw a highway patrolman and lunged forward to lean on the horn?

"Do you think your life might have been different if you hadn't been introduced to guns so young? If you hadn't learned to shoot and had access to weapons?"

"You ain't one-a them gun-control nuts, are ya?"

"No."

"Good, cuz those people piss me off. Winchesters, Colts, Smith and Wessons, they built this country. Pioneers used 'em to fight Indians, outlaws, and rattlesnakes."

"Right," I said. "But are you aware that gun accidents killed more pioneers than Indians or outlaws did? They didn't have air rescue or trauma centers. Alone in the wilderness, a branch or a twig would catch on their gun and the thing would go off. A lot of lonely unmarked graves out there."

"Tell me about it. How d'you know all that?" she said.

"Researched a piece on gun safety after a rash of accidental shootings in Miami."

"I like Miami," she said. "I'd go back there. Everybody's packin'. You don't feel out of the ordinary when *everybody*'s got a gun."

The flat landscape flashed by. I fought the urge to lean back for a moment to rest my eyes.

"I'm not a bad person. I wouldn't call myself real religious," she was saying. "Dabbled in Satanism as a kid, wore a pentagram, and all that shit, but I had a real religious experience over in Clearwater—you know, where the Virgin Mary appeared in the finance company window?"

"I read about that."

"Me too. Heard about it and went there. Saw a sign, said VIRGIN MARY PARKING, and drove right in. People come from all over the world to see it, thousands of 'em. You can see 'er, plain as day, when the light hits it. You can see 'er. I could feel the energy. The entire parking lot is coated with wax from all the people burning candles. You should see it," she said.

"But the experience didn't change your lifestyle or cause you regrets?"

"I'm not a bad person," she repeated. "Write that down. Every one-a them brought it on himself. Only regret I ever had," she said, raising her voice, "is I never got to know my mother better before she was taken from me."

"How about the people who raised you? What are they like?"

"Good, churchgoing, God-fearing folks. Damn, did I drive them nuts. I was just a little girl who wanted her mama."

She lapsed into a morose silence, sipping from the bottle. A highway patrolman passed, southbound, as we crossed into Seminole County. He glanced our way. He appeared to tap his brake and I held my breath. Keppie watched in the rearview but he continued south.

She began to curse at the radio signals, fading in and out, and at other motorists, gusts of momentum in a gathering storm. She finally switched off the radio in a fit of pique and focused on me. "What the hell you think you're lookin' at?" she demanded.

"Nothing," I murmured. "Think I'll rest my eyes for a while."

I washed my swollen face at the next rest stop, where she bought sandwiches and soft drinks from a vending machine. She drove to a nearby picnic area and parked near the last wooden table, in the shade near a small lake. We were the only ones there. Everybody else was inside the air-conditioned restaurant. Keppie said she needed to stretch her legs. She strolled up and down a paved pathway between the picnic area and the traffic rolling off the north and southbound lanes into the rest stop. She had that bad-girl look that turns men on. Several truckers and male motorists ogled as she stretched, tossed her hair, and strutted back and forth, like the mating dance of an exotic bird. A big sports utility van, a Lincoln Navigator, pulled in, the driver giving her the eye. A guy in his late twenties or early thirties climbed out. He was tall and rangy, with tousled hair, wearing blue jeans and a T-shirt. His little boy was with him. The father gave her a wave and she smiled.

A few minutes later they came out carrying sodas and sat at the next table.

He smiled.

"Hi there," she said.

The little boy was playing, chasing a duck who apparently lived on handouts and made his home in the lake. He trotted over to our table. An adorable child in a Pooh-bear shirt and little striped shorts, he was about four years old, with a fine-featured sensitive face and serious brown eyes. He drew shyly away when Keppie rumpled his curly hair.

"Hey there, champ." She crossed her long bare legs and looked up at the father flirtatiously from under her lashes. "What a gorgeous boy, just like his good-lookin' daddy." Her voice dripped southern honey.

He got up and introduced himself, then straddled the bench at the end of our table, pushing his sunglasses up to the top of his head. His eyes were hazel, and his friendly smile similar to his son's shy grin. His name was Jeff.

"Where's the mama?" Keppie asked.

"Divorced," he said. "I get Joey for two weeks in the summer. We're going to Disney World." His gaze grew troubled as he looked at me.

"What happened to her?"

"Long story. This here's my cousin, Britt." I was surprised she used my name. "I just hadda come on down to help her git outa a bad marriage. Real bad, as you can see. She's got this abusive husband. Hadda git her outa there before the SOB kilt her. Takin' her back up home to kin."

"Sorry." He glanced at me, pity in his eyes, then refocused on her.

My armpits felt wet and sticky, but the heat agreed with her. The skin between her breasts glowed slick and glossy. He shifted his seat and moved closer. She leaned forward, mimicking his body language.

The dance was unmistakable.

"We're running late," I said nervously. "We better hit the road."

"We got time," she murmured, with a sidelong glance at me.

She turned back to Jeff.

"I think she stayed with him so long cuz the sex was good," she told him, lowering her voice.

The little boy was chasing a butterfly now, darting in and out among the wildflowers.

"I'm more a free spirit," she said. "I believe you should enjoy sex whenever you can, anytime, anyplace, and then just move on; you don't try to tie a man down or make demands."

"I'm with you there," he said. "Be a cold day in hell 'fore I ever tie the knot again, I can tell you that. But I'm surprised a beautiful, sexy girl like you isn't married."

Take your child and get the hell out of here! I willed, trying desperately to catch his eye. He was mesmerized.

"I mean, sex is a gift God gave us to enjoy. He is a loving God and meant for us to love one another in every way. Ain't that right, Britt?"

I stared at him and surreptitiously shook my head. She caught it.

"Britt ain't in a good mood, cuz-a what she's been through," Keppie said sympathetically. "Poor Britt, she just wants to go home. We'd be on the road already, but I couldn't help notice you goin' past and sorta hoped you'd stop by to say hello. Nice car you got there, always liked those SUVs, plenty of room inside."

"Want to see it?" His voice sounded husky.

"Sure, come on, Britt."

We followed Jeff to the Navigator.

"How am I doing?" she whispered, swinging her hips.

"No," I said, stricken. "Don't." She patted her handbag with a warning look.

They sat in front. He turned on the radio and the air-conditioning. Next thing I knew they were necking.

I sat in the back with little Joey, who was hugging a Beanie Baby, a little black Scottie dog.

"We going, Daddy?" he piped up.

"Not just yet, boy." He sounded out of breath.

More heavy breathing, some thrashing around, and giggles from Keppie. "No," she finally purred, and pulled away. "Not here. Way too public. But I know a place, it ain't far."

"What about them?" He indicated us with a jerk of his head. "Can they wait for us here?"

"No, I don't wanna leave Britt, but she can come along and watch the baby for us."

He didn't hesitate. I held the child's hand and tried to catch the father's eye in the rearview as he drove like a lamb to the slaughter.

"You got one-a them childproof locks for the back? I don't want nobody fallin' out," Keppie cautioned.

I heard the metallic click. The rural roadways, bordered by piney woods, all looked the same. I watched for landmarks and tried to count the turns.

"Here," she said. "Turn right in here." The rutted dirt road was barely visible. Trees and bushes slapped the car on both sides.

Joey's eyes were wide.

"Hope this don't scratch my paint job," Jeff said doubtfully.

"Don't you worry, baby." She touched him, causing him to throw his head back for a moment, eyes closed.

"I don't think we should go down in there," I ventured. "We might get stuck."

"Shut *up*, Britt, you are such a worrier." Her tone was teasing, her glance chilling. "This here's a good spot," she said.

"We're gonna leave 'em back there?" he murmured.

"Too many snakes and skeeters for them to walk around." She pulled her midriff top off over her head.

I heard his sharp intake of breath, the rustling of more

disrobing, and the whir and motion of the seat as he adjusted it as far back as it would go.

The fool, I thought, my heart pounding. The stupid crazy fool! Oh, my God. I had hoped we'd have the chance to run. Joey looked around restlessly. "Lean back and sit by me," I coaxed. "What's your doggy's name?"

"Scottie," he said, his little brow furrowed.

Up front a muffled exclamation from Keppie. "You rascal! You gotchur jimmy hat all ready. How'd you know you were gonna find me today?" She chuckled. "But we don't need it, ya know."

"Uhhh, you sure?"

"I'm clean. Ain't you?"

"Sure."

"Let's take a nap," I told Joey. "Close your eyes."

"No," he murmured, a frown forming as he looked at the shadowy woods closed in around us. "I don't like it here."

"We'll be going soon. I know where to see some real puppies," I whispered in his ear. "Maybe we can go play with them." His hair was sweet-smelling, soft and silky.

The raw sounds and smells of sex came from the front seat.

Keppie's hair and bare shoulders appeared between the head rests astride her victim.

"Oh, Jesus," he said. "Oh, yeah! oh, yeah! . . . You're really something," he murmured weakly.

"Ain't it the truth, baby?"

"Hey, what are you doing!" he demanded suddenly, voice startled.

I closed my eyes and held on to the child.

"Come on, come on, come on!" The unspent urgency in her voice told me what was happening. "Git out, git outa the car!"

"What the hell . . . ?"

"I swear to hell, I'll cap you right here," she said. "Now, now! Git out! Take your goddamn shirt."

Eyes big, he picked up his T-shirt and opened his door. "This is a robbery, ain't it?"

"Out! Git out!"

He slowly exited, hands high in front of him.

"Put the shirt on."

I sat up and leaned forward. "Keppie," I begged. "Please don't."

She crept across the front seat, ignoring me, the gun in both hands. She slowly followed him out of the car, chest heaving, eyes narrowed, jaw set, her face ecstatic. Sunlight filtering through overhanging trees cast dappled patterns of light and shadow across her naked skin and his bewildered face.

He pulled the shirt on, still naked from the waist down.

"I shoulda known. This is a robbery, right? You gonna take my car?"

"Technically," she said softly. "It's more than a robbery. Yeahhh." The word was a long soft sigh. "I'm taking your car. Down on your knees, you son of a bitch."

"Daddy!" The boy began to whimper.

"Hush." I peered frantically over the seat to see if the keys were in the ignition. They were not. I couldn't see them anywhere.

The man knelt. Scared now. Did he know? Did he remember the news stories, the other victims?

"Look," he pleaded. "Take my wallet, take the car. All I wanna do is raise my boy. He's a good little citizen, and I want him to grow up good and have a good life."

Keppie laughed, a bubble of infectious mirth. "Shoulda thought-a that," she crooned. She wore the rosy glow of a woman in a state of arousal.

"Take it. I'll just tell the cops it got stolen from the rest stop. I won't—"

I clasped the child to me, burying his face against my chest. He struggled at the sound of the shot, but I held him tight. Closing my eyes, I clamped my hands over his ears before the second shot.

It echoed, resounding through the silent woods. The brief thrashing and labored breathing that followed were not unlike those heard minutes earlier. They ended quickly.

Somewhere birds soared through shining skies, stars rose, and planets whirled. Somewhere, gentle souls dreamed of peace. But not here.

Thirteen

"HE JUST DIDN'T GET IT."

Shrugging bare shoulders, she leaned back against the car seat, breathing deeply, the gun still in her hand.

"That was good," she murmured. "Real good." She looked numb, in a fugue state, and remained that way for a good ten or fifteen minutes, with only the woodland sounds around us, while I tried to keep Joey calm. "Shit," she finally said, disturbing the quiet. "I need a drink, and the bottle's in the other car." She lit a cigarette and smoked in silence. I feared her moods. There was nothing to stop her from killing us both.

I prayed that someone heard the shots and called for help, but gunfire in this remote area would probably be attributed to hunters or target shooters.

Eventually, she raised her head, eyes clearing. "Git out," she said dully, "and take him with you." She pulled on her thong panties and released the backseat lock.

"I don't want him to see—"

"Oh, shit, Britt," she said wearily. "Don't start playin' goddamn Mother Teresa. He's old enough to see his daddy screw a stranger, he's old enough for this."

I held the boy's hand tightly. His father lay crumpled

about twenty feet from the car, bleeding into the roots of summer's thirsty green growing things.

Tears blurred my vision. "Oh my God! Look what you've done."

"Daddy, Daddy!" The boy tried to run to his father, but I held on to him. He tried to fight me but he was too small.

"What's done is done," Keppie drawled, buttoning her shorts, cigarette dangling from her lips. "I can't call bullets back, now, can I?" She glanced at me. "I just needed some love," she crooned. She rolled her eyes and tossed her hair back, laughing. "Now you got to help me with him."

"What do you mean?"

"We don't want him found right away."

"Why? You didn't care about the others."

"I got good reasons." Then she focused on Joey. "He ain't comin' with us."

"We can't leave him here. We've got this child now." My voice sounded shrill. "He's too little. He's only four."

She sighed. "You're right. Step away from him, Britt." She raised the gun.

"No! No! You can't!" Instinctively, I pulled him to me. "He's just a little kid. He didn't do anything!"

She paused and lowered the gun, her eyes changing. "Why, Britt, I do believe you are absolutely right."

Could I trust her? I swept him up in my arms, watching her fearfully.

"Guess you're his mama now," she said cheerfully, "so protect your baby. Go sit him down in the car while we take care of his daddy."

He kicked and protested, calling for his father, as I strapped him into his car seat. "Please," I whispered. "Please be good. Don't upset her, sweetheart. It'll be all right." I left him whimpering in the car.

Keppie, gun in hand, was exploring the nearby woods. "We're in luck," she said. "I thought it was up in here."

She had found a jagged fissure, an open wound in the ground. The sinkhole, there for some time, had already swallowed several trees and undermined the roots of a live oak that lay toppled nearby. Vines and weeds had tangled and merged across its gaping mouth. Push them aside and it was impossible to see bottom. Step too close and the sides crumbled, like my life collapsing in on me. In times of drought, water levels drop in underground rivers and streams, causing the soil above to cave into the void. In populated areas, sinkholes swallow cars, buildings, and sections of highway. This one would swallow a man.

"Come on, Britt."

Insects had already discovered the body, busily buzzing around it. She twisted a college ring with a blue stone off his finger.

"Grab his arms!"

I swallowed and tried hard not to look at his face. His skin still felt warm to the touch, his blood sticky on my hands. I thought of home, my life, the people I loved. I thought of the child whose muffled cries came from behind the closed doors of the SUV and did what I had to do.

"Hurry up!" Keppie panted, swatting mosquitoes. "Nobody in their right mind'll come back in here till the weather cools," she gasped, dragging him by the ankles.

We slid him into the sinkhole feet first.

Nothing that could identify him went into the hole with him. She kicked leaves and pine needles around the bloody scene, then went through his things.

"Hoo-ha! Lookit all this plastic, includin' American Express, all with his initials instead of a first name. Knew I liked that man."

She erupted in another happy exclamation when she found his PIN number on a scrap of paper in his wallet.

"Glory be, we hit a mother lode." She also took a large folding knife from the glove box and slipped it into her pocket.

Her arm draped casually over the seat, she smiled, as if discussing the weather.

"I'm makin' it clear to you now, Britt, that the first time you defy me, or try to leave 'fore I'm ready for you to go, I will kill you—after I off young Joey here. Anytime, anyplace, I'll slit his little throat like he was a chicken. Count on it, and if you wanna be responsible, try me."

She meant it.

"When I go back to write the story," I said, "can he go with me?"

"Sure. Think I want 'im? If I'd wanted a kid, I'da had one."

The SUV bounced off the dirt road back onto the highway. As Keppie floored it, picking up speed, hundreds of great southern white butterflies swarmed across the road ahead. I remembered the nine-mile cloud that had fluttered across St. Lucie County in June of '86. But before I could speak, she accelerated, leaving the road behind us littered with dead and dying butterflies.

Back at the rest stop we transferred our things into the SUV and took the turnpike north, beneath dusty rolling skies pressed like lead against the dull terrain.

Joey sat quietly, eyes wide, strapped in his car seat in the back, clutching his Beanie Baby.

"Where'd you git that?" Keppie asked him.

"Grandma," he muttered, lips pursed, trying not to cry. "Where's my daddy?" he demanded.

"He's gone to be with Elvis," Keppie said jauntily, and took a hit from the bottle. "Now, where were we?" She turned to me as though after a brief interruption. "Let's see. Write this down. First, I want you to say that I am always in control of my mind to an extent, as everyone is—to an extent. . . ."

Hands shaking, I opened the notebook to a clean page. I felt no reportorial instincts. I glanced back at Joey, his eyes closed, as though dozing, and saw dead children. The girl, age five, was walking home from kindergarten; the boy, age seven and holding his big brother's hand, was crossing Biscayne Boulevard on the way to buy ice cream. Stray bullets found them both. But that was Miami, where streetlights are bullet-proofed, entire families dodge fusillades and know when to hit the floor, and mothers pray to God to bullet-proof their babies. Joey did not reside in a shooting gallery like so many inner-city kids. How had he come into harm's way? Was I to blame?

"You paying attention, Britt?" Keppie sounded irritated. "I mean you're like the only person who understands all this, who knows what I've been put through."

"We both lost our fathers at a young age," I said quietly, pen in hand. "How do you feel about what you've done to Joey?"

She raised a casual eyebrow, then gave a quick nod, as though acknowledging the question as legitimate. "I guess I've changed his fate in some way. Don't know if I've hurt him or helped him. But I do believe I've prevented him from livin' through a lot more pain with the father he did have. You know"—she reached for her cigarettes—"it's easier to know your father is dead than knowin' he is in a living hell and havin' to live through it with him."

"I don't understand. Why do you—"

"Who said you had to?" Her tone was sharp. "Just write that down like I tell you. That's why you're here."

After dark we bought more chicken and found another bungalow-style motel.

Keppie made sure the manager saw Joey when we registered. Nobody was looking for two women with a child.

I examined my face in the mirror of the small windowless bathroom. My nose and cheekbone were bruised and swollen, my hair tangled and matted. My eyes were the worst. Would they ever see the world the same way again? My mind was beginning to misfire. Stay calm and rational, I thought, fighting for control. It's the only way to get us out of this alive. Hysteria is highly contagious. If Keppie caught it, we were dead. I forced myself to eat something and coaxed Joey. He ate some chicken, and drank milk, but then threw up. Keppie watched in disgust as I quickly cleaned up the mess.

"You see? 'Nother lesson learned. Be careful what you ask for, Britt, you may get it."

"He'll be all right." I wiped his face. "He's got a little heat rash on his chest. Probably because it was so hot back there in the car."

"Jesus, Britt." Her nose wrinkled in distaste at both of us, hands on her hips. "You look like the wrath of God. I don't even wanna be seen with you. Take a goddamn shower and wash your hair. I'd be too embarrassed to send you back to Miami looking like that. Wash up the kid, too, and leave the door open."

Keppie tuned in the TV while we bathed. I looked deep into Joey's bewildered brown eyes and held his hands as the water ran into the tub. "What's your mama's name?" I asked urgently.

"Mommy," he said.

I checked the water temperature, helped him undress, bathed him, then wrapped him in a soft bath towel. "Be brave, sweetheart," I whispered in his ear. "We'll get out of this. You and me, together." His little arms slid up around my neck in a tentative hug. I held him so close I felt our hearts beating.

He sat on the closed toilet seat, his face serious, while I showered. It was good to be clean. My eyes were closed in the stream of warm water when Keppie screamed, a startled, high-pitched cry. I cut off the water, snatched a towel, and held it around me, heart pounding. Had the police arrived at last?

"Britt, Britt! Come quick!" She burst, breathless, into the doorway. She had undressed. I wished she would keep some clothes on in front of Joey. "Come on! Come on!

Get on out here!'' she squealed. ''You ready for this? We're on *America's Most Wanted!*''

A bad composite of the Kiss-Me Killer, eyes, chin, and hairline all wrong, shared a split screen with my mug shot, filed at police headquarters for my current set of press credentials.

''Montero is a Miami newspaper reporter who apparently set out in an attempt to interview the killer,'' the voice was saying. ''These unlikely companions are believed to be traveling together in a white late-model American-made sedan, possibly a Monte Carlo or Ford Galaxy. It is unknown whether Montero is being held hostage by the killer or is a willing participant in her flight to avoid justice. But police do want to question her in the case. In what is believed to be an authentic sighting, the two were spotted laughing and talking in a Denny's restaurant in central Florida twenty-four hours ago.''

''Hadda be them goddamn truckers!'' Keppie muttered bitterly. ''I knew it! Sonsa bitches. I shoulda shot their fat asses! They were askin' for it.''

''The public is warned to make no attempt to approach them, as the Kiss-Me Killer is believed to be armed, violent, and extremely dangerous.''

''Violent!'' she howled indignantly, hands on her naked hips. ''They call *me* violent? This whole damn country is violent!'' She paced the room angrily, hair and bare breasts bouncing. ''The world is violent. Mother Nature is violent. And they call *me* violent!''

''The reward for arrest and conviction in this case has reached the two-hundred-thousand-dollar mark.''

Her right eye closed, left eyebrow raised, she punched the air like a cheerleader. ''Awwww right!''

''Anyone with information is asked to call local law enforcement or *America's Most Wanted.* Help us take down this dangerous serial killer, believed responsible for at least seven brutal murders, before any more lives are lost.''

Her growing notoriety seemed to thrill her, as though the exposure had elevated her to star status.

"I didn't look so good," I said dismally. "They think I'm an accomplice, because we were talking and laughing."

"Ain't that a hoot? You gonna have a lotta 'splainin' to do, Britt. Can't deny, you did help me git ridda that dead body." She admired the blue stone in Jeff's college ring, now adorning her right index finger.

Patty Hearst went to prison, I thought, for crimes committed with her kidnappers.

"We're okay here," Keppie was saying. "That woman never even looked at you when we checked in. She was busy making goo-goo eyes at little Joey here. That's my good boy!" She scooped him up and twirled him around the room.

He began to cry and she handed him to me. "What a piss-poor little crybaby," she said in disgust.

I rocked him until his sobs stopped. His soft curly hair was still damp from his bath and his skin felt warm. Too warm? Did he have a fever? What would I do if he did?

Giddy at her new fame, Keppie celebrated with tequila, even used a glass. She wanted to sit out on the small screened-in porch wrapped around our tiny cabin and insisted on leaving Joey in the closet.

"Just so we know where he's at," she said as though it were perfectly logical.

I reluctantly bedded him down on the closet floor with a pillow, blanket, and his Beanie Baby. "What if he starts screaming?" I asked her.

"Then we shove a sock in his mouth," she said matter-of-factly.

I left the door ajar, a chair pushed against it so he couldn't crawl out without knocking it over.

We were surrounded by woods and a dark sea of sky that glittered with far more stars than are visible over

Miami's city lights. A sliver of young moon hugged the horizon as Venus blazed to its right.

Keppie reclined on a creaky wooden lounge chair, voice low and almost dreamy. "What do you think's out there, Britt? Little green men? Aliens from outer space?"

"The only aliens we worry about in Miami aren't from outer space."

"Miami. You really like that place. I like to keep moving, see new things, new people."

The Milky Way arched toward the summer triangle. Tears sprang to my eyes. Was anybody in Miami looking at the sky and thinking of me?

"You got the notebook?"

I held it up.

"Good," she said. "Write this down. I seen a UFO once, big as life, amber lights just floatin' above the treetops out behind my Grandma Bass's place just this side-a Gulf Breeze."

"Probably a helicopter."

"Shit, no. I know a goddamn helicopter when I see one. This didn't make a sound, just hung around the same spot for a good five minutes, then disappeared—*pssst*—just like that, into a cloudbank. I knew what it was. They got more sightin's 'round Gulf Breeze than anyplace in the entire world. Never understood all these people complainin' they was abducted by aliens. They want to take me in a flying saucer, I'd be first one aboard. Damn right."

"I wonder what they'd find if they probed your mind."

Keppie guffawed. "Who knows?" She reached over and cozily patted my knee. "Maybe where they come from, I'd fit right in."

Keppie wanted Joey restrained for the night, even though he could not reach the door lock. I didn't want her to lock him in the closet, so we compromised. She handcuffed me to the bed leg, looped a rope around his neck, and knotted it to the cuffs. If we tried to untie it during the night, the cuffs would rattle enough to wake her.

He slept beside me, fitful and feverish. Was he sick or reliving the trauma he'd endured?

Exhaustion weakens your defense against relentless thoughts. I had to rest, but the world always seems worse at night. Distractions of the day fade, enabling dark thoughts to creep out of the corners of your mind and grow into monsters of your own making. The mind is caught in circular thought patterns, obsessing on fear or pain that builds in intensity along with your emotions. No surprise that more people die in the dark hours before dawn.

The homeless I had interviewed on Miami's streets said what kept them awake nights was not the heat, the rain, the rats, or the mosquitoes. It was fear: the uncertainty of how to stay alive without being raped, beaten, or murdered. I was one of them now.

Nightmarish flashbacks of the woods and dread of what was to come kept me awake. I had always believed the human race to be resilient, brave, and basically good. How, I wondered, had Keppie become so different from the rest of us, for whom fantasies are enough? What made her act them out?

I prayed that my fears and fatigue would disappear at dawn. I had to think clearly enough to keep myself and this innocent child alive.

My face did not look as bad in the morning. The swelling had subsided, and Keppie insisted I try to cover the bruises with makeup. I wore fresh underwear, a pair of the new shorts she had bought, and a bright yellow T-shirt that said FOLLOW ME TO FLORIDA, THE SUNSHINE STATE. We stopped at a general store, where Keppie purchased a dog leash and fashioned a harness for Joey. He submitted stoicly, standing stiffly as she buckled it around him. No one knew he was missing, I thought, with growing despair. He and his dad had been en route to Disney World. No one would miss them until they failed to return. It was up to me to save him.

Keppie was in a talkative mood, chatting about her victims as we waited at the drive-through for Burger King breakfasts. I took notes.

"Man of God, my lily-white ass," she said, discussing the preacher. "Pious and pompous as all get out. Hah! Then he wants . . . well, you know." She jerked her head toward the backseat as though suddenly sensitive to Joey's presence. "I sure baptized him." She smirked. "Shut his scripture-spouting mouth for damn sure."

"And the sheriff?"

"I'd seen him around, always undressin' you with his piggy eyes. Had a couple drinks in a café up there. Went out to the parkin' lot to get somethin' outa the backseat of a car I had borrowed from an acquaintance. I'm bendin' over, in a short skirt. He cruises by, gets a eyeful, and pulls up.

"The tag is stolen, he says. I say, Like hell. He says, Come with me. Like he's arresting me. All the way up to the jail annex he's talkin' 'bout how good-looking, how sexy, I am. He grabs a feel and says we kin probably work this out. 'Magine how many times he done that over the years? Had his own kingdom up there. Well, hoo-ha, the king is dead! Shoulda kept a hand on his gun insteada his cock. Make sure you tell that one right."

We pulled off the road into the shade of some live oaks to eat our biscuits, cheese, and sausage, milk for Joey and coffee for us. Keppie kept the engine running, air conditioner blasting, as the temperature climbed faster than the sun in the sky. She poured the contents of five sugar packets into her coffee, took a small sip, then tore open number six. Maybe it was sugar that made her unpredictable and homicidal. I had reported a cotton-candy defense, an armed robber who pleaded insanity on grounds that eating five cones of cotton candy the night of the crime drove his blood sugar so high he wasn't responsible for his actions.

"You ever had your blood sugar tested?" I asked Keppie. "Any diabetes in your family?"

"Britt, quit talking trash and pay attention. I'm strong and healthy as a bull, like my whole family."

Except they're all dead, I thought.

"Now where were we?" She patted her lips with a paper napkin. "Oh, yeah. The four-one-one on that fella at the rest stop in Alachua County. He was headed for a job interview, in advertisin' or somethin'. Had a wife and babies at home, 'sposed to be looking for work. Seen his wife on TV later. Pretty little thing was cryin', said the last thing he told her was that with any luck he would land the job. Well, he got lucky, all right."

She nibbled at her biscuit.

"I tell you, Britt." She sipped her coffee. "They was asking for it. Like that guy in South Beach with his big greasy paws. Here I am conversin' with somebody, he elbows his way up, and the next thing you know," she said indignantly, "his sweaty paw is gropin' my thigh. And I say okay. He's asking for it."

"What about the man you were talking to at the time? Why not him?"

She shrugged. "Wasn't a bad guy, hurtin' over some woman, pourin' out his heartaches. We was havin' a nice conversation."

"What about?"

She winked slyly. "Lotsa things. Then that purty boy. Never mentioned modelin', lied through his teeth, said he was a writer and lived alone. I could see a woman lived there. What'd he think, I was stupid? . . .

"They was all askin' for it. They hate us." She downed the last of her coffee and crumpled her empty food wrappers. "It's war. You got to live by the golden rule: Do unto others before they do it to you."

She brushed crumbs off the seat.

"Your turn." She hit the signal and pulled out onto the roadway. She wanted to know what it was like growing up with a mother.

"Well, the mother-daughter thing can be complicated, at least with us. She's never liked my line of work. She thinks I'm like my father, accuses me of being a risk taker."

Keppie rolled her eyes. "Well, Britt, don't you think that, just maybe, the woman's on to something?"

"She's into high fashion; that's what she does for a living, and she's got this talent for laying guilt trips on me. I guess I embarrass her. She didn't want me seeing my dad's family when I was little and got all evasive when I tried to find out what really happened to my father—"

"The bitch!" Keppie said indignantly. "When we get back to Miami, I can get rid of her for you."

"What?"

"You want her gone, I can do it."

"Are you crazy?" I yelped. "Don't even joke about that! I love my mother!"

"Well, will you make up your damn mind?" she retorted angrily, and stomped the gas, brow furrowed.

The radio news on the hour had no reports, either about us or about a missing child. Top story was death-row inmate Ira Jonas. Final appeal denied, he was about to die in Florida's electric chair.

"Son of a bitch," Keppie muttered through clenched teeth. I thought at first she was cursing at traffic. "Those bastards," she said. "Those bastards."

"What do you care about Ira Jonas? He killed an old couple in a robbery at their little store."

"Sittin' in Old Sparky is no way to die," she said.

As if her way was better.

"You heard how they botched that last execution." Her foot hit the gas, and the SUV leaped forward through traffic.

"It may have been messy, but not botched. I mean, the guy is dead. The end result was achieved."

"Hang 'em, shoot 'em, inject 'em!" She swerved past a produce truck and tailgated a delivery van. "Anythin' is better! That man didn't git electrocuted, he burnt up!"

The solemn legal process had erupted into an incandescent spectacle as foot-long blue and orange flames erupted from the condemned man's head, startling both witnesses and executioner. It still seemed more humane than what happened to the man's victim, an eighty-six-year-old widow, raped, stabbed twenty-six times, and left to bleed to death.

Despite protesters seeking a change, the electric chair remains in use. With all its wires, meters, electrodes, sea sponges, and leather straps, it's an archaic throwback, which is part of its unique and terrible beauty.

"The problem," I said, "is that it's hard to test. You can't ask volunteers to sit down and try it out."

Keppie never cracked a smile.

"I think it's fixed now," I offered.

Her only response was to kick the accelerator way up past the speed limit, the first time I had seen her do that.

She's scared, I thought, aware that a date with Old Sparky looms in her future, if she's got one.

Flying low on a curve, outdistancing everything else on the road, we hurtled up on an accident scene on the far side of the divided highway. An ambulance was departing. Three highway patrol cars with blue flashers were clustered to the side, where an accordioned silver-color car with a plastic luggage rack on top had apparently slammed into the rear of a semi-tractor truck. Luggage was strewn across the roadway and the grassy shoulder. The truck had begun to smolder and billow black smoke.

Keppie took her foot off the accelerator, too late. Swerving to avoid other motorists slowing to gawk, she cut off a Toyota Corolla and shot across two lanes. Horns blared. Drivers hit their brakes. She had to be doing ninety. The eyes of a trooper at the accident scene followed us, his head turning. He shouted something to the others and ran for his car.

I caught my breath.

"Oh, Jesus!" Keppie said. "Shit!"

"Maybe he's not coming after us," I said fearfully, praying he was.

The trooper rolled into a wide U-turn across the median into the northbound lane.

"Goddammit!"

She floored it again and leaned on the horn to blast an elderly driver out of our path.

"Here we go!" she whooped, foot to the floor, eyes on the rearview.

"Where? Where are we going?" Joey said.

"It's okay, sweetheart. Just hold on." I checked to make sure he was secure in his car seat, then tightened my seat belt.

The trooper's siren wailed behind us.

This is it, I thought. We will be rescued or die.

"Listen," I pleaded, scenery flashing by so fast it made me queasy, "all he wants is to write you a ticket. The car isn't reported stolen."

"Shut up!" She weaved in and out of traffic. "You saw how he eyeballed us. Somebody musta spotted us and dropped a dime." She glanced in the mirror. "We can lose this sucker. This baby can outrun them."

I closed my eyes as we cut off a driver who leaned on his horn, then opened them as another driver careened onto the shoulder to get out of our way. Joey's eyes were wide, his mouth open, pudgy fingers grasping the sides of his car seat.

The speedometer clocked us at 110.

"Take it!" I screamed. "Just take the damn ticket! The registration's in the glove compartment! Take the ticket! It's not worth getting us killed!"

"Ain't it?" She never let up on the speed. We passed

one exit, then another, like a jet on a runway about to lift off.

We were pulling away from the trooper's car, but he still followed, lights flashing, siren blaring.

"Hoo-ha!" she cried, as his siren grew fainter and we continued to outdistance him. Suddenly the siren's scream was upon us, startling us both. Her grin faded. Another trooper had appeared, not fifty feet away, racing along an access road parallel to the highway, nearly pacing us. More blue flashers ahead: a local sheriff's department car, approaching in a southbound lane. He slowed down and bounced onto the median to cut us off.

It was all over, time to stop and surrender. Anybody could see that. Despite my own fear and panic, I was struck by Keppie's expression. No fear. Intense, centered, excited, but never afraid. She groped on the floor with her left hand, brought up the gun, and wedged it in the map holder on her door.

Please, God, I prayed, *please don't let her shoot at the cops.* The SUV's dark window tint made it impossible for them to see the child seat or me. Shot at, the cops would return fire.

"Don't," I pleaded. "They'll kill us."

"Shut up," she said.

We rocketed past the deputy crossing the median. He fell in three car lengths behind us as the trooper sailed off the access road onto the highway, right with him. The original FHP car brought up the rear, less than a quarter mile behind. The sirens, blaring horns, and screaming brakes around us all chorused in a wild cacophony, and a dark shadow suddenly enveloped us, appearing overhead and swooping down like the angel of death.

Fourteen

"THAT IS A FUCKING CHOPPER!" KEPPIE shrieked. "Not a UFO! See, I *can* tell the difference!"

The police. How did they get a chopper out here so fast? They must know who we are! For a wild elated moment I expected Ojeda to be aboard. They had come at last.

"They ain't cops!" Keppie yelled.

I squinted up through the windshield. WSTR 950-AM RADIO, NEWS-TRAFFIC-TALK was painted on the helicopter.

"A news chopper!" I said. They must have been in the air already, to cover the traffic accident we saw.

Keppie jabbed the radio button.

". . . our traffic news chopper at the scene of that serious car-truck collision on I-Seventy-five at the junction with Flamingo Road is now monitoring a police chase in progress. We take you to Maynard Swan in the WSTR Traffic Copter. Maynard?"

"Yes, Alex, we're over the fleeing car in the north-bound lanes of I-Seventy-five at Suwannee Boulevard, where the FHP and county deputies are involved in the high-speed pursuit of a black SUV, could be a Ford Expedition—"

"Asshole!" Keppie shrieked.

"Looks like this may have started out as a routine traffic stop, but the driver refused to pull over. The pursuit has reached speeds well in excess of a hundred miles an hour. So you motorists out there, steer clear of this area, use alternate routes, because this could get messy. We'll stay with it, Alex, keeping you and our listeners informed of the outcome of this chase."

"Look out!" I cried, gripping the door handle as Keppie weaved between lanes, forcing a Greyhound bus into a skid as the driver hit the brakes.

Joey sobbed.

"Whoops! The driver of the black SUV nearly ran a Greyhound into a ditch. This suspect shows no signs of slowing down, so, drivers, if you see this pursuit headed your way, pull off to the side and let them by."

Surreal. We were listening to our own live police chase on the radio. If we crashed and burned, would the last voice we hear give a live description?

"Turn it off!" I said.

"Hell, no!" Keppie cranked up the volume. Chopper rotors in stereo beat the air overhead and reverberated through the speakers of the car's surround-sound system. I felt the vibrations in my gut.

The chopper suddenly vaulted into the air, soaring high ahead of us for a bird's-eye view.

"Okay, Alex, this chase is now approaching County Line Road. We've been in communication with the sheriff's department and hear that deputies are positioned up ahead to stop this runaway pursuit before someone is injured.

"Police are at the junction just south of the Seminole Trail exit, where northbound I-Seventy-five narrows to two lanes. That's where they'll roll out the spike strip, right into the path of that fleeing SUV, and we've seen what that can do, folks. Those spikes will instantly blow out the suspect's tires, ending this pursuit. Amazing no one has been injured yet. This is gonna be a sight to see. We're staying with it, Alex.''

''Shit. No exit between here and there.'' Amid the heat of the chase, Keppie's words were cold, her voice oddly calm.

Helpless, my heart racing, I considered trying to force her to a stop, but struggling for both the wheel and the gun was suicidal at these speeds. I couldn't control both her and the car. Time, the enemy, accelerated faster and faster, like an amusement park ride run amok.

Joey's sobs had stopped. His pinched face was chalk white.

As the SUV ate up the highway, we saw the roadblock, ahead, where the pavement narrowed and jogged to the right. Other motorists were being waved off to the side. I had seen spikes used in Miami. Police roll the eighteen-foot strip across the road and block the shoulders with vehicles. The fleeing car is channeled across the spikes and disabled, a quick and easy stop to a high-speed chase. Cops snatch the strip out of the road before pursuers run over it.

Two cars blockaded the right-hand shoulder. Another was positioned at the edge of the wide median to the left. The low, sloping, grassy area beyond it was bordered by soft shoulders, too wide to block completely. No place to go except straight over the spikes. How far, I wondered, could she drive on rims?

''Here they come, Alex!'' bleated the radio voice. ''The end of the road for this fleeing driver!''

I expected Keppie to slow down, but she never took her foot off the gas. We roared directly toward the spikes. Four cops scrambled for cover in case she spun out of control. At the last moment she wrenched the wheel to the left, off the road, directly at the cops. The torque snapped my head back and Joey started to scream. A deputy crouching at the roadside dove and rolled to escape being hit as we veered past his patrol car onto the soft median, wildly spinning tires spitting grass and mud high in the air. The four-wheel drive kicked in as we slid, tires fighting for purchase. Lost traction slowed us down to twenty miles an hour, and I breathed again. Two officers came running, guns drawn, but Keppie spun the wheel and we were back up on the highway before they reached us. They scattered again as the county car and the FHP cruiser skidded toward the spike strip, brakes screaming. One spun twice, ran over it, and slammed into the two county cars positioned on the shoulder.

"Uh-oh, uh-oh, uh-oh!" the traffic reporter was screaming. "Un-believable! Alex, the SUV managed to swerve onto the median and avoid the strip. But hoooo-weee! An FHP and a deputy's car ran right into it. One of 'em has struck two other county sheriff's cars. They could see the strip, Alex, but couldn't stop in time. The officer assigned to remove it from the roadway apparently had to abandon his post and run for cover when the fleeing driver nearly ran him down."

"Any injuries, Maynard?"

"Not clear at this time, Alex. The third pursuit car did avoid the spikes by following the suspect onto the median but appears to be stuck there in the soft grass. The SUV made it back to the road and is still on the run. I tell you, Alex, this is one for the books."

We continued to race the copter's shadow north as Keppie crowed in jubilation and Joey screamed for his mother.

"I'll bounce that brat right down on the pavement head first, he don't quit that yelling!" Keppie shouted.

"Joey, Joey, Joey. Hush, sweet boy. Hush, it's okay. Isn't this fun!" My voice shook. "Like Mr. Toad's Wild Ride at Disney. Be quiet now, sweetheart." I reached over the seat to try to soothe him. "It's okay."

Face wet, nose running, he choked back the sobs but continued to make a soft, one-note moaning sound.

The chopper still hovered over us, and somewhere far behind another siren wailed.

"Can you tell us what's happening out there now, Maynard?"

"The suspect's black SUV is continuing to travel northbound at a high rate—"

"Gotta take a break now, Maynard. Folks, we'll return to our bird's-eye account of this live police chase, in the aftermath of a serious accident, following these messages."

Keppie suddenly left the highway during the commercial, kicking up a cloud of dust before turning onto a narrow road into a wooded area. Pines and oaks towered around us, branches embracing overhead in a natural fretwork of boughs, leaves, and pine needles. We still heard the chopper but couldn't see it through the trees.

We were somewhere near Ocala National Forest. Was this it? The one-lane roadway curved, then ran alongside the main road we had come in on.

Obviously familiar with the area, Keppie drove off the road, taking a trail used by hunters and campers on all-terrain vehicles. It led into dense woods. Gold and green leaves and branches slapped and scraped our windows. Joey was quiet again. Hoping he was asleep, I looked back. Eyes wide in the dim light, he was sucking his thumb. I hadn't seen him do that before. If I thought it might settle my nerves, I'd try it myself. I loosened my seat belt as the SUV lumbered through the woods.

"Whatchu doing?" Keppie demanded.

"Looking for his Beanie Baby, his little Scottie." I plucked it off the floor in the back and placed it in his hands. "Here you go, Joey."

"Thank you," he murmured faintly. "Want some juice now, please."

"Not right now, honey."

The weather, "hot and muggy," followed noisy commercials for Piggly Wiggly Markets and an automobile dealership; then the annoyingly cheerful Alex returned.

"Okay, back to Maynard Swan, our traffic spy in the

sky. How goes it? What's the situation out there now, Maynard?'' Ear-splitting bursts of static followed.

''Are you there? Maynard?''

''Alex, can you hear me? The suspect crossed the county line, then exited I-Seventy-five, taking off into the woods, near Camp Town Trail, apparently still headed north. We can't see the SUV at this point but we're over Camp Town Trail waiting for it to emerge back onto the roadway.''

They watched north-south, as we crunched east through the underbrush. What would happen when these dense woods became impassable even for this vehicle? Drained, my knees shook. We would have, should have, been in police hands by now. I cursed the reporter for screwing up a police operation, aware of the irony. At least we were still alive. So far.

''Can you clear this up for us, Maynard? How does this pursuit relate to that serious car and truck accident out there at the exit? Or is it linked at all?''

''Not absolutely clear at this point, Alex.''

''Sure, blame the wreck on us too,'' Keppie said derisively.

''We'll be coming in to refuel shortly and be back in the air for rush hour this afternoon. Just stay tuned to Nine-fifty on your dial, WSTR. We'll get you home safely. Back to you, Alex.''

''Thanks, Maynard, for keeping us posted on all the action out there on our highways and byways. Now let's have a look at the national news. A House-Senate committee today—''

Keppie cut off the radio. The SUV pressed through the foliage like a huge animal. We saw no one, but there was evidence of campsites used by weekend hunters and hikers, even a few small cabins, unused this time of year because of the heat and unbearable mosquitoes. After nearly two hours, we stopped in a small clearing. Joey was asleep. I envied him. The engine idling, Keppie sipped tequila, stretched, rolled her head, and rotated her shoulders.

"Well, how'd I do?" she asked, her smile arch.

"Outfoxed 'em again," I acknowledged. "Were you scared? I was."

Her eyes narrowed. "Nah, I was too damn busy."

"Did—"

"Shhhhhh." She raised her hand, eyes half closed as though listening.

I heard nothing.

"Okay," she murmured softly and nudged the gas. We emerged from the brush into brilliant sunlight and a four-lane highway. She glanced both ways, then barreled across all four lanes into the woods on the far side. Trees closed in behind us, blocking out the familiar sights and sounds of civilization. In seconds we were safely swallowed up by the forest. We had not seen a single vehicle.

"While we talked, you were listening for a break in traffic so we could cross without being seen," I said. "Amazing. I never heard a sound."

She shrugged. "You didn't know the road was there. I grew up in this kinda country, been in and outa here lotsa times before. Never could've done it without this here vee-hicle." She patted the walnut-accented dashboard fondly, the first time I had seen her demonstrate affection for anything.

She appeared to meander aimlessly across dirt paths and trails, knowing all the while exactly where she was and where she was going.

"Here we are," she announced, an hour later, as she stopped in a small clearing at the foot of two giant live oaks.

"Where?" I asked.

"Home. Don't wanna take the car out there for a while. It's too risky."

Joey stirred in the back. "I have to go pee-pee," he said.

Keppie nodded. I got out and unbuckled his car seat.

"Come on," I told him.

"Be careful out there," Keppie teased. "There's black bears in these woods, and snakes, maybe even a mountain lion."

"It's okay," I whispered, as he clung tightly to my hand.

An unfamiliar yet strong emotion overtook me. I could hang tough myself, but I had neglected to childproof my heart.

Kneeling in the pine needles, I hugged him. "Everything will be all right," I promised. He hugged back, his little body warm and soft against me, his brown eyes trusting. Each of us was all the other had. In this beautiful but desolate place, there was no chance on earth that Ojeda, the cops, or a rescue team from *America's Most Wanted* was suddenly going to appear. Nobody would find us here.

The woods were silent except for bird songs, the buzz of insects, and the occasional rumble of a distant jet. If this was the Ocala National Forest, a park ranger might stumble upon us. I rehearsed a plan: scream a warning, snatch up Joey, dash for cover in the woods. But rangers work alone. What if Keppie killed him or her? She would hunt us down. She knew where we were. I didn't even know which way to run. How fast could I go with Joey? How far were we from the safety of other people? I felt helpless. I could take chances, but I couldn't endanger him.

I brushed a mosquito from his cheek and smoothed his hair as we walked back to the car. That was when he began calling me by name.

"You mean you want to sleep out here tonight?" I complained. "Why not go back to one of those cabins we saw? It shouldn't be hard to get inside."

Keppie tossed her head. "This is the place. We stay in the car."

"What about food . . . water?"

She shrugged. "A little stream runs back behind those trees. We can wash up and get water there."

"Is it safe to drink?"

"Safer than getting shot."

We had a small cardboard carton of Animal Crackers the motel manager had given Joey, a few cellophane-wrapped Saltines, and two unopened bottles of tequila along with the one Keppie was drinking.

That was it.

Keppie wanted to save the battery, and without the car's air-conditioning, the woods were stifling, swarming with stinging insects, gnats, no-see-ums, and mosquitoes.

Keppie changed into a shirt and jeans. I dressed Joey in little denim trousers and a long-sleeved pullover, touched by whoever had packed his small suitcase with such care. His mom? Or the dad now gone forever? I pulled on the jeans I was wearing when all this began. It seemed so long ago.

I sat on the open back of the SUV with my notebook as we resumed the interview. Joey played nearby, stirring up pine needles with a stick and making trucklike noises. Keppie stretched her legs and smoked, the gun in her waistband, watching us.

"Thank God you didn't shoot at those cops," I said. "I was really afraid you would."

"Has the sun fried your brain?" She snorted. "The hell of it is, you shoot at cops, they're goddamn sure to shoot back. Them sons-a-bitches'll try to kill you!" Her voice rose in indignation, at law enforcement's insensitivity and lack of fair play.

"Well, when I saw you reach for the gun, I assumed—"

"Hell, I wasn't gonna use it on *them.*" She leaned against the SUV in a smoker's stance, cigarette close to her lips, the other arm across her waist, its wrist supporting the elbow of the hand with the smoke. Her eyes glittered in a shaft of sunlight that back-lit her soft streaming hair.

I felt sick at what she had intended. She would hate jail, but she was no suicide, she was a survivor.

"There's no reason to use it," I said calmly. "Nobody here wants to hurt you. All I want is to go back to Miami and write your story. Now." I looked down at my notebook, the only security I had to hold on to. "What do you dream about, Keppie?"

Frowning, she took a deep drag on the cigarette, then smiled and licked her lips, exhaling smoke. "I dream about being lost in a wilderness," she said slowly, "where there are a lot of guns and men and you can smell blood in the air." She cocked her head, curious eyes meeting mine. "Wonder what that means?"

I shrugged, scribbling notes.

"Come on," she offered. "Let's take a walk, wanna show you somethin'."

"Come on, Joey," I called, and he came running. Light slanted through the trees. Nearly five o'clock. What were they doing in Miami? Was McDonald searching for me?

Twice Keppie hesitated, to study her surroundings for a moment, then slightly changed direction. A tiny tree frog leaped onto her shoulder, and she casually shrugged him away. These woods all looked the same to me. How would we find the car again?

In a tight dark tunnel of pine trees, she pushed back some dead branches, tearing away a heavy curtain of spiderwebs. "Looky here," she said.

I gasped. A human skull lay in the thicket, bones strewn around it.

"This here's Stanley," she said with a grin. "The man was really hung, but he don't look so hot to trot now, does he?" I stepped in front of Joey. A scalp with strands of dark hair still clung to the skull. Spiders with silver streaks darted across faded scraps of fabric, all that remained of his clothes.

"Had a body by Budweiser," Keppie was saying. "Shoulda heard him scream when he came—and bellow once he got gut-shot. Hey, Stanley.'' She addressed the scattered bones. ''What the hell happened to your legs? I'll be damned if it don't look like some wild animal's done run off with 'em.''

''Daddy?'' Joey said, from behind me.

''No, baby,'' I said. ''Let's go back.''

My eyes shifted skyward at the sound of a plane. Police, I prayed, focusing on a patch of blue between two trees. It was a sleek military jet, a lawn dart leaving a vapor trail behind.

''It's what men have been doing to us for years,'' Keppie said flatly. ''Killin' us and leavin' us in places like this. Bones in the wilderness.''

The body had been in this lonely place long before this recent murder spree. How many more were there? I wondered, with growing horror.

Next to her, Charles Manson had to be a ray of sunshine.

'' 'Bye, Stanley,'' she called cheerfully, releasing the branches that snapped back in his direction. ''Don't know what I'm gonna do with you,'' she chided, manicured hands on her hips. ''First, your balls are gone and your dick; then I come back and it's your arm; now it's your legs. Try to pull yourself together and stay put now till I come back, you hear?'' She laughed like a giggly teenager.

Joey balked as we left and kept looking back over his shoulder. ''I wanna see,'' he said.

''There's nothing to see, sweetheart,'' I said.

''I want my daddy. He got shot, got shot in the head,'' he piped up. ''In the woods. I saw it.''

''Ain't no big thing, son,'' Keppie told him, reaching out to tousle his hair. He pulled away fearfully. ''Ya gotta get used to it, boy. People die all the time.''

Joey asked for juice again on the way back to the car. He had missed lunch; now it was time for his supper. ''I wish we could've stopped for supplies,'' I told Keppie.

"At least we could have gotten him some food, water, and insect repellent."

"Sorry 'bout that," she said.

"Let's go," I urged. "I'm worried about the mosquitoes. You saw the warnings in the paper about the encephalitis outbreak up here. There's a medical alert in twenty-seven counties between here and Miami. Mosquitoes spread it. They've even canceled night baseball games."

"How quick does encephalitis kill you?"

"I don't know, but it's pretty fast. You get a headache, pain, then seizures. Your brain swells—"

"Bullets kill you faster," she said.

"But you're just as dead," I said. "The mosquitoes carrying it are like vampires, creatures of the night, the hungriest and most active between dusk and dawn. We still have a few hours of light. We can dump the car someplace close to a town, walk to a motel, or take a bus."

"I'll take my chances with the skeeters," she said. "They ain't killed me yet."

I wanted out of these steamy insect-infested woods. No place in Florida is more than sixty miles away from salt water, yet there was no hint, no breeze, no fresh smell of air from the Atlantic or the Gulf of Mexico. The heat dulled me into a near stupor as sweat streamed from every pore.

We plodded to the little stream. Keppie brought a paper cup and drank but I refused to drink or allow Joey to. To get sick would be a disaster. I couldn't picture Keppie nursing us back to health.

"If you ain't the goddamnedest worrier!" she said. "You just know too much for your own good."

"There are phosphate plants and paper mills in this part of the state," I said, "along with sewage treatment plants and garbage dumps. We don't know what's upstream."

She stood ankle-deep in water, paper cup in her hand, one hip slung over to the side, hair streaming down her back. "The water's the least of your worries. You graspin' the big picture here, Britt? Think I'd drink it if it wasn't safe?"

"You do a lot of things other people wouldn't do."

She grinned, raised her cup in a mock toast, then drank.

"She's drinking it," Joey protested. "I want some too."

"No, honey, this water might be dirty," I said. "Here, sit down." I helped him take his shoes, socks, and pants off so he could wet his feet, then soaked a T-shirt and dabbed his face and throat to cool him off.

"You see, my folks who raised me did the best they could," Keppie said, as we resumed our interview back at the SUV, "but they just couldn't stand havin' me around. Their kids were scared to death of me. I was outa control."

"In what way?" I asked. We sat under the open hatch, facing the forest.

"Well, I started smokin' and drinkin' at 'bout ten or eleven years old." She swallowed from the bottle, leaned back, and swung her feet up onto the floorboard. "I'd been shopliftin' since I was nine. Had tons of stuff under my bed. Boxes and bags full. All kindsa stuff I didn't even need or want, just took it for the thrill of it. And I'd carry a big ol' nail around in my pocket. Whenever I seen a nice car, I'd run the nail right down the side. Sometimes I'd write some other kid's name in the paint with it. Hah!" She gave a little half laugh. "Used to follow the mailman around and steal people's mail, throw it away, just for the hell of it. All kinds of stuff like that. What really got to 'em was the fires. I liked settin' fires when I was a kid."

"You mean playing with matches or cigarette lighters, that sort of thing?"

"Nah, *fires*. I'd pile a buncha papers or clothes outside their door when they was sleepin', pour on lighter fluid, and strike a match to it. Shoulda heard 'em scream. It was comical."

"My God, you could have burned the whole house down," I said, scratching the mosquito bites on my ankle.

"Oh, I did that once. Red Cross hadda put us up at a motel."

"What did your folks do?"

"Had me in and outa therapy, hospitals, juvenile court. I told ya, I drove 'em nuts."

She caught me eyeing her cigarette and smiled.

"Nothin' to worry 'bout now," she said. "Grew out of it. Just a stage, I guess. Thought about it when you ragged on me for smokin' in bed."

"So your childhood was troubled," I said, nodding.

"Hell, no. Aside from losin' my mama, I was happy as peach pie. It was my mama's sister, my Aunt Mary Alice and her husband, my Uncle Harland, my new parents, that was troubled. I was fine, but she was cryin' all the time and he was always bent outa shape. Used to stay up nights talkin' 'bout what to do with me. Didn't think I heard 'em, but I did. Thinkin' back, I guess they were too scared to go to sleep." She chuckled.

"What finally happened? When did you leave home?"

"Last time I ran away I was 'bout sixteen, just never went back. They were probably hopin' I wouldn't, though I know they'da took me in if I showed up. You see, they promised my mama they'd look out for me. And you gotta give 'em that, they always kept their word. They're good Christians. Sometimes I call 'em or drop a line, just to let 'em know I'm alive. Probably scares the shit outa them, thinkin' I might show up some day."

"How do you see your future? What do you think is ahead?"

"For me?" She shrugged. "Well, I don't plan much. Plans never tend to work out. I'm not one-a those people who knows exactly where she's 'sposed to be and what she's 'sposed to be doing five–ten years from now. Might say I live for today but I have hope for tomorrow. You know what hope is?" She brightened.

"Tell me your definition."

"Hope," she said, swallowing another hit from the bottle, "is a memory of the future. Write that down." She wiped her lips on her sleeve and gazed skyward. "Every day I wake up with strong feelings of hope. As long as I do, I know there's a future."

"I wanna hamburger," Joey said, interrupting. "Please."

I gave him an animal cracker. "Mine," he said, and reached for the box with both hands. He whimpered as I pulled it away.

"We're playing a game," I said. "We're going to see how long these crackers can last. You eat the tiger and we'll save the elephant for later."

Dry tiger crumbs caught in his throat and he coughed. "Milk!" he gasped, between spasms that reddened his face.

"We don't have any right now." I patted his back.

"Let's go get some." His little voice was raspy.

"We can't right now." I cuddled him and wished for rain.

It elated Keppie to hear on the radio news at six that the search for the Kiss-Me Killer had focused on Atlanta, after a reported sighting there. Georgia police were on alert.

I coaxed Joey, who was hungry and cranky, to settle down in the back of the SUV, while Keppie sat up on the hood reading a tabloid. Though I was as wrung out as a wet dishrag, hair hanging damp and stringy, the heat merely coated her skin with a glossy sheen, curling tiny tendrils of hair around her forehead and neck, adding to her luminous look. Who would believe somebody who looked like her could spread so much misery to so many?

She caught me watching and met my eyes with a heavy-lidded seductive gaze that made me acutely aware of every curve beneath my wet clinging clothes.

Trees obscured the setting sun, and night fell like a

rock. No lights, no highway sounds in the distance, only night birds, insects, and small scary creatures rustling in the brush. We left the car windows open so we could breathe, but the mosquitoes were a nightmare. When I draped clothes and a blanket over the windows, the heat was suffocating. We desperately needed air, but when I took the clothes down, the mosquitoes swarmed. Their high-pitched whines filled the car.

"Blow some cigarette smoke back here," I begged Keppie, who was in the front. "It'll help keep the mosquitoes off." I fanned Joey with one of her tabloids.

While he slept fitfully, I entertained visitors. I felt their eyes in the dark. I am young to have so many ghosts. They usually appear in public places and familiar neighborhoods. Sometimes I see the homely profile, familiar bulk, and shambling walk of Dan Flood, the veteran cop with a long memory and a passion for old cases. About to call out his name, I remember he's gone. As I pass a video arcade or a pickup basketball game on some inner-city court, I glimpse Howie's awkward and stick-thin shadow. I stopped my car once, happy to see the spunky abandoned teenager again, then painfully remembered that he, too, was gone—his potential and brave heart stilled forever by misguided police bullets. My friend Francie appears at the wheel of a speeding patrol car or in a flash of blue uniform around a corner, though I know a sniper's bullet found her through the smoke and chaos of the riot. Her dog, Bitsy, is my only inheritance, except perhaps for the one my mother accuses me of, my father's attraction to lost causes. His presence has always been with me, strong and comforting in times of danger. But not now. Others came and went throughout this endless night, but not him. Had he forgotten me? Had the final resolution to the mystery of his death freed him from earthly bonds? Had he left my life forever?

I listened to Joey's breathing, fearing it might stop. Beads of sweat sprang to life on my scalp, worming their way toward my forehead like tiny maggots. Staring into the dark, I saw another ghost. The young father on his way to Disney World with his little son. They would be there now, had he not chosen to stop at that time, at that place. Had he not seen Keppie.

His last words echoed. "He's a good little citizen, and I want him to grow up good and have a good life." If we survive this, I promised the ghost, I will see to that and make it happen.

Dozing at last before dawn, I dreamed I was having sex on a hot and sultry long-forgotten Fourth of July. The sheets were damp and rumpled against my skin, the darkness smelled like our bodies, and sheer drapes billowed in a breeze bearing the scent of frangipani. I looked eagerly at my partner's face, hidden in shadow—and awoke with a start, Keppie's face close to mine.

"You awake?" she whispered, her palms on my knees.

"What do you want?"

"You know."

Fifteen

I CLOSED MY EYES, HOPING THIS WAS YET ANother nightmare. Her hot breath singed my cheek.

"No way," I whispered.

"Gimme one good reason."

"I can give you lots," I hissed. "Mosquitoes have bitten me half to death, which does nothing for my libido. I'm straight. I'm sleep-deprived. There's an innocent child in the car. And last but not least, your lovers' life expectancy is usually about three and a half minutes. Those reasons good enough? If not, I can come up with some more."

Her laughter caused Joey to turn in his sleep. "You'll change your mind," she murmured confidently. "I've seen you look at me. I know you want it."

"I'll let you know when," I said, and turned over, knees together, arms across my chest.

I never went back to sleep, exquisitely aware of every movement in the car. Keppie was restless. She got out and I heard her walking around, spotted the glow of her cigarette in the dark, and heard her humming some mournful country-and-western song.

The pale and misty woods echoed with bird calls one minute, sweltered in sudden daylight the next. Life in the woods, with towering trees and dense summer foliage blocking out the rest of the universe, left me claustrophobic.

Dehydrated and speckled with red mosquito bites, Joey cried forlornly. He wanted to watch cartoons.

"Show me a TV set," Keppie told him, stretching and yawning, "and we'll turn on the 'toons. Go ahead, boy, just run out there in the woods; you find the set and we all can watch."

Joey sobbed and clung to me.

"Jesus Christ!" Keppie snapped. "That little bastard's enough to make a woman swear off motherhood."

"We've got to get him some food and water," I said. "He's feverish. He's too little for this. I feel miserable myself."

She cut her eyes at me and sneered. "You had your chance last night. I'da made you forget food and water. You'd feel a helluva lot better. What is wrong with you people? I went without eatin' for seven days once. Didn't hurt me none."

"Why?" I reached for the notebook. "What happened? Why did you fast?"

"No reason." She shrugged and tuned in the radio. "Just wanted to see what it felt like." No mention of us on the news. There was trouble in Bosnia, a small plane crash near Orlando, and the governor had signed Ira Jonas's death warrant.

"They're itchin' to pull the switch, can't fry the poor bastard fast enough!" Keppie raged.

"He was convicted nearly fourteen years ago," I said.

She turned off the radio and stormed out of the car. She checked beneath the hood, then slammed it down with a crash. "Okay! I'm sicka your bitchin' and moanin'. We're hitting the road! We're outa here!" She glared at us and frowned. "But first take him on down to that stream, wash him up, and comb his hair so he looks half decent. You too. I ain't takin' either one-a you anywhere lookin' like that."

Half an hour later, washed and in fresh clothes, we again lumbered along forest trails in the SUV.

"Shoulda waited till after dark," Keppie groused. "But I can't deal with all this whinin' and complainin'. Rattles my damn nerves."

Joey looked listless in his car seat.

"We're going for breakfast," I told him. "Want some juice and cereal?" He nodded mournfully.

"You know what I've been craving?" I told Keppie.

"I know, baby. I know." She raised a wicked eyebrow.

"No, for Pete's sake. A big juicy mango." I leaned back, imagining it. "Skin the color of a sunset, sweeter smelling than flowers. A shame they're so messy."

"Easiest way is to git naked and eat it in the bathtub," Keppie said, steering the SUV around a huge petrified stump, artifact from some ancient hurricane. "My mama won prizes for her mango chutney. Had rows and rows of glass jars lined up, all ruby, green, and gold."

When she finally stopped and lowered the windows, I nearly wept at the welcome *whoosh* of passing traffic. Back in the real world at last. She waited for a lull, eased onto the road, and drove toward the outskirts of a small town.

"There's a place," I cried.

She eyeballed the small convenience store, passed it, and pulled off the road. I carried Joey as we walked back.

"Get some insect repellent and calamine lotion," I said, as she tossed items into a little basket.

My parched lips tingled at the cooler. Forget flavored iced tea, cappuccino, and diet soda, all that orange- and purple-flavored water. What my body craved, needed to replenish itself, was water, good old aqua—designer label, spring, purified, or, worst-case scenario, just plain tap—straight up and ice cold.

Even Joey lifted his flushed face from my neck, blinked, and began to look around, as though sensing the presence of food and drink.

Hands shaking, I twisted the cap off a cold and sweaty water bottle, fed Joey small sips, and then took a long draft myself. We carried the supplies back to the car and raised the hatch. Keppie had bought white bread, billowy, cloud soft, and full of empty calories. She slathered on mayo with a plastic knife, heaped on the lunch meat manufactured from some mystery animal, and fixed sandwiches that tasted so good I nearly moaned with pleasure. We had milk, water, potato chips, and bread-and-butter pickles. Keppie had also stocked up on the latest tabloids and local newspapers, which she devoured. Our story was on an inside page.

"Looks like I been real busy." Georgia police were investigating possible links between the Kiss-Me Killer and a homicide outside an Atlanta night club and reports of a sighting farther north, in Marietta.

She removed the license plate from the SUV with a screwdriver and folded both inside a newspaper. We strolled back to the convenience store, to buy a few more things and use the rest room. Then I bent over Joey, brushing off his clothes and helping him with his grape juice as, behind us, Keppie switched tags with a parked Chrysler LeBaron.

Back on the road, a new tag on the SUV, I asked where we were headed as she turned south.

"Sure as hell ain't Atlanta," she muttered. "Know where I'd like to go? Ochopee."

"Down south, out in the 'glades? Why there?" My heart beat faster. Ochopee was only about sixty miles west of Miami.

"They just had another skunk ape sightin'," she said. " 'Cordin' to the paper. Tour guide and a buncha British tourists seen it."

No wonder police were confounded trying to track her. Her elusive trail was based on whatever curious events or tourist attractions captured her imagination.

"Seven feet tall, covered with hair, and he smelled bad,

like a skunk.'' She glanced back at Joey in his car seat. ''He was watchin' 'em, lurkin' behind a veil of Spanish moss and spidery air plants drippin' off the cypress trees at the edge of the swamp.''

''He's Florida's Bigfoot, the Sasquatch of the swamp, the Abominable Snowman of the subtropics,'' I said. ''There've been stories for years. He's an urban myth that people see after a couple of six-packs.''

''Has to be somethin' out there. Everybody who seen it can't be lyin'.''

''Some reporters think it's a local character playing games to scare tourists.''

''Well, he better be fast and hold onto his ass, cuz one-a these days he'll scare some tourist with a gun.''

I visualized a headline: KISS-ME KILLER SLAYS SKUNK APE. Would they have sex first?

I felt giddy. We were out of the woods and rolling south, toward home, toward Miami, wheels singing on the road. Buoyed by a sense of relief and optimism for the first time since we dropped Joey's father down the sinkhole, I nearly joined in as she sang along with some country song on the radio about ''wild whiskey and rum.''

Then another news report on Ira Jonas plunged her into a tirade.

''Somebody with balls could go right over there and bust him the hell out.''

''Off Death Row?'' I asked.

''That guy in Texas escaped.''

''Yeah, but they found him dead.''

''At least he died trying, not when *they* decided he would die. He cheated 'em! Probably woulda made it if he had outside help. Bonnie and Clyde did it once. Broke in and rescued a cousin or somebody.''

''But look what happened to them.''

''Not till later. Jesus Christ, Britt! Land a chopper inside the walls, step off guns blazing, those corrections officers'd run like rabbits.''

"Where would you get a helicopter?" I asked. "They cost hundreds of thousands of dollars. How would you fly it?"

"You don't go out and buy one, for Christ's sake! You take a ride in one-a them sightseeing choppers, hold a gun to his head, and the pilot'll do anythin' you say. I swear, I don't know how you've lived this long. You ain't got a resourceful bone in your body."

Who cared enough to carry out her fantasy of a Death Row rescue? I wondered. No one who knew her.

She lit a cigarette. "Death Row inmates don't get to work like other prisoners. It's a bitch. One shower a week. No exercise with the others. Fucking lousy. Specially when somebody don't really belong there."

"Are you saying Jonas is innocent?"

"Hell, I don't know shit 'bout his case. I'm just sayin' that sometimes somebody who's there shouldn't be."

She meant herself, I thought, incredulous at how she could think she was anything but a winning argument for capital punishment.

Keppie exited the turnpike in Palm Beach, went east to the Atlantic Ocean, and drove along the beach. My eyes eagerly drank in the sight of endless blue water, always different, always the same. They had thirsted for that as much as my body had for water.

South Florida is more year-round playground now than winter resort. We cruised with Bentleys, Rolls-Royces, and BMWs, down Worth Avenue, past small elegant arcades and Mizner buildings with tiny passageways and exclusive shops tucked beneath the stairs, past French bistros with New York waiters wearing black tie and white aprons down to their ankles.

"This is my style," Keppie said, and parked at the marina. We strolled along the boat slips to see the lavish multimillion-dollar pleasure craft from all over the world and the old money elegance of the yachtsmen in whites and navy blazers.

"Let's go," Keppie said. "We got us some shopping to do. . . . Now, you listen," she warned, as she strapped Joey into his little harness. "I'm dead serious. You run off or cause any kinda commotion and he'll be with his daddy again quicker than this." She briskly snapped her fingers. "Wanna take responsibility for that, you just try me, girl."

"I understand," I said. "But why stop here? Why not just go on south?"

"Because I am in the mood to shop," she said.

The first sales clerk did not take us seriously until Keppie had her wrap up a $400 pair of designer cargo pants and a silky little $320 blouse that went with it.

The clerk snapped to attention.

We shopped a swath along the avenue where pampered pooches lap fresh water from tiled doggie bars while strolling with their owners. Keppie used credit cards and cash, stopping three times to hit ATM machines, as we loaded the car with shopping bags and boxes. Keppie gravitated to casual chic: Lily Pulitzer pastels that showed off her tanned legs and sang out that the wearer was not a tourista and a little fifteen-hundred-dollar Nantucket handbag that was dainty but large enough to accommodate a gun.

She kept Joey at her side. When his little harness raised eyebrows, she spoke sadly about his "disability."

"I have to keep him close by at all times," she explained, her sweet face troubled. "It's life-threatenin'. His seizures come on all of a sudden, just like that. I keep his medication right here." Patting her purse, she turned to me, smiling. "He's got my sister here to thank. Without her, he wouldn't be alive today."

Tomorrow, I thought, we'll be near Miami, on my turf. The advantage will be mine.

At a motel, we filled our small room with her newly purchased treasures, including a five-pound box of Godiva chocolates, a sterling silver comb and brush set, handbags, high heels, and little strappy sandals.

She had bought clothes for us all. Joey got cotton pjs in a puppy print and a three-piece ensemble: striped shirt, cotton pants, and a little fishing vest he would probably outgrow in weeks. We were Keppie's captive audience as she modeled the clothes, striking poses, flashing new diamond stud earrings and a gold bangle bracelet.

We bathed and dressed to go out. She fussed even more than usual with her hair and makeup; then we paraded to the car in our new clothes—on our way to dinner, I thought. Instead, Keppie drove to the big glassed-in convention center. On the marquee: 23RD ANNUAL ORCHID SHOW.

''Always wanted to see one-a these,'' she said, steering us to the box office.

Perfume and aftershave mingled with the delicate fragrance of thousands of species on display. Orchids everywhere, in every shade.

Only eighty miles from home, I scanned the crowd hoping to see a familiar face, while Keppie struck up a conversation with a stranger. The badge on his blazer identified him as a judge.

''Were you aware that orchids are the largest family of flowering plants in the world, with about twenty thousand species?'' he asked her.

I did not hear her response, but the flirtatious lilt to her laugh chilled my blood. I turned to stare, and my mouth dropped open. I wanted a familiar face, but not his. The classic profile and prematurely silver hair belonged to Sanford Rutherford DeWitt, grandson of a robber baron, heir to a vast fortune, a senator's son, a governor's brother, and a criminal defendant.

An oft-married playboy, DeWitt had been tried on a highly publicized rape charge three years earlier. The victim, a fledgling photographer at a little shiny sheet that covered Palm Beach high society, said he had invited her to photograph him at his mansion, where she was assaulted, overpowered, clothes torn, camera broken.

Inexperienced prosecutors had been blitzed by his flamboyant defense team. They claimed the act was consensual, that she liked rough sex and he had merely accommodated her. The jury acquitted.

"They embarrass me," Keppie tittered shyly. "I can't hardly bear to look at 'em." She erupted in a bubbly giggle. Was she blushing?

"Did you know," he said, demeanor distinguished, mellifluous voice sly, "that the word *orchid* is from the Greek word *orchis,* which means testicle? See the way some of the bulbs are shaped? And see there"—he gestured toward a display—"that bloom resembles a vagina."

"I thought I was the only one who saw that." Her shiny lips were wet. "I thought it was me! That I was oversexed."

The glitter in his eyes matched her own.

I scrutinized a yellow orchid surrounded by beefy dark green leaves. The thing did resemble a pelvis. I'd never noticed that before. Some blossoms were pristine and virginal, others swollen, bloated, and conspicuously sexual.

"Here's a phalaenopsis," he said, slowly and distinctly shaping each syllable. "It blooms for six weeks." He leaned forward and spoke intimately in her ear. Her diamond earring, bought with blood money from one of her victims, twinkled and winked under the artificial lights.

"Can't say that ain't stayin' power," she murmured seductively. She arched her back and brushed against him.

Good grief, I thought. Both predators; they deserved each other.

"Melody, Melody!" She caught my arm with girlish exuberance.

Melody? Did I look like a Melody?

"You hear what he just said?" She pointed to a display of baby plants, naked roots dangling. "Look at 'em, just look at 'em.'' Her cheekbones reddened. ''I can't stand it.''

''Hybrids, dendrobium,'' he said. ''See their little stamens and pistils?''

She gave a delightful little shriek. ''Oh, God! I can't take it. I love it when you talk dirty.''

Laughing, he barely glanced at me, so absorbed was he with Keppie.

What if I fled into the crowd, out of the building, and flagged down a patrol car? Would she dare hurt Joey in front of all these people?

Keppie turned, as though hearing my thoughts.

''This is my cousin, Melody,'' she told DeWitt, ''and her little boy, Joey.''

Joey gazed up, bewildered. He'd been talking less and less. Keppie whispered flirtatiously to DeWitt, her eyes meeting mine over his shoulder, the long fingers of her right hand curling around the nape of the child's neck. Stoic, the little boy blinked but never flinched.

She would do it. Joey would die for nothing, I told myself. We were so close to Miami and what I hoped was freedom. I believed she really was about to let us go.

''Here, this is it,'' DeWitt said, ''the one that looks the most like the female sex organ.'' He steered Keppie toward another booth, his hand at the small of her back. ''It's called the Dracula Vampira.''

''Oh, God!'' she gasped. ''My favorite!''

He stepped away briefly to confer with a matronly woman also wearing a judge's badge. ''Do you know who that is?'' I muttered to Keppie.

''I read the newspapers,'' she murmured. ''Ain't it a hoot?'' She glowed like a bride as he rejoined us. ''I 'member where I've seen you,'' she said, gazing up at him. ''Yes, you must be a yachtsman. I'm sure I saw you at the marina.''

He nodded, eyes relieved. ''I do have a little pleasure craft moored there. You like to cruise?''

"Oh, I'm dangerous out at sea. I feel so free and open, nothin' but sky and water—and the right person, a-course."

Her eyes shone expectantly.

"What about tomorrow?" she said. "I'd just love to see your . . . pleasure craft." The words fell from her lips like an obscene phrase.

A SWAT team could have swarmed the convention center, rounded up the usual suspects, and stomped every last obscene pistil and stamen to pulp beneath their boots and he would not have noticed.

"Come hungry," he said. "My chef will whip up something special."

"I'm always hungry," she murmured, licking her lips. He kissed her hand; their eyes locked.

"What about dinner?" I asked, as we climbed back into the SUV in the parking lot.

"We'll pick something up," she said absently and checked the time.

I unpacked the take-out chicken as Keppie parked in front of the TV. I had forgotten. Ira Jonas was to die tonight.

Candlelight marchers protested outside prison walls. They held hands and sang "We Shall Overcome."

"They're almost all relatives, pastors, and loved ones of Death Row inmates, people with an ax to grind," I commented.

Across the street, kept at a distance by deputies, death penalty supporters shouted insults and carried signs saying AN EYE FOR AN EYE, JUSTICE!, and REMEMBER THE VICTIMS.

"A lot of them are cops, relatives, or victims' rights advocates," I said.

Keppie didn't answer. Eyes glued to the screen, she sat cross-legged on the bed closer to the door, the gun tucked between her legs under a pillow she rested her elbows on, the tequila on her nightstand.

Her hits on the bottle became more frequent as a perky girl reporter did a live stand-up outside the prison disclosing the menu for the condemned man's last meal. He would not die hungry. He had ordered a dozen shrimp with cocktail sauce, rare prime rib, baked potato with sour cream, corn on the cob, and a hot fudge sundae.

"Sounds good," the solemn anchorman said, promising to return later for more live reports from the death watch.

Keppie peeled off her new clothes, carelessly tossing them into a corner, unlike her usual fastidious behavior. She paced the room in panties and a lacy bra, gun in one hand, bottle in the other, drinking, smoking, ignoring the weather and sports reports. Joey and I brushed our teeth and I tried to tell him a bedtime story, but, unnerved by her erratic pacing, I couldn't think of one.

"Tell me." He touched my cheek as we lay together on the bed.

"It's your turn," I said. "You tell me a story, sweetheart."

"Mommy is looking for me and Daddy," he began, as I cradled him in my arms. "She's crying 'cause she can't find us anywhere. The good angels are crying too. Their wings shine and they live in the blue water. They wanna save all the good boys and girls. But the bad angels hide in the woods. They have blood on 'em and they're strong. If you let 'em see your face, they kill you." He nodded solemnly. "They're fighting."

"And who wins in the end?" I asked.

"Nobody knows," he said.

I didn't remember fairy tales being that grim.

"Gimme your wrist." Cigarette smoke spiraled around Keppie as she stood over us.

"Do you have to do this?" I pleaded. "I'm not going to give you any problems. I've got enough to write the story now. We're almost finished."

She snapped the cuff around my wrist without answering, locked me to the grillwork of the ornate headboard, and took her seat for another live report from the prison.

"With no word from the governor," the anchorman said, "it appears as though the death sentence will be carried out on schedule tonight."

It was.

The lights dimmed, and a long slow sigh rose from the protesters. Supporters, still relegated to the far side of the street, cheered.

A department of corrections spokeswoman stepped into the TV lights to announce that the execution had proceeded smoothly, without a hitch. Jonas spoke no last words and was pronounced dead three and a half minutes after the first jolt of electricity.

The prison gates swung open minutes later and a white hearse glided into the dark, amid jeers and sweet voices raised in "Amazing Grace."

A death-chamber witness was interviewed, the victims' grandson, a boy who grew into manhood awaiting justice.

"I looked him right in the eye," he said. "He knew who I was. Our family finally has closure, tonight." I hoped they did.

"Why did they kill the man?" Joey asked. I didn't think he had been paying attention.

"Because he was bad," I said softly.

"Was my daddy bad?"

"No." I hugged him. "He wasn't bad, sweetheart. Sometimes bad things happen to nice people."

Keppie shot me a sharp look, pointed the remote, and abruptly turned off the TV, plunging the room into darkness. "Shut up and go to sleep," she said, words slightly slurred.

This was the first time I had seen her feel the liquor. It worried me that she was still walking around with the gun.

"Are you all right?" I asked.

"No. Life is shit, then you die."

"Other than that?"

"Scattered," she said, sounding weary. "I'm just scattered tonight." Her cigarette glowed in the dark. "I'm just fucking pissed."

"At who?"

"The whole fucking system that screwed me over."

I heard her take another hit from the bottle. She hadn't touched the food.

"There's chicken left," I said. "Why don't you eat something?"

"At least he got his goddamn last meal."

"Why did Jonas upset you?" My free hand groped for my notebook and pen.

"I goddamn guarantee you, I don't give a flying fuck about him." The cigarette flared. "See DeWitt tonight? Hot to trot, huh? Son of a bitch really raped that girl, didn't he?"

"Probably," I said quietly. "I believed her."

"Money and politics. See how fucked the system is? He walks free and my mother's in her grave."

"How did your mother die, Keppie?"

"I was just a little girl. Nothing I could do. She loved me."

"I'm sure she did. You must have been a beautiful child."

"Everybody says I take after her. Look just like her."

"What was her cause of death?"

"They took her from me."

"Was it sudden? How did she die?"

"The bastards took her."

"Who?"

"Said terrible things 'bout 'er. Just like all the things they say about me."

A chill swept my body.

"What did they say about her?" I whispered.

"All kindsa shit!" I heard the bottle. "Then they took her."

"What killed her?"

"Murdered. Somebody killed her."

"Oh my God, who?" This explained so much, I thought. The pain of a victim's child.

"They claimed it was one of the others. Nobody knows."

"What others?"

"They said she killed them; then one of the others killed her."

"Keppie?" The handcuffs rattled against the headboard as I sat up. "Tell me your mother's name."

"Rita Lee. Rita Lee Hutton."

I knew before she said it. "Oh my God," I said. "I know all about her."

"Fuck you. All you know is what you read in the damn newspapers."

I slumped back on my pillow, dizzy, as my head spun in the dark.

Sixteen

EVERYBODY KNEW ABOUT RITA LEE HUTTON. One of the few Florida women sentenced to Death Row, her story was splashed across front pages for years. I remembered the pictures. Her mug shot. The wedding portrait provided by tearful relatives. Tender photos of her and her baby daughter.

Rita Lee Hutton, a prim and pretty Gainesville housewife, dubbed the Black Widow by the press.

Despite the untimely and painful deaths of her husband, her tiny son, her father, an uncle, and her minister, the wholesome beauty was never a suspect until the demise of her new fiancé. She had nursed them all devotedly, slept in their hospital rooms, and kept vigil at their bedsides, hand feeding them her warm homemade soup and smooth egg custard. When the last death was diagnosed as arsenic poisoning, the other bodies were exhumed. All poisoned. She inherited minor amounts from some, but for most no motive existed. Prosecutors attributed it to pure evil. Jurors agreed.

The Black Widow was sentenced to death and relatives adopted her little daughter, changing her name.

Rita Lee Hutton never kept her date with Old Sparky, but she did die on Death Row, apparently strangled by another inmate. Rumors, never proven, hinted at sexual aggression and perversion.

Dr. Schlatter had actually mentioned the woman in one of our conversations.

"I had no idea she was your mother," I said, in a hushed tone.

"I'd think you'da figured it out by now," Keppie said bitterly.

Terror struck me. Was Lottie right? Are some people simply born evil? Is there a genetic propensity for violent behavior, a murder gene? For the first time, I thought it possible. The mother fed poison to males with whom she had relationships. The daughter used bullets.

Keppie's obsession with Old Sparky, which I had thought sprang from her own fears, was that of a little girl spinning fantasies about how she could have rescued the mother taken from her.

What a story! But would I live to write it? What about Joey? My stomach churned with fear for him. The more I understood Keppie, the more frightened I became. Her mother killed her husband, father, child, and lover with no signs of remorse.

What chance did we have?

When Keppie's regular breathing signaled at last that she was sleeping soundly, I took the ballpoint pen apart, removed the cartridge, and tried to pick the lock on the cuffs. Difficult in the dark, impossible when I dropped it. Stretched over the side of the bed, trying not to wake Joey, I groped the carpet for the cartridge. My fingertips brushed it, just out of my reach. When Keppie saw it, she would know.

I never slept. By morning only one thing was certain. Aware of the risks, I had refused good advice from people who cared and placed myself in jeopardy. But Joey was a total innocent swept up in this homicidal madness through no fault of his own. No matter what happened to me, I had to save him.

* * *

Keppie displayed no signs of a hangover or dulled reflexes; in fact she seemed surprisingly cheerful, given the night before. I found it impossible to look at her without seeing the old mug shots of her mother. They shared the cheekbones that could cut glass, the watercolor eyes, and cheerleader looks. In her daughter's face, Rita Lee Hutton must have seen herself looking back.

Alert as ever, Keppie spotted the twisted ballpoint cartridge on the floor.

"What's this?" She held it up.

I stared innocently. "Must be from my pen." I snatched up the empty shell from the nightstand, scrutinized it, and looked annoyed. "I thought I told him not to play with that."

Joey's eyes widened, mouth opening in protest.

"Let me get him into the bathroom," I said, and swung my legs over the side of the bed before he could speak.

Keppie unlocked the cuffs and stepped back, barefoot, watching me. I saw her examining the lock for scratch marks as I whisked him into the bathroom.

"I didn't—" he said.

"I know, baby. I know you didn't. You're such an excellent boy, you're so good." I hugged and kissed him, sat him on the side of the tub, and turned both water taps on full blast. "Now listen to me," I said softly. "It's very important. Are you listening?"

He nodded, with an apprehensive glance at the door, which stood ajar. "We're going in the car later, and when we get out I'm going to put you on the sidewalk, and then I want you to run, run away as fast you can. Don't stop. Promise me you'll do that?"

He nodded, wide-eyed.

"You look for a policeman. Tell everybody you need a policeman. Tell the policeman you were with Britt, tell him—"

"Wha'chu guys up to in here?" Keppie pushed the door wide and leaned against the frame, cigarette in hand, the gun in her waistband.

"I'm telling Joey we might go for a boat ride today. Think we might?"

"Could be." She regarded me thoughtfully. "Could be. Wha'chu doin' with the water?" she glanced at the open faucets.

"Running a tub, for a bath."

"You have to put the plug in first," she said.

She watched us every moment after that. My only other chance was when she called DeWitt at eleven. She laughed and chatted on the phone, sitting between us and the door, the gun in her lap.

"Remember, Joey," I whispered. "You run as fast as you can. You promised me."

"I will," he said.

" 'Bye, handsome," Keppie cooed to DeWitt. "See you then. Can't wait."

She didn't want to go out for breakfast, so we used the coffee maker in the room and nibbled rolls and butter left from our chicken dinners the night before.

"With all we talked about last night, I think we've just about wrapped it up." I tried to sound casual. "The tri-rail runs from here to Miami. Why don't you just put me and Joey on the train? And we'll be out of your hair. Then I can get back to the paper and start putting the story together."

She cocked her head, as if to say, You think I'm stupid? "Not yet, Britt. Not yet." She was painting her fingernails a rosy new shade called Pink Pleasure.

"Why not?"

Inspecting her handiwork, she frowned. "You know where I'm gonna be and who I'm gonna be with."

"You mean DeWitt? I won't say anything."

"Oh, right." She flashed me a dark look. "Just like you weren't gonna bring the cops in the first place. Screw me once, it's your fault. Twice, it's mine. Only way I can let you go is to do it when I got me a head start."

"How can we arrange that?"

"I'll think on it and let you know. Maybe I'm gettin' to like having you and the kid around. You know, breakin' up is hard to do." She grinned.

She would never let us go. When Joey was publicized as a missing child and no longer an asset, she'd kill him.

Keppie insisted we pack everything for her date with DeWitt.

"I always wanted to cruise the out islands," she said.

"I don't think that's what he has in mind," I said.

"We'll see."

No way could I let her take Joey on that boat, I thought. It is too easy to become lost forever out there, too easy for a body to be swept away in the Gulf Stream, that relentless river that rushes through the sea.

The marina was only minutes away. Keppie stopped in front of a row of newspaper racks as we arrived. I had to act now. Once Joey ran, I would stop her from firing the gun, try to take it away. If I had to shoot her to protect him, I would. She took the keys, as usual. As she fed quarters into the machines, I turned like a madwoman, lifted Joey free from his car seat, opened the door, and thrust him out onto the sidewalk.

"Run, Joey! Run!"

I slipped out and shoved him toward a corner teeming with pedestrians.

"Run!"

He did, for several steps, his Beanie Baby Scottie dog clutched under his arm. Then he stopped and looked around, bewildered. He turned, ran back, and threw his arms around my legs. My heart broke. He was too little, too lost. I was all he had in a world full of evil and sinister strangers. I sat down on the curb, hugging him, then glanced up apprehensively at Keppie.

"See, you are his mama now," she said cheerfully, her purse held in front of her so I could see the gun. "You best protect your baby."

* * *

Sanford DeWitt beamed at Keppie, looked a bit startled to see me, and was downright disheartened at the sight of Joey clinging to me tearfully. But he bounced right back. "My housekeeper will take good care of the boy back at my place while we take our little cruise and dine aboard the *Playtime*. She's great with kids. He'll have fun," he assured us, lowering his voice, "and be out of the way. My driver can take him."

"Great," I said quickly. Joey's life expectancy would be longer with strangers than with us.

"Oh, noooo." Keppie pouted sweetly. "The poor baby cries and carries on so when we try to leave him. He's been through too much lately. Melody and his daddy just split up. I hoped your boat might be big enough," she said, wide-eyed, "that we could put him down to sleep and still be alone. It is, isn't it?"

He smiled proudly. "That it is," he said. "See for yourself, the *Playtime*." He gestured, the flourish of a man unveiling a work of art.

The magnificent white vessel had to be more than a hundred feet long.

"Nice." Keppie tossed her hair flirtatiously, eyes meeting his. "We can take a trip around the world in that, can't we?"

"Indeed." He draped a tanned arm around her shoulder and planted a kiss on her forehead. "Let me take you aboard, show you around. Now, no high heels, right?" He made a point of checking out our legs. "The decks are teak," he explained. "Just had them redone."

"Is that a—"

"Yep, a helicopter pad," he said. "A jet ranger, out being serviced at the moment."

Keppie flashed me a triumphant look. "We were just talkin' 'bout choppers the other night," she drawled sweetly.

Keppie's belongings were carried aboard by a crew member and stowed in a handsome stateroom with its own bath. She told DeWitt we were changing hotels and didn't want to leave them in the car.

The *Playtime* had all the comforts of a rich man's home: gleaming woodwork, highly polished brass, expensive art, antique furniture, a large-screen entertainment center, and softly playing mellow jazz.

"How big is your crew?" I asked.

"Normally seven," DeWitt said. "But I'm making an exception today. Thought a little privacy might be nice. After some help casting off, only the captain and I will be aboard. We'll putt-putt about a little bit, have dinner, maybe catch a little moonlight later, and who knows?" He gazed into Keppie's eyes, his arm around her slender waist. "When we're ready to come back in, Rudy'll radio ahead so we have crew waiting."

Rudy, the captain, was ruddy-faced and rugged-looking. Middle-aged, with a German accent and pale eyes and hair, he wore a perpetual frown. How many of these romantic little cruises had he participated in? I wondered.

"Hope you girls brought your bathing suits," DeWitt said, as the *Playtime* motored away from the dock.

"Bathing suit?" Keppie hooted. A sea breeze lifted her hair as she leaned back against the rail. "I never wear one." She winked at DeWitt. "Best way to swim in the ocean is just git naked and dive in."

"Seems like your answer to everything is just get naked," I murmured.

"Try it sometime," she said. "You don't know what you're missin'."

The sea was brilliant turquoise, the clear sky a perfect blue. Longingly, I watched the shoreline recede through the porthole of the room with our luggage, where I tried to coax Joey into a nap.

Losing sight of land scared me. Soon there were voices and a rap at the door.

Both held champagne glasses; DeWitt had brought one

for me. They insisted I join them on deck for canapés. A small round table draped in linen had been set with china, napkins, and a tray: Boursin cheese and granulated peanuts with a grape garnish, bay scallops with basil cream cheese, and dried apricots with rum cream cheese and macadamia nuts.

Keppie bounced all over the *Playtime*, bubbly and energetic, flattering, flirting, and curious, as DeWitt and the captain demonstrated the sophisticated navigational, radar, and radio equipment and explained how charts are read.

They didn't see that she was too eager to learn. They loved it. We saw other boaters less frequently as we moved into deep water. Though busy, Rudy seemed less sullen, his sidelong glances hinting that I might be the reason. Were we expected to pair off? A good idea. Alone, I could persuade him to radio for police and the Coast Guard. I returned his looks with a smile. These men had no idea of the company they were keeping, I thought. Once they knew, they'd be less arrogant.

The fiery summer sunset painted the water a shimmering gold with blood-red rivulets. Nature's dramatic beauty added to my fears of the dark at sea.

Lights approached from the south and the captain stepped out of the pilot house to inform DeWitt, who used a pair of high-powered binoculars.

"The Coast Guard," he said, "is paying us a visit."

A blue strobe light began to spin as the craft drew closer. My heart pounded crazily as we were hailed.

"United States Coast Guard! Stand aside and prepare for boarding!"

"What do they want?" Keppie asked quietly.

"Routine inspection," DeWitt said. "No problem."

My spirits soared.

"I'm going down below, to be with Joey," Keppie said abruptly. "I don't want him alone."

"No, I'll go," I said.

"No, Melody. You stay here and rest easy, knowin' I'm

with him.'' She drew her index finger across her slender throat as she brushed by, a small gesture that froze me where I stood.

The patrol boat, a 41-foot cutter, drew alongside. I held my breath. DeWitt had slipped into his navy blazer. He waved and picked up a battery-powered hailer.

''Ahoy, lieutenant!'' His voice boomed across the water. ''Sandy DeWitt here! How goes it, protecting our borders?''

I stared imploringly toward the uniformed men on the cutter's deck.

''Sorry, sir, didn't recognize your vessel at first. You haven't seen a leaky boatload of Haitians, have you?''

''Not yet. We'll be on the horn to you if we do.''

''Thank you, sir. Carry on.'' The friendly guardsman saluted and waved. The cutter pulled to port, then into a 90-degree turn, its wake trailing like a rooster tail in the water.

Sandy waved back, smiling.

''Listen to me,'' I said urgently. ''This is serious. Can you—''

''Melody?'' Keppie interrupted. ''Joey doesn't look so good.'' She stepped gracefully out on deck, purse in hand. ''You better have a look at 'im.''

''Nothing to worry about,'' DeWitt called after me, as I flew down the spiral staircase to the stateroom. ''It was just routine. They know me. . . . Seeing the Coast Guard upset Melody,'' he said, turning to Keppie.

Joey sat whimpering on the bed, legs spraddled in front of him, hands clutching his throat.

''Are you all right, honey? What's the matter?'' I gently pulled his hands away and gasped. A scratch stretched ear to ear, the skin barely broken by the tip of a razor-sharp knife. A warning, to show what she could and would do.

I scrambled to the porthole to see our last hope of rescue vanish on the horizon.

Seventeen

THE PUSH OF A BUTTON RAISED A DINNER TABLE out on deck, as a crescent moon climbed the sky. We were anchored in forty feet of water about a mile offshore. Stars shone clear and bright as our hair ruffled in the sultry summer breeze and candles flickered behind the protective glass of hurricane lanterns.

My heart and stomach ached. I filled a plate with hors d'oeuvres for Joey—mushroom quiche, lobster in crispy phyllo triangles, miniature Beef Wellington in puff pastry—took it down, found him asleep, left it, and went back up on deck.

The captain served, then joined us at the exquisitely appointed table, with bone china, elegant silver service, crystal champagne glasses, and Dom Perignon on ice. Salad, a main course of Chateaubriand, then crème brûlée, its satiny heart hidden beneath a sweet crisp crust.

I had no appetite. I had trouble swallowing, drank some wine, then wanted more. I resisted the sudden desire to drown my fear and stress. Blood would be shed tonight. I had to keep my senses if I didn't want it to include mine.

My panic escalated as Keppie prattled about cruising the remote islands of the Bahamas and the Caribbean. No one would search for her there, I thought.

The predators grew more amorous; he sensuously sucked crème brûlée from her fingers, then her lips. Their foreplay did not go unnoticed by Rudy, who got into the spirit of things and fondled my knee under the table.

Keppie discarded her blouse as she and Sandy DeWitt merged into a single lounge chair. Silver moonlight glinted off her bare breasts. Their laughter subsided into more intimate sounds, and I knew how this night would end.

"No, no," I heard him protest good-humoredly at one point. "No way can we head out to the islands tonight. We'll be back in port by dawn. We still have plenty of time."

The captain and I remained at the table. As Sandy tossed his shirt aside, I removed Rudy's hand from my thigh and gripped it tightly. "You have to stop them," I whispered urgently. "She's dangerous. She's a killer. You—"

He held up one hand like a bored traffic cop who has heard it all. "I know you're jealous," he said earnestly. "You have to learn to live with it."

"Shit. Listen to me. Go call the police, the Coast Guard, now."

"The Coast Guard was here." He spoke with the exaggerated patience of a doctor who deals with the deranged. "Why didn't you say something then?"

"Because she would have killed Joey."

He rolled his eyes skyward as if to lament being stuck with the crazy one. "Keppie told us about your problems, especially when you drink. Did you take your medication?"

"Oh, for God's sake," I muttered. "You've heard of the Kiss-Me Killer. That's her!"

"Yes, and I am Carlos the Jackal."

He thrust his hand under my blouse and squeezed my breast hard, as though his rude advance might dispel my madness and hallucinations.

I pushed him away. "Somebody's going to die tonight!" I whispered.

A shadow appeared in the doorway. Rudy cursed under his breath and lurched to his feet, breathing hard.

"Mommy?" Joey stood there, sleepy-eyed.

"It's me, honey, Britt." He ran to me.

"I had a bad dream," he said, clinging to me. "I woke up and you weren't there."

"I'm here now."

"The bad angels came out of the woods. . . ."

I held him and stroked his hair.

"Let's take a walk." I steered him briskly away from the lounge, where Keppie straddled Sanford Rutherford DeWitt in a precoital embrace.

Rudy discreetly disappeared below deck as Joey and I walked around the side of the yacht, out of sight.

I heard intimate laughter and a moan of pleasure, aware of what would follow. We stood at the starboard rail, staring at the shoreline. Night had fallen. The sky was a diamond-studded vault overhead. We had cruised south from Palm Beach. The lights of what I thought might be the Hollywood Beach Hotel glimmered in the distance. So near, yet so far. Then, across the water, carried by sea breezes, came soft, gently musical sounds. Straining my eyes in the darkness, I saw nothing. But I heard it. I knew it was there. And I knew what it meant. I had to seize our last slim chance. Now or never. I snatched a seat cushion from a deck chair and stepped over the rail. I braced myself, reached back across, and swept him up in my arms.

"I love you, Joey," I whispered, clinging to the railing with one hand. "Don't be afraid. I'll take care of you." Holding him tight, I let go and jumped.

We hit the water feet first, down, down, as though we would never stop. I let him go for a moment to try to stop our descent, then fought my way to the surface, groping wildly for him. He surfaced, choking and sputtering, a few feet away. Trusting and brave, he never cried out.

"Hold on to me," I told him. "No, no, not like that." He thrashed in panic, lunging at my neck with a death grip, pulling us both under.

I held him away from me, treading water. "You have to help me, Joey," I gasped, spitting out seawater. "You have to kick and paddle. We have to get away."

He clung to my belt as I tried to get my bearings. The cushion bobbed nearby. I caught it and tried to slide it under him like a belly board. "Hold on," I said; "now, kick, kick." We swam for our lives, his hand on my shoulder, toward the sounds I had heard, toward shore. I stopped to catch my breath and glance back at the *Playtime*. No hint of alarm.

Desperately searching the black water, I saw nothing but darkness, unable even to discern where heaven and the sea met. Had I been hallucinating? I was a strong swimmer, but when I stopped to rest and tread water, I heard only the sea. The shoreline seemed no closer as the current swept us north. The lights of the *Playtime* were barely visible in the distance. Almost imperceptibly, the wind had begun to pick up speed and the waves became more choppy.

Joey began to choke and gag. "Spit it out, spit it out," I gasped. We had both swallowed too much seawater already. I swam toward shore again as powerfully as I could. When I had to stop once more to catch my breath, we seemed no closer. I remembered the dead Cubans, eight men and women who died of hypothermia in these same offshore waters when their small craft capsized, but that was December when water temperatures were in the 50s. Tonight the sea was a warm bath with more frightening prospects. Tiger sharks and hammerheads frequent these heated waters. Weeks earlier a shark had killed a small boy, bitten him in two, as he played in full sight of his parents in the shallow surf off Vero Beach.

I wanted to weep but could not spare the strength. Should we have remained aboard, safe at least for the moment? Then I remembered the Texas Death Row escapee and Keppie's words. He died trying, on his own terms, not when his captors decided it was time.

But Joey, I thought, gasping, eyes burning. How unfair to him. From time to time, I rolled over to float on my back. Each time he panicked because he had to readjust his grip on me. The night was beautiful. We could see the constellations. A thunderstorm rumbled and lightning flashed to the east, far out at sea, its energy kicking up the surface of the water. I hoped to God it wouldn't come our way. Mechanically, I swam, treaded water, and listened, swam, floated, and listened, swam, treaded water. Could I keep us afloat till dawn? I didn't think so. Even if we survived the night, no one was searching. Who would find us?

The threatening thunderstorm blew by to the south. I thought of my mother, McDonald, Lottie, and Mrs. Goldstein. Would anyone ever know what happened to me? If our bodies were found, they would think we were refugees, lost at sea. Would they examine the labels in our clothes and realize they were purchased days earlier in Palm Beach? My fingerprints were on file, but how would they ever identify Joey?

My throat burned and my sinuses seemed about to explode. Joey was sputtering, swallowing more water. To my horror I found that the cushion had lost its buoyancy. Waterlogged like us, it was about to sink. Exhausted, strength spent, my entire body ached. I couldn't stay afloat much longer. Where were they, the voices I had heard? A wave broke over our heads. Blinded, choking, and gagging on saltwater, I opened my eyes and there he was. Still with me after all. *Estamos juntos*. My father's naked skin glistened in the waves, his open arms beckoning. I struck out toward him, but he was gone. Then like an answered prayer, I heard them again, the gentle sound of voices speaking softly in patois, Haitian boat people, illegal aliens in a quest for freedom, trying like us to survive in a sea of night.

Their boat creaked in the water close by as I floundered. "Help us," I choked, spitting out water. "Please."

A woman cried out in fear and dismay. Frightened voices began to babble.

"Help," Joey cried out.

A weak flashlight beam splashed onto the water near us. "Here!" I begged weakly. "Here."

Then the light, weak as it was, found us. Hushed discussions, arguments, angry, frightened debate followed. At the end, they did not leave us. They tried to help. Their leaky, overloaded boat was too crowded to take us both aboard. Two people were already bailing with rusted pails. But a woman did reach out and drag Joey in, amid protests from her companions.

"Mommy! Mommy!" he cried weakly. Somebody threw me a line, a frayed rope to which I clung.

After more than an hour, my feet touched bottom. Eyes watering, I thanked God. Men, women, and children leaped from the rickety wooden vessel, splashed ashore, fled up a sandy beach, and scattered into the darkness. I staggered several steps and collapsed sobbing, slumped in the shallows.

"Britt!" Joey cried.

I crawled forward, onto the sand where they had left him. Gazing back at the dark sea and limitless horizon, I realized with awe what a miracle it was that we were alive. Mind reeling, I stared in disbelief at the lights, the familiar skyline. We had landed at the southernmost tip of Miami Beach. I was home, home at last! Overcome by relief and exhaustion, I gave in to the urge to rest. Only for a moment, I thought, as Joey curled up on the soft sand beside me.

Powerful lights in my eyes woke me. "They're alive!" somebody shouted. "Call rescue and INS!"

Two burly Miami Beach cops were dragging the rickety boat out of the surf up onto the beach. "*¿De donde eres?* Where are you from?" demanded the one shining the light into my eyes. "*¿De donde eres?*"

I blinked up at him, disoriented. "*The Miami News*," I said.

Eighteen

"WE'RE SAFE NOW," I TOLD JOEY IN THE AMBULANCE. "These people will take care of us."

He struggled when we were separated in the emergency room. "No! No! Stay with me, Britt! Stay with me!"

I hugged him and kissed his cheek. "It's all right," I said. "It's just for a little while. I'll be close by. They just want to make sure we're okay." I appealed to a nurse. "He's been through so much," I said. "Please . . ."

She smiled. "Don't worry. We'll take good care of him."

"How is she? Where is she?"

I heard McDonald's voice. Was he a dream? No, he was real, standing over me, lean and long-legged, strong jaw, cleft chin, his silvery blue eyes filled with concern.

"Hey, Brenda Starr."

I reached out for him, aware I looked awful, eyes red, lips swollen, wearing a paper gown they gave me in the emergency room. He didn't seem to notice.

"I thought I'd never see you again," I croaked, my voice raspy, throat raw from swallowing seawater. I wept as we hugged. "You were right. I'm so sorry, so sorry."

He shook his head and held my face tenderly in his

hands. He looked exhausted, tears in his eyes. "I was wrong not to stop you," he said. "I never should have let you do it."

"But I wouldn't listen. . . ."

"I should have kidnapped you myself." He held me, stroked my hair, kissing my forehead. I was home at last.

"Joey," I murmured against his shoulder. "The little boy; we have to call his mother. You won't believe who the killer is. I know her name. I know where she is."

Urgent voices and sounds, the crackle and static of police radios, came from the other side of the curtain. "I hate to do this," McDonald said, "but I have to leave you for a while now. The detectives need to talk to you right away. Later." He gently kissed my lips. "Welcome home, love."

"I tried so hard to get back to you," I said tearfully.

"Well, you sure took your time." He winked, our eyes connected, and he was gone.

Ojeda and Simmons, two prosecutors, and some other cops were already there. I filled them in fast, between tears and hugs from my mother and Lottie, who arrived minutes later, followed by Fred Douglas, my editor, and Mark Seybold, the paper's lawyer.

The detectives worked fast, hoping to save DeWitt. Efforts to raise the *Playtime* by radio and cell phone failed. Because the yacht was equipped with multichannel radio and satellite television and Keppie was a news junkie, the paper agreed to temporarily withhold the news that we had been found. That gave police and the Coast Guard time to launch an intense air and sea search. If she believed we'd drowned, she would not alter her plans, vague though they were.

When I asked to see Joey, Ojeda said the Division of Children and Family Services was taking him into protective custody until his mother arrived.

"No," I objected. "I can't let strangers take him away. It's not—"

"That's how the system is set up," Ojeda said. "Work with us here, Britt."

"Well, then, I have to see him, to explain and say goodbye," I insisted.

A caseworker had already left the hospital with him, they said.

I burst into bitter tears. "He'll think I abandoned him," I grieved. "He saw his father murdered. He was taken by strangers. How could you let strangers take him again?"

"There was no alternative. Now let's focus, we're working against time," the detective said impatiently. "Nothing about this whole thing has been easy on anybody."

"Well, where the hell were you?" I demanded of Ojeda. "You promised nothing would go wrong! Why did you let any of this happen?"

"Shit happens," he said. "We don't have time to go into that now. You need to help us."

He was right. I wanted nothing more than to see them stop Keppie.

Debriefing for hours, they bombarded me, repeating the same questions over and over.

They took me home that afternoon. The T-Bird was being held as evidence. Still numb, I was greeted by Mrs. Goldstein with open arms, chicken soup, and chocolate chip cookies. Bitsy was beside herself. Even Billy Boots abandoned his usual aloof feline demeanor and came running, tail straight up. Thrilled to see them, to be surrounded by things familiar, and to be alone at last, I wanted to kiss the floor. My bed and soft comforter beckoned, but I showered and changed to drive a borrowed car to police headquarters to make official statements under oath, in the cases in which I had direct knowledge.

Before I did so, flowers arrived from McDonald. The loving card did not say *I told you so*. It moved me, but my thoughts were with Joey. Did he think I had deserted him?

I worked with the police and the Coast Guard, poring

over maps, downloading all I could remember. My notebook was at sea somewhere, still aboard the *Playtime*, along with Joey's Beanie Baby. I could still hear him asking for it on the way to the hospital.

They found the SUV parked where I told them Keppie had left it. But they did not find her, the *Playtime*, or the missing playboy. The Coast Guard search, called off at dusk, resumed at dawn.

Joey's mother would arrive in Miami the following afternoon. Detectives and a child psychologist had spoken with him. He did well for someone so young, they said, corroborating much of what I had told them.

He and his mother were to be reunited in the chief's office, where pictures would be taken. City officials like to take pictures at positive events, they are so rare. I asked to be present.

I arrived early. Joey ran to me, the only familiar face in the room. "Britt! Britt!" he called and climbed gleefully into my lap. I held him tight.

"I will always remember you," I whispered in his ear. "Your mommy is coming to take you home today. I love you, Joey." No time to say more.

A woman's voice resounded in the corridor. "Where is he? Where is he?"

Joey slid from my lap, eyes wide.

She burst in, a pretty, plumpish bottle blonde.

He stood shyly for a moment, then rushed across the room. "That's my mommy! My mommy!"

"Thank you, Saint Jude," she cried, sweeping him up in her arms. "Thank you, Saint Jude, for answering my prayers, for bringing back my baby!"

She spun him around, her eyes squeezed shut, expression ecstatic.

"When they didn't call every night like his daddy promised, I knew something was terribly wrong. I was sure Jeffrey had kidnapped him, that I would never see my baby again, so I prayed to Saint Jude, the help of the hopeless. I knew Saint Jude would bring him back. He saved my baby!"

I watched without a word. There was so much I wanted to say, but she took her son and left. I wanted to run after them, to remind her not to let him ride a bicycle without a helmet, to warn him never to talk to strangers, to make her aware of all the trauma he had suffered, and to tell her what a brave and good child he was.

I didn't. He gazed at me from over her shoulder, her lipstick smeared on his cheek, his brown eyes solemn as they went out the door. That was the last I saw of him.

I went back to the office, surprised by my sense of loss. Ignoring the stares, I went to the wire room and stood at a counter, wondering where Keppie was as I leafed through the newspapers published in my absence. I needed to become grounded again, to get back to business.

The planet had continued to spin in my absence. Life in Miami had continued at its usual frenetic pace. There is no business like the news business to make you aware of how insignificant any one individual's pain or tragedy is in the grand scheme of things.

The Marlins lost. Liberty City drug wars killed four. A man burned to death when an irate ex-lover torched his apartment. Robbers killed an unidentified woman on the street. Police cars racing to a call startled a motorist who assumed they were chasing him. He panicked, pulled over, leaped out, and ran. He made it safely across two lanes. A semi nailed him in the third.

Our justice team of reporters had finally made the front page with the investigative piece they had worked on for months, a probe into possible bribery and jury tampering in a major drug case. A tipster told the reporters and the FBI that the jury foreman had received a quarter of a million dollars to guarantee no conviction, with a hundred-thousand-dollar bonus for acquittal. The accused drug kingpin had been found not guilty. The jury foreman spent lavishly after the trial, despite a modest salary. His former girlfriend admitted he had brought the cash home in a satchel, saying it was payment for his work. A grand jury was now calling in his fellow jurors for testimony. I turned the page. Wait a minute. I went back to the story. Didn't Althea serve on that jury?

I carried the papers back to my desk. My messages included several from her, some from the day I left. That seemed so long ago. The most recent was marked URGENT: *I pray you are all right and come home safe, Britt. I know why now. I know the motive. Please call me.*

Was her sudden revelation linked to the investigation? But how? I scanned the newsroom for members of the investigative team. None in sight. I dialed Althea's number. No answer. For a woman who wanted help, she was as difficult to reach as ever.

I continued thumbing through the papers, right up until that morning's final. Local section brieflys included a three-year-old drowned in the family pool, new drug death statistics from the medical examiner, and the name of the woman killed two days earlier in a street robbery.

The lines leaped off the page as though in bold-faced type.

> Althea Albury Moran, an Orange Bowl queen in the early 1970s, has been identified as the victim shot to death in an apparent random robbery after leaving Jackson Memorial Hospital following a day of volunteer work.

I reread it, reaching instinctively for the telephone to redial her number.

It rang, but I knew she wouldn't be there. Ever.

I called her daughter.

"Jamie, this is Britt, from the *News*. I just saw the story. What happened?"

"Are you all right?" She sounded bewildered. "I didn't know you were back."

"What happened?"

"We don't know." Her voice broke.

"What happened?" I demanded, my voice rising.

"The other reporters were already here," she said.

"What other reporters?"

"From your paper." She sobbed.

So did I.

I washed my face in the ladies' room and looked for Fred. His office was empty.

"I need to talk to him, it's important," I told Bobby Tubbs at the city desk. "Where is he?"

"In a meeting with the justice team," he said. "Looks like somebody murdered a major witness in their bribery case. Glad you're back, Britt."

I crashed the meeting. An investigative reporter had called Althea days earlier. She had acknowledged being the last holdout for guilty during deliberations. The foreman's high-pressure persuasion had changed the guilty votes of several other jurors, and he had finally talked her into making it unanimous. As she and the reporter talked, she had recalled overhearing the foreman's side of a phone call he had made. He had seemed upset that she did, but she didn't think it important at the time. Apparently it was.

The reporters arranged to tape an interview at her home. Althea was not there. An FBI agent's card was in the door, with a note asking her to call him. She did not.

She was already in the morgue, ambushed and shot to death as she left the hospital.

"Looks like she didn't understand the significance of what she overheard, but the suspect apparently thought she did," said Joe Bloss, the hefty bearded investigative reporter who led the team. "When he heard the FBI was investigating him, he must have thought she tipped them off. He apparently took out a hit on her with a couple of two-bit lowlifes he met in a bar.

"One is talking, and it looks like there may be murder indictments by the end of the week. Helluva story," he said. "We're running with it tomorrow."

"Britt?" Fred interrupted. "You knew about these other attempts on Althea Moran's life?"

"Yes. I looked into it, talked to her, went out to her house. I've got a whole file I put together—"

"Then the city desk knew about this?" He scowled, perplexed.

"No. I didn't mention it to the desk. I didn't know . . . the cops didn't believe her and I wasn't sure. Then the Kiss-Me Killer story broke and I got sidetracked."

"Too bad," Fred said gravely. "We've had the jury list for weeks. We discussed it at news meetings. Her name would have rung a bell."

I saw the looks they exchanged.

"You know it's standard policy for reporters to keep the desk informed of everything they're working on," Fred said, his eyes cold.

"Nobody knows that better than I do—now." I swallowed hard. "I'm sorry."

I blamed everybody, myself the most, then the police, Althea's relatives, even the World War II vet with rheumy eyes and a thirst for cheap wine, spinning lies about killing enemy soldiers, self-absorbed and totally unaware of how the threads wound in the skein of our actions can disrupt the fabric of a stranger's life. Had it not been for him, I would not have been as skeptical. I had been so absorbed with my own image and chasing the bigger story that I had failed her.

Sanford Rutherford DeWitt was found that afternoon, aboard the *Playtime*'s lifeboat, afloat off Walker's Cay in the Bahamas. Naked, he had been shot like the others. A predator himself, he'd been no match for Keppie. She, the yacht, and the captain were still missing.

We broke the story, identifying her to the world at last,

Keppie Lee Hutton, serial killer, the daughter of one of Death Row's most infamous inmates. I attended Althea's funeral that afternoon.

Keppie's story launched a media frenzy unlike any since the Versace case. Now, along with the police and the FBI, a rabid press trailed her wake.

Searchers found the body of Joey's dad with the help of dogs. They continued to search for the unidentified remains of the man she called Stanley. Mary Alice and Harland Travis, the aunt and uncle who had raised Keppie, were besieged, their modest upstate home surrounded by microphones, sound trucks, and network correspondents. I opted to remain in Miami, piecing together new developments for the main story each day.

A Navy plane en route to the torpedo testing range in the deep trough just east of Andros Island spotted a burning vessel adrift at sea. The burning boat was later identified as the *Playtime*. No sign of Keppie or the captain. However, a vacationing schoolteacher from Massachusetts and his fifty-two-foot sloop were reported missing a short time later from a nearby island.

I jumped each time the phone rang. It would never end for me until she was found, I knew that now.

My updated map had red pushpins all the way out into the Bahamas like the twisting path of some killer storm or other freak of nature. I painstakingly reconstructed our interviews and continued to anchor the breaking story.

The missing teacher reappeared, shot dead on the sandy beach of one of the small islands that freckle the Caribbean east of St. Martin, where a wealthy retiree and his forty-one-foot trawler were reported overdue by anxious relatives.

The big story I had wanted was all mine. But it had lost its appeal. Curiously repelled, too emotionally involved, I was loath to face the questions in the eyes and on the lips of other reporters.

When Keppie was finally arrested, using Sandy De-

Witt's American Express Card in Barbados, the press corps descended on its capital city of Bridgetown. I was not among them. The *News* sent Janowitz.

Eager to escape the islands, where executions are by hanging and the steps to the gallows do not take twelve to fifteen years, she waived extradition. With jurisdictional problems in their cases, island authorities were willing to see her tried first in Florida. Brought back in manacles and leg irons, Keppie looked unperturbed at the airport, smiling flirtatiously and laughing intimately with her armed escorts. I watched her on TV and studied the newspaper photos.

Keppie had noted my absence from the media mob scenes and asked for me, Janowitz said.

Being back on the job was good for me. I turned my files and interview notes with Althea over to the justice team. They did not invite me to join their growing coverage of the crimes that resulted in her murder. I didn't blame them.

McDonald took me out to dinner after my annual evaluation by Fred. Both Althea's story and that of the Kiss-Me Killer figured prominently in Fred's analysis of my job performance at the *News*.

"I'm surprised he wasn't even harder on me," I said, picking at my salad. "I never should have become so involved in the murder investigation. I should have reported the story, not become a part of it; that was my mistake. I didn't listen to people who knew better."

"What did he write in the evaluation?" McDonald asked. "How tough was he?"

"He rated me high in initiative and enterprise and good in writing skills," I said, "but flunked me as a team player. We agreed that I have to work harder to build a closer relationship with the desk, keep them informed, and remember that reporters do not work alone or make their own judgments. I have to check in with the desk several times a day and write memos about everything I'm working on,'' I said. ''It's penance, even though, I swear, I've learned the lesson: Life is a team effort.''

''Been meaning to talk to you about that,'' he said, his smile sly. I felt the sizzle as our eyes met.

''Don't try sweeping me off my feet,'' I warned, as he poured wine into my glass. ''You might succeed. And nobody knows better than me that it's not always good to get what you wish for.''

''I'll go slow,'' he promised, ''and sneak up on you.''

I dream of Joey often and still reel from the more important lesson that has forever changed me. Having seen it myself, I know now that evil is real, that some people are born with a dark genetic defect, difficult to diagnose and impossible to fix. I believe in the murder gene.

My dreams about Joey are always the same. We are together, struggling to survive in a black sea where the sounds of the waves are screams, the smells are gunpowder and blood, and a battle rages. Dark angels engage in fierce combat against bright angels from the blue water. I awake with a prayer that the angels with wings of light will prevail.

Nearly a month after her return, Keppie's court-appointed lawyer called.

''Everybody wants to interview her,'' he told me, ''from Larry King to Geraldo to Barbara Walters. I've strongly advised her against it—but she wants to talk to you.''

I am too busy on other stories, I said. Weeks later, working late one night, I picked up my telephone and heard a familiar voice.

''Hey there, Britt. I've got a story for ya. When you comin' to interview me again?''

Her words sent a shudder through me. ''I think we did enough interviewing,'' I said.

''Look, I'd come out and meetcha somewhere, but we been there, done that, and I'm kinda tied up at the moment.'' She chortled. ''Why don'cha come on over here? You know you miss me, babe. Said yourself you always have more questions. Come on,'' she coaxed. ''You're the only person I know in Miami, 'cept for that little prick of a lawyer they gave me. Dumb little son of a bitch. He's scared to sit in the same room with me. How the hell am I gonna get a fair trial? When you come,'' she added confidently, ''bring a coupla packsa Benson and Hedges.''

The jail was noisy, as always. Slams of metal on metal resounded like gunshots as electric locks were opened and closed from an elevated control room. They searched me, took my purse, and led me to a private visitor's cubicle divided by a wire mesh screen. I sat on a wooden chair, waiting for her to be brought in. Two corrections officers and a supervisor escorted her. Her face lit up when she saw me. She wore a pink jumpsuit, identifying her as a high-risk inmate, unlike the drab attire worn by other prisoners. Pink was a good color for her; it picked up her rosy complexion. She glowed.

''How ya been, babe?'' She greeted me casually. ''Looking good.'' She leaned in close to the screen to peer at me. ''Too bad there's no touchin','' she murmured, ''but we had us some good ol' times, didn't we?'' She smiled, with a lascivious wink at a corrections officer, a middle-aged woman who remained stoic.

Her restless energy, vivacious edge, and raw sexuality had not been dulled by captivity. Even the jail food she had dreaded seemed to agree with her. Her slim frame had filled out a bit.

''I gave them the cigarettes to give you,'' I said.

''Thank you, ma'am,'' she said cheerfully. ''Thought you were dead, but you made it back. Little Joey, too. What'd I tell you? We could be sisters, you and me, we're so much alike. Survivors, that's us.''

''If I were you,'' I said quietly, ''I wouldn't count on

staying a survivor. You're looking at the death penalty from a dozen different directions.''

''Aww, Britt.'' She shook her head at my silliness. ''They won't 'lectrocute me. Who would sentence a pregnant woman, a young mother-to-be, to death?'' She leaned back in her chair and fondly patted her stomach.

I stared.

''True fact. Can't wait to be a mama.''

''Who's the father?'' I whispered.

''Damned if I know.'' She gave an exaggerated shrug. ''Maybe Sonny. Coulda been Joey's daddy, or that pretty boy, that model on South Beach. Hell, doesn't matter.''

Another child, I thought, who will grow up without a father, with a mother behind bars.

''Nobody's gonna send the lovin' mother of a little baby to the 'lectric chair. And, if they do''—she shrugged again—''at least I've left somethin' behind. A little part of me will still be here. I can feel it,'' she drawled. ''It's a mother's instinct. I know it's a girl. . . .

''I'll still be around,'' she called as I left. ''One way or the other, I'll be back.''

Acknowledgments

I am grateful to the usual suspects, consultants, generous friends, and co-conspirators: the brilliant Dr. Joseph H. Davis, Marilyn Lane, Arthur Tifford, Ann Hughes, D. P. Hughes, Ruthey Golden, Reneé Turolla, Gay Nemeti, Marie Reilly, Miami Police Lieutenant Gerald Green, Officer Eladio Paez, John Wolin, Dr. Valerie Rao, Sam Terilli, Arnold Markowitz, Cynnie Cagney, Charlotte Caffrey, Bill and Amalia Dobson, Dennis Vebert, Karen and Bill Sampson, and Steve Waldman; to my editor, Carrie Feron, and my agent, Michael Congdon. All of them, the best and brightest.

If You Enjoyed *Garden of Evil,*
Then Sample the Following Selection from

YOU ONLY DIE TWICE

The new Britt Montero Novel
by Edna Buchanan

HOT SAND SIZZLED BENEATH MY FEET. AN END-less turquoise sea stretched into infinity. Bright sailboats darted beyond the breakers, their colors etched against a flawless blue sky. Playful ocean breezes kissed my face, lifted my hair off my shoulders and ruffled my skirt around my knees. The day was to die for. Too bad about the corpse bobbing gently in the surf.

Her hair was long and honey colored, streaked by brilliant light as it swirled like something alive just beneath the water's glinting surface. She seemed serene, a full breasted, narrow waisted mermaid, with long slim legs, an enchanting gift from the deep.

I wondered if she had been caught by the rip current, that fast-moving jet of water racing back to the sea, or did she tumble from a cruise ship or a party boat? Perhaps she was a tourist unaccustomed to the sharp drop off only a few feet from shore. But if so, why was she naked?

She was no rafter drowned in a quest for freedom, a new life, or designer jeans. Her polished fingertips and toenails gleamed with a pearly luster, as though smoothed to perfection by the tides. She looked like a woman who had had a good life. None of the grotesqueries that the sea and its creatures do to dead bodies had happened yet. Obviously, she had not been in the water long.

I had heard the initial radio transmission on the "floater" while at the Miami Beach police public information office, where I had been plodding dutifully through a stack of computer printouts, compiling crime statistics zone by zone. The *Miami News* art department intended to create a locater map for Sunday's paper, to accompany my piece on the crime rate. A tiny black dot would pinpoint the scene of each rape, murder, armed robbery and aggravated assault.

I hate projects involving numbers. If words are my strength, decimal points are my weakness. Calculating the number of violent crimes per 100,000 population has always been problematic for me at best. Was it 32 crimes per hundred thousand, 320 or 3.2? A live story on a dead woman was infinitely more interesting. My statistic-loving editors would not agree. But a stranger's death fueled my imagination.

I identified with her, more than with most victims. We were close in age, and I had planned to body surf and sunbathe along this same sandy stretch today. Instead I had reluctantly agreed to finish this DBI (Dull, But Important) project on my day off. Now fate had brought me to the precise place I had yearned to be, sun on my shoulders, sea breeze in my hair—but this was not the day at the beach I'd had in mind.

I watched, along with a small crowd and two uniformed cops, as a detective trudged toward us across the sand. Emery Rochek was an old-timer, one of the few holdouts who had not opted for guayaberas when dress codes were relaxed. Unlit cigar clenched between his teeth, his white shirt was open at the throat, his tie loose, beneath a shapeless gabardine jacket that flapped in the breeze. Emery handled more than his share of DOAs, mostly routine deaths. Young cops wanted sexier calls, I knew, not reminders of their own mortality. Emery never seemed to mind the unpleasant tasks that came with a corpse.

"So, you beat me here, Britt," he acknowledged, his voice a gravelly rumble.

"I was at the station working on a story about the crime rate. I heard it go out."

Emery chewed his cigar. His smelly stogies came in handy to mask the odor of corpses gone undiscovered too long, though his colleagues fiercely debated which stench was worse. No need to light up here. This corpse was as fresh as the sea around her.

"Well, lookit what washed up." He regarded her, his shaggy eyebrows lifted in mock surprise. "Whattaya waiting for, the tide to go out and take her with it?" he asked the cops.

"Thought maybe I should leave her the way she was 'til you guys took a look," one said.

Rochek shook his head in disgust as the two cops left their shoes and socks on the sand, pulled on rubber gloves and waded gingerly into the sun-dappled shallows. They dragged her unceremoniously ashore, water streaming from her hair. Her pale, half open eyes stared at the sky with a hopeful almost prayerful look. Her only adornment, a single gold earring, the delicate outline of a tiny open heart.

An excellent clue, I thought. Distinctive jewelry always helped indentify the dead. But this woman's youth and beauty assured that she was no lost soul. I was sure her identity would be no mystery. I expected a frantic spouse, relatives, friends, to appear momentarily, frantic with grief, hearts breaking.

"A great body is a terrible thing to waste," one of the cops muttered.

Emery straddled the naked woman, cigar still clenched between his teeth, tugging her one way, then the other, seeking wounds or identifying marks. I watched, painfully aware that the dead have no privacy.

"Hey, Red." Emery glanced over my shoulder to acknowledge a newcomer, elbowing her way through the growing throng of gawkers.

Lottie Dane had arrived, the best news shooter in town, and my best friend. Her red hair whipped wildly in the wind as she strode across the sand in her hand-tooled cowboy boots, twin Canon EOS cameras, wide angle lens on one, a telephoto on the other, slung from a leather strap around her neck.

"Geez, who is she?" Lottie murmured, shutter clicking, camera whirring. "She's so young."

The big eyes of a small boy were fixed on the dead woman's breasts. He was runty and pale, at the forward fringe of the crowd, wearing baggy swim trunks a size too large. Where is his mother? I wondered, as a beach patrolman brought the detective a yellow plastic sheet from his Jeep.

"What do you think?" I asked Emery, as he peeled off his rubber gloves.

"No bullet holes, or stab wounds," he said. "We'll know more when we get a name on her. Most likely what we have here is an accidental drowning."

"Is the ME coming out?"

He shook his head. "The wagon's on the way." Medical examiners didn't normally go to drownings these days except in cases of mass casualties, obvious foul play or refugee smugglers who routinely dumped human cargo off shore—sometimes too far off shore.

"My Raymond saw her first!" The little boy's proud mother finally made her appearance. She wore big sunglasses, a bikini that exposed a hysterectomy scar on her glistening belly and pink hair curlers under a floppy sunhat. She smelled strongly of coconut scented suntan oil and spoke in a New York accent.

Raymond, pail and shovel forgotten, still stared at the sheet covered corpse.

"Unbelievable," the mother told all who would listen. "Raymond kept trying to tell me, but I didn't pay attention. That kid is always into something.'' She shook her head smugly. ''I shoulda known.''

She and Raymond's father, she said, had partied on South Beach 'til the wee hours. He was now in their hotel room, convalescing, nursing a hangover and yesterday's sunburn. She had brought Raymond to the beach, intending to nap and work on her tan, but her son gave her little rest.

''Mommy, mommy, there's a lady with no clothes on,'' she quoted her pride and joy. ''I was half asleep,'' she said. ''Thought it was another one of them damn foreign models, you know, stripping topless on the beach. Most got nothing to show anyhow. The worst are the ones with their nipples and belly buttons pierced,'' she complained, snorting in disgust.

She had waved Raymond away, she explained, with a warning not to look. But the boy persisted. ''He's tugging at me. 'Mommy, mommy, it's a dead body!' Wouldn't gimme a break. Finally, I take off my little plastic eye shields, sit up, and, my God! It is a goddamn dead body! Ya can't even take your kid to the beach any more! His grandma is always nagging, saying the beach is bad for 'im, nagging about sun screen, the sand fleas and jelly fish. Now this! What the hell is going on?''

I approached the boy, aware that it would be tough to compete with the naked lady. ''Raymond? My name is . . .'' The child reluctantly took his eyes off the corpse and stared up at me.

''Does she have wings now?'' he asked. ''Can she fly? Like on TV?''

I swallowed. ''I don't know. I hope so.''

His mother had used the cell phone in her beach bag to dial nine one one. But Rochek said she had not been the first to dial police. The initial call had come from a housebound resident on the twelfth floor of the Casa Milagro, a high-rise condominium, he said. A regular caller who liked to scan the horizon with high-powered binoculars, he had spotted the body riding the incoming tide facedown.

Murmurs suddenly swept the crowd. A sighting. Something floating just beyond the breakers, a hundred yards down the beach. A man broke into a run, pursued by several others who splashed into the sea in a race to retrieve the prize.

"Take it easy. Don't kill each other over it," Rochek shouted after them.

A young Spanish-speaking man with a killer tan and astonishing pecs, flashed a triumphant smile as he waded out of the surf waving the trophy above his head like a banner. It was a rose red bikini bathing suit top.

The detective dangled it by its thin strap, then held it up for me to scrutinize. "Whattaya think, Britt. Her size?"

"Looks about right. Only one way to tell if a bathing suit fits."

"We'll try it on Cinderella at the ME office. No sign of the bottom half. Some pervert probably thought it was a souvenir," he said.

Lottie left for a feature assignment at the Garden Center. I knew I should go back to headquarters. Instead I walked the sand as far north as 34th Street, looking for an unattended beach towel or lounge chair the dead woman may have left, along with her personal belongings, but found nothing. That didn't mean they hadn't been there. It would not be unusual for them to have been stolen.

Rochek was talking to a physical fitness buff in his late seventies when I got back. A local who had been around for years, the man jogged, did push ups and head stands on the sand each day, then swam miles along the beach, rain or shine. I occasionally encountered him in the supermarket. Slightly hard of hearing, he spoke loudly, with an eastern European accent.

"I saw her." He nodded, gesturing broadly. "This morning. She vas svimming, right there." His gnarly index finger indicated a deep blue spot in the water opposite a row of pastel hotels and condos. "She looked like a good svimmer. It was early, vhen it looked like rain, before the sky cleared up. There vas almost nobody on the beach."

"She was alone?" Rochek asked.

The man paused. "There vas another svimmer. A man in the vater. I thought he was vid her, but," he shrugged, "maybe not."

He had not seen her arrive or leave, could not describe the other swimmer, or even say for sure what color her bathing suit was.

"I was exercising," he said. "I vastn't paying attention. I guess the guy vastn't vid her . . ."

"Why do you say that?'" Rochek asked.

"Vell, if he was vid her," he shrugged and extended his hairy arms, "vhere is he now?"

"Good question."

"You think they both got in trouble and there's another body out there?" I asked. I knew women have a higher fat-muscle ratio than men, whose leaner bodies are less buoyant. If both drowned, she would likely surface first.

We stared at the sea, valleys and troughs, rising and falling like the ebb and flow of life, with all its pain and joy.

"Terrible." The old man shook his head. "A terrible thing. She was young, so attractive."

Azure sea and sky normally refreshes my spirit. Instead, sadness washed over me as I walked back to my car, illegally parked at a bus stop, my press identification prominently displayed on the dash. Head throbbing in the blinding sun, I felt thirsty and dehydrated.

I sat in my superheated T-Bird, wondering if her car was parked nearby. If so, the meter must have run out by now. Expired, like its driver.

The woman's image haunted me all the way back to the *Miami News* building. What were her plans when she awoke this morning? Did she have a premonition, a bad dream, any clue that this day was her last? How many hearts would break, how many lives change because this one ended prematurely?

Bobby Tubbs was in the slot at the city desk. His chubby face wore its perpetual scowl of annoyance. "Did you get the stax for the art department? They need them right away."

"Sure," I said. "I've a story for tomorrow. A drowning on the beach, an unidentified woman."

"Keep it short," he snapped, after I filled him in.

I double checked the figures, turned in the crime statistics, then went over my notes on the dead woman.

I made some calls. The beach patrol reported no other victims, no rescues and no evidence that rip currents were to blame.

My lead depended on who she was. I was sure she would be identified by deadline. But I was wrong. A medical examiner's investigator returned my call at six P.M. She was still Jane Doe, and would not be autopsied until morning. I called Rochek.

"Nuttin'," he reported grimly. "Do me a favor, wouldja, kid? Put her description in the newspaper."

"That's why I called."

"Good girl, you're a woman after my own heart." I heard him flipping the pages of his notebook and imagined him adjusting the gold-rimmed reading glasses kept in his shirt pocket.

"Les' see. You saw 'er yourself, probably early thirties. Nice figure, good looking, Five feet, four and a half, weight 121. Hair blondish, a little longer than shoulder length. Eyes blue, bikini tan line. Nice manicure, good dental work. We'll know more after the post."

"And the earring," I reminded him.

"Yeah, we shot pictures," he said. "Maybe you can put one in the paper if we don't have her ID'd by tomorrow."

"Do me a favor," I said. "If you find out who she is

before our final, at one A.M., call me so we can change the lead.''

''You'll be home?''

''If I'm not, leave a message.''

I led my story with a police appeal to the public for help in identifying the victim.

Lottie stopped at my desk, her turned up nose sunburned, hair frizzy from the humidity. ''So who was she, the floater?''

''No clue,'' I said.

Lottie frowned. ''Think she just swam out too far?''

''Could be, or maybe she had a seizure.'' One of my first stories at *The News* had been about a teenager from Brooklyn who drowned in a hotel pool in full sight of witnesses who thought he was playing. They didn't realize he was suffering an epileptic seizure. ''Maybe she lives alone,'' I mused, ''and nobody will miss her until she fails to show up for work tomorrow. Then somebody will see the story in the newspaper and put two and two together.''

''She didn't look like the type who'd live alone,'' Lottie pointed out. ''Somebody who looks like her . . .''

''We live alone,'' I reminded her.

''Damn it to hell, you never miss the chance to rub it in, do you?'' She laughed.

''Don't knock it. With our jobs and the hours we keep,'' I said wistfully, ''maybe we're lucky.''

As I left the newsroom, I sw that some wag from the photo desk had posted one of Lottie's unused prints on the newsroom bulletin board. Skinny little Raymond, standing knock-kneed in the sand, clutched his pail, his little shovel in the other hand, the covered corpse lay in the foreground. A caption had been added, a Miami Beach tourist slogan: *Miami, see it like a native.* Not humorous, I thought, glaring around the newsroom. But the usual suspects were all hunched over their terminals. I yanked the photo off the board and locked it in my desk.

As I drove home through the twilight's tawny glow, I

wondered what the story would reveal about the dead woman tomorrow. That's the beauty of this job, I reminded myself, it's as though I live at the heart of an endlessly complex novel, rich with character, ripe with promise and rife with mystery.

I took Bitsy for a long walk, over the boardwalk. We sat in the moonlight for a time, watching the surf, then strolled home along shadowy streets.

No messages waited.

In the morning I called the Miami Beach detective bureau but Rochek was out, across the bay at the medical examiner's office they said. I took the MacArthur Causeway west, dodging the tourists in their careening rental cars as they eyeballed and photographed the cruise ships. The Ecstasy, the Celebration and the Song of Norway were all in port readying for departure to destinations such as Cozumel, Ocho Rios, Half Moon Cay, St. Lucia, and Guadeloupe, the ships and trips that dreams are made of.

The cheerful receptionist at Number One Bob Hope Road said Rochek was "with the chief, down in the autopsy room." She called for permission, then waved me on.

I left the soothing pastel lobby through the double doors, descended the stairs, and went through the breezeway into the lab building, my footsteps echoing along the brightly lit hallway. Poster-size photos of the towering oaks and resurrection ferns along the Witlacoochee River in Inverness lined the walls. The chief medical examiner shot them himself in a place as unspoiled today as when Chief Osceola and his band of warriors holed up there during the second Seminole War. U.S. Army Major Francis Langhorn Dade led his troops into an ambush at the now historic battleground there. On bad days in the city I often wonder if Miamians brought themselves bad karma by naming the county for a leader whose sole claim to fame was being massacred.

I passed the photo imaging bureau, the bone and tissue

bank and found the three people I was looking for at an autopsy room station: the chief, known worldwide as "the titan of medical examiners" and the genius who masterminded this one-of-a-kind building, the scowling Miami Beach detective, and the star attraction, the woman who had brought us all here.

She lay supine, her body incandescent, bathed in the powerful light from sixteen overhead fluorescent bulbs. The wooden block positioned beneath her shoulders had tilted her head back, exposing her throat. Her internal organs had already been scrutinized under the glare of a high-powered surgical lamp on a stainless steel dissection table rolled up beside her.

The fiberglass and epoxy resin tray on which she lay was neutral gray for color photo compatibility and designed to facilitate X-ray transmission. Mounted on wheels, it was custom-built for minimal labor, guaranteeing that the bodies it transports need only be lifted twice: on arrival and departure.

The autopsy had been completed, the Y-shaped incision in her torso and the inter-mastoid cut that ringed her skull loosely sewn shut with a running stitch of white linen cord. Despite the procedure, every surface was scrupulously clean, no drop of blood spilled. Spotless instruments gleamed, and the chief's surgical scrubs and apron remained immaculate, a matter of pride with the man who acknowledged my arrival with a cheerful nod.

"Hey, kid," the detective growled. He too, wore an apron. He stood near the woman's head, just outside the splash zone.

"Got an ID on her yet?" I slipped out my notebook.

"Not a single call. Not even the usual nut cases who wanna chat. Zip, zilch, nada."

"Huh." I was surprised. "Maybe she was a tourist . . ." I stepped closer, then stopped short. My jaw dropped.

"What happened to her?" I gasped. When I last saw her, the dead woman had been haunting, as ethereal as

Botticelli's Venus emerging from the sea. Today she looked like the loser in a nasty bar fight. It was not the autopsy incisions; I was accustomed to them. What shocked me was her nose, her knuckles and ears, all raw and scraped, and the ugly red-brown bruising on her wrists, forearms and legs.

"Nothing new." The chief spoke briskly. "Abrasions and other injuries are almost invisible on moist skin and don't show up right away. They become noticeable after the body is dried off and refrigerated. Drying tends to darken wounds."

"But her eyes," I protested. Still slightly open, the whites had turned to black on either side of the irises.

"*Tache noir,*" he said. "Black spot. Though to be literal, it's actually dark brown. Another part of the evaporation process. Common in sea water drownings."

The changes in her appearance made me queasy.

"The water's five percent salt dehydrates the tissues causing *tache noir,*" he was saying. "Salt water, being hypertonic, draws out the moisture. When the tissue dries, it's dark brown."

"But what are all those marks, fish bites?"

The chief shook his head. "I'm afraid not."

"The news ain't good." Emery nodded at the doctor.

"It appears our detective friend here has himself a homicide," the chief said pleasantly. "She was murdered."

"Why me?" Emery sighed.

I was not sympathetic. She, after all, was the one murdered.

"So," I said, "you mean somebody attacked her, then dumped her in the water?"

"No," the chief said. "As I was just apprising Detective Rochek, she was deliberately drowned." The chief consulted his notes. "Those bruises on her wrists and upper arms were inflicted as she struggled, fighting against being submerged. See here?"

He turned her head to one side with a gloved hand.

"See the bruises on the back of her neck? That's where someone grabbed her from behind and slightly to her left, and pushed her head down. See the marks? His right hand was here," he demonstrated, fitting his own fingers over the bruises, "on the back of her neck. Fingers on the right, thumb on the left. You can see some little horizontal, linear fingernail abrasions that also showed up after she was dry, where his nails penetrated the skin on the back of her neck as she twisted, trying to escape his grasp."

Chills rippled across my skin, and the room, a constant seventy-two degrees, seemed colder. My heart thudded as I imagined her panic, her gasps, her struggles to breathe as she inhaled water. I nearly drowned twice. Once in a dark Everglades canal in a car, later in the ocean, the bright lights of Miami in sight. Somehow I survived both experiences. But nobody had been deliberately holding my head under water.

The chief was pinpointing injuries to the woman's left arm, ". . . bruising beneath the skin, about a centimeter in diameter, three or four fingernail abrasions here, where he apparently grasped her wrist with his left hand to stop her from flailing and grabbing at him. There are visible bruises on the flexor, the underpart of her left wrist, and another fingernail mark."

"None of them were visible at the scene," Rochek said morosely.

"The guy swimming near her," I said, "it had to be him."

"Could be," the detective said.

"How did he do it?" I asked. "A healthy young woman struggling to survive in the water had to be difficult. Why didn't anybody see them, or hear her scream?"

"Looks like he used a scissors grip from behind, wrapped his legs around hers, pinned her ankles together," the chief said, "then he used his own body weight to submerge her. Her body supported his while he held her down."

''How long does it take to drown somebody like that?'' Rochek asked.

''Two to three minutes. She'd be struggling of course, choking and ingesting sea water. Most likely unable to scream out for help.''

The thought of this woman's terror, helpless in her last moments, both infuriated and saddened me. She had been savagely attacked in the ocean, like in the movie *Jaws,* but this savage predator was a man.

''All these bruises and abrasions,'' the chief mused, peering thoughtfully, ''makes it difficult to be certain what's post and what's anti mortem. Some are obviously the result of the wave action, as it swept her body back and forth on the sandy bottom.''

''What else?'' Rochek peered over his little half glasses, notebook in hand.

''See here?'' The chief pulled down her lower lip to expose pinpoint hemorrhages. ''On the inside of her lip, a linear abrasion in the shape of a tooth. He apparently did it when he grabbed her face, to push it underwater or keep her from screaming.

''And on the earlobe here, a one millimeter tear where an earring was lost, ripped off with some force. She still wore the other when found.''

''What about the bathing suit?'' I asked.

''That top could be hers. It fits. No way would a swimsuit simply fall off in the water,'' the chief said. ''The killer either deliberately removed it, or accidentally tore it off in the struggle.''

''Was she raped?'' I asked.

''There was no trauma to the genitalia,'' the chief said. ''The rape workup was negative, but of course that doesn't rule out sexual battery.''

''What started out as a simple drowning,'' the detective said, his voice resigned, ''is now a whodunit and a whoisit.''

Our eyes met across the dead woman's body. Only we

three cared about what happened to her, I thought sadly, and only because our jobs demanded it.

I really do care, I thought, gazing at the empty shell of her ruined body. You must have wanted to live as much as I do.

"You will catch the SOB who did this," I said. "Right, Emery?"

"No way to find the motive and nail the perp 'til we know who got killed," he said. "We need her name." He turned to the chief. "Whatdaya say, Doc? Got anything else here to help me out?"

The chief frowned and picked up her chart. "Her dental work looks excellent. Porcelain veneers on numbers eight and nine. Good work. Expensive, sophisticated. We'll have Wyatt take a look and do an impression. And we'll have a set of prints for you shortly."

A thin, olive-skinned morgue attendant had joined us. He uncurled and stretched out the fingers of the corpse's right hand, inked them one by one, then pressed and rolled them into a spoon-like device lined with narrow strips of glossy fingerprint paper.

"She had a bikini wax," I murmured out loud, "and her hair . . . when you release her description, be sure to mention that she has frosted highlights, probably done in some high-class salon. See those lighter streaks? They cost big bucks and half a day at a beauty salon. Somebody might recognize that."

"So that ain't natural, from the sun? Humph." The detective peered more closely at her hair. "What else? How was her general health, doc?"

"No signs of disease, prior injuries, surgeries or chronic conditions. But there is one other thing that might help. She was a mother."

"She has children?" I was startled. "How can you tell?"

"She had some stria—stretch marks—on her abdomen,

and the cervix of her uterus showed an irregularity. The nipples tend to be a bit darker, as well."

"How many kids?" the detective asked. "More than one?"

"No way to know." The chief shrugged. "But she'd been through at least one pregnancy. Possibly more."

A child, or children, were left somewhere out there without a mother. Why does no one miss her? I wondered, as we turned to leave.

Birds sang in the sunny parking lot outside and traffic thundered along the nearby expressway, as Rochek filled me in on what little he knew. Her condition indicated that she had died four to five hours before her body surfaced, setting the time of death at between 5:30 and 6:30 A.M.

"Probably closer to six, when that elderly guy said he saw her," I told Rochek. "He's a good witness, a creature of habit, probably right on target about the time. I always see him when I run in the morning. You can set your watch by him."

He gave me two photographs, black and whites, a close up of the earring, shot with a small ruler beside it to demonstrate scale, and a mug shot of the corpse.

"I'll try," I promised, frowning at the second picture. My editors harbor an unreasonable prejudice against seeing dead people in the morning paper, when readers are at the breakfast table. "They probably won't go for it," I warned.

Maybe it wouldn't matter, perhaps the right message waited in the newsroom. Just because Rochek had no calls didn't mean I wouldn't. Some people will talk to cops but not reporters—and vice versa.

Unfortunately, none of my messages were in response to the morning story. The only new clue came from an unlikely source. My mother.

I had comp time for working on my day off and had arranged to meet my mother at La Hacienda for lunch.

Her convertible was parked outside, the top down. At

age fifty-three, she looked stunning in a crisp pastel suit. Her bubbly chatter was full of news about her burgeoning social life, her high fashion career and the new winter cruise wear. I was grateful that she didn't criticize my clothes, my job or my love life.

My favorite, a delectably seasoned crisp crusted baked chicken with moros and green plantains, was wonderful. Lunch was uneventful until I fished through my Day Timer for my credit card, and the photos, tucked inside, fell out.

"Oh," my mother said, picking one up to study before handing it back. "Those are my favorites."

"Of course, the Elsa Peretti open heart. Exclusively for Tiffany's." She shrugged. "Everybody knows that."

"You're sure?"

She stared as though I was not her only child, but an alien creature from some third world planet. There are times I am sure I was the victim of a maternity ward mix-up. We are so different.

"Excuse me," I said, "you recognize this earring?"

"Of course," she chirped. "They're a signature design for Tiffany's." She reached out to snatch up the second photo.

"Good god!" She squinted at the image. "Is this woman . . . alive?"

"No," I murmured unhappily. "Not anymore."

She slapped it face down on the table like a playing card, shoulders aquiver in an exaggerated shudder.

"What happened to her? No, no," she held up one hand like a traffic cop. "Please. Don't tell me. Spare me the details."

She studied me in pained silence for a long moment, her expression one of suspicion. "What on *earth* would you be doing with a thing like this?"

I realized again what a disappointment I must be to her. Most women my age happily share baby pictures, while my handbag revealed close-ups of corpses.

Appetite gone, I pushed away my caramel flan and fortified myself against the usual barrage with the dregs of my *cafe con leche.*

Instead, she turned up one edge of the photo with a beautifully manicured fingernail to take another peek, her expression odd.

"Gruesome." She grimaced as she turned the photo face up. "But I swear, something about this poor creature . . . Who is she?" She raised her eyes from the picture to me, her look questioning.

"You think you know her?" I leaned forward. "She's the unidentified woman found drowned yesterday at the beach."

"I saw your story," she said pointedly, as though somehow it had been all my fault. She stared again at the photo, closed her eyes for a moment, studied it again, then pushed it toward me. "I guess not. Her own mother wouldn't recognize her, I'm sure."

"You know," I said quickly, "it's entirely possible that you do know her. You meet so many women, the fashion shows, the models, the buyers, your clients. She may have moved in those circles. Here, take another look," I urged. How ironic, I thought, if my mother could help solve this mystery.

She shook her head emphatically. "No!" She refused to look at the picture again. "It was just a passing thought." She was strangely silently as we walked to her car. A quick hug and she was gone. Her car flew out of the parking lot, tires squealing.

I showed Bobby Tubbs the earring photo which he agreed to run with the story if space was available. "I also got a picture of the victim," I said cheerfully.

His head jerked up, eyes narrowed. "Is she dead in the picture?"

"It's not that bad," I said. "We can touch up the nose a little."

"I don't want to see it. Gedit the hell outta here!" Fuming, he spun in his swivel chair, turning his back to me.

"Putting it in the paper may be the only way to reunite her with her loved ones . . ." I said to the back of Tubbs' head.

"*Don't* even think about it," he barked, without looking up from his editing screen.

Of course, I thought about it. Missing people intrigue me. Perhaps because my father was missing for most of my life, or because human beings lost and never found baffle me. The words of a long dead comedian, Myron Cohen, haunt me: "Everybody's got to be some place."

I turned in the story, stuffed a handful of business cards in my pocket, reminded the desk that I was still owed comp time and departed for the day. I drove to the Beach, parked ten blocks south of where the dead woman was first spotted and began to hit the hotel lobbies, trudging from one to the other, inquiring about any woman guest or employee who might be missing.

I pressed business cards into the hands of front desk clerks, managers and bartenders, asking them to call if they heard anything.

I continued until I was ten blocks north of where she had been found. At sunset, I beeped Rochek. We met, shared drinks, ate a pizza and compared notes.

Our victim matched no missing persons reports, county, statewide or even internationally, Rochek reported. He had checked on cars parked overtime or towed from the beach since her final swim. None were linked to a missing woman.

The detective had also visited Tiffany's. I imagined him, with his smelly cigar and unperturbable swagger, shooting questions at the staff. The earrings could have come from any one of more than 150 Tiffany stores in the U.S., and world capitals such as London, Paris, Rome and Zurich. She might not have purchased them herself.

"She looked like the kinda broad guys buy presents for." He sounded wistful.

"Wanna bet the call will come tomorrow?" I said.

"From your lips to God's ears, kid." He raised his glass.

But the call did not come the next day or the day after.

"Every right turn I make is a dead end. It's like she dropped outta nowhere," Rochek complained at our next strategy session, a week later. Her fingerprints had come back NIF, not in file. No criminal record. "It's like she came to Miami to die. What the hell she had against me, why she did it on my watch, I dunno."

"Maybe she's a foreign tourist and folks back home haven't missed her yet. Did you talk to Wyatt?"

Dr. Everett Wyatt, one of the nation's foremost forensic odentologists, sent one of the nation's most savage serial killers to Florida's electric chair by identifying the bite marks he left in the flesh of a coed victim.

He shrugged. "He says her dental work looks like it was done in the states."

"Jeez," I said. "It's like she was scooped up in a flying saucer and dropped off here."

The morgue was overcrowded, as always, and Rochek told me the administrator at the medical examiner's office was talking burial.

"We don't come up with answers soon," the detective said, "they're gonna plant her in Potter's Field."

The prospect made me want another drink.

Twice a month backhoes dig trenches and prisoners provide free labor as the cheap wooden coffins of Dade's destitute and unclaimed are buried in graves marked only by numbers. Stillborn babies sleep forever beside the impoverished elderly, jail suicides, victims of violence, AIDS victims and unknowns without names or any one to mourn them. They use numbers in the county cemetery, otherwise known as Potter's Field, in hope that a John, Jane or Juan

Doe will one day be identified by a loved one eager to claim and re-bury the body. That rarely happens.

"No way," I said.

"Right." His jaw squared. "Somebody must miss her."

He took it personally. So did I.

"How can somebody like you and me just get lost?" I groused to Lottie the next day. She had dropped by my desk and pulled up a chair after deadline for the first edition.

"Maybe she wasn't like you and me."

"If she shopped at Tiffany's regularly," I said, "she wasn't. But rich people are missed quicker than the rest of us. Where the hell are her relatives, her neighbors, co-workers, her boss, her best friend? Hell, you'd think her hairdresser would report her missing, if nobody else did. She looked like high maintenance."

"Dern tootin'. By now, she's due for a touch-up, a manicure, another bikini wax."

That evening, a much anticipated date with the man in my life, Miami Police Major Kendall McDonald, ended badly. The first sign was when I thought he was reaching for me. It was actually his pager in the glove compartment.

The beeper sounded as we dined on excellent food at a barbecue at the home of a policeman friend. The night was soft around us, with music in the air and the pungent aroma of citronella candles burning to repel mosquitoes.

He returned from the phone, his expression odd, and spoke into the ear of a homicide lieutenant who reacted as though he'd been gunshot. They exchanged whispers and expressions of disbelief.

"What's happened?" I asked expectantly, as McDonald took his seat beside me.

"Nothing," he said, eyes troubled.

That was his final answer. I hate secrets. During the drive home I coaxed, but he lectured me on ethics. One thing led to another. At my place I stepped out of the car, marched to my front door and turned my key in the lock as his Jeep Cherokee pulled away.

Why, I thought, *am I my own worst enemy*?

Ignoring the blinking red eye on my message machine, I took Bitsy for a walk. Each time a car slowed down beside us, I hoped it was him, but it never was. *Why does this always happen?* I wondered.

Back at home dressed for bed, I was warming a glass of milk in the microwave, when someone knocked softly.

I smoothed my hair and threw open the door, smiling and relieved.

My visitor's balding dome shone in the moonlight. "You ain' gonna believe this, kid."

"Emery, what are you doing here?" I clutched my cotton robe around me and glanced at the clock. "It's one A.M."

"You tol' me to call you if I got a break. You didn't answer. I was passing by and saw your lights."

I swung the door open wider and he stepped inside.

"I got the ID of the mermaid," he announced. "Been working the case all night. Thought you'd wanna know. It's a hell of a thing."

"How'd you find out who she was?" Eagerly, I led him into my little kitchen. He looked rumpled and needed a shave. "Want coffee?"

"No, but I could use a stiff drink. I'm heading home after this. You expecting somebody?"

"No." I took out a bottle of Jack Daniels. "How's this?"

"Perfect. Nothing on the side." He looked puzzled. "What's with you, kid? Didn't you ever learn to check who it is before you open your door in the middle of the night? You of all people."

"You're right. I wasn't thinking."

We sat across from each other at my kitchen table. Him with the booze, me with the milk. Our notebooks in front of us, the air electric with anticipation.

"I knew you'd do it," I said as we raised our glasses in a mutual salute. "Where is she from?"

"Right here." He took a swallow, then sighed. "Miami, born and raised."

"Amazing, how come she wasn't identified sooner?"

"Because the corpse that we fished outta the drink that day was a dead woman." Fondly, he contemplated the amber liquid in his glass.

"So? We knew that." I frowned and put my pen down.

"She was a homicide victim . . ."

"Emery," I implored impatiently.

". . . more than ten yeas ago. She was *already* dead." His gaze met mine. "Ran her prints again, this time through local employment records. Came back a hit. Her prints positively identify her as Kathlin Ann Jordan, murdered in 1991."